Skin and Bone

Skin and Bone

ROBIN BLAKE

Minotaur Books
New York

SKIN AND BONE. Copyright © 2016 by Robin Blake. All rights reserved. Printed in the United States of America. For information, address St. Martin's Press, 175 Fifth Avenue, New York, N.Y. 10010.

www.minotaurbooks.com

Library of Congress Cataloging-in-Publication Data

Names: Blake, Robin, 1948– author.
Title: Skin and bone : a mystery / Robin Blake.
Description: First U.S. edition. | New York : Minotaur Books, 2016. | Series: Cragg & Fidelis mysteries ; 4
Identifiers: LCCN 2016021611| ISBN 9781250100962 (hardcover) | ISBN 9781250100986 (e-book)
Subjects: LCSH: Coroners—Fiction. | Murder—Investigation—Fiction. | Great Britain—History—1714–1837—Fiction. | Preston (Lancashire, England)—Fiction. | BISAC: FICTION / Mystery & Detective / Historical. | GSAFD: Mystery fiction. | Historical fiction.
Classification: LCC PR6102.L347 S57 2016 | DDC 823/.92—dc23
LC record available at https://lccn.loc.gov/2016021611

Our books may be purchased in bulk for promotional, educational, or business use. Please contact your local bookseller or the Macmillan Corporate and Premium Sales Department at 1-800-221-7945, extension 5442, or by e-mail at MacmillanSpecialMarkets@macmillan.com.

First published in Great Britain by Constable, an imprint of Little, Brown Book Group, an Hachette UK company

First U.S. Edition: October 2016

10 9 8 7 6 5 4 3 2 1

For Gus Alexander

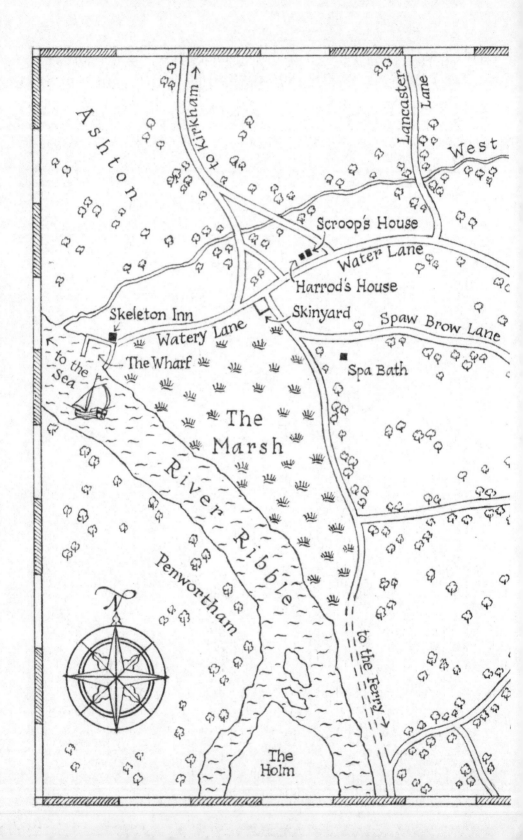

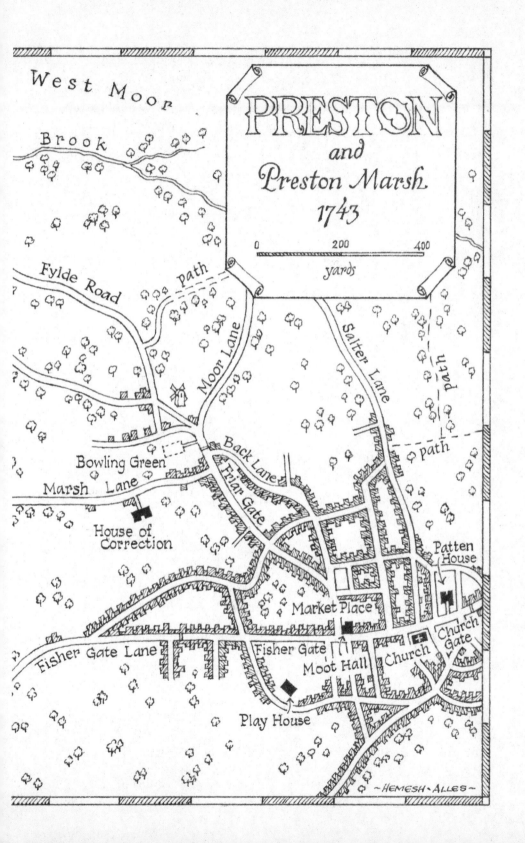

West Moor

Brook

PRESTON
and
Preston Marsh
1743

0   200   400
yards

Fylde Road

path

Moor Lane

Salter Lane

path

path

Bowling Green

Back Lane

Marsh   Lane

Friar Gate

House of
Correction

Patten
House

Market Place

Church
Gate

Fisher Gate Lane

Fisher Gate

Church

Moot Hall

Play House

~HEMESH·ALLES~

Skin and Bone

Chapter 1

IT WAS A DAY on which the sun was a disc of polished brass, and flocks of white cloud chased each other cheerfully across a blue field of sky: the perfect September afternoon for a game of bowls.

I was on the green by Friar Gate Bar and just about to cast my second wood. My opponent's two bowls lay temptingly together like a pair of cherries just in front of the jack, and I planned a drive shot that would crash violently into them both, shooting them away to one side and the other while mine, with luck, would come to rest in their place and win the end. I grasped the wood firmly in my right hand, took up the bowling position with care and swung my arm. Then I heard a voice shouting my name from the direction of the Greenkeeper's hut and it sounded as rough as the caw of a raven.

'Mr Cragg! Mr Coroner Cragg!'

The rhythm of my stroke was naturally disturbed. The wood left my hand awkwardly and was, in effect, lobbed rather than rolled. It therefore bounced off the grass, disastrously lost its momentum and came to rest far short of my aim. My opponent, James Starkey the stationer, crowed in delight.

'Ha! Ha! That's another end to me, Titus. You owe me two shillings and fourpence, unless you want to play again for double the stake.'

I don't much like triumphalism in sports. A man should win a game with as much grace as he loses one.

'No, I'll play no more,' I said, opening my purse and counting out the money. 'It seems I am needed elsewhere.'

The footing-plate that marked the playing position of that final end was placed on the opposite side of the green to the hut, from where a raggedy young woman now came striding towards its crown, stopping there to shade her eyes against the glare of the sunlight. She turned this way and that to survey the four or five pairs of bowlers that were ranged around the circular and slightly domed green – the field of play. Some of them cursed her for a pest. But she was no respecter of the rituals of the game.

'They say the Coroner's playing here. Which is he?'

'He is me,' I called up to her, raising my hat to make myself seen. 'Who's asking?'

'A corpus has been found and you're needed to come.'

I shook hands with Starkey and hurried towards the woman. I did not know her and so had to ask her name. It was Ellen Kite, and she was the daughter of a skinner and a skinner herself, since at Preston women as well as men work in that separated and unwholesome trade. The rank smell that came off her, as off all skinners, was the reason they kept to themselves and were little seen in town – a powerful compound of rotten blood and stale urine, with more than a hint of manure added in.

'It's a babby, Sir, and a newborn.'

'Where was it found?'

'At the skin-yard. You must come.'

She led the way as we left the green and, turning away from the town, hurried along Spaw Brow Lane, the lower and less frequented of the two ways from the town that went towards Spaw Brow, and below it the wharf where sea-going vessels came and went on the tide, as well as river boats that plied between Preston and the southern half of the county along the River Douglas Navigation. The top of the Brow commanded a view over the Marsh Mill Dam, the Marsh itself, the wharf with its few ships, and the whole estuary as it runs and broadens westwards to the sea.

I paused there and, looking down, saw below me the small brick house built halfway down the slope for the outflow of the spring that supplied the bath. A hundred yards below that lay the curious structure of the bath house itself, a little temple of cleanliness with its domed roof, key-pattern decorations and semi-circular porch supported by six round columns. The style was inspired no doubt by the Classical world's love of bathing in company but, if its first founders a generation ago had hoped the habit would be adopted by all prominent citizens of Preston, they have been sadly disappointed. The bath was successful for a while but had then suffered a painful decline and now stood locked and unused on its hillside station.

The bath stood beside a steep rutted track to which it gave its name. Cold Bath Lane descended from the bath house to a crossroads – the way ahead led to the township of Ashton and beyond that the small town of Kirkham; the one on the right took you back to Preston by the more level route of Water Lane; and the left-hand road led to the river bank and the wharf.

The skin-yard stood at this crossroads and behind lay a grassy water-meadow that stretched a hundred and fifty yards to the river's edge. This was known as the Marsh and Prestonians had for centuries enjoyed the right to graze their cattle, sheep and goats on it. The skin-yard itself was enclosed by a ten-foot wall and entered through an arched gateway. A group of women had gathered a few yards from this gate and were in animated conversation amongst themselves while, under the arch itself, there was a second group of both men and women standing more silently. The two groups were quite distinct. The mixed group were Ellen Kite's fellow workers from the tannery within; the females were local women that lived in the cottages scattered around the crossroads and along Watery Lane. It was these women that I came to first.

In my experience, an infant that's been found dead has power to bring out the community of women like no other unexpected corpse. When I arrived at the place, there must have been above a dozen of them, gathered in a conspiratorial circle. There would have been only one subject of their muttering: which young woman had been secretly pregnant? Which girl of the parish had turned whore and then done away with her ill-begotten child? One of the women, a tall, gaunt one called Hannah Parsons who was the wife of Jem Parsons the bath-house keeper, was leading the discussion, hissing that they must leave no stone unturned, no secret unrevealed, until they had found who had done this killing.

'Now, ladies,' I said as Ellen left me to join her friends next to the gate. 'What is the matter?'

The women started talking all at once and the words came to me in such a gabble that I understood nothing. I pointed to Hannah Parsons.

'Hannah, you speak. This is about the dead infant, I take it.'

'Yes, Your Honour,' she said.

'Was it any of you that found it?'

'No, it was them inside the skin-yard. We heard a shouting and a caterwauling, so we came out to see what it was about. They were saying they'd fished a baby out of one of their tan-pits.'

She wrinkled her nose in what I took to be disgust for the skinning trade and those who worked in it.

'Now they won't let nobody near. They won't let us in, or bring it out for us to see it.'

I spoke to her firmly.

'Well, that is quite right, Hannah. A body that's found is for me to look at first, and is not to be removed from the place unless I say so. Now, do any of you have anything to tell me about this matter? If so, you must do so.'

They glanced around at each other. No one spoke up.

'Very well. But please understand that if you do think of any-thing – anything definite, mind! – I must be told. In the meantime you should disperse to your homes or your work.'

I added the last injunction largely as a matter of form, for I knew they would not obey.

I now walked across to the skinners, who numbered a dozen at most. They had gathered around Ellen Kite and were questioning her. As I drew near my nose was assailed by the same pungency that emanated from the clothes of Ellen Kite, but multiplied. It was the smell that set these folk apart in every way from Hannah and her friends, who considered themselves more proper, even if no richer. I strove not to betray any sign of displeasure as I came near.

A man of middle age stepped towards me and tipped his hat.

'How do, Coroner? Barney Kite.'

'Ellen's dad?'

He neither confirmed nor denied it, but only said,

'Follow me. I'll show it thee.'

Within the gateway arch, and built as part of it, was a small stone lodge with a single room below and another above. It was halfway to ruin, the thatch sagging, the ceiling pocked by rot, the interior damp and draughty. With the whole company in attendance I was led inside and shown a trestle table in the lower room. Walking ahead of me, Kite reached the table and grasped the square of sack-ing that covered it. With one movement he pulled it away to expose a tiny dirt-caked heap of human remains.

It was clear that this was, indeed, a newborn. Its body was wrapped in what appeared to be a piece of sodden filthy linen, but its head was exposed. I stooped to look more closely. Smears of stinking mud lay across the face, whose features were yet hardly formed. The eyelids were shut, but the round mouth was a little open and the nose was flat. I was suddenly almost overwhelmed by a rush of pity at the sight of those closed eyes and parted lips. I stood upright once more.

'What happened? Does anyone know how this poor thing came here?'

I looked around at the faces surrounding me. They were uniformly anxious, but otherwise blank. I addressed the one who had earlier seemed to put himself forward as their leader.

'Mr Kite, can you explain the circumstances?'

'By some wickedness, we suppose, the babby got into one of the handler pits,' he said. 'Our Ellen found it this afternoon.'

His daughter was standing next to him. He hooked an arm around her shoulders and pulled her tightly to him.

I said, 'Ellen, I need to know exactly where this was. Will you show me? No! No! The rest of you stand off!'

Her father released her and she preceded me out of the lodge.

The skin-yard was about half an acre in extent. The central part comprised the area of the tanning pits, each about ten feet square and lined up in three rows. Above them were erected frames from which hides were lowered for soaking in the tanning fluid. As we reached them, I turned to survey the whole perimeter of the yard. Against the surrounding wall a run of sloping roofs had been pitched to make a kind of gallery. This sheltered tuns and troughs and stone-topped work tables, as well as further racks for drying or storing hides. There were also fires burning here and there, heating great iron pots which steamed sulphurously into the afternoon air. This air was everywhere rank with the smell of decayed vegetation, rotten flesh and manure, a smell which evidently came from the tanning liquor inside the pits.

Ellen led me directly to the nearest pit.

'It were this pit I found it in.'

'Your father said it is a handler pit. What is that?'

'That's a pit where we start off the hides, where the ooze is weakest.'

'The ooze?'

'What's in the pit. Hides go from pit to pit, with the ooze getting stronger every time, see?'

I saw that each of the pits was slate-lined, and that the frames surmounting them were equipped with crude winching machinery, operated by turning a wheel. By this means the hides were dipped and brought out of the ooze, which was a dark brown, like coffee.

'How long do the hides stay in this pit?'

'Twenty weeks. But meantime we must handle them every day, which is what I came to the pit to do after my dinner.'

'Handle them? What's that?'

'We wind out the hides and stir up the ooze.'

She pointed to a long-handled paddle lying beside the winching wheel.

'Why do you do that?'

'If you don't the goodness settles at the bottom and the leather doesn't cure properly all the way up.'

'So when you stirred the pit you found the remains?'

'Aye, it came up on the paddle, like. I just took it out and laid it on the side. I was right shocked. I shouted for me dad. He came and carried it into the gatehouse, and sent me up to get you.'

'I see. That means you are the first finder, Ellen, and shall go down in the record as such. You shall have to swear a deposition and in due course give evidence at the inquest into what you found and how you found it. Will you be able to remember everything that happened?'

Ellen, who was quite a presentable young female under her noxious grime, nodded and tapped her temple.

'Don't worry, Sir. I've got over the shock now. It's all in here.'

Passably intelligent, too, I thought, as I indicated that we should return to the gate.

'The baby must be kept for examination,' I said on the way, 'but not here. It must be somewhere safe and in the vicinity.'

I looked up the hillside that rose above the skin-yard. The bath house, like a domed and pillared temple, was in clear view halfway up, and it occurred to me at once that, unused and secure, this was the obvious place in the neighbourhood. I hurried back to the gatehouse, gathered up the dead baby and took it out through the skin-yard gate. The local women were still waiting in a huddle, like harpies.

'Is your husband up at the bath?' I asked Hannah.

'No, he's gone to town,' she said.

'I need somewhere to keep the body safe, as near as possible to where it was discovered. The bath will serve my purpose. Do you have a key?'

'Aye.'

A few minutes later, with the tiny body resting on my upturned hands, I led a small procession up Cold Bath Lane. When we reached the place, Hannah unlocked the doors and the two of us went inside. The others gathered around the porch to await whatever might ensue.

At the time I am describing – the autumn of the year 1743 – the Preston spa had been closed to all business for a long time and, entering it now with my dismal burden, I could see why. What once, twenty-five years ago, had been an airy and modern interior now looked gloomy and decrepit. The previously white walls were mottled with black and blue mould; the plunge-bath was half-full of dirty water, its bottom a thick layer of sludge; the window panes – set high in the walls to prevent folk peeping at the bathers' nakedness – were cracked and grimy.

There had been talk that the bath was to be furbished up again, with investment provided by Lord Grassington, a member of the county nobility. But there had been legal objections to the scheme from the Corporation, which owned the water supply, and the water which had once filled the bath now merely ran through beneath the building and into the conduit on the other side so that a faint subterraneous rushing sound was heard at all times.

Entering the desolate place now, I decided the conversation should continue solemn and so, though I was curious, I did not ask Hannah Parsons how matters stood between Lord Grassington's project and the Mayor. I only told her I needed a room and some receptacle in which the baby's remains could be kept safe. She conducted me around the simple building, which consisted of half a dozen rooms – apart from an entrance hall and the plunging room under the central dome, there were the keeper's little hutch, a cupboard-like tiring-room for changing out of one's clothes, the jakes and the tiled sluicing room. The sole features of the latter were the open fireplace with its great water cauldron hanging above the blackened grate, wooden benches arrayed around the wall, a stone sink and a drain hole in the middle of the floor.

'Shall this be the room where you inquest into the babby, Mr Cragg?' she asked, her voice lowered for the first time.

'No, but I shall keep it here, Mrs Parsons. A body waiting for inquest must lie as close as possible to where it was found, making this place very suitable. The spa is not in public use, and the sluicing room is cool and has a stout door, which is a most important consideration. We can't risk the little one being taken away, as without it I am unable to proceed to inquest and in that case we may never know the truth.'

Hearing this her face took on a sudden intensity.

'And that we *must* know, Mr Cragg. This is murder and whatever harlot-whore did it must pay – and she will! Every woman in the world – every honest woman – will say yes to that with me.'

I moved over to inspect the sink. Its interior, and the tap that had once filled it, were cobwebbed and perfectly dry, while a wooden lid leaned against the wall alongside. I felt confident that here my little victim would come to no harm.

'Please would you brush out this sink?' I asked.

While she went to find a brush I walked restlessly around the room. I remembered times when I had been in here with my young friends, all of us naked and covered in soapsuds while the keeper dipped a bucket in the cauldron that he kept steaming over the burning logs. For a halfpenny a time he would hurl the water at us with gusto, laughing at how we cried and jumped around at the shock of the soaking. I had much enjoyed going there in such company, on one of the alternate days in the week when it was reserved for the use of males. But soon enough, as domesticity supervened, I found less and less delight in jumping into icy water, or in having the bathhouse keeper hurl buckets over me that he always claimed would contain hot water, but generally proved scarcely tepid. It became so much more agreeable to enjoy a weekly soak in my own kitchen fireside tub, with my own Elizabeth on hand to scrub my back.

But now I thought how sweet it had been to be young and slippery with soap, and to stand laughing with arms wide to welcome the force of the hurled water against our bodies. I looked down at the dead baby in my hands and felt another pang of sorrow. Whether it was for this bud of unfulfilled humanity, or for my own lost and irrecoverable youth, I cannot say.

Hannah returned with brush and pan, and cleared the sink of its webs and dust, after which I placed the baby inside. Then I lifted and covered it reverently with the sink's wooden cover.

'Hannah, I expect you to lock up and safeguard these remains to the utmost of your ability. It is getting late now and I can do no more today. But tomorrow I shall return with someone to help me examine it and we shall begin our investigation into this distressing event.'

So I went outside to find the skinners shifting around and talking together urgently. They wanted to get away to their work before nightfall, but were uncertain in case I required them to remain. I told them at once that I didn't and as they began to turn away, I called Ellen Kite to me.

'Ellen, I shall be obliged if you would come to my office in Cheapside first thing in the morning. With the help of my clerk Mr Furzey I shall take your deposition.'

She gave a bob of a curtsey, a politeness at odds with her mired and noxious working clothes, and said, 'I come to market every Wednesday with my brother, Sir, bringing some of our leather goods to sell. As soon as we have the stall set up I'll come to your door.'

So they all went down the lane in a troop to their skin-yard. Beyond them the orange sun was already sidling towards the west where, in a couple of hours, it would lower itself, as into a bath, below the horizon.

Chapter 2

T HE CORONER'S DUTY is to enquire into unexpected deaths, and I find it incomprehensible that my colleagues in other parts of the country imagine they can do this without medical assistance. How can you distinguish poisoning from the morbid failure of an organ, or tell deliberate suffocation from a natural death, simply by consulting law books? The second of these distinctions was one I was going to have to make in the case of the baby found in Cold Bath Lane and so, rather than going directly to the office, I headed first for the Fisher Gate lodgings of Luke Fidelis.

My friend Dr Fidelis divided opinion in the town. He had come to Preston seven years earlier after learning his trade in Europe, principally at the university of Leyden where (as he once told me) there were always new ideas about disease fermenting like beer. But arriving back in Lancashire he found medical innovation far from popular, especially with the old ones in authority. 'Tried and tested, never bested', they would say; or 'The old way's God's way and novelty is devilry'.

Fidelis was all for stirring things up and would not hold his tongue about what he called the many useless and probably harmful practices of our more conventional physicians. He would produce lucid and (to the unbiased ear) not unpersuasive arguments against blood-letting, or cupping, or the timing of treatment by astrology, with the paradoxical result that his own methods came under adverse scrutiny by others. If Fidelis saw Preston's other doctors as stuck in provincial ignorance, they regarded him as a dangerous foreign-educated upstart.

But my friend had two qualities that stopped his practice from landing on the rocks: his good looks, which recommended him to many female patients (and a few male ones); and his habit of being – not on all, but on many of the more important questions – in the right. Even had I not already found him a good and stimulating friend, that would have been enough for me to seek his advice when the occasion demanded it.

In answer to my knock a servant came to the door of bookbinder Lorris, at whose house Fidelis occupied comfortable lodgings on the topmost floor.

'Doctor's gone out of town, Mr Cragg,' she said. 'He's riding upriver seeing patients.'

'That is inconvenient. When do you expect him to return?'

'Well, he's been gone two days, and said he'd be back after three.'

'If he returns earlier would you please tell him that I would like to consult him at his earliest convenience.'

'I hope you are not unwell, Mr Cragg,' said the maid.

I assured her I was quite well, tipped my hat and set off up Fisher Gate towards the office adjoining my house on Cheapside.

Here I briefed Furzey on what had been found at the spa, and dictated a note about it to the Mayor. It was expedient to keep the Chief Magistrate of Preston informed of my doings as Coroner, since I may in due course have to apply to him for fees and expenses, or to refer a criminal matter on to him.

'We should have a visitor here in the morning, one Ellen Kite,' I said as Furzey began tidying the writing desk in preparation for going to the home he shared with his mother. 'She is our first finder and an intelligent young woman, though I fear you may nose her as she comes through the door.'

Furzey grimaced.

'*Nose* her? How's that?'

'She is from the tannery at the bottom of Cold Bath Lane.'

Furzey slid from his stool and took an upright chair, which he carried to the window next to the outer door and set it down there.

'Then when she comes she shall sit here with the window open and as far from my writing desk as may be.'

'What kind of mother has so much hate for her child that she throws it into a filthy tan-pit? Am I looking for a shameless whore, Lizzie?'

Elizabeth and I were in our parlour after supper, playing a game of piquet.

'No, Titus. You are looking for someone capable of shame. A respectable girl, even a poor one, who risks too much by having a baby unmarried. She might be cast out of her employment by it, or miss her chance of marriage. It is not an immoral girl who hides her condition and secretly gives birth.'

'Legally speaking, the consequence for such a woman is terrible: she is a murderess. That is what I am now looking for, in law. A murderess.'

She looked up from her cards with a frown. I forestalled her objection.

'I know, you rightly object,' I went on. 'But the law on this is inflexible. There is a statute of King James the First, which was made specially to cover these cases. It lays down that any girl who conceals the birth of a child, if that babe subsequently dies, is presumed by the law to have murdered it.'

'But that law is so monstrous, Titus! Babies are stillborn through no fault of the mother. To be hanged for murder of a stillborn child cannot be justice.'

'Logically, you are right. It's a fallacy, a case of *cum hoc ergo propter hoc*. However, I think the law when it was instigated was meant to serve some other object than logic – or for that matter justice.'

'What do you mean my love? What other object can a law have?'

'Moral policy, Lizzie. The Act was meant to stop carnal vices, and specifically to prevent young girls playing at hazard with their maidenheads. What could be a more terrifying prophylactic against immorality than a hanging?'

'Well I do not like it when morality has a fight with justice. It makes me anxious. But the truth must be found out anyway. You must discover if the baby died before it was born.'

'I agree, though it is difficult. The old law is much muttered against nowadays; even the Lord Chief Justice in London is known not to like it. I think if the bath-house baby was indeed stillborn we may save some poor girl from the gallows.'

Ellen Kite jangled the office bell at nine o'clock in the morning. Furzey had brought his mother's perfume bottle into work. As I came through from my inner sanctum, I found him hastily preparing for our visitor by sousing his pocket handkerchief with lavender and civet.

'Why do you look at me?' he said, looking up. 'My mother'll tell you. I cannot abide a rank odour, me. I am made ill by it.'

He hurried to throw open the window, then went with handkerchief at the ready to admit the witness. As he swung the door open he clapped the fragranced linen to his nose and gave her a muffled greeting.

Ellen walked in with confidence. She wore her cleanest dress and had perhaps, before dressing, washed her body, for there was no sign of yesterday's miasma about her. Unable to smell anything but old Dame Furzey's civet, however, Furzey was not to know this and continued with the handkerchief clamped under his nostrils.

Ellen looked at him with curiosity, and then at me.

'Ah, this is my clerk Robert Furzey,' I said. 'Perhaps he has a nosebleed. Will you sit?'

I closed the window and, dragging away the chair that Furzey had put there, repositioned it more centrally. Ellen settled herself while Furzey looked on from behind his handkerchief, his eyes incredulous of my actions. I pointed towards his desk.

'Furzey to your writing, if you please,' I said.

My clerk shook his head but did as he was told, though without removing the handkerchief. I waited as he slid on to his stool and, with his one free hand, selected a sheet of paper from the drawer, put it in the writing position and dipped his pen.

I said, 'Now, Miss Kite . . . or is it Mrs?'

'I am not married, Sir.'

'Very well, but perhaps I may call you Ellen.'

'That's all right.'

'So, Ellen, please will you tell us everything that happened yesterday after your dinner, from the moment you approached the tan-pits?'

'You mean when I went there to handle the ooze and found the babby?'

'Yes.'

So, to the accompaniment of Furzey's squeaky quill, she told how she had first raised the hides from the liquor by means of the lifting gear, and then taken the paddle and dipped it, pushing it right down to the bottom and stirring up the sludge that had settled there. She had then started moving crabwise around the pit, all the time stirring so that no part of the tanning liquor would remain undisturbed, and had reached halfway around when she felt the slight weight on the blade of the paddle. Lifting it she did not know what she had scooped up – perhaps a dead bird such as a duck. Only when she deposited it on the ground was she able to look closely. Then she had vomited up the whole of her dinner.

'It was not a duck, Sir, but a babby. Cold, stiff and sodden in its filthy wrapping.'

'And so you called for your father.'

'No, I screamed for him.'

'Had you seen a newborn baby before, Ellen?'

'Yes, Sir. When my sister had hers.'

'And have you seen a dead baby before, a newborn or stillborn child?'

'No. Never ever.'

'But you were in no doubt, all of you who saw it, that this baby was dead.'

'Of course! How could it be alive, under the ooze?'

'And can you think of anyone to whom this poor dead baby might belong? Do you know of any girl or woman from the skin-yard or round and about that had just given birth?'

'I don't know of any, no Sir. No one in skin-yard, and round about there's only Mrs Scroop that lives on Water Lane.'

'Good heavens! Has Mrs Scroop produced another little Scroop? Surely not so soon. It only seems the other day she had her last.'

'That were last year, Mr Cragg. This babby came yesterday, so we've heard.'

Mrs Helena Scroop was the wife of Abraham Scroop, one of Preston's richest merchants, a dissenting Protestant and member of the Corporation. She had given birth a dozen times – the new addition would make it a baker's dozen – but only half of the children lived to be weaned. Scroop's fortune was built on what other people do not want – ordure, rags, bones, scrap leather, bits of metal. He dealt with the tannery, selling to them and buying off them, so it was natural enough for the workers there to see him from time to time and get his family news.

'Well if it was born yesterday that would have been after this poor little one. So there's no one else you can think of? Of the women you see every day, for example, in the skin-yard. Could any have been with child and given birth, without your knowing?'

'No. Everyone in this town knows everything that happens here, either now or tomorrow. Happen it's some stranger, a peddler-woman or a loose girl chucked out of her parish and wandering the roads.'

'That does happen, indeed. Has any such person been seen recently around Spaw Brow?'

After a moment's thought, Ellen shook her head.

'No. Crazy Daisy's been by the skin-yard with her mats and potions to sell. The day before yesterday, I think it were. But that's the only woman or girl from out of town that we've seen very lately, as far as I know.'

I knew Daisy by reputation, a poor woman living out on the south side of the estuary, towards the village of Hutton. With her son she made mats and brooms at home, which she hawked around Preston whenever she could wangle a free passage with a boatman coming on to the wharf on the tide. It was difficult to tell Daisy's age. A long time ago she had been a midwife, and she also made draughts and poultices from herbs.

'She still sells her medicines, then?'

Ellen smiled.

'To anyone fool enough to buy.'

'And you can't think of anyone else from outside Preston, apart from Daisy, who was seen here in the past few days?'

'Not to my knowledge.'

'But there is a difficulty, is there not? If the culprit is someone from outside the skin-yard, someone who brought the baby in – in the middle of the night shall we say? – would they have been able to do so? Was the gate not locked at night?'

'Yes, it's locked, but not until ten o'clock.'

'Whose job is it to lock up?'

'Me dad's.'

'And do you all sleep inside – all the skinners I mean?'

'We do.'

'There is just one last thing. How often do you handle the ooze in the way you have described?'

'Every day.'

'At the same time?'

'Yes, right after me dinner.'

'And can you be sure that, had it been in the tan-pit on the previous day, Monday, you would have discovered the baby then?'

'Oh yes. I see what you're saying, Sir. If it had been there on Monday, I would have found it then. I'm sure of that.'

I rose from my chair and signalled to Furzey that he might stop writing.

'Well that would seem to be the sum of it, Ellen. Thank you very much. Now, about the inquest: you will receive a summons to give evidence. You are the first finder and your evidence is the most important of all. You shan't be afraid to speak up in front of many people?'

'Oh no, I'll not. I do sell in the market, you know. I'm not afraid to talk in front of folk.'

It was perhaps half an hour after she left us that I decided to give myself and the dog Suez a stretch of our legs. Tuesday's pleasant weather had now given way this morning to gusting winds and flurries of rain, forcing the stallholders of the market to protect their wares under awnings of tarpaulin, which flapped and slapped in the wet breeze. I pulled my hat firmly on to my head and we set out. As soon as we entered Market Place the spaniel was attracted to the sound of voices raised even above the raucous cries of the sellers. I followed him as he bounced towards the disturbance.

'You've got no right!' I heard a female voice shout as I approached. It sounded like that of Ellen Kite. 'You are a bully and a bastard, Mister!'

A small crowd had gathered around a trading table, which was the subject of the argument in progress. On the one hand were two Corporation officers, and on the other was Ellen and a dark young man that I took to be her brother.

The market had always had two official days of trading – Friday and Saturday – but traditionally it had been permissible to sell certain goods, though unofficially, on Wednesday. This was the day on which townspeople or outlying villagers used to bring the surplus produce of their gardens to market, and would sell at the same time sundry home-made items – pins and pegs, toys and needlework. Over time this Wednesday event had grown into a substantial fruit and vegetable market, but the selling of household manufactures continued to be tolerated, if not licensed, as long as it kept within limits that did not overlap with the business of the licensed stallholders.

The row that Suez and I had encountered was over a complaint against the Kites by the Constable of Preston, Oswald Mallender. He had come dressed in his grubby greatcoat and shabby hat and holding his tipstaff, and brought with him the more consequential figure of Abraham Scroop of Water Lane, father of the newborn that I had only an hour before heard tell of. In addition to being a burgess of the town, Scroop was one of the market regulators, with the official title of Searcher and Looker of Leather.

He was one of those men who liked to exceed others in everything possible. Therefore his carriage had wheels of greater diameter than any other in town, his house had taller windows and his servants wore the most splendid livery.

'This stall is unlicensed,' Scroop was saying, with a wag of his forefinger, 'and the goods you are selling are of such low quality that they bring disgrace to the leather trade of Preston. As Searcher of Leather I therefore order this trash – not for the first time – off the market place forthwith.'

Jonathan Kite, a young man of impressive physique, was breathing heavily through his nose and evidently trying to control his temper.

'We have the right to sell here. We have always enjoyed the right, like these other people.'

Scroop raised his finger.

'Mr Kite, I am telling you – and Mr Mallender here will second me – that you must produce a trading licence, and if you cannot do so you must clear off out of the market.'

Kite turned and appealed to the stallholders nearby.

'Licence? Who has a licence? None of us has a licence on a Wednesday.'

'I am not concerned with any others. As Looker and Searcher of Leather I am concerned only with the commodity you are selling, to wit, leather goods. Stuff as inferior as this lowers all Preston's leather in the eyes of the world. More reputable producers—'

'More reputable? That's your cronies on the Corporation. I know what you're playing at.'

'Playing at, Mr Kite? Do not think I am playing.'

Kite took a deep breath and lowered his voice.

'Just let me explain, Mr Scroop, as I have explained before, that these here are not *meant* to be things of high quality. That's the whole purpose of this stall. It's for people who do want bags and purses, but at a price they can afford.'

At this point Mallender intervened.

'Now see here, Kite. You are nothing but a tanner. Stay within your appointed task. Do not sell to the public but only to your proper craftsmen and let them make something superior – something worthwhile – out of your crude product. Know your place, Kite, and you may do well. Exceed your place and expect the Corporation to strike you with an heavy hand. An heavy hand, Kite.'

He looked at Scroop, who nodded. Mallender reached into his pocket and produced a paper, thrusting it upon Kite.

'I therefore and by the authority granted me by His Worship the Mayor and the honourable bailiffs do serve you with this notice, that you must present yourself at the next Court Leet in front of His Worship to answer the charge of knowingly selling tawdry goods at market, without licence and contrary to the reputation at large of this ancient borough.'

Beside himself with frustration, Jonathan Kite kicked the trestle of his table so hard that it wobbled and then collapsed, tumbling the display of leather artefacts in a heap on the flagstones.

Mallender tut-tutted, then said, 'Now, now, violence shall not avail, you know. Please be sure to present yourself at Court on Friday week.'

He and Scroop retreated and the Kites knelt to retrieve their sale goods. Suez darted forward and seized a purse in his mouth, running away to the other end of the market, where with a jerk of his head he threw it in the air, seized it again as it landed and began biting it vigorously. By the time I caught up with him the purse resembled chewed meat. I brought it back to the Kites.

'I am sorry – sixpence, is it?'

I produced a coin and handed it over.

'Eh, Mr Cragg,' said Ellen, dropping the sixpence into her apron pocket. 'You're a lawyer. This is the third time in three months we've been dragged before the Mayor's Court. It's just for the fine, I'm thinking. They want the money. Amercement they call it, right? An injustice and a damned outrage, we call it.'

Chapter 3

HALF AN HOUR LATER, after giving Suez a scolding at home and
consigning him to the care of our servant-girl Matty in the
kitchen, I set off with a purposeful stride for the bath house.
Although I still hadn't heard of Fidelis's return, there was no post-
poning my examination of the baby. It had to be done today, with
or without my friend's help.

Going through Friar Gate Bar I hesitated at the turning into
Spaw Brow Lane, then decided against the narrow and now boggy
route that I had taken with Ellen Kite on the previous afternoon.
Instead I walked on and took the longer but firmer thoroughfare
of Water Lane. Because it led down to the western border of the
Marsh, and so on by a causeway to the wharf, as well as to the
township of Ashton and the agricultural country to the north of
the Ribble estuary, Water Lane was a fairly busy road. A number
of cottages stood by the wayside, as well as fly-by-night stalls
selling bacon, cheese, butter or eggs. But interspersed with these
were the gates of more prosperous dwellings and in one of the most
prosperous lived the fruitful Scroop family, with its latest new-born
addition. Coming to it, I was seized by an impulse to ask how the
new baby thrived and turned in at the gate.

A young serving man came to the door. He had a broad chest,
quite startling red hair and a livery coat of dark red. The fellow did

not want to let me in, which he emphasized by himself coming out into the rain and closing the door behind him.

'Mrs Scroop has just given birth, Sir,' he told me in a pronounced Irish accent. 'The house is very quiet with all the children save the oldest sent away. Mr Scroop orders expressly that there are no visitors allowed in except the doctor.'

'Is Mr Scroop himself at home?'

'No, Sir, he is from home this morning. He is arranging a dinner to be held tomorrow evening in town. Now, if I may—'

'I merely called to give Mr and Mrs Scroop my congratulations. The little one thrives, I hope?'

'I believe so, Sir.'

'And Mrs Scroop?'

At that moment the door behind him opened and I saw the substantial figure of Dr Basilius Harrod with his medical wig, black silk stockings and bag grasped firmly in his meaty, stub-fingered hand. The doctor stepped out, his face split in a broad smile and his eyes, looking as kindly and wise as ever, seeming to sparkle with delight in the rightness of everything.

'Well, well! It's Titus Cragg! What brings you here young Titus?'

I had known Harrod since my earliest childhood. He and his wife had been among my parents' friends, and he had naturally been our family physician. Long a widower, Harrod now lived with his seventeen-year-old son Abel and operated a substantial practice, though the younger doctors like Luke Fidelis saw him as fatally attached to outdated methods. I liked him. As a friend he laughed a great deal but, as a doctor, he never made light of sickness or discomfort, always speaking of them in a quiet but authoritative tone.

'I was passing the house and thought I would pay my respects at this happy time for Mrs Scroop,' I told him.

Harrod's smile broadened further as he glanced between myself and the footman, who took this as his dismissal. With a bow, he withdrew to the house and closed the door. The doctor took my arm and guided me to walk with him along the short gravelled drive towards the gate.

'It is not a happy time for Mrs Scroop, I fear. Or not in the eyes of the stars. A thirteenth child born under Virgo. She is full of dread, though I impress on her that Virgo is as often positive as it is negative. In the stars, as in the bodily fluids, balance is all, is it not?'

'You have told me so in my youth many times, Doctor Harrod. Did you attend the birth?'

Harrod laughed heartily and slapped my back.

'Well, I did, Sir, but it was a damned near-run thing. Mrs Scroop was out of Preston until yesterday, visiting with relatives in Yorkshire. Her labour pains first came on at Burnley as she made her way back and she barely arrived home before the beginning of the birth itself. I have just been in to see mother and son, the last call on my round this morning before dinner.'

Harrod's house stood in its own grounds on Water Lane immediately beside that of the rather larger and more modern residence of the Scroop family.

'And the child thrives, I hope,' I said as we walked along, leaving both houses behind us.

'He was born in such excitement, Cragg, but do you know? He is the quietest baby I ever delivered.'

'That is good, is it not?'

'Lusty complaint at being born is the characteristic of babies. That this one complains little, or not at all, merely increases Mrs Scroop's anxiety, and to an extent that of myself also.'

'Still, it must make life easier for the wet nurse, having no squalling in her ears.'

'Mrs Scroop is a remarkable woman. She will have no wet nurse near, but gives suck herself. Now, my boy, what of you? May

I hazard a guess at the business that takes you down Water Lane? Coroner's business, is it?'

So I told him of the other newborn baby, the one now lying cold in the bath house, and of how it had been discovered. Of course he had heard about it, as the news had already flashed up and down Water Lane by the end of the previous afternoon. He asked me two or three pertinent questions as to its appearance, which I answered as best I could.

'But I am on my way now to make an inspection of the body, Doctor. You would not care to take a look yourself, I suppose? A professional medical opinion might be convenient.'

The idea of asking him came to me quite unexpectedly but, in the absence of Fidelis, it seemed a good one. Harrod was a man of long experience. Curiosity in such matters is extremely strong in all of us and I did not expect Harrod to decline my invitation – which he did not.

'I don't suppose I shall be of much use to you. I am nothing but a booby where legal matters are concerned. But with that proviso I shall be glad to accompany you, of course.'

We set off together as renewed gusts of rain hammered our faces.

'I would say this girl-child was definitely stillborn,' said Dr Harrod. 'Quite definitely.'

We had collected the bath-house key from the Parsons and were now standing in the sluicing room, on either side of a small table that I had found and carried in from the bathkeeper's kennel and placed the body on. I had asked Hannah Parsons to wash the mud and filth from the dead baby, and this she had attempted to do, but with only partial success. Opening the wrapping linen, I saw that the worst of the caked mud was gone, but there were still streaks of grey dirt all over the skin.

'My first question, in such cases,' I said, 'is whether this is a premature birth. A stillbirth.'

I had seen many stillbirths and they almost always appeared more like skinned rabbits than human beings. This, on the other hand, seemed a fully formed baby girl.

'To my eye, this does not look a premature birth,' I said. 'Yet you say she never breathed?'

'Oh, no. She was ripe and ready to be born but when it happened she breathed not a sip of breath. Died in the womb before she had the chance.'

'What leads you to that conclusion, Doctor?'

'Forty years of experience leads me to it. There is a certain colour, a certain quality or texture, shall I say, about the skin. Then there's the way the mouth is . . . I cannot put it into words, but I assure you I am right. I would stake my reputation on it. My entire reputation.'

Dr Harrod was speaking with conviction, in the way that he always had when talking of matters within his professional scope. Yet he had not approached the body with anything resembling the attention that Luke Fidelis would have given it. Harrod had bent his head to it just once, breathing in through the nose as he did so, as if sniffing. Then he had straightened his back and whistled a faint tune a little uneasily through his teeth. When I suggested he might like to turn the baby over and see the other side, he recoiled.

'Touch it? Certainly not, Titus. And I would recommend that you do not do so. Not its bare skin. That might be dangerous. Troubled spirits can be transferred in that way – from it to you. You should avoid acquiring a troubled spirit at all costs, believe me. I have seen men go stark mad by it – mad far beyond the power of medicine to control.'

'Hannah Parsons has already washed it,' I pointed out.

'Oh, she merely held it under the falling stream outside, I expect. I doubt she handled it directly.'

He turned away from the table and began to circulate around the room while fluttering his fingers and resuming his whistling. Finally he paused beneath the high window and gazed up at the sky.

'I must make my way home now, young Cragg,' he said, turning back to me after a few moments. 'My boy is a hungry animal and must be fed to time. I hope my attendance here has been helpful. And please—'

He held up his hand.

'Don't think of a fee. *Pro bono publico*, my friend. I take much satisfaction in assisting public officers in their duties when I can. Good day to you.'

With these amiable words Dr Harrod hurried away from the bath house leaving me staring at the baby on the table, wondering what to do next. Fidelis would of course have scorned the reservation about troubled spirits. Yet I was disturbed by Harrod's urgency and the compelling manner of his warning, and held back from touching it directly. I did, however, see that I could use the linen cloth to turn it so that the other side would be exposed. Gingerly I got my hands under the cloth and, through it, grasped the body, rolling it inside its wrapping until it lay on its front. I raised the cloth once again, straightened my back and, in that instant, I realized I might have to change my whole view of the case. The back of the skull was horribly wounded, as if from a heavy blow.

But I had no time to consider the matter, for now there was a hammering on the bath-house door and a voice calling my name. I went out through the plunge room and the changing room to the entrance hall where I pulled the heavy door open. Luke Fidelis stood beaming at me on the step.

'Greetings, my friend. As you see, I am returned.'

'And in high spirits, evidently.'

'Why not? In two days I have removed a bladder stone the size of a plum, lanced a plague of boils, pulled a mouthful of teeth, rebroken a crookedly set fracture, played at cricket with farm boys and been kissed by a blacksmith's daughter. Who'd be a doctor of law when they might be one of medicine?'

'Who indeed?'

'Well, this is a delightful place.'

He tethered his horse and came in stretching his arms wide to indicate that he referred to the building.

'The Lorrises told me that you had been enquiring after me, and then Furzey told me you were here. I have to go on to Penwortham by the low-water ford, and since this is on my way and low tide is not for another hour, I saw no reason not to come and find you. What a perfect little temple of health and yet I have never been inside it before. Shall we make sacrifice to the goddess Hygenia while we are here?'

'Sacrifice has already been made, Luke, and discovered nearby. There has been unpleasantness.'

'Hah! You are no stranger to that.'

'It is a baby, Luke.'

He stopped laughing at once and followed me to the sluicing room where I showed him the infant body, lying with its injured head exposed.

'She was found in a tan-pit in the skin-yard below,' I told him. 'By this, it looks as if she's been struck, or maybe had her head dashed against something sharp-edged.'

'Yes, that is possible. But not necessarily when the child was living.'

Fidelis bent to look more closely at the wound, delicately taking the head between finger and thumb, and twitching it this way and that to catch the light. Then he returned the body to its back and inspected the stump of blackened navel string projecting no more than an inch from its belly.

'That is interesting,' he remarked as he took from his bag a leather roll containing his instruments.

'How is it interesting?'

'All in good time,' he said, as he carefully unwrapped the body, opened the roll and laid it out on one of the benches by the wall. Then he took forceps and a scalpel and returned to the newborn while I sat on the bench beside the instruments and watched.

'The question we should address first is whether this little girl was born alive, or dead.'

'Yes, I have already—'

'Because, according to the answer, some poor young woman's neck will or will not be at hazard – am I right?'

'We do not yet know who the mother is,' I said, 'but, according to the law, a murder trial need only show that she was with child and gave birth in secret. She can then be assumed, legally speaking, to be a murderess, whether or not she made that wound in the head, or did other harm to him.'

Fidelis appeared to make an incision in the baby's chest and was now opening it. He stopped and looked at me.

'Assumed? That is extraordinary. The two do not necessarily follow.'

He returned to work as I explained about the law of 1624. His reaction was not unlike Elizabeth's.

'It is a travesty of reason, never mind justice.'

'I agree, but it is not my business to interpret Acts of Parliament. I only have to do the Coroner's job: determine whether the death be stillbirth, accident, or murder and, if the latter, by whom. Can you tell if the child died in the womb?'

'Not from just looking.'

I deliberately did not tell him of Dr Harrod's method and

opinion, for I did not want him to be influenced into producing a different conclusion out of pure contrariness.

'How, then?'

'There is a test, though not always conclusive. Bring me a bucket of clean water, if you please, and we shall try it.'

I found a bucket which, as the taps inside the building were dry, I took outside to fill from the spring which fed the bath house's water supply and otherwise flowed through a channel underneath the building and into a conduit beyond. The water I brought back was clean and clear.

'Put it down there, Titus.'

Fidelis pointed to one of the wooden benches where the light from the window most strongly played and I put the bucket down. Once I had let it go the water jiggled, and the sheen of light across its surface chopped and sparkled. I looked questioningly at Fidelis and he said.

'We must wait until it settles.'

When he was satisfied that the water in the bucket was as still as he wanted he picked up something from the table where he had been working, which seemed to be a small whitish scrap of tissue.

'One of the baby's lungs,' he told me, holding it up with all the solemnity of a fairground magician preparing the audience for his next trick. He brought the tiny lung to the bucket and, with a care that I would like to describe as fond, but perhaps I should say precise, he placed it on the surface of the water, then stood back.

I looked at the little white fragment as it turned gently on the surface of the water, and then at Fidelis.

'What?' I said.

'Do you not notice? It floats.'

'Yes,' I said. 'I see that. But I don't see what it means.'

Fidelis sighed, picking the lung from the water and taking it back to the table.

'Well, I'm sorry to say it means we are no further on.'

Now producing a tinderbox and a candle stub he lit the wick and held the flame close to the tiny head. Bending his head down beside it he seemed to be trying to see inside the mouth, nose and ear holes.

'There's something interesting there, too,' he said, straightening his back. 'It might prove more informative than the floating experiment.'

'Tell me more.'

But Fidelis looked at his watch.

'Not now. It requires further examination and I do not have the time today. The tide has already turned and I must cross the river by the ford to Penwortham, where there is a boy with a possibly mortal fever.'

'But you say we have not finished here. And I am burning to know the meaning of these things you have been doing.'

My friend was threading a needle.

'The living come before the dead, Titus. And, if I do not go now, the ford will be impassable for ten hours.'

'The inquest is tomorrow afternoon.'

'So, I will close this little one up and take him with me. I shall make the examination in the meantime.'

I was horrified by this suggestion.

'Take him with you? Impossible, Luke! The body must always lie as near as possible to where it was found. It must not be removed until the jury has viewed it. I forbid you to take it with you as if it were no more than a . . . a sample of merchandise.'

Fidelis sighed.

'Very well. I shall have to return here in the morning. Will you join me? I can be here by ten o'clock.'

Five minutes later I was legging him up into the saddle. As he wheeled the horse, I grabbed hold of the reins again.

'At least tell me what you noticed about the navel cord. You said it was interesting.'

'Yes. It suggests an important possibility.'

'What is it?'

'That the mother of our poor mite did not give birth alone.'

'There was an accomplice?'

'I would not go so far. Perhaps an attendant.'

He tightened the rein, I let go, and he clattered away down Cold Bath Lane.

Chapter 4

'DON'T YOU DARE to deny it, Kathy Brock, you dirty murdering bitch! You dropped the babby, you kept it quiet and then you killed it.'

I had walked down Cold Bath Lane and was about to rap on the door of the Parsons' house on Water Lane in order to deposit the bath-house key. Through the door I could hear the voice screeching in fury and recognised it as that of Hannah herself.

Instead of knocking I turned the door handle and stepped inside. The room was filled with women, two of whom had laid hold of a young person of perhaps seventeen and were pulling her roughly this way and that. She struggled under their mauling whilst crying out that their accusations were untrue – a plump girl of short stature, and dressed in the style of the skin-yard, which I recognised from the garb of Ellen and the other tanner-women that I'd met the previous day.

Kathy Brock continued to struggle and cry out, as the women dragged her across the room to a settle and pinned her down upon it.

'Let's have a look at her. We'll soon find out if she's thrown a babby.'

'Get her jugs out. See if they're giving milk.'

Hannah stepped in front of Kathy. She grabbed the bodice of her dress and, with strong arms, ripped it wide open. I was vainly trying to make my voice heard against this violation but the women were babbling encouragement to their leader and were too far in fury to hear me, let alone be stopped from what they were doing. It seemed to me they cheered as the bath-house keeper seized the poor girl's exposed dugs and worked them between her fingers, squeezing and pulling as her victim squealed in pain and embarrassment. Despite my renewed protests, I was suddenly quite unable to suppress my curiosity. I wanted to know for myself whether milk was coming forth. So instead of looking decently away I craned my neck.

No milk appeared.

'Well she's dry but that proves nowt,' said Hannah. 'We must have a look lower down.'

This was finally too much. As two of the women grabbed Kathy's skirts to pull them over her head, I bellowed,

'STOP THIS AT ONCE!'

Describing the scene to Elizabeth later, in our parlour, I used a rather boastful tone and military metaphors. The women had been startled not only by my unexpected presence but by the fury of my voice, and I had immediately seized the initiative. Charging straight into the melee, I forced my way to the centre and stood at bay in front of the girl, ready to repel any further attacks by the women and telling them to calm themselves while Kathy collected herself and pulled her clothing together. Then I raised her up and escorted her through the hostile ranks of her accusers to the door, from where I sent her on her way. She was crying, but at least she could return home without being further molested.

'Titus, my love, you were a proper Don Quixote,' said Elizabeth, as she worked on a complicated piece of embroidery. 'You hero-ically hacked your way through an army of sheep.'

My wife's laughter was too musical to my ear to be truly offen-sive, even when I was mocked. So I only said, 'You should read that great book and you will see the difference. Poor Don Quixote was deluded; I was saving an innocent girl from a vile examination.'

'How do you know she is innocent? Did you question the girl?'

'No. She was much distressed. I sent her on her way.'

'Yet those women suspected the girl.'

'Yes, though without evidence. I put that to them afterwards and they had little to say in their own support.'

Elizabeth relented.

'Well, Titus, it was cruel of them to persecute her if it really was for no reason, and so I think you did right to let her go without further distressing her.'

'But why *did* the women take matters into their own hands like that? If they suspect Kathy Brock they ought to call in the law.'

Elizabeth grew serious as she considered the question, but did not stop working her needle.

'I think because, being women, their suspicion was magnified by passion. We women find it hard to believe that the magistrates who enforce the law can ever regard the birth of a child with the same concern as we do, because they are men, you see.'

'But last night, when we spoke about secret pregnancy, you defended girls guilty of it.'

'I defended poor women held to be murderesses without a hearing, when all they've done is deliver a stillborn child.'

She lowered her sewing to her lap.

'To give birth, and then to *kill* your child deliberately – that is so different! It lies beyond my powers of forgiveness, or those of any of my sex. If the tannery girl that those women seized had committed such a crime, she would deserve to be exposed and punished. She would have refused God's charge of giving life to immortal souls.'

Her mocking tone had long gone and, now, tears were glinting in her eyes.

'My dearest wife,' I said, kneeling by her chair and clasping her hands. 'You are not yet thirty and God is merciful. It is not too late for you – for us – I am sure of it.'

Going out at half past six I went straight to one of my favourite resorts – Sebastian Sweeting's bookshop on Church Gate. After Elizabeth's brief tears – she is never down-hearted for long – we had changed the subject and spoken of what had happened in the household during the day, and laughed over one or two domestic trivialities. However, I had in mind a gift for Elizabeth from Sweeting's to cheer her further. I also, not incidentally, thought that a visit there might afford me some enlightenment in the matter of the baby now lying in Cold Bath Lane.

In truth, every visit to that bookseller was in some way enlightening and the snuff that he gave out to his customers was excellent also. So, as soon as I had entered, the two of us snuffed and sneezed companionably, and then Sweeting asked by way of conversation if I was engaged as coroner in the matter of the dead baby newly discovered. I had been hoping he would.

'You have heard about this?' I asked.

'Naturally, Titus. It's spoken of all over town. But no one knows who its murdering mother is.'

'We don't know if it is a murder at all, you know, but you are right to wonder who the mother is. I am holding the inquest tomorrow. I hope for a decisive verdict, though I cannot be sure of one. I find it hard to understand the case myself, and so will the jury. What sort of young woman, a girl as she may be, kills a defenceless baby, and one that is her own flesh and blood, having come out of herself?'

I paused. Sweeting was squinting at the ceiling, his brow creased. I had deliberately planted a seed, but would it grow? Whenever one put a question to this remarkable bookseller, whether on politics, religion, history or natural philosophy, he regarded himself as challenged to recommend a book on the subject. He almost invariably succeeded.

'I think I have something where this question is addressed,' he said at last.

He rose and ambled to the back of the shop, disappearing into some inner recess where shelves reached from floor to ceiling, crammed with his stock. He returned carrying a single volume, which he opened. He riffled through a few of the pages. At last, with a grunt of satisfaction, he placed it in my hands.

'This is *The Fable of the Bees*, or *Private Vices, Public Benefits*,' he said. 'I fancy you will find something to the purpose there.'

'I've heard of this book,' I said. 'Is it not a notorious tract justifying vice, depravity and crime?'

Sweeting rubbed his hands together in relish.

'The same. Divines and philosophers everywhere have condemned it as satanic. Rather pleasingly, I think, the author's name is Mandevil: he is dead now and feeling the bite, according to some, of his master's red-hot pincers. In his lifetime, however, he never repented but issued half a dozen editions of the book, with more matter added in defence of his case to each of them. This one is the last and the most complete and, if you want to know, I think he occasionally writes good sense. Another pinch of snuff?'

I took one.

'And does this Mandevil talk directly about women that kill their babies?'

'He does.'

'And says it is permissible?'

'The book begins as a poem like a Fable of Lafontaine,' said Sweeting, avoiding the question. 'It is about a beehive where all the features of human society are found in small. Mandevil was a physician in London, but originally a Dutchman I believe. He may or may not have gone to the devil but he was a clever fellow who understood much about the human mind, and why people do good or evil. Here, let me see.'

He took the book from me, found a page and handed it back.

'Here is the introduction to his lengthy explanation of the poem, which he published to continue the argument with his detractors.'

I read the first sentence.

'"One of the greatest reasons why so few people understand themselves is that most writers are always teaching men what they *should* be, and hardly ever troubling their heads with telling them what they really are."'

I looked up at Sweeting. He always had the keenest eye for the taste of his customers.

'You knew that sentiment would appeal to me, did you not?'

Sweeting answered with a complacent smile.

I went on, 'And you will warrant that he writes of mothers killing their babies?'

'If he doesn't, you may return the book without charge.'

'So what does he say?'

Sweeting merely shrugged. It was, after all, his business to sell me the book, not to tell me its whole contents. I sighed.

'How much, then?'

'Half a guinea.'

'I'll take it. Now, there's something else that I need. I have seen it announced in *The Gentleman's Magazine* that there is a newly Englished *Don Quixote* from the London booksellers. Have you got it yet?'

Sweeting repaired once more to an inner recess of the shop, and came back with two bound volumes in quarto size that he placed on the counter for my inspection.

'A guinea for the set,' he said. 'I have been trying to get it in sheets for personal binding, but the booksellers delay and delay in sending them. There is so much more profit in the bound edition

and it is selling like smuggler's brandy, according to my correspond-
ent in London. It seems that Quixotic fever is prevalent there.'

'Who is this latest translator?'

'A very surprising one: the court and society painter Mr Jarvis,
now dead. I am told that he had been quietly working on it for many
years, though no one suspected him of understanding Spanish. He
was a friend of Dean Swift and did his portrait. A very vainglorious
fellow, but I find the work to be in good clean English.'

He took another pinch of snuff while I glanced at two or three
passages. Sweeting was right. It looked good reading.

'And there are more than fifty plates illustrating the story,' he
added. 'They are not by Jarvis, but Mr Vanderbank, which is a
good thing as he's the better artist.'

I made up my mind all at once.

'Put it on my bill along with the bees book. It is for my wife.
She compared me this evening to the Don as a joke and I intend to
answer by requiring her to read the novel.'

'That will be no hardship.'

'No, but I am hoping it will instruct her about the difference
between her husband and a crazy knight of old Spain.'

Sweeting began making up my purchases into a paper parcel.

'And now you shall bring her to be as supple as a glove, though
you find her harder than a cork tree.'

The remark caught me by surprise.

'I am sorry, Sweeting?'

'It is Sancho Panza's promise to Don Quixote, you know, when
he supposedly takes the Don's messages of love to Dulcinea. It is
surprisingly poetical, don't you think? I hope this gift has the same
effect on your wife. I'll have the boy take the books over to your
house right away.'

* * *

From Sweeting's I walked the few yards to the Turk's Head, on the chance that Fidelis had returned from Penwortham and was dining there. The coffee house was in an uproar of noise and jollity. A long table at the far end of the room was laid to a dinner for twelve of Preston's citizens, presided over by Abraham Scroop, whose home I had called at earlier in the day. Seeing no sign of my friend I stopped the coffee house proprietor Noah Plumtree as he passed by with a steaming haunch of meat for carving.

'Have you seen Dr Fidelis, Noah?'

'No, Mr Cragg. He has not been in for a few days.'

I gestured towards the banquet.

'And what is this? Can Abraham Scroop be celebrating the birth of his son?'

'No, Sir. Mr Scroop has laid on a dinner in honour of Captain Strawboy there, who is to be partner in his business.'

'Really? Scroop and Strawboy? That seems unlikely.'

'Unlikely but rather lively, don't you agree?'

The guests ranged around the table were merchants, most of them solidly prosperous members of the Corporation. They wore clothes with as many buttons and braids of gold and silver as ever they could afford. Some, like the former Mayor Ephraim Grimshaw, were fat and florid, with goitrous necks and bulging eyes. Others were thin, grey skinned and made angular by years of devotion to their ledgers. All were in the process of becoming communally and bestially drunk.

The young man sitting in the guest of honour's place to Scroop's right was of an entirely different stamp from these citizens. His name was Charles Strawboy and he was dressed in a plum-coloured military coat. He, in fact, held a commission in the army as captain of engineers, though he had been on half pay from his regiment for the past three years. Tall, slim and vigorous, Strawboy had regular features and an abundant head of black hair worn simply – with no wig or buckled side-curls. His dress was fashionable but far from foppish. His blue eyes flashed with humour and his voice was a rich baritone, confident and unaffected. Not surprisingly, half the ladies of Preston were anxious to know him.

I had met Strawboy once or twice when he had first come to town towards the end of the previous year. At that time he was accompanying Lord Grassington, and the pair had placed before the Corporation projects which, they claimed, would be of great benefit to all. One had indeed been for the renovation of the spa, but they had also proposed various other schemes: a bridge across the river to Penwortham, it seems, and a permanent stand for the racecourse on Preston Moor, with other useful civic improvements.

For a moment Strawboy caught my eye looking across the room at him, and he fractionally raised an eyebrow before returning his attention to some bombast of Grimshaw's, and then to Scroop as he rose to his feet and called for a toast. At this point James Starkey came in from the street. I had not seen him since we had played bowls.

'Cragg!' he said clapping me on the back. 'No doubt you want to discuss a return match after my victory yesterday.'

'No, I just came in to see if—'

'Success at bowls is as much a matter of courage as it is of accuracy by eye and hand, you know. To succeed one must seize the wood with all the mettle of Prince Rupert in the field.'

'Yet Prince Rupert lost in the end.'

'Very well, I could say Oliver Cromwell. It matters not. What matters is that a game of bowls is exactly the same as life and society. Striving and winning – that's the stuff of life, you know.'

'Is that so? Well, I was just listening to Mr Scroop's address to his guests—'

'And passion. One does need passion. Let me expand on this. Can one truly say that bowls is really exactly the same as life? I argue, Sir, that practice, experience and natural ability all get one so far. But guts, Sir, they are the secret of real success, they are all that counts, whether on the bowling green or in the counting house, the court room, the field of battle et cetera. You see it is my contention that . . .'

It took some time to extricate myself from Starkey's company, and then not without engaging to play bowls with him in the near future. By the time I had done so, Scroop's speech was over and he had sat down.

When I went home and presented the *Don Quixote* to Elizabeth, she gave a shout of delight, and hugged me saying she would go to bed and begin reading it immediately. I took *The Fable of the Bees* into my library in order to do the same. I was hoping it might answer the difficult question of how and why a woman might kill a baby.

I was soon absorbed in the book. I found that I was not faced with the darkness of a 'Satanic Bible', as Mandevil's enemies had called it. On the contrary, *The Fable of the Bees* contains much ingenious satire, with the argument lying under that many of the things which we call individual vices are really good for our society. So, vanity and greed lead people to spend money and thereby to increase general prosperity; gluttony improves agriculture; self-love generates virtue and heroism by making us sensitive to how others perceive us; and lust, of course, is needed for the generation of our species.

I found that only a part of Mandevil's purpose was satirical; he also rationally expounds his philosophy. Telling people 'what they are' was full of peril, though, and he risked much. I only fully understood why so much ordure had been poured on to him by his enemies when I came to his remarks on the sexual feelings of the female. Mandevil goes some way beyond what society calls proper when he writes of a woman's 'secret wishes', meaning of course in the bedroom. A woman's desire, says he, is 'the grand truth of the matter which modesty bids her, with all her faculties, to deny'. The author was lucky not to have been banged into the stocks for that – and yet he is right. Women may enjoy a bedding as much as a man; Elizabeth enjoyed one as much as I did; and I thanked God for that.

Not surprisingly after such reading, this was on my mind as I went up to our bedchamber, but I was a little put out to find that Elizabeth had on her mind a man quite other than myself.

'The projector Captain Strawboy is in town again,' she said, laying her book down as I came into the bedchamber.

'I know. I saw him tonight. He was being dined by Abraham Scroop and a dozen of Preston's finest.'

She sighed.

'Such a waste.'

'Of food?'

'Of a man, Titus, and an unmarried one. He is too fine a fellow to spend his time gluttonising with the likes of Abraham Scroop. He should be dancing at assemblies or playing music and, in between times, fighting a duel or two.'

'He and Scroop are to be business partners, I've heard. It surprises me that Captain Strawboy concerns himself with projects. When I last heard, he was in line to inherit Lord Grassington's estates.'

'He still is,' she answered. 'That is why Scroop cultivates him. They say his dearest wish is for the Captain to marry one of his daughters.'

'That would be a stroke of luck for Strawboy.'

'More so for Scroop and his daughter. The Captain is not only handsome, he has many useful connections being not only heir to a title, but a friend to my Lord Strange and other bigwigs all over the county.'

'You are well informed about the Captain's affairs, my heart.'

45

'The ladies buzz with news of his return, you know. The captain is such a favourite.'

But later as I lay waiting for sleep I wondered: what could a projector such as Strawboy do for a merchant like Scroop? Strawboy was a military engineer. What did he know of rags and bones, scraps and ashes?

Chapter 5

IN THE MORNING, before making my way to the bath house to meet Fidelis, I slipped into the office and made out a summons for Kathy Brock to give witness at the inquest later in the day. I regretted now that I had not already taken a statement from her. Her neighbours' accusation, I still believed, had been based on nothing but prejudice whipped up by Hannah Parsons. But my wife's tears of the day before still lingered in my memory. If Kathy had done this thing she must certainly be openly exposed. But, by the same token, if she were innocent she should have the chance to defend her good name in public.

Stuffing the completed summons into my coat pocket, I hurried away to the bath house. Passing the gate of the Scroop house on Water Lane, I saw that a carriage stood before its door and that a troop of children of descending height were going from it into the house: it was the brood of Scroop children returned from their temporary exile. They were being ushered into the house by their eldest sister and by a man I recognised as Captain Strawboy who, when the last of the children emerged, tucked her arm in a friendly way into his. He was laughing and trying to jolly her with a pinch of her cheek, which she did not appear to like, pulling away from him. It is not true that youth is always blithe, I thought. It can be surly enough, too.

I found Fidelis waiting for me with his horse at the bath-house door. Short of sleep, he looked pallid.

'I enquired after you last night at the Turk's Head,' I told him.

'I did not come back to Preston last night. I've come directly from the boy's bedside, and have kept a long vigil.'

'You saved his life?'

'He'll live, probably, though not by any clever work of mine. His fever was abating naturally as I left him.'

He went ahead of me into the sluicing room, where he moved the table that we had used the day before to a position beneath the window.

I said, 'So what are we here for now? Whatever it is, I hope you will be able to give your opinion at last about whether the little one was born alive, or dead. By the way, I did not tell you yesterday that I already had an opinion on the matter. Dr Harrod had a look at the remains before you came yesterday, and his opinion was—'

'Harrod?' my friend interrupted. 'You cannot have shown *Harrod* the body?'

'I did, while you were gadding about the Fylde kissing wenches and playing football.'

'It was cricket, Titus. But of all people, not Harrod!'

'There's no call to make that sour face. Harrod offered his services freely and, as I had no intelligence on when you would return, I accepted him.'

'The man's a perfect charlatan. He's never looked inside a body; I would be surprised if he has ever *touched* a body.'

'He certainly seemed reluctant to—'

'He just passes out nostrums and talks about the stars and the balance of the humours. I suppose he *might* have heard the news that blood circulates around the body, since that was demonstrated when his grandfather was a boy. But his prescriptions follow no reason except that of the ancients – and they thought the heart was a species of furnace. You cannot seriously have asked him!'

'He was our family physician for thirty years. We all liked him.'

'I like my tailor, but I won't ask him to set my broken leg.'

I admit that I was stung by his scorn and sulked a little. I regarded Harrod as an honourable fellow and he had undeniably long medical experience. Fidelis however could not let the matter go.

'So what arrant nonsense did Harrod tell you? I know in advance that it was nonsense.'

'He told me he was certain that the little girl was stillborn, Luke.'

'I would wager a month of fees that he made no examination.'

'He assured me that he could tell from the general appearance.'

Fidelis gave a scoffing laugh.

'Then what did he say about the injury to the head?'

'Nothing. He never saw it.'

'Ha! Charlatan. Of course, he would know nothing of the floating test we performed. The lung-in-water test.'

'He made no test at all. Is the lung test a new thing?'

'By Harrod's standard, it is. It is the test for stillbirth that they do at St Thomas's Hospital in London. It is commended in his book by Dr Cheseldon.'

I had never heard of Cheseldon but my respect for the test was a little increased by knowing that it had appeared in a book.

I said, 'I watched what you did, Luke, but I'm damned if I know what it all meant.'

'Well, this is how it works. It is surmised that if the baby drew breath then air has been drawn into its lung, and some of that air will still be present in the organ's hundreds of tiny pockets, even after breathing ceases. This will then bear the tissue up in the water.'

'Making it float.'

'Exactly.'

'Which in this case it did, meaning that the baby did draw breath. So your test proves Harrod was wrong, does it?'

'It is not my test.'

'Cheseldon's test, then.'

'Yes, Cheseldon's test. But no, it does not prove any such thing, unfortunately. I would love to show up Harrod's idiocy but here is the difficulty. If the lung sinks, I would take that as proof positive that the baby never breathed. But if the lung floats there is more than one possible reason for that, especially if it is performed some time after death.'

'And that is?'

'Putrescence.'

'I don't understand you.'

'Putrescence produces air from the dead tissue, or something like air, but foul-smelling.'

'You mean like a fart?'

'More or less. Your fart is made in the gut by much the same process, supposedly. Van Helsing in Holland invented a word for this foul air: he called it "gas". And this gas, it has been averred, if present within the tissue might have the very same effect as air; it might buoy it up in water.'

'So even if the baby never breathed there could be air in the lung because of putrescence.'

'Not air. Gas.'

'Which means that yesterday's floating test left us no further along.'

'I am afraid not. As I say, it is only conclusive if the lung sinks to the bottom of the bucket, meaning no breath and no gas either.'

We may not have been any further along, but I admired Fidelis's willingness to think fresh thoughts. Certainly Dr Harrod was not flattered by the comparison. Fidelis had fearlessly handled the dead little one, had looked inside it and carried out a test, which would be the basis for his deposition before my inquest. Harrod had disdained even to touch the remains, and had given his opinion in one short sentence. My regard for our old family physician had begun slightly to diminish.

'Well,' I said, 'even if your test—'

'Cheseldon's test.'

'Cheseldon's test. Even if we could have used it to show that the baby breathed, we would still have no proof of murder. A child can die naturally or by chance at any time: of disease, for instance, or from falling. What is your conclusion about the wounded head?'

'I have not got one. I have nothing to show how it happened – whether the baby was deliberately struck and so murdered, for instance, or that he died by accident.'

'I, on the contrary, feel quite sure that it was an accident. I propose that the injury occurred when the body was cast into the water, by hitting the side of the tan-pit perhaps.'

'Why are you so sure?'

'Because no woman will batter her newborn child, Luke. If she wanted to kill it she would smother it, or drown it.'

He sighed and opened his medical bag.

'I will not contradict you, but I would like to do some more work on the body nevertheless.'

'You are going to open it again?'

'Yes, I noticed something yesterday that warrants investigation. It may be nothing; it may on the other hand be highly significant. In order to be sure I must carry out a dissection.'

'Do you require me to help?'

'No, I can work alone.'

'Then I shall stroll a little. I want to visit the Skeleton Inn to ensure their readiness for the hearing. Then I must go down to the skin-yard and serve a summons.'

I left Fidelis preparing for the operation – unrolling his instruments and setting them out ready for use, removing his coat and rolling up his sleeves, then bringing the wrapped body of the child to the table.

'This will take me about an hour,' he called after me.

The Skeleton Inn, which overlooked our small river harbour on the edge of the Marsh, may well have seen more prosperous days but was now ill-kempt. The upper room that Furzey had engaged for the afternoon's inquest was the best they could provide, yet I found it a gloomy, unpleasant chamber. The squeaking floor undulated, the walls were nowhere vertical and the ceiling was low and ribbed with rough-cut black beams. Still, it would have to serve. I left some instructions with Clarkson the innkeeper about seating for myself, Furzey, the jury and the public, then walked out again and quickly along Whatery Lane towards the skin-yard at the Marsh's edge.

I first strolled all the way around the yard's circumference, outside the surrounding wall. This was a good deal higher than a man and, though the cracks between the masonry grew weeds and it was ragged around the top, it was nowhere breached and couldn't easily be climbed over. I concluded that the skin-yard could be entered without difficulty only through the main gate on the lane.

This was a high and solid double gate, but it was furnished with a small inset porter's door. I found it lying open, and stepped through. The smell in the air this morning was so sharp that I involuntarily coughed and put my hand to my nose. The pungency was enough to convince me that Van Helsing's fart gas might indeed exist and that I was at this moment filling my lungs with it.

A man whose age was hard to determine walked towards me. He wore a leather apron and carried a leather bucket. I knew little enough of leather, and how it is made, but looking at him I was prepared to believe that his weathered and pugnacious face had also somehow been tanned along with the hides he worked.

'You clap your palm to your nose, Mister,' he said. 'Offends you, does it – the smell?'

'Not offends, but it is strong to be sure. You must be bothered by it yourself, working in the yard day by day.'

He tapped his bulbous nose.

'This here is an amazing organ. It can make friends with the worst. What is your name and business, Sir?'

I told him my name and that I was on Coroner's business, at which he bowed and told me grandly, as if laying claim to the throne of the Holy Roman Empire, that he was Daniel Gogarty and that his family had worked in the skin-yard for four generations. In a gesture that he seemed to have learned from watching plays, he threw up his free arm and circled it, to encompass not only the breadth but the whole history of the skinners' domain.

'When we came here,' he said in a ringing voice, 'there were ten, no, there were *a dozen* master tanners that worked these pits. Those were the days – the great days, the days of plenty.'

He took a step towards me and presented two fingers to my face.

'Now there's just a couple of master tanners left in the skin-yard of Preston – that's meself and Barnaby Kite.'

He frowned over his fingers like a man baffled by fate.

'Is that not enough?' I asked.

'Oh aye, it is enough. It is enough – for *now*. But soon even that will be too many.'

He edged nearer still, lowered his face and then rolled his eyeballs up to look at me. His proximity filled my nose with the skin-yard smell in pure concentration, and I could not prevent my gorge from rising.

'The time is coming,' he stated in a voice of portent, 'when there will be no more skinners in Preston, none at all; when we shall cry, as Jerusalem cried, that the adversary hath spread out his hand upon all her pleasant things, and the heathen entered into her sanctuary. I see it as if in a vision. Our days are few and ruin cometh after.'

'Oh come-come. How shall you be ruined? There will always be call for leather, I know that.'

I edged as imperceptibly as I could away from him. He seemed half crazy. He shook his head, as if the woe lay heavy on him.

'Do you not know also that there is call for improvements? For enclosure and engrossment? For manufactories and tolls? Many things, none good, and all blown into this town on one man's bad breath.'

There was a brief silence, then Gogarty's expression changed. His eyes narrowed in suspicion, while his lips tensed and relaxed in a sucking motion. I began to wonder if he was more than half mad.

'And now we find *you* come here. Or rather, you come *here*. What is your purpose? Are you for us, or against?'

'I am neither,' I told him. 'It is really nothing to do with me. My only business is to enquire into the circumstances of the child's body that Ellen Kite found here.'

It was as if his mind, having wandered for some moments, recollected itself.

'Oh, aye! I know that. Babby in tan-pit. Coroner sent for. Inquest today.'

He paused for a moment of thought, then went on.

'I won't go. I never leave the skin-yard, me. But young Ellen, she'll speak up, and very well she'll do it.'

'I have no doubt of that. And here she is in person!'

With some relief I saw Ellen Kite crossing the yard with a young man. They had been carrying a tub between them but as soon as she caught sight of me, she spoke to the youth and they put the tub down. Now she was coming on towards us.

'Are you here to remind me of the inquest this afternoon, Mr Cragg?' she asked. 'I haven't forgot, you know. And I'll wear my cleanest clothes.'

'No, no, Ellen, it isn't that. I just wanted to know more about your work here – to inform myself of how the skin-yard is operated.'

'I'll show you round, shall I?'

She looked about until she spotted a boy of about thirteen.

'Joseph!' she shouted, pointing at the tub she had left. 'Help Michael with that.'

The boy jumped to, and from this I saw that Ellen was a young woman of some authority in this confined world.

'Well, these are the tanning pits,' she said, taking me on a circular walk around them as she explained that the dark brown and foul-smelling solution in which they steeped was prepared with bark brought from the Welsh and Cumberland oak forests, pounded up and mixed with urine and faeces (those of dogs being especially efficacious) and all boiled in hot water to make a vile but necessary soup.

'There's eighteen pits here but we only work twelve at the minute. They hold six different strengths of liquor. We start the hides off in the weaker and we move them every couple of months to the next stronger one, and so they slowly get tanned.'

'Why don't you use all these pits?'

'We are too few to work them. Once we made three qualities of leather, now there's only two. One's the cheap sheep hide that we turn into the bazal for working wear – aprons like this one I'm wearing, and gaiters and the like; the other's the cowhide that's stronger and goes for shoe leather and saddlery.'

She beckoned me on and we walked past two stacks covered by tarpaulin.

'Them's the bark stacks, and here's where the hides are scraped.'

A middle-aged woman was standing at a slate table and working a palette knife back and forth across the inside surface of a fresh hide. This produced pink curls of meat and lumps of white fat.

'That's me mam.'

The woman looked up and smiled for her daughter.

'We waste nowt, mister,' she called without ceasing to work.

'The lean she's scraping off makes what they call tanner's meat,' her daughter added. 'We sell it for dog food at a penny a pound. The fat we keep and use. We render it for tallow, which we rub into the leather to make it supple.'

And so we proceeded around the edge of the skin-yard, past the shallow lime pits where the hides were dipped to remove the hair; the bark mill, where the oak bark was crushed; the salting and soaking vats for preserving untanned hides; the stretchers, the drying frames and currying tables. None of this gear was new and much of was in ill-repair. By the end of our tour, as we walked past the lean-tos in which the skinners lived and arrived again at the ruined lodge beside the gateway arch, I was well versed in the art and labour of leather-making.

'Daniel Gogarty seemed to be saying there is one set on destroying the skin-yard,' I said. 'Is this true?'

Ellen's face screwed up as if she'd taken a mouthful of vinegar.

'That's Abraham Scroop, the bits and bones merchant. He buys our scraps off us for his business, but he's not liked here. He's been boasting for years that he can run the skin-yard better than us, but it only means he wants the profit. This place supports three families at the present – that's the Kites, Gogartys and Brocks. But this is town land and if Scroop has his way the Corporation will kick us families out and give it over to his family.'

'If they did, he would happen have you work for him. He would need those that have the skill.'

She spat.

'Work for him? I'd rather dig graves.'

I took out my watch.

'Well I must go. It is near the time of the inquest, where I shall see you again, Ellen. But wait! I almost forgot my other purpose in coming down here.'

I produced the summons from my pocket.

'Will you give this to Kathy Brock? I thought I would see her here, but have not.'

'What is it?'

'A notice, like the one you got, requiring her to attend the inquest as a witness.'

A look of concern slid across Ellen's face, like a cloud's shadow on a cornfield.

'Oh! But she is not here, Sir,' she said. 'She has gone away this morning.'

'Where to?'

'To her uncle in Wigan.'

Chapter 6

RETURNING TO THE bath house I found Luke Fidelis washing his hands in the bucket of water he had used the previous day to test the baby's lung.

'You have finished the dissection? What do you conclude?'

He fished a small towel from his instruments bag, dried his hands and, his voice edged with triumph, said, 'I have found something extraordinary.'

'Go on'

'I think it proves this baby was born alive, and it gives reason to believe that she was outwardly healthy.'

'Tell me!'

Fidelis seemed to be considering whether to do so, enjoying the moment like a horse trader that weighs up a buyer's offer. He said at last, 'No, let me think a little more and make sure of it for myself. How long have I before the inquest starts?'

'Forty minutes.'

'Then I shall go to the writing room at the inn and set down my findings now. There is nothing like writing something down to make it clarify.'

'Luke, this is intolerable! It can only take a few seconds for you to tell me.'

'No. I'll give you my findings from the witness chair and not before.'

He closed his medical bag and strode out of the room, his lips compressed in a thin and perhaps mischievous smile. There had always been this theatrical side to my friend's character.

He left me thinking of the consequences of what he had confided in me, that the baby had lived and been well. If it were true, it would be more than ever necessary to find the mother of this child, and more than ever difficult to do so. While a girl that had concealed a stillbirth might overcome her shame through remorse, a murderess would be more intransigent. Then the thought of Kathy Brock, fleeing to Wigan, came to my mind. Was I wrong about Hannah Parson's allegation after all? Had Kathy indeed given birth to this child? And had she now gone away to evade the inquest and the exposure of the truth?

The Skeleton Inn's gloomy upper room was crowded and smelly as I opened the business. I regretted even more its lack of dignity as the setting for legal proceedings. The small dormer windows, filthy-paned, let in such little light that I was forced to ask for candles, while the timbers creaked like a ship as the people crowded in. The landlord, his establishment destitute of benches, had found trestles and laid floorboards across them to create half a dozen wobbling forms for the public to sit on, and these had been filled so tightly that those occupying the ends sat braced to avoid being forced to the floor.

The skinners, led by Barnaby Kite and ranged together along the foremost of these makeshift benches, were receiving foul looks and prejudiced comments from those behind them. But it was the constitution of the jury that gave me more concern. As I administered their oaths I thought them an unpromising lot. Like so many sailors in the King's service these were pressed men, and not necessarily suited to the intended task, or even willing to perform it. But the naval captain had the advantage over me by being allowed to whip his men into shape. Jurors cannot be forced to work well – to understand the evidence or come together in their thinking. They are presumed to have no faults, and to be rational and right in their hearts. It is a most foolish presumption.

A summons to serve on a jury is often welcome: it raises the pulse of one's monotonous life and offers a few hours off work, with food and drink provided. But soon enough Jack's remembering the way Georgie-Porgie looked at Jill; Georgie-Porgie rekindles an old quarrel with Tommy Tucker; and Dr Foster frets over missing the coach to Gloucester. The group of twelve men that I cast my eye over today looked not immune to discontents of this kind. All lived or worked in the immediate neighbourhood, and would know each other pretty well. A group of six that included Jacob Bull the wheelwright, Peter Johnson the signwriter and John Talbot the potter were innocuous enough. Not so Leonard Tiddy the nurseryman and William Trent the fuller. These were neighbours and brothers-in-law and but brothers in little else, since it was well known they could agree on nothing. Nor would Old John Borthwick be easy to handle. He had been court tipstaff in his day and so reckoned that he knew more about the law than the Lord Chief Justice. His son Young John sat compliantly beside him, and would not dare go against his father. Finally I was disconcerted to see that Furzey had chosen to summon Bartholomew Lock. He was supervisor in Scroop's business, and well known to be exacting in his own work and loudly opinionated of everyone else's. Beside him sat Laurence Jones, his meek assistant and acolyte.

I trooped them all up to the bath house to carry out the viewing. Inside the sluicing room they stared in fascinated horror at the table on which the baby's remains were displayed.

'The little babby's been all injured and stitched up again,' said John Talbot. 'A shame, I call that.'

'The doctor has examined him, John,' I explained. 'He needed to open the skull.'

'The doctor cut open its head? He didn't ought to do that.'

'It was necessary. You will hear his evidence later.'

'Dr Harrod, is that?' asked old Borthwick.

'I refer to Dr Fidelis.'

'But I've heard Harrod's got his evidence to give an' all.'

'Yes, he is on the list.'

'So there's two doctors we got to hear,' said Lock. 'That'll double the lies we'll be told, then.'

In order to steer the matter back to the pathetic object before us I took hold of it and gently turned it face down.

'I ask you all to look carefully. Notice the injury to the back of her head. See?'

They craned forward as one, mouths hanging open.

'Did Doctor do that, an' all?'

This was Leonard Tiddy.

'No. It was there when we found it. Later you will hear Dr Fidelis's opinion on that also.'

Bartholomew Lock was unimpressed.

'And shall we hear the doctor's opinion on the national debt and the war?'

By the end of the viewing most of the jurors had had something to say. This is usually the case. When death is present in company the natural thing is to cover the discomfort with chatter, not to any useful end, but aimlessly and sometimes facetiously. There was one, however, who did not say a word, and that was Jacob Bull the wheelwright. As we made our way out of the room I saw that Jacob's eyes gleamed with tears. His wife had given birth to a stillborn only a few weeks before.

Returning to the inn we found the room full of people jostling each other for space. Not improving matters were some of the older ladies of quality, who considered it necessary to venture out on formal occasions – which they deemed this to be – in their hooped skirts and with fans to mask their faces. Struggling through this press to reach my chair I found my way blocked by Dr Harrod.

'May I be first to give evidence, Cragg? I am called to a lady – Lady Rickaby, you know – who has a horrid case of an abscess on her leg and I must change the bandage.'

I pointed out that, by invariable tradition, the opening witness must be the first finder of the body – in this case Ellen Kite.

'Oh! Then call me second, Cragg, you must.'

Not only had Fidelis expressed his scorn for the old physician's judgement, but the evidence of the two doctors was going to be directly contradictory, leading the jury into an impasse which might infuriate them. Here was my chance of avoiding that outcome.

I said, 'I am perfectly willing to forego your testimony entirely, Doctor, if you must hurry away. We shall, after all, have that of Dr Fidelis and—'

He waved his hand to dismiss my suggestion.

'No, no, it is my duty to testify. Relieve Dr Fidelis if you like, but I had better have my say.'

In the Coroner's chair one learns diplomacy; I did not press the matter.

'Very well, Dr Harrod, I shall call you to the chair after Ellen has spoken. But I shall also then call Dr Fidelis. Now, if you would be so kind . . .'

I manoeuvred my way past him and reached the somewhat wobbly table behind which Furzey and myself had our station.

The examination of Ellen Kite was not hard. I had the deposition she had made and used this to lead my questions. The result was that the court heard almost exactly the same evidence as she had given Furzey and me on the previous morning.

'No,' she said in answer to my final question. 'I don't know any girl round here that's got in the family way – not without she's been married. Not lately, I mean.'

'Thank you Ellen. You may go back to your seat. Dr Harrod?'

Approaching the witness chair, Dr Harrod turned his head this way and that, with an expression suggesting mild surprise that there should be so many there to listen to him. Before sitting down he removed his hat and in one movement swept the chair seat with it as if to remove a coating of dust. Then he sat down, settled himself comfortably, cleared his throat and turned his face with its pleasant expression towards me.

'Dr Harrod,' I began. 'Please tell the court of your inspection of this dead child.'

'I saw it in your company, did I not, Mr Cragg? It was yesterday morning at the bath house up the hill there. As we have just heard, that is close by where it was found.'

'And when you saw it, what did you conclude?'

'I concluded that it was born dead. A sad but not uncommon occurrence, as we know.'

'How did you form this opinion?'

'As I said to you at the time, Sir, I have practised medicine for forty years and I know the appearance of a stillborn.'

'So you made no physical examination?'

Harrod laughed in his easy, light way.

'Oh, no! There is really no need. I saw the whole matter in one glance – the texture of the skin, its colour, that sort of thing. I suppose some poor girl must have had the baby on the sly, out of wedlock naturally, and finding it born dead thought she might get away scot-free of her indiscretion by quietly disposing of it.'

'Is that a common occurrence, in your experience? Surely it is not easy to be pregnant without the, er, well, the pregnancy showing.'

'I give you my opinion, that is all. But if I may further suggest, you should look for a girl who is naturally fat. An obese girl. Such a one can easily conceal her pregnancy even down to the day of its birth. I have seen that before, indeed I have.'

'Thank you, Dr Harrod. You are excused. May we have Dr Fidelis now?'

Once Luke Fidelis had taken his seat I went straight to the point.

'Dr Fidelis, what testimony do you have for this inquest about the dead infant?'

'Very significant testimony, Sir. Unlike Dr Harrod, I made a thorough *physical* examination of the body.'

'And what can you tell us?'

'It is a neonate. A newborn.'

'We have heard the opinion of Dr Harrod that the child was born dead; that it never breathed. Do you agree with him?'

'I do not. I am certain this child was alive when its mother was delivered of it. In addition I believe it was most probably born in good health, and there are indications that the mother did not give birth without knowledge, or assistance.'

'Assistance?' I interjected. 'You think she may have been attended at the birth?'

'That is one possibility. I noticed straight away that the navel string had been tied and then cut through in the proper way. It was not torn or bitten apart as I have seen in cases where a girl gives birth alone and ignorance and desperation hold sway. I do not say the mother did not do this herself, of course, but whoever did was acquainted with the correct way to prevent excessive bleeding, and had the necessary equipment to do so.'

'What else did you find when you examined the body?'

'I saw an injury to the back of the skull, a wound. It could only have been caused by a blow from a hard object or by the head being dashed against a hard surface.'

'So this injury could have been a result of the body being thrown down, as for instance into the tanning pit and perhaps striking the slate facing its sides?'

'That is a likely explanation.'

'Did you see any other superficial injury?'

'I did not. But looking into the cavities of the body and, coming in particular to the ears, I saw that one of them was stopped with congealed blood. I supposed at first it had been a chance bleed, perhaps following from the injury to the head already mentioned.'

The room, which with the restless audience had so far been full of whispers and creaking timber, was becoming quieter now, which I found was often the case when Fidelis gave evidence. There is no doubt that the cogent way in which he spoke, and the uncommon knowledge he deployed, made him a compelling witness. Even Basilius Harrod had waited to hear him, for I saw the old physician standing beside the top of the stairs, his hand cupping one ear. The demands of Lady Rickaby and her abscess could not override his professional curiosity as to what Fidelis might say.

'And was it a chance bleed?' I asked.

'No. There was nothing of chance about it, and nor was it natural. But I could not determine the truth of the case without opening the head. That I did this morning.'

'What did you find?'

The room was completely silent now, and straining to hear.

'That the ear had been assaulted, Sir. The ear-drum was burst through and the whole hearing apparatus destroyed. Beyond the ear the tissue of the brain itself was grievously damaged.'

'Good heavens! How was this done?'

Fidelis straightened his back and drew in a long breath through his nose. He looked around the room like an actor about to deliver a decisive line.

'I concluded that someone had pushed an instrument into the baby's ear far enough to penetrate the brain.'

There was a communal in-drawing of breath around the room, and a few exclamations of horror. I was no less surprised and horrified than the rest.

'What sort of instrument was that, Doctor?'

'I cannot be precise unless it be found. The best I can tell you is that it was narrow and pointed and at least four inches long. A bodkin, perhaps, or something like. The injury was such that it could only have been caused by such an instrument.'

'So the injury to this newborn child was in your opinion no accident but done on purpose.'

'I do.'

'And what could that purpose have been?'

'One only: to kill the baby without leaving an outward trace. And that is why I conclude this was never a stillbirth, as Dr Harrod has averred, but the calculated murder of a baby girl that gave all the appearance of being perfectly healthy.'

At the sound of the word 'murder' a new flux of whispers thrilled through the audience.

'Thank you for your evidence, Doctor. You may step down.'

Fidelis rose from the chair and forced his way to the back of the room, which now seemed more tightly packed than ever. As he did so the volume of comment and speculation rose to a crescendo around him.

I let the noise continue. I needed time to think. Fidelis's dramatic evidence meant that I must after all face the possibility I had discussed with Elizabeth, and also read about in the author Dr Mandevil: a newborn foully murdered at the hands of its mother. What troubled me was the way of the killing. Could a poor fraught young girl – that is all I could conceive her to be – have overridden the prime instincts of motherhood and treated the flesh of her own flesh in such a vile and deliberate way?

I quietened the court.

'I would like to inform the jury that there was to be one further witness, but it appears that she has left town to visit relatives. This was before she could be served with a summons, so I place no particular construction of guilt on her absence. I must tell you, however, that she was asked to give evidence because suspicion had fallen upon her in this locality. It is a suspicion for which there is no evidence that I know of – but I am prepared to hear from anyone present who can assist the court.'

I looked expectantly around, and added, 'The girl's name is Kathy Brock.'

The name brought exclamations of dissent from the row of skinners, and a new round of murmurs from all parts of the room. Then Hannah Parsons was on her feet.

'I will speak, Your Honour.'

'Very well. Come up.'

Hannah sat very primly in the witness chair as I administered the oath, then broke out with, 'Mr Cragg, if not for you, this slattern would have been heard today.'

'Why is it my doing, Hannah?'

'You know well, Sir. We women took her up for a questioning yesterday. You saw fit to stop us and send her on her way, and so she made her escape. Why did you do that?'

'I had to. You were treating her roughly.'

'Not roughly enough – not if she'd done this.'

'So tell the court. What were your grounds for suspicion of Kathy Brock?'

'She was talked about as a slattern. And she were as fat as you like. Dr Harrod's said it: she might have been with child and nobody knew. It deserved having a talk with her, we thought, so we did, until you stopped us.'

'And what did Kathy say in reply to your charges?'

'She denied it, of course. But we saw the guilt in her eye.'

Through most of this evidence – if you could call it that – the row of skinners were muttering in discontent. Now Barney Kite called out.

'Scurrilous! You've got no proof, not for any of it – none!'

I held up my hand to silence him and fixed the witness with a severe look.

'Can you give any substance to this charge, Hannah, beyond what you think was a look in her eye?'

'I've said what I had to say, that's all.'

She left the chair accompanied by a scattering of applause from the room. I looked along the bench on which sat the skinners.

'Is there anyone here that can speak for Kathy, in her absence?'

A small woman of perhaps forty raised a timid hand. Her quavering voice was almost lost in the room's groundswell of noise.

'I'm her mother, Your Honour.'

'What is your name?'

'Margery Brock.'

I motioned her forward and she sat herself uneasily in the witness chair, while I administered the oath.

'Had Kathy been with child in recent weeks, to your knowledge?'

'No, Your Honour.'

'Might she have been, secretly I mean? She is quite a tubby girl, is she not?'

'She is a little tubby like you say, Sir, but I am her mother and I would know anything like her carrying a babby. Last time I did, any road.'

'The last time? You mean she has been with child before?'

'Oh yes, but that were last year, not this.'

A flurry of whispering swept through the room.

'Last year? She was expecting a child last year, you say?'

'Yes, Sir.'

'What happened to this child?'

'She miscarried after five months, you see. It never lived.'

'And you were about to say – you knew of that pregnancy?'

'Yes, I knew all about it – she confessed it. She would have told me an' all if it happened again. We were that close, since her father left us.'

'When she confessed that pregnancy to you, did she tell you what man she had been with? Did she name the father?'

'She wouldn't ever say, Sir. After the babby'd dropped untimely, I said no more about it.'

'Did you suspect anyone of being the father?'

'We had no idea.'

'Who is "we"? You and your husband – you and Kathy's father?'

'No, Your Honour. Like I said, he's left us these seven years.'

'Where's he gone to?'

'He's dead, Sir. I'm a widow.'

Almost from the start of Margery Brock's evidence I had begun to sense unrest growing at the back of the room. I had taken no notice in order to concentrate on the witness, thinking it must be occasioned by her story. But now the true cause of the shifting of feet and whispering became suddenly apparent. Immediately after Margery Brock had told me of her widowhood, loud comments were heard and, simultaneously, I smelled the reason: there was smoke creeping up between the floorboards around the stairwell wall.

And then someone yelled in a hoarse, urgent voice, 'Fire! Fire!'

Chapter 7

AS THE UPROAR INCREASED, Margery Brock looked at me, uncertainly.

'Shall I go on talking, Sir?'

'No, Margery, I believe we may have to resume later.'

Smoke was seeping into the room, not candle smoke or tobacco, but acrid unaccustomed smoke, puffing up from somewhere around the stair top. Then, all at once, there came through this haze a rushing sound, followed by crackling, and intermittent flickers, and peeps of orange light. There were cries of dismay, which gave way at once to shrieking and screaming, as people surged towards the stairhead, and soon enough began to fight to get there, for the stairs were the only means of leaving the room. I saw fists pummelling and elbows scything. But it seemed that the fire was on or in the stairwell itself and, taking an increasing hold, it threatened to block the way out entirely.

Furzey and I, the jurymen and the row of skinners, and indeed the whole audience, had jumped to our feet and turned towards the events occurring at the far end of the room. I cannot speak for the others, but I experienced at first an odd sense of detachment, and no urgency. With a solid wall of perhaps thirty or forty agitated people between myself and the flames there was in truth little I could do to get to the burning stairs.

A few brave ones launched themselves downward into the smoke and flame to reach safety unscathed, but soon enough the stairhead became congested with those who hesitated, lacking the courage to take the plunge. This was not surprising. As far as I could see the flames were now visible and the heat was increasing. Moments later a curtain or a hanging caught fire in the room itself, blazing upwards and conducting the fire towards the ceiling. The crowd around the stairhead immediately retreated and the make-shift benches collapsed to the floor before the surge. Here and there in the commotion I saw more than one lit candle knocked over, which could only add to the danger, though a greater peril would come when the flames got into the roof. Once the thatch caught fire properly we would all undoubtedly roast to death, or die in a matter of minutes under the collapse of flaming timbers.

My feeling of calm detachment lasted no more than ten seconds, but time in extremity plays extraordinary tricks and the period seemed much longer. Then I came to my senses and saw that the room was fast filling with smoke, and that the screams were combining with thick and raucous coughs. Something had to be done if everybody in this overcrowded room were not very soon to perish. As people began to crowd back from the burning end of the room, I looked to my right and left.

'The windows!' I shouted. 'It's the only way out.'

I was, of course, not alone in reaching this conclusion. Barnaby Kite and his daughter were opening the nearest window on our left-hand side, and others were doing the same further down the room. Furzey and I made for the casement on the right. We tore away the curtains and got the window open. A gust of untainted air was sucked into the room and we breathed it gratefully.

Leonard Tiddy the nurseryman, coughing and looking stupefied, was the closest of the jurymen. I grabbed his arm and pulled him towards us.

'Now, Len, out you go and quick about it.'

Still looking dazed, he hesitantly raised one of his legs towards the opening.

'Don't be daft, husband,' screeched Mrs Tiddy who had come from the body of the audience to join him. 'Stick your head out first, and be quick.'

He did so, and with a heave on the belt of his breeches Furzey and I propelled him through the aperture and on to the roof, down which he slid, followed immediately by his wife, and so we proceeded with the next, and the next. Now, throughout the smoke-filled room, men and women were diving out of the windows and sliding down the eaves, before tumbling the ten or twelve feet to the ground, where hands had gathered to catch or pick them up. No doubt injuries were sustained, but every broken pate or dislocated shoulder was yet a life saved.

However, as each frightened choking body was defenestrated, the air that was sucked in through the open windows steadily fed the flames and the fire was now roaring both behind and above us. I caught hold of a curtain and pressed it to my nose between shouting instructions.

'Be orderly, don't press! You must go out head first! Head first!'

Chunks of plaster were dropping here and there from between the beams of the ceiling, showing that fire was now taking hold in the roof cavity. The heat was actually toasting my cheeks and singe-ing my wig. But at last, within three or four minutes of the first signs of fire, the evacuation was virtually complete. On my order Furzey had gone out, too – I had a foolish notion that I should be last to leave – and so I took a lungful of fresh air and turned for a final look around. The stairwell and all of the far end of the room was burning steadily. Dust and smoke threw a gauze film across the scene but I could see that the room was in chaos, with the planks and trestles that had made the audience's benches being overturned and strewn around the floor. Everywhere possessions had been abandoned – hats, bags, wigs and several hooped skirts stripped off by their wearers as being impossible to fit through any of the windows. The finer, more mature ladies present at the inquest must have descended to the ground in their drawers. I looked up. The ceiling was largely in place, but I knew it would entirely collapse as the fire spread along the thatch. I fancied from the sound that the roof ridge was already burning along much of its length.

I was just about to go through the window when it occurred to me to make quite sure that I really was alone and so I peered through the smoke one more time up and down the room. One of the hooped skirts was moving and seemed fuller, or rather less collapsed, than the others. I went to investigate, and found that it still had its wearer inside it, a small woman in middle age who lay half-conscious, overcome by smoke, with the skirt ballooning up around her legs. I hooked my hands under her armpits and dragged her to the window.

She would not go through while still wearing the hooped skirt, and I decided on desperate measures. A penknife lay on the presiding table with Furzey's writing gear and this I seized. Pulling up the woman's outer skirts, I used the blade to attack the complicated, stiff and cage-like petticoat beneath, sawing at it in a circle around the waist so that it sheared off and could be pulled free of her body. I lifted her out of it with no difficulty and thrust her through the window. Then, pausing only to sweep up the inquest papers from the table and stuffing them in my coat pocket, I dived through myself.

We slid down together until there was nothing under us, and I heard a cheer as we dropped into the receptive arms of a crowd of helpers. We were laid on the ground and there I remained for what must have been several minutes, coughing and regaining my senses, which felt scattered and not under immediate control. Recovering myself at last, I propped an elbow beneath me and saw that the woman I had rescued was being attended where she lay on the ground. The man bending solicitously over her had abandoned his coat; his shirt was torn, his dark hair was wild, and his breeches and stockings were scorched and smutched.

'Will she live?' I called out.

'Oh yes,' said Luke Fidelis, looking round at me. 'You certainly took your time to bring her out, but she's remarkably unscathed.'

The survivors of the fire were sitting and lying in various degrees of shock, injury and undress along the stone jetty which extended from the front door of the inn into the river. A few ships were berthed there, and it had been their crewmen who had saved the building from total destruction. No sailor lets fire prosper and, well trained as they are to combat it, they reacted to the sounds of alarm with speed. Smartly running a pair of pumps ashore, they had thoroughly hosed the conflagration until its vigour waned and was finally reduced to smouldering. By the time the town's own engine arrived from its station under Moot Hall, the inn was a steaming, hissing shell, without a roof but with most of its blackened walls, floors and timbers still in place. The little Customs House and warehouses nearby were unscathed.

The first part of the pier was edged on either side with a low wall and I found Furzey sitting on one of these with three of the jurors. Having assured myself of their well-being, I thanked my clerk for his staunchness at the inquest room window and had a short conversation – in wheezing tones – about the inquest itself. There was no question of concluding it that day and I asked Furzey to prepare a full report on the health of the jurymen, so that I could decide when to resume the hearing. Where we would do so also remained undecided.

I was mortally tired and all at once overwhelmed by the desire to see Elizabeth. Usually she attended my inquests but, mercifully, had been prevented this day by the need to bring her father to the barber's to have one of his few remaining teeth extracted. At the very moment I was silently thanking God for my father-in-law's toothache when I heard my wife's voice calling to me.

'Titus! Here you are, and alive and well!'

I looked up and saw her walking towards me. Then she was clasping me in her arms, holding me tightly.

'Oh Titus, Titus, my love, we heard that the engine had been called out, and where to, and I so dreadfully feared the worst.'

'I am not hurt, except that my lungs pain me a little from the smoke. I am not burnt and I came down chute from the roof without harm. I believe sailors from these ships here caught me as I fell.'

'Then God bless Jack Tar. Are you ready to come home?'

At six o'clock, I was sitting beside the parlour fire in my nightgown, with my head nightcapped and woollen blankets warming my shoulders and knees. Elizabeth had dosed me with three spoonfuls of syrup of violets for my cough, and my feet were soaking in a hot preparation of mustard, salt and hartshorn, which she swore to be sovereign against all shocks and distempers. I was in this embarrassed condition when Luke Fidelis came in.

'You are well ministered to, I see,' he said.

'I have the best of care.'

He picked up the bottle of medicine from the table beside me, read the label, then replaced it without comment before changing the subject.

'I have spent all the afternoon at the wharf.'

'Were you dealing with casualties? Were they bad?'

'There were no deaths, many sore lungs from breathing smoke, a few sprains and bruises and one or two cracked bones from falling off the roof. A fortunate outcome, so far.'

'How did you escape the fire yourself?'

'I was standing near the top of the stairs, listening to the mother's evidence. When the smoke appeared I was one of the first to run down. A dozen or so others followed but the stairs quickly became impassable. We therefore roused the sailors from their ships and all stood around the building catching people off the roof. It was good sport.'

'It did not feel like that from where I was. Does anyone know how the fire started?'

Fidelis shrugged.

'Not that I have heard, but there's no mystery. The house was antique and made of wood. It could have burnt at any time.'

'But it didn't. It burnt in the middle of my inquest.'

'That weighted the chance, no doubt. There were more people than usual inside, more drinkers and more people smoking pipes jostling for space, knocking over candles.'

'Yes, I suppose so. Crowds are careless. What of the woman I saw you treating, the one I'd pushed out of the burning room before I came down myself?'

'She recovered and went away. A gentleman friend was at hand to do the gallantries and escort her safely. She is a visitor to town.'

'You will review her?'

'I shall not. I was warned off. She told me she would see no one in Preston but Harrod. The women has more than a touch of haughtiness and she hints at high connections.'

Elizabeth came in and bustled around me.

'Now, Doctor, is this a medical call, or just a friendly one?'

'I came to talk about the inquest.'

'Perhaps not tonight, though,' she said gently. 'Poor Titus's voice is much strained and his breathing is so tight from the smoke. It pains him to talk.'

I almost interrupted, but then I thought, there are times when it is best, and it is even pleasant, to be a patient and have someone else decide matters on one's behalf – especially when that someone is a loving woman. So I rested quietly in the chair as Elizabeth tactfully showed my friend out of the door.

'Nothing like this has happened to me before,' I said in my croaking whisper.

I had been in bed some time, but sleep never came. Now, when it was past ten o'clock, Elizabeth had come in to join me. She had brushed her hair, cleaned her teeth and put on her nightdress, in which she looked as pretty as a primrose.

'Nothing like what?' she said as she slipped in beside me.

'The inquest today being interrupted – stopped – so violently.'

'How far did it get, then, when the fire happened? Oh, but don't tell me if it hurts you to talk.'

'The fire broke out as we were coming to the end of the evidence. And, as it happened, we had just heard something very unexpected, something which might have changed my idea of the case. It is frustrating.'

'Do tell me, Titus. If it does not pain you too much to speak.'

'No, I can speak, and I want to tell you. You remember that I meant to call the girl Kathy Brock as a witness, after she had been accused by those women of being the dead child's mother? Well, I was unable to serve Kathy with the summons, you see, because she took herself off this morning to Wigan, to visit some relatives. Just like that. I had meant to give her the chance to answer her unjust accusers, but she'd upped and left town. What do you make of that?'

'It certainly looks a very convenient visit to Wigan, if she wished to avoid speaking at the inquest.'

'But that isn't the only thing: Margery Brock her mother came forward, quite unexpectedly, after most of the evidence had been heard. She meant to defend Kathy, but she only made the matter worse. She stoutly denied that her daughter had been pregnant recently, but ended by blurting out that Kathy *had* been with child before, last year in fact, but miscarried.'

'Oh no! Poor Kathy. Who was the father?'

'Margery Brock claimed not to know, and I was just about to cross-question her on the point when the shout of "Fire" was raised.'

'That is frustrating, as you say. And, oh, poor Kathy!'

'Yes, poor Kathy, but if she had been pregnant before, perhaps she was again.'

'It does not necessarily follow.'

'It is suggestive. And the real nub of the matter is that Luke had already given evidence that proves deliberate murder in this case absolutely. This is not the legal presumption of murder that you and I talked about the other night. This baby was unquestionably born alive and deliberately killed.'

'How unquestionably? Did anyone see it happening?'

'No, but Luke saw it after the event.'

She laughed merrily.

'What a wizard he is! Did he look into a glass ball?'

'No, he looked into the body.'

I told her about the injured ear and brain that Fidelis's dissection had found.

'But that is horrible! Who would have done such a thing?'

Her hands had gone to her cheeks and her voice was hushed in horror.

'The mother is the most obvious suspect.'

'No, Titus. Would a woman who has just given birth do that – a desperate woman, as she would need to be? I can imagine her smothering the baby or even dashing it down in a fit of madness. But for her to kill the baby in such a way seems impossible. The violence is too . . . precise. Too deliberate.'

'Well, if she did not do it, she must have an idea who did. And that in turn might make her terribly afraid – afraid enough to run away.'

We lay together quietly for a moment, just holding hands. Then she said, in a whisper, 'If there be a house in Paradise for the people that are murdered, I hope there is a very comfortable apartment reserved there for those that die before ever they *are* people.'

'Does not your religion call them holy innocents, and say that they lodge in limbo?'

'Yes. The priests say it is because they have never sinned, so it is a kind of blessing that they die. I call that rubbish! A baby dying is sad because it never learns what it is to be a person. It isn't just that they don't know sin. They are ignorant of everything human: of learning, laughter, beauty, taste. They will never solve a puzzle, or make a drawing, or sing a song, or write a letter. They will never love as we love, or reflect as we reflect, or know any of the things that make us what we are.'

She let go of my hand, clenched her fist and beat the covers.

'How can some women not see that, Titus? How can they not want to hug the baby in their arms, and watch it grow to enjoy those things? And how can some be so wicked as to even countenance that it be stopped from ever really being!'

'It is impossible to understand.'

'My church says those babies are innocent of sin, but really that is not the point. They are – what do you call it? – potential. Yes, potential for *everything*. But that everything will never be. It is a world that dies with them.'

'My love, I see you have thought deeply about this, and of course you are right. Any woman who does this knowingly and deliberately must be extremely wicked.'

Chapter 8

'CLARKSON IS HERE TO see you and wants money,' rasped Furzey, with his head round my door. 'You're a fool if you pay him a penny.'

James Clarkson was a lanky and (on this particular day) a drooping fellow with plum-purple lips, a bloodshot eye and a sickly sallowness of complexion. When I had seen him yesterday, before the destruction of his inn, he had been a strutting, red-cheeked braggart.

'You see a man ruined, Mr Cragg,' he stated gloomily. 'You were there, so you know what happened. I have nothing now in the world and I'm very much in need of money and therefore I'm collecting what I can of it. So I am here for my fee in your use of my upstairs room.'

'How much are you asking, Mr Clarkson?'

'The full amount is four shillings and sixpence.'

I didn't much like James Clarkson, but I was still surprised. His ramshackle establishment had burnt down and stopped my inquest, and yet he had the brass to ask for the whole amount of the room charge.

I said, stiffly, 'You will remember we were contracted for the room between the hours of two and six in the afternoon. In the event, we were unable to use it beyond four and could not finish our business. I would therefore say that half the fee is due at most and certainly no more.'

'Half, you say? That's less than I had hoped.'

'It's all you will get, and I am being generous.'

'Now, see here—'

He had raised his finger for emphasis, but then in his mind the point collapsed. He drooped a little more.

'Well it's better than nowt, which is all I shall likely ever again earn out at the inn.'

'You had no insurance?'

'No.'

'The lease may be worth something, even with the building in its present state.'

'I've borrowed against it. I shall be lucky to escape prison.'

Clarkson now became more agitated and a little more upright.

'Now see here, Mr Cragg, whoever started that fire should be prosecuted. I deserve satisfaction on that account. The arsonist should restitute me.'

'Arsonist, you say. That is a serious charge. Who do you mean? Did you see someone setting the fire?'

'Not exactly. I was in the pantry when the shout went up. But there are those that wish me harm. The wolves have been prowling around me for more than half a year. Now they have torn out my throat.'

'That is strong language indeed, Mr Clarkson. Who are these enemies?'

'I will name no names, not until I have proof.'

'That is wise.'

'But I mean those plotting to have me out of the Skeleton Inn by any means, and the inn destroyed.'

'Why would they wish for that, Mr Clarkson?'

The colour had returned to his cheeks now and his voice was more fervent.

'Improvement and Profit, Mr Cragg. The great pagan gods that rules those vultures' hearts, and which my inn stands in the way of. Chasing them, they will let the rest of us go to hell. For the proud are risen against me, and the assemblies of violent men have sought after my soul.'

This talk of wolves and vultures, attack and ruin – I had heard like words from the mouth of Dan Gogarty in the skin-yard only yesterday morning. Did Abraham Scroop, then, have designs on the wharf as well as the tannery? Or was Clarkson referring to someone else?

He rose from his chair and stood, more upright than before. He seemed to have charged himself with a little courage now.

'You will pay me the money?'

'My clerk will give it to you. You will be asked to sign a receipt.'

'Thank you. I hope to have like indulgence from Moot Hall, where I go from here. In spite of all, I shall ask for an advance of money to rebuild. I shall tell them the Skeleton Inn is needed by this town, greeting mariners as they moor up and giving shelter to travellers from the sea.'

'I wish you luck,' I said, feeling a little sorry for the man in spite of myself.

I saw him back into the outer office and instructed Furzey to pay over two and threepence in exchange for a receipt. My clerk had come to work in the morning with his voice no less hoarse than my own, and a bottle with the word 'Lohoch' written on the label, from which he took periodic draughts. The contents had edged his lips with a black rime, from which I guessed the preparation included liquorice.

'Aye,' he'd whispered, 'it's the mother's linctus: licky and rosewater and gum. Says it can't fail to do me good – I don't think. But since I *must* come to work, I go on swigging it all the same.'

Now he pouted his blackened lips rudely at Clarkson and reached for the cash box and receipt forms.

'Innkeepers do talk about warm hospitality, Mr Clarkson,' he croaked, shovelling out the cash. 'But they should not mean scorching. They should not mean searing a man's lungs. Here's your money.'

When Clarkson had gone I reminded Furzey of my request that he visit the jurors and see how each of them fared so that we could restart the inquest. The day was Friday. If possible I wanted to do this on the following Tuesday – it could not be before – but first we must know if our jurors were well enough to attend. He agreed with some enthusiasm: Furzey seized any opportunity to be away from his writing desk.

'And while you are doing that, I shall go back to the skin-yard. I fancy Mrs Margery Brock has more to tell about her daughter.'

It was beginning to drizzle as I came up Spaw Braw Lane and caught my first glimpse of the mastheads and pennants of the ships tied up at the wharf. At the brow of the hill, the hulls of the vessels themselves came into view and I saw how, as the bottom of the tide approached, the deeper-draughted vessels had been grounded on the mud and were canted at various angles out of the vertical. These would not be sailing anywhere until high tide returned.

I saw, too, the buildings alongside the dock and the blackened shell of the Skeleton Inn amongst them. In spite of the rain the wharf was bustling, particularly around one of the largest of the ships. Her rail leaned against the jetty's stonework as she was pre-pared, evidently, to catch the top of the tide.

Then the tannery, more immediately below me, became visible but, by contrast with the quayside, I could see little activity there. The usual ribbons of wood smoke were rising from its fires, and a lone figure was crossing the yard, bent under a load, but no one else could be seen at work.

I found Margery Brock five minutes later, sitting under shelter with Ellen Kite, Mrs Kite, Ellen's mother, and a third woman whom I had also seen at the inquest. They were sitting around a thick wooden table working on cowhide. One of them pierced holes along the edge of her piece of leather with an awl, while the others sewed the pieces together with big needles and thread almost as thick as string. All three looked equally dejected and all spoke in the same hoarse manner as I did.

'None of us that were in the fire can speak, hardly. We're that smoked in the lungs.'

'I am the same myself, as you can hear.'

'You were champion-like yesterday, Mr Cragg, you and Mr Furzey, helping folk through the windows to get out. We are grateful, don't think we're not.'

'That is kind of you, Ellen. But I did no more than my duty, and no more than you yourself and your good father. Now, it's Mrs Brock I came down to see. Could we . . . ?'

The other three women left us with good enough grace. The delinquent's mother stayed where she was but looked uneasy.

'What's it about?' she asked.

'I would like you to enlarge a little on the evidence you were giving to the inquest when we were, as you know, interrupted. You had just been telling us that your daughter had previously been expecting a child, and that was only last year.'

She looked suspiciously at me.

'Do I have to tell you about it?'

'No, I cannot compel you to speak now. But you may have to when the inquest starts again. If you can answer my questions now it makes it easier for both of us. It saves me from wasting time putting the wrong questions in court, and it saves you the worry of facing the unexpected.'

'Oh, I see. All right.'

'So, did you have any suspicions about who the man was? Or

maybe it was a boy that she'd been with. Was it one from here in the skin-yard?'

'Oh, no. Not from here. It must have been a boy she saw in her job.'

'Her job? But her job was here, was it not?'

'Not then. She'd been working out. She started when she were twelve, as a domestic.'

'A servant? Who did she work for?'

'It were at Mrs Scroop's, housemaiding. It were like hard spit in that house, so she told me, with all them children. But she were doing all right, so we thought, until one day she just came out with it – she wanted to chuck in and come back to work here. In the end I got out of her why and she confessed it all.'

'So you think it was someone in the Scroop household responsible for this pregnancy?'

'I reckon it were some lad that called there – a milk-boy, or maybe someone that worked for Scroop that came and went to the house.'

This was not unlikely: Scroop's yard was perhaps three hundred yards from the house, up the road in the direction of Preston.

'You never found out?'

'She kept it close who she's been with, never said a word.'

'Now, I want to know about Kathy's visit to Wigan. People are saying that she went there to avoid appearing at the inquest. Is that true?'

'Oh, no, Your Honour. She's gone to look after my brother Terence's children and that's the honest-to-God truth. His wife's leg's broken, see? She's got five young'uns. He wrote me asking for Kathy to come and help.'

'Can you show me the letter, if you please?'

'No, I put it on the fire.'

'What is your brother's name and occupation?'

'He's the town Headborough. Terence Pitt.'

'You don't mean the Constable?'

'Yes.'

Having gathered this interesting information I left the skin-yard and turned my steps to the left, along Watery Lane. I meant to have another look over the site of yesterday's events, for Clarkson's accusations had aroused suspicions of my own and I knew that, should anyone die as a result of the fire, I would have to hold an inquest into the circumstances.

The inn was a desolate sight. Smoke had blackened its walls, which were of wattle and daub over a wooden frame. The door and windows had been smashed in. The roof was entirely gone except for its beams, charred and thinned by flames, which reared emptily above the structure like scorched bones. It had been called the Skeleton for years. Now, it was one.

A few yards from the main door, which opened directly on to the quayside, a woman in her middle years, and with her head covered by an old grey blanket, was sitting on a heap of fishing nets and cork floats, bemoaning her lot. A team of boys and girls – her children no doubt – were carrying bundles out of the ruined inn and depositing them around her; the worldly belongings, I supposed, of the Clarkson family.

'Mrs Clarkson, do you know me?' I asked.

'We are thrown out and nowhere to go,' she wailed, not so much to me as to the world in general. 'We are destitute. We are houseless. Oh, improvidence! Oh, cruelty!'

'I am the Coroner, madam. If you please, I must take a look inside.'

I retreated, not thinking she was likely to converse rationally, and went in by the damaged doorway to carry out my inspection. I was in what had been the common room, where everything had been battered and soaked by the sailors with their fire hoses. The centre of the ceiling had collapsed, leaving a gaping wound through which appeared the sky filled with rolling slate-grey rainclouds. I went over to what remained of the stair, which stood to my right at the east end of the building. The casing remained in place, but the treads and handrails had all gone, burned away, so that I looked up in effect at another hole in the ceiling, through which showed, once again, the sky. Walking around the staircase I opened the small door set in its side, which gave access to the triangular under-stairs cupboard. The door itself had burned on the inside and the wall opposite was also fire-damaged. The floor of the cupboard into which the stairs had collapsed was filled with charred wood and wet ashes.

In the wall at the other end of this large room were set the fireplace and chimney, the only stone-built parts of the structure. I examined this from all sides and found little evidence of direct fire, except where one would expect to find it, in the fireplace itself. The kitchen was reached through either of two doors on each side of the chimney. Here, too, the floor of the room above had collapsed, and there was much confusion and damage. Above it had lain the private family apartments which, with no remaining thatch above them, were now open to the elements. The stair that led up to them, however, was only lightly scorched. It was clear to me that the flames had spread along the roof from the eastern end, and that the seat of the fire had been there, in the cupboard below those stairs.

Outside again I interrupted the children in their work and gathered them around me, a little way from where their mother continued to complain.

'Does anyone know how this fire started? Did any of you see anything?'

They looked up at me, a circle of pinched, dirty faces.

'Did you see anyone standing by the cupboard below the stairs there. Or even opening the cupboard itself?'

No one had seen anything of the kind.

I fished in my purse for a sixpence, which I pressed into the hand of the eldest of them.

'Buy some bread and cheese with this. No need to tell your parents where you got it: just say you found it inside, on the floor.'

'The fire was started deliberately, you know,' said Luke Fidelis.

It was the same evening and I had been sitting by the fireside in my library, turning the pages of Mandevil and digesting the baked trout I'd had for supper. At nine my friend came bustling in, eager to talk over with me the matter of the fire.

'I hope I do not disturb you,' he went on, 'but I've just returned from seeing my young patient – he does well, by the way – and as it was low tide I have again waded the river by Penwortham Ford. As it brought me ashore near the Marsh, I had a look around the remains of the inn. It is arson, I have no doubt, and worse, too, I dare say.'

'I don't know what you mean by worse,' I said, as I poured him a glass of claret and handed across the tobacco jar. 'I agree it is possible that the fire was set deliberately. I was there myself this morning and saw the state of things.'

'And you agree that the mischief began in the staircase: in the cupboard below the stairs, to be precise.'

'Yes, it looks likely.'

'It is the perfect place to set a fire if you wanted to prevent the people upstairs from escaping.'

'As what – an act of malice?'

'Of attempted murder.'

'You go too far. It may yet have been an accident.'

'How could a fire have started accidentally inside a cupboard? No, Titus, we are looking for an arsonist.'

'Not me, Luke. The innkeeper, Clarkson, is certainly doing so. He goes about saying the fire was set on purpose to drive him out of business. We shall see if he can give substance to that claim, but since nobody died in the fire, I am not professionally concerned with it. The days are gone when coroners inquested mysterious fires for their own sake.'

'Although if this one happens to have been set deliberately to interfere with your inquest, you *should* be concerned.'

He was right about that, and yet the idea was incredible to me and anyway I was tired of the subject; I wanted to talk about Kathy Brock.

'The future of the inquest itself is greatly more important at the moment. The girl Kathy Brock's sudden journey to Wigan: let us look at that.'

I bent, lit a spill from the grate and passed it across. His handsome face looked fixedly into the flickering light of the fire as he pulled on his pipe.

'This gives the appearance of running away,' he said, puffing a cloud of smoke. 'And if she did flee, it does not strain the wit to find a reason why.'

He offered the burning spill back to me but I shook my head.

'You forget I've breathed enough smoke in a minute to last me a month. And yes of course, I see what you are saying. I was with her mother today, a simple soul. She told me she'd had a letter from her brother saying his wife had broken a leg and would Kathy come to attend their chirping brood.'

'You have the letter?'

'It no longer exists. She burned it, she says.'

'Ah!'

Luke brooded for a few moments, watching the flames as they danced impishly around the firelogs.

'Without that letter, it is easier to say that Kathy did not want to speak or be questioned about this dead baby in public, which would be tantamount to a confession. What do you make of Kathy?'

'I hardly know her. I saved her from the rough treatment of Hannah Parsons, but she did not stay for a conversation. Her mother looks a straightforward woman, but . . .'

'Is not to be trusted underneath? I agree, but there's only one way to prove it.'

'I know. So: will you come to Wigan with me?'

Chapter 9

THE ROAD FROM Preston to Wigan is a toll road of seventeen milestones. It begins where Church Gate ends and branches away to the south along a sunken or hollow way that descends after less than a mile to the ancient bridge at Walton, which at that time, unless you counted Robert Battersby's ferry, was the only dry crossing of the Ribble for miles. It was not yet nine on Saturday morning and we had paid the toll and were over the bridge. For a few miles we cantered, until the road began to grow boggy and rutted and we were forced to walk our horses. The road was like this all the way along our twenty-mile journey – for a certain stretch it would be well-maintained and level, and then would sink to a disgraceful condition of holes and protruding rocks that broke the axles of coaches and the legs of horses.

Where our progress was slowed, we were able to talk, and I told Fidelis of my reading in *The Fable of the Bees*.

'Mandevil the author is enamoured of paradox. He loves to point out that vice can produce good, while much virtue results in evil.'

'Ha! His vicar cannot have liked him.'

'He was constantly denounced from the pulpit.'

'Not many clergy are known for their love of paradox.'

'The reason I am telling you about Mandevil is that he makes some remarks pertinent to these enquiries. He looks into what sort of young girl might murder her bastard child and comes to a surprising conclusion: that she is more probably virtuous than vicious.'

'The conclusion would go with his philosophy. But it must all be a vast joke, surely.'

'Maybe, but I am not sure. Elizabeth said something similar only the other day – that any such killer would act out of shame. Now we all think of shame as a very proper emotion, which only afflicts virtuous people. So if a girl feels extreme shame after conceiving a bastard, Mandevil puts that down to her extreme sense of virtue. And *that* will send her to extremes to cover up the offence. Murder, of course, is the extremity of extremes. Hence murder proceeds from extreme virtue.'

'Well, we'll shortly be able to put Dr Mandevil's ideas to the test in the case of Kathy Brock. How old did you say she is?'

'Seventeen.'

'And her uncle is the Constable of Wigan, is he?'

'Yes.'

'I wonder if that will prove help or hindrance.'

'The real difficulty is to know how to approach him. If I present myself officially as the Preston Coroner, he will likely have not a word to say to me.'

'We will devise a stratagem.'

The town of Wigan, a borough old as Preston, was Preston's equal in proudly minding its own business. But in its treatment of strangers the people there were peculiarly hostile, there being nothing they liked more than to use red tape against anyone that dared to settle in town without permission, or even to sell a sheep or a bolt of worsted in the market. First they took them to court and fleeced them with a fine, and then they turned them out on their ears.

We had passed through the village of Standish and could see the massive tower of Wigan parish church rearing ahead of us at several miles distance, like a castle keep. A skinny fellow appeared in front of us, perched on a roadside gate. As we came level with him he swept off his hat.

'Fine morning, good sirs.'

We gave him acknowledgement and continued on our way, but he leapt down and was soon stumbling and panting along beside us, a tatterdemalion figure in hooped stockings and a buffin coat.

'You goin' to Wigan? Take my advice – don't go with money in your pocket.'

We ignored him as best we could but did not shake him off.

'Thieves they are. I lost every coin I had to them, not to mention my Henrietta.'

It being impossible to ride safely above a walk, as the road for several hundred yards ahead was strewn with rocks and pits and severed by fallen-in tunnel-drains, we had no choice but to listen to his yammering complaint and to the expected request for money that would surely follow.

But in fact it was not money that he wanted.

'Do a small service for a man down on his luck. It'll take you but a minute or two.'

We reached a part of the road where a side-walk had been created beside the quagmire, from a layer of slag from the local ironworks. This smooth, metalled path presented the chance to get away and I was on the point of giving a kick to my horse's flanks when the fellow said, with sudden desperation in his voice, 'Just seek out the pinder for me. Goes by the name of Terence Pitt.'

Startling at the name, I glanced at Fidelis, who arched his eyebrows.

'You know the gentleman?'

'I do know him. I would not call him a gentleman. Scoundrel,

94

maybe. He took me up by a trick. I went into Wigan town last market day, see, with my little Henrietta. I know what you're thinking, but she goes everywhere with me. I have her always on a string and she trots along beside me sweet as beetroot. And then Pitt strides into the market like Pontius Pilate. He has two henchmen with him, one at each of his elbows, and no sooner do they clap their eyes on me and Henrietta than they seize us shouting I'm a stranger coming to market and must be put in irons. Well, no sooner do they lay hands on me than my Henrietta gets free and starts running about. Oh you should've seen her! You wouldn't believe it with her short little legs but she runs like a hare. This way and that under the egg-stalls till they capsize and spill their eggs, under the women's skirts till they're shrieking, under the horses till they're rearing and kicking. But the horses never lay a hoof on her, she moves so quick and lish. My darling Henrietta, she is, my little gilt.'

'Your guilt? What are you guilty of?'

'No, no, Your Honour. Henrietta's my gilt, my little pig. And I hope you will help me to get her back.'

'What is your name?'

'It's Spungeon. Jasper Spungeon. Jass.'

'Well, Mr Spungeon, er, Jass, perhaps you would tell us where to find this Pitt?

'Why, in the house by the pinfold outside town at the far end of Wall Gate.'

We came into Wigan along Wigan Lane where the famous battle had been fought that finally ended the civil war in the last century. Ranged alongside the road as we neared the town were workshops where men smelted copper and iron, and the acridness of burning coal stung our nostrils. Reaching the town by the street called Standish Gate we passed the great parish church (which I will admit far exceeds Preston's in grandeur), and entered Wall Gate where we spotted the sign of the Bear's Paw Inn. It looked a good place in which to feed the horses and ask for directions.

The landlord, Simon Freckleton, had a loud voice and did not stint to pass judgement on his fellow man.

'Terence Pitt?' he said when asked about him. 'He's a ruffian who thinks he's on his way to being a gentleman. But he's not: he has no manners and his father was nowt but a labourer though he bosses our people as if they were animals, and he bosses our animals, too, come to that, seeing as he's pinder as well as constable.'

He gestured with his thumb rubbing against his fingers and tempered his voice to a confidential hiss.

'And he makes a business of it, if you take my meaning.'

'You are suggesting he is not ruler-straight?' put in Fidelis.

'He's about as straight as a pig's tail. When you arrest a man, or confiscate an animal, it should be because it's the right thing to do, not to turn a shilling. A fine is a fine, not a ransom. A lot think the same of Mr Pitt around this town.'

He took us out into the street and pointed along Wall Gate.

'The pinfold's down there, at the town's end and off the road to the right. His house is by it, as you'll see. You won't need your horses – it's a walk of less than a mile.'

Fidelis led the way with a determined stride.

Having left the mass of houses behind us we came to a sign that pointed away from the road and along a lane to the pinfold, where the house of Terence Pitt also lay. We made our way down it and after two hundred yards the house came into view, and beyond it a collection of hutches, stalls, byres and paddocks variously inhabited by animal species.

By means we had guessed from Freckleton's insinuations, Pitt had evidently made himself a man of consequence in the town. In addition to his power over people as their constable, he enjoyed the pinder's job of arresting stray and vexatious animals, which could be returned to their owners in return for a fine. If an owner failed to come forward to pay, the beasts would be sold and the profit split with the Corporation. Much the same system of ransom was no doubt in force for his human prisoners, enabling Pitt to milk his position vigorously. Thus, though he had neither an education nor a trade, he lived in a modern residence on three floors, with sash windows and, above a painted front door furnished brightly with prosperous brass handles and knockers, an elegant fanlight.

The plan we had settled on was to pose as two travellers accidentally importuned by a stranger. Moved by his tale of an impounded pet piglet, we had agreed to his request that we call on Mr Pitt and ask on what terms the animal might be released. While discussions continued we would no doubt be invited into the house and there, perhaps, meet Kathy, the real object of our visit.

The door was wrenched open by an impatient hand. It was that of the pinder himself, who now faced us brandishing a chicken bone. Across his ample chest a linen napkin was spread, tucked at the top into the collar of his shirt.

'I'm dining. What do you want?' he said, with small attempt at civility.

He listened with evident impatience as I explained about our meeting with Jasper Spungeon and the matter of Henrietta the pig. His laugh when I had finished fired a volley of chicken shreds out of his mouth.

'You're too late. The man attempted to bring that little pig to market without a trader's licence, making it my bounden duty to confiscate the creature.'

'Respectfully, Sir, Mr Spungeon can convincingly show that he never sought to sell the pig at Wigan Market, and that your arrest of the pig is a misunderstanding.'

'I don't misunderstand, Sir. I never misunderstand. The day I am found to misunderstand will be my funeral day.'

'But has Spungeon not the customary right to have his case heard and, if successful, to redeem his property?'

'He would have that right, except that the piggie is now earmarked for my own table and will be killed, stuffed and roasted next Saturday week, on Mrs Pitt's birthday.'

'His rights—'

'The Devil take his rights. He is a foreigner, like you gentlemen, and no one of consequence in Wigan will speak up for the rights of foreigners.'

He put the chicken bone to his mouth and with two slashes of the teeth stripped away the remainder of the chicken flesh. Then he waved the bare drumstick in the direction we had come.

'Now, you will leave my property while I return to dinner. Good-bye.'

The door slammed as suddenly as it had opened.

'A very disobliging fellow,' said Fidelis as we retreated the way we had come.

'He is clearly a petty tyrant, with a regrettable disregard for a man's rights. But I wish we had not played Henrietta the pig as our opening card. It turned Pitt against us immediately. Perhaps I should have declared myself and my business, and asked outright for Kathy Brock.'

'That would not have worked. You've seen the man. He's taken the girl in, she is of his family. He would have denied she was there and sent us packing anyway.'

We had reached the main road, which I glanced along in the direction of the town. A rather plump young woman was coming towards us with a basket hooked over her arm.

'Good heavens,' I said, 'isn't this Kathy?'

I hurried towards her. 'Are you not Kathy Brock, of Preston?'

Her eyes widened and for a moment her mouth dropped open.

'Who's asking?'

'Kathy, do you not know me? I'm Titus Cragg and the last time we met I rescued you from the attentions of a mob of accusing ladies near Marsh End in Preston. This is Dr Luke Fidelis.'

Her face relaxed a little as she remembered, and her shoulders dropped. At the roadside there was a mossy water trough with a stone seat alongside it and I gestured towards this. Kathy, who was obviously not unintelligent, took my meaning at once and allowed herself to be led there. A brass cup on a chain hung above the trough.

'Let's sit here for a moment, shall we?' I suggested, gently taking her basket from her and placing it on the ground.

We sat in a row on the bench with Kathy between myself and Fidelis. Turning towards her I noticed the girl's pallor, her deep breathing and the glisten of a teardrop in the corner of her eye.

'Why did you run away from Preston, Kathy? Is it because that dead child was yours after all, as the women thought?'

Kathy would not meet my gaze, but stared down at her basket, sniffing.

'No, Mr Cragg,' she said in a voice hardly audible over the trickle of water into the trough.

'I have spoken to your mother, you know. She told me about your miscarriage of a child last year, after you'd been working at Mr Scroop's house.'

Kathy pressed her knuckles to her mouth.

'Did it happen a second time, Kathy? And did you not this time reach full term, give birth in secret and, being ashamed at being caught out conceiving a second bastard, did you not kill it, or have it killed?'

'No! No, that's untrue, I can swear to it.'

'All of it?'

She rose suddenly and grasped the drinking cup, which she dipped and raised to her mouth, swallowing noisily.

'Kathy, tell me at least this: is your mother's testimony the truth?'

She let the cup drop and it clanked noisily against the stone. But instead of answering my question she rested against the parapet and, a more composed figure now, asked her own slyly spoken one.

'Would it be that you have been to my uncle's house already?'

'We have.'

Her face registered immediate concern.

'And did you ask for me? What did he say? Was he vexed?'

'We did not mention you. We pretended we were there about a different matter.'

'I am right glad you didn't say my name. My uncle is very pettish if anything bad is said against what he calls the family honour – his own honour, really, as he thinks of it. He does not want his sister's daughter to put a stain on that.'

'How would she, Kathy? What have you done to threaten your uncle's honour?'

'I'll tell you, Mr Cragg. I'll tell you everything I know. But not now.' She pointed to her basket. 'I'm bringing my uncle's tobacco from town. If I don't come home with it now he'll be very vexed.'

'So when will you tell us, Kathy? If we wait here, will you return after you have taken home your shopping and talk to us then?'

'I can't. I've much work to do with the animals in the pinfold, feeding and mucking them out. If I don't do it, I'll surely be beaten. He always keeps an eye on my work.'

'So when?'

'Not today, any road. But tomorrow after church, there's a chance. My uncle has quarrelled with the vicar and he stays away from the service. My aunty is poorly. So I'm to go in charge of my cousins, but I can give them the slip after.'

I glanced at Fidelis.

'In that case we could stay the night at the inn. Unless you have to get back, Luke.'

Fidelis shook his head.

'No, I will gladly stay.'

So it was agreed that we would see Kathy at the churchyard in the morning.

'You must not come near me outside church,' she warned. 'Just follow me and I'll lead the way to a place where we can talk in private.'

'Very well. But do not let us down, Kathy, or I shall be obliged to seek you in your uncle's house after all.'

Fidelis rose and approached Kathy.

'You say your uncle will beat you,' he said, 'if you don't do your work.'

He reached out to take a gentle hold of her head, tilting it slightly to catch the light. Then he touched an area of faintly discoloured skin beneath her left eye.

'I see he has already done so,' he added. 'Go now, quickly. We do not want to see any more such evidence tomorrow morning.'

Chapter 10

AT THE BEAR'S Paw Inn we were just in time to secure a room. Shortly afterwards, a coach from Yorkshire rolled into the inn yard in need of some repair, and the passengers, facing an unforeseen overnight stay in Wigan, snapped up the remaining accommodation. Coming out to the inn yard to see to the stabling of our horses, we found many of these travellers gathered around Freckleton, listening to his account of one of the curious sights of the region – a burning well that lay beside the road towards Warrington, yet within two miles from where we stood. Freckleton proposed himself as their guide to this marvel, in return for a small fee of threepence apiece, at which half a dozen of the passengers got out their purses.

'The famous Burning Well of Wigan – I have never seen it,' I told Fidelis.

'Then you certainly must,' he said. 'It is a wonderful phenomenon.'

So we were admitted to the party in return for our sixpence and Freckleton went inside, returning with a long-handled copper pan and a candle-lantern. Thus equipped, we set off on our expedition.

The well lay a hundred yards from the road, and was constructed exactly as you would expect, with a low circular wall of dry stone around it. First, our guide invited us to gather around this parapet and look down into the well. Black water glinted back at us from about three feet down.

'It's not much, is that,' said one fellow. 'It's just a water well.'

'But notice the bubbles coming up from the depths,' said Fidelis.

'Is the water hot, then? Is it boiling?' asked one of the ladies.

'Try it,' said Freckleton with a booming laugh. 'Stick in a hand. Don't be afraid.'

She peeled off her glove and very gingerly did so.

'It's cold as ice,' she reported and we all dipped our own fingers to verify it. I sniffed mine when it was still wet and fancied the moisture smelled a little like marsh water.

Freckleton leant down into the well and scooped a panful, from which he drank a little before offering it around. Most of the party held back until Fidelis accepted his offer.

'Delicious!' he pronounced after taking a draught, with a smack of his lips.

'Just so,' said the landlord. 'It drinks like normal water, with no ill effect.'

One or two others took small experimental sips and agreed the water was indeed potable.

'Now,' said Freckleton, 'if one of you gentleman would oblige by kindling a flame for the lantern, I shall kindle for you a singular surprise that cannot be obtained from your usual water well.'

He bent to scoop several times more until he had lowered the well level by a foot. Then he took a rush from his pocket and, opening the now burning lantern, set the rush alight. This he flourished and told us to observe him closely.

Very slowly he lowered the burning rush into the well until it almost touched the surface. All at once a ghostly flame licked upwards from the water and then stole across the surface until it was burning all over, with the dancing blue flicker of brandy flame. Several of the party gasped.

'Suspend an egg in that, or a leg of chicken,' announced Freckleton, 'and it'll cook it for you, will that.'

'But how *does* the water burn?' asked one of the ladies. 'It is against nature. Is it bewitched?'

Looking down in fascination, the same question came to me. I was reminded of the 'lake with liquid fire' into which Milton's Satan plumps at the start of *Paradise Lost*. I even fancied I could see the miniature forms of tortured wraiths twisting in its flames. However, the smell was not sulphurous, as hell fire should be, but more like the iron smelters' fumes we had met along Wigan Lane.

For a whole minute the party stood entranced, except for Fidelis, whose attention quickly wandered. He picked up the saucepan in which the water he had drunk still remained.

'See here,' he said to get our attention. Taking the rush from Freckleton he reignited it in the fiery pool and applied it to the water in the pan.

'As I thought,' he said with satisfaction. 'Outside the well, it does not burn. However, if we were to empty the well of all its water, I fancy the earth inside the hole would burn, or seem to burn, just as much as the water. But let us confirm whether if this water will perform one of its more usual offices.'

With a single jerk of his arm he threw the pan's remaining contents back into the well. Immediately the flames were doused. Freckleton raised his voice.

'Now, Sir, there's no cause for that!'

'I am sorry,' said my friend with sardonic emphasis. 'Have I broken the spell?'

On the return journey I walked with a young curate, who told me he was on his way to visit his sick mother in Cheshire. He was complacent about what we had just seen.

'There is nothing new, Sir. The same is mentioned in *De Rerum Natura*, you know. Wells that bubble and generate fire.'

'Lucretius?'

'The same. The Epicurean.'

'I don't know much about him.'

'He was a contemporary of Caesar. I fancy they were school-fellows. It is a while since I looked through the poem. A great work, of course.'

'Of course.'

'Utterly godless, mind you. He maintains the soul is made of atoms and not immortal – among many other impieties.'

Seeing this clergyman was a reader I took the opportunity to ask him about the booksellers of York, and he told me that there were half a dozen of them, all with well-stocked premises in the city centre, close to the Minster. We chatted on about books and booksellers for the rest of our walk, until Freckleton led us through the arch and into the inn yard. At this moment I looked round for Fidelis and did not see him. I had been so absorbed in my conversation, I had not noticed that he had left us.

'Have you seen my friend?' I asked the landlord.

'He wanted me to recommend him a good apothecary,' said Freckleton. 'Perhaps he's gone there.'

I could not imagine what Fidelis wanted with an apothecary, unless it was on some professional business of his own. He did not enlighten me on his return after half an hour, but simply said he was hungry and strode ahead into the dining room, where we made good company with the Yorkshire travellers. Afterwards the landlord regaled us with the history of his inn, and in particular of the hirsute foot for which it was named, and which he kept pickled in a jar on the dining-room mantelpiece. Then his wife brought in a tray of locally made curiosities, carved out of the hard coal particular to the area, which they call cannel coal – little trinkets and pillboxes, and even a pen standish complete with inkwell and quill-box. In every case the objects were coloured deepest black, and highly polished.

'These look exactly like jet,' I said.

'They are pure coal, Sir,' said the landlady, now bringing out a spotless white cambric handkerchief. 'And happen you buy, for instance, this necklace as a present for your wife, you'd be afraid it'd smutch her neck, wouldn't you? Watch this then.'

She picked up the necklace and rubbed it vigorously with the handkerchief, then showed him the result. He expected it to be blackened, but the white cloth was unmarked.

'That is remarkable.'

'So you'll have it? Only fifteen shillings.'

I whistled.

'As much as that!'

'Oh come, Sir! I bet it's no more than what you spent on that wig you're wearing. Just think how charming these will look around your wife's neck.'

I picked up the necklace and let it run through my fingers. Elizabeth had a most beautiful neck and she would indeed look charming wearing those glistening, faceted beads.

'You are right,' I said. 'I'll take it.'

Next morning, in the magnificent surroundings of Wigan's Church of All Saints, I sat in a packed pew surrounded entirely by parishioners. Fidelis, as a papist, had taken himself off to find a mass somewhere else. When we reached the sermon, it became obvious that Pitt's quarrel with the vicar was far from resolved.

A thickset and combative sort, he preached on a text from Psalm 18: 'Therefore hath the Lord recompensed me according to my righteousness; according to the cleanness of my hands in his eyesight.'

'How righteous are ye?' he thundered. 'How clean are your hands? Truly you must reflect on your lives. For all of us know there is one amongst us – one, at least! – who stands accused of unrighteous exercise of his authority in our town and of sullying his hands in the matter of fines and amercements. As a result, he no more comes to the house of God, but only the women and children of his family attend this divine service. I would remind him, and you all, of the words of the psalmist, "with the merciful, show thyself merciful, with the upright man show thyself upright". But remember also,' – and now he lifted an admonitory finger – 'that these words are reversible; that under God's adamantine law, the *unmerciful* man can expect only to be treated *unmercifully* and the *crooked* man *crookedly*.'

At these words the congregation began whispering and many turned to look at the bench in which Kathy sat. There was, of course, no sign of Terence Pitt or of his wife. Like all preachers, and much envied by lawyers, the vicar enjoyed the luxury of conducting his arguments without answer or protest.

As we spilled out of the church, I kept a close eye on Kathy. After lingering a minute or two to speak to one or two fellow worshippers – friends, perhaps, giving her words of comfort for the vicar's wounding remarks – she spoke rapidly and vehemently to the children, and pointed up at the church clock. As her cousins began a game of hide and seek among the graves, she hurried out of the churchyard and I followed. I caught up with her halfway along a narrow weind or lane, where she ushered me into a damp and mossy ginnel between two backyards. Here we held our conference.

'Now, Kathy,' I said firmly. 'Your story, if you please.'

'I must be quick, Sir. I can only leave the children ten minutes, but I hardly know where to begin.'

'Begin with what your mother told me. Is it the truth?'

A bald question, but we had no time for nicety. She responded, to give her credit, in the same way.

'Some of it. I admit I went with a man last year, but I learned my lesson after. I keep clear of lads now, I do.'

She spoke quietly but in a rational, even way, and her hands moved and gestured precisely to emphasise her words.

'But you ran away from the inquest. What other reason could there be to do that, if not that this dead baby was yours?'

'One, Sir, and a very good one.'

'What is it?'

She thought how best to reply, mouth set, head still and expressive hands clasped together.

'You must tell me, Kathy.'

'It is that I don't feel safe. I'd rather have the fists of my uncle, I think, than what certain people might do to me if I ever spoke out at an inquest about my time working at the Scroops'. I'm afraid all my plans and schemes'd be ruined for ever.'

'Plans and schemes, Kathy?'

'Yes, for my life, Sir. You see I know what I want and it's not to be dipping hides in shit and paddling it for the rest of my days.'

'Why, then, did you leave your job as a maid? Did you not like it?'

'Oh, I liked it. To work in a fine big house was everything I wanted.'

'Why, then?'

She took a deep breath.

'I will tell you my story, but you must not try to make me tell it in public. If you do, I'll deny you.'

She jabbed the air. Although her body ran a little to fat she had the neat, sinewy fingers of a seamstress, small-boned but capable and strong.

'Go on, then.'

'As you know I were maid at the Scroops in Water Lane. The eldest girl is Harriet and she's fifteen. She's very close, that girl, so you'd never know what she was thinking some days. But she seemed to like me. We used to play cards and laugh very merrily together. But one day Miss Scroop fell poorly and Dr Harrod came in from next door to see her. Well he spent an hour with her and came out saying she had the colic and a disordered stomach and prescribed some medicine. That wasn't right, Sir, for truth to tell she'd got a babby starting.'

'Good heavens! Are you suggesting that in reality Harriet Scroop was pregnant, that Dr Harrod did not spot it and so she gave birth in secret?'

Her hands had made small fists. Now she opened them and showed me her palms.

'I don't know all that. But I do know she'd got a babby.'

'Miss Scroop confided in you, I suppose.'

'No, she never. But a few weeks later, after the bouts of sickness had passed and the family thought her cured by Harrod's medicine, she told me privately of certain changes in her body. Well, she didn't understand them, her, but I knew they meant she was carrying – I knew before she did!'

'What did you do? Did you not inform her?'

'I didn't dare to, no, Sir. I thought she'd just have to find it out for herself. I gave notice of leaving instead. I couldn't bide there, not with such knowledge in me. Now, Sir, I must go home. I have a story ready for why I've come away after church, but it will not do if I am missing too long.'

We were due to ride straight back to Preston, but Fidelis had still not returned. I went up to the room and, sitting down a little impatiently to wait, opened *The Fable of the Bees*. Twenty minutes passed, and another twenty. Then I read the author comparing 'the virtues of great men to your large china jars; they make a fine show but look into a thousand of them and you'll find nothing but dust and cobwebs'. I was still laughing when the door of the room crashed open and there was Fidelis. His face was flushed from effort, his clothing was disordered, but a wide triumphant smile lit his face.

'Good God, Luke! What have you been doing?'

He did not reply but, as he came into the room, I saw he was dragging behind him a sack, which seemed to have something alive in it, since it writhed and squealed as it slid across the floor.

'Can you guess what I've brought you?' he panted.

'Whatever it is, there's quite a stink off it.'

'That is an ungallant remark to make about a young member of the fair sex.'

The neck of the sack had been tied with baling twine. Fidelis undid the knot and was on the point of showing me what he had when, jerking and wriggling with new force, the sack slipped from his grasp. In a trice a round pink missile launched itself into the room. Its velocity was such that it skidded and skittered across the wooden floor until, finding its feet, it could turn around and face us with defiance in its eyes. Fidelis extended his arm towards it.

'May I introduce our poor little princess of pigs, the kidnapped and abused Henrietta?'

I pointed incredulously at his burden.

'You mean this is Spungeon's pig?'

'Certainly it is. I have re-abducted her. I cannot find it in my heart to let that ruffian Pitt eat her.'

'But what are we going to do with her?'

'Return her to her master, naturally.'

'Yes, but in the meantime, Luke?'

As if wanting to know the same thing, Henrietta sat on her haunches, looking at Fidelis, then at me, then back at Fidelis. She had that appraising wariness common to the species. Fidelis stepped towards her making a high-pitched wheedling noise and, not for the first time, I saw the unusual rapport he had with animals. In the manner of someone taking an indulgence, Henrietta allowed him to scratch the back of her neck. Then she jutted her head forward to get him to tickle her chin.

'She is really very tame,' said Fidelis. 'However, I have got a powder from the apothecary that will induce a deep sleep. She will give us no trouble on the way.'

'Apart from the smell.'

And so we smuggled a sleeping Henrietta out of Wigan in her sack, lying across the crupper of Fidelis's horse. Having gone two or three miles along Wigan Lane we began looking out for Spungeon so that we could reunite them, but he did not appear.

'We will have to take the pig home with us,' Fidelis said.

Chapter 11

BY THE TIME Wigan was ten miles behind us we had given up
hope of meeting Spungeon on the road and begun discussing
what to do with Henrietta once we'd arrived in Preston. So, naturally, it was at this point that our man came into view ahead,
walking in the same direction as ourselves. We drew alongside him,
and saw that he proceeded with his head down and feet dragging,
as if dejected. I concluded he was missing his pet – a humour that
was about to change, for Fidelis now took hold of the sack that he
carried and swung it down to him.

'Here, Spungeon, my friend!' he called, startling the fellow out
of his reverie. 'A gift from Wigan, and it's not made of cannel coal.'

Spungeon grasped the sack, lowered it to the ground and began
to open it. But we did not wait to see the result of Fidelis's good
work. By the time the sleepy Henrietta was revealed to her master,
we had kicked our horses on and it wasn't until we had forged
some way ahead that a burst of joyful hosannahs rang out behind
us. As these faded, Fidelis's mind reverted to the subject of Kathy's
testimony, which I had related to him first on the previous evening,
and now a second time, at his request, during this ride.

'Kathy's story is striking in respect of Harrod, is it not?' Fidelis
now said, as we came to yet another part of the road where it was
necessary to walk the horses. 'It proves my point entirely.'

'Your point about what?'

'About the Stygian depth of Basilius Harrod's incompetence: not to have seen that Harriet Scroop was with child.'

'It would, if it's true that she was. I am reserving judgement on that, for the moment.'

'Do you know the girl, Harriet Scroop? Is it likely she could have strayed from the virtuous path?'

'I don't know her, but Elizabeth might. I will find out.'

At home, in our parlour, Elizabeth twirled around in excitement after I'd fastened the new necklace in place for the first time.

'Oh! It's beautiful, my love,' she said, turning to the pier-glass and fingering the bright beads. 'I'll wear it at Saturday's Assembly. Everyone will admire it.'

She kissed me and ran into the kitchen to show Matty, whose appreciative cries rang through the house. A few minutes later Elizabeth returned to me, bringing tea.

'Now tell me, what was so charming about Wigan that made you stay a night away from your loving home?'

She poured my tea and I began to tell her about the excursion, laughing about Henrietta, wondering at the mystery of the burning well and growing serious over my conversation with Kathy Brock.

'She claimed that Harriet Scroop was with child? She's only a child herself.'

'Not exactly. She is old enough, I think.'

'Just old enough. But is it likely? The girl is so serious, and so close, and not particularly well favoured by nature – in her appearance, I mean. She's a nervous, inward girl. I'd say she wasn't spirited enough to speak to a lad, never mind lift her skirts for one.'

'It happens every day.'

'Well, I know, but coming from that respectable Bible-reading family, I do find it very hard to believe.'

'Kathy worked as a maid at the house. She tells me she got to know her young mistress rather well.'

'But can you believe any of Kathy's story? She's likely making all this up about Harriet, to get the attention away from herself.'

Next morning I went directly to Water Lane meaning to speak to one or both of Harriet Scroop's parents. I took a special note of the young footman, who had spoken to me superciliously in the previous week, wondering if I could discern in him anything of the character of a seducer. He was not a bad-looking young fellow, but I was no further on with my speculation by the time he showed me into the morning parlour to, as he said, await Mr Scroop's pleasure.

Going in, I found, to my surprise, that Captain Strawboy was seated at a table under the window, writing busily in a notebook.

'Captain!' I said. 'How do?'

He stood as I came forward and we shook hands. Strawboy was effusively friendly. We had met during his visit to Preston in the previous year, although we did not much know each other.

'What brings you to this house, Mr Cragg?'

'A little legal matter, that is all,' I said.

'And are you recovered, I hope, after the unfortunate events of last week when the Skeleton Inn was burned? I know you were in the thick of it.'

'I thank you, Captain. I am quite recovered. Are you also waiting to see Mr Scroop?'

The captain smiled with a degree of complacency.

'No, I'm fortunate you know in that I already see Mr Scroop at breakfast, dinner and supper.'

'Ah! You are in residence.'

'For a few days only, on this occasion. With Mrs Scroop's new baby, and all the children now returned, the house is in a disturbed condition.'

'We have inns in town, of course, where you might be more comfortable.'

'Well, I have been in the army long enough to find inns less pleasant than a billet such as I have now. In family accommodation, one is better fed, I find, and more gratified in every direction. It is also more convenient in this particular instance, as Mr Scroop and I are working together on a project.'

'Oh? What is that?'

'Well, to put it briefly, we intend to repair the production of leather in this town. To reform it root and branch. It will of course be necessary to curtail the privileges of those inefficient and indeed scandalous families of tanners who presently work the skin-yard. But I have no doubt the Corporation will be persuaded by our case. The whole trade must be established on a more businesslike footing. It is crying out to be done. I suppose you heard what was found in one of the dye pits the other day?'

'As a matter of fact that is why I'm—'

'They are a blot on the town, those people. I say the sooner we extirpate them, the better.'

The door opened and none other than Harriet Scroop came in. She was a round young woman and much as Elizabeth had described: tight around the mouth, rigid about the shoulders, wan about the eyes. There were no apparent signs of her recent alleged dishonour – but then, I thought, what would such signs look like? Harriet did seem a little embarrassed except that this, as I soon perceived, was far from being anything to do with me – I was scarcely acknowledged – but caused by the presence of Strawboy in the room. Harriet blushed when she set eyes on him, put her hand to her lips, then burst out, 'Oh, Captain Strawboy, let us have your company in the nursery for a game of cards. I would not . . . only my sisters send me, to ask you kindly to come in and play with us.'

Strawboy smiled indulgently.

'What are the stakes in this game of cards, Miss Scroop? Do you play high?'

She blushed more deeply.

'Why, there are no . . . no stakes, Captain. That you should suggest such a thing!'

'None at all? That is exceedingly virtuous of you. Good Lord, I never play cards unless it's for stakes, you know.'

He made this declaration in a firm, though not in an unkind, way.

'I find the game is empty, you see, if there is nothing to lose, and nothing to win. I would find it lacking, you know, as a . . . well, as a gun that has no bullet, I suppose.'

'Oh, then I beg pardon,' said Harriet, dropping a curtsey. 'I regret I have disturbed you.'

Seeing she was about to withdraw, I said, 'Miss Scroop, I have a little business with your father. Do you know where he is? Or I can speak with your mother in his place, if he is not at home.'

'My mother is with the baby. We have not yet found a nurse, so she is . . .'

'I see. Then of course I shall not inconvenience her. And your father?'

At that moment the red-headed footman reappeared. He had the answer to this last question.

'My master regrets,' he said, 'that he is called away on business and cannot see you today.'

I tried to spot anything between the servant and Harriet, but she seemed as indifferent to his presence as he to hers.

I took my leave in some frustration, though my visit had not been entirely wasted, I thought, as I made my way back to my office. I had after all seen Miss Scroop, and I had found out something about her: that she gave every sign of being not unaffected in the presence of Captain Strawboy.

Furzey was at his writing desk. His smoked voice sounded somewhat better, but his humour did not.

'I have had no sleep from coughs,' he told me. 'I should not be here at work, as I shall certainly make more mistakes than usual in my writing, and have to do it over.'

'You never make mistakes,' I said. 'And I am glad to see you as we must talk about where to reconvene the inquest.'

'I'm thinking we should hold it in the fire station.'

I laughed.

'I'll leave it to your judgement, Furzey. Now, have you copied the Arkwright tenancy agreement yet? I am due to see Mr Arkwright at eleven o'clock.'

So I spent the morning immersed in dull legal work, but my mind would not let go of the puzzle presented to me by Kathy Brock's statement. In spite of what Elizabeth had said about Harriet Scroop's timidity, I supposed it was possible she had been with child, though the circumstances were hard to imagine. Even less easy to believe, though, was that she would have been capable of killing the child and dumping it in a pit at the skin-yard. That would seem to me the act of a very different type of young woman: one that was indeed more like Kathy herself.

At dinner Elizabeth suggested we go together to Avenham Walk, as it was a pleasant afternoon. This amenity had been created by the town almost half a century ago, when the land had been purchased and laid out for promenading. Gravelled and guarded by iron rails and within it an avenue of lime trees, it extended southward the length of a spur of land to the south of Fisher Gate and a little below it. At the end of the walk was a matchless view of the south, across the river to the fells in the east and the flat mosslands in the west. Immediately below was the river, and beyond, snaking away directly southward, was the road up which Fidelis and I had travelled only the previous day.

The walk was being enjoyed by a few groups of people, whom we greeted as we met them. One pair of ladies I knew quite well – my client Miss Colley and her neighbour and friend Mrs Bryce.

'Oh, Mr Cragg!' exclaimed Miss Colley, her bright eyes shining. 'How fortunate that I could not attend Thursday's inquest as I usually do, owing to a slight indisposition. I should never have survived in the fire, you know. I should have been burned to a crisp.'

'No, Miss Colley,' I assured her. 'No one was burned, or not seriously, though it was a close run thing. I hope the accident will not keep you from attending our inquests in future.'

'Accident, you say?' said Mrs Bryce. 'It was no accident, that.'

'Do you have any information, Mrs Bryce?' I asked with a bow in her direction. 'For if so, I should be most grateful if you would speak out.'

Mrs Bryce sniffed.

'It was more in the nature of the general opinion, Mr Cragg, and what the fellow Clarkson's been putting about.'

'I have heard that. He has been to see me, loudly complaining.'

I raised my hat and we passed on, and, reaching the end of the walk, lingered for a few minutes to admire the view.

'Somewhere in that country roams poor Jasper Spungeon and his Henrietta,' I said.

Elizabeth laughed merrily.

'I hope they're not poor, but prospering,' she said. 'I like him very much for his devotion to that animal.'

We turned and, halfway back along the walk, saw Ephraim Grimshaw and Mrs Grimshaw in earnest conversation with a diminutive lady whom I did not at first recognize. Then as they approached nearer to us it struck me.

'It's that woman,' I murmured to Elizabeth. 'The one that I got out of the fire at the last minute. I must ask how she does.'

I let go of Elizabeth's arm and darted eagerly forward, not noticing that she was trying to restrain me.

'Dear lady,' I said to the stranger, having greeted the Grimshaws and received in reply a barely civil grunt from our former mayor. 'I hope you remember me. I was fortunate enough to help you the other day out of the fire at the Skeleton Inn.'

The woman's face was rigid, pained. She sniffed, met my gaze and then jerked her head to the side, saying nothing. I don't know what I expected: gratitude, perhaps; a friendly look at the very least. I did not expect to be cut dead.

'That is Lady Rickaby, a widowed sister of Mrs Grimshaw,' whispered my wife, as the three of them swept past without another word. 'She has come from Leamington for a few weeks' stay. I should have mentioned it to you: she's been complaining all over town about how you treated her.'

'How I treated her? I recollect that I saved her life.'

Elizabeth was laughing.

'Dearest, did you cut off her hoops?'

'Indeed I did. She *would* have been burned to a crisp else.'

'Her dignity is gravely affronted.'

'Because I saw her legs?'

'And her drawers. She will not forgive you for that, I'm afraid.'

I joined my wife in laughter, putting my arm around her shoulder and hugging her close. Neither of us could have foreseen that, as things would turn out, this was no laughing matter.

Elizabeth and I parted at the top of Cheapside, where she went home and I hurried into the Moot Hall. Mayor Thwaite was in his business room, standing at a table strewn with a disordered heap of papers and open ledgers. Jack Thwaite, who was now coming to the end of his term of office, was a shoemaker with a considerable trade, though its success depended largely on the acumen of his wife Margaret. Thwaite did not lack cunning but he was unsystematic, hasty in everything and full of bluster. His mayoralty had had little to commend it.

He frowned at me, bunching together his remarkably bushy eyebrows.

'This is a bad do, Cragg, this unfinished inquest. Very bad. We need to close the matter, which means establishing that the murderess is this girl who's run off to Wigan. You can't trust anyone in Wigan. That she went to relatives there puts her guilt beyond question, so people are saying, and I agree. Her mother admitted in your court that she's a slut. But it seems you cannot do what the people and I require.'

'No one wishes to conclude the inquest more than myself,' I said, in a tone that I hoped was conciliatory. 'It is not yet certain that Kathy Brock killed this baby, though it's true questions have been raised that need answering.'

'Then get them answered, Sir.'

'But first there is the matter of the fire that interrupted the hearing. I fear we have an arsonist in our midst. If I restart the hearing too soon, we may be in danger again.'

'You have evidence of this arson?' The tone of his voice lay somewhere between a bark and a growl.

'Innkeeper Clarkson is convinced it was arson.'

'That is not evidence. Clarkson's complaint is known to the whole town by now. He's even been up and down here with it. I don't believe him, nobody does. He is a deluded wastrel and a desperate man, who will make any allegation if it saves him from the charge of his own negligence. That is what most likely caused the fire.'

'So you will not act? You will not investigate?'

'There is one matter concerning the fire that I *will* look into, Cragg, and it is not this imaginary arsonist. It touches on your own conduct.'

'My conduct? How so?'

'You must know what I am referring to.'

'I do not.'

'Lady Rickaby says that you assaulted her. Dishonoured her. She says you took advantage of the circumstances, being alone together, and behaved in a manner that must disgust any decent person.'

'I removed her underskirts.'

'My God, you admit it!'

'I had no choice: it was to save her life.'

'She said you did it out of lascivious and lustful motives.'

I laughed.

'I don't know how she knows that. At the time she was unconscious, more or less.'

'Unconscious! So you admit that, too. And you laugh barefaced at it. You took advantage, Sir. And you shall answer for it. In the next few days you shall receive a summons to present yourself in front of Court Leet. We shall hear from the lady then. And we will decide if you are a fit person to hold public office. That will be all, Mr Cragg.'

I left Moot Hall with a light heart. The whole thing was absurd to me, and absurdity is always funny, I find. Just as amusing was Furzey's doom-laden response when, back in the office, I told him of Thwaite's threat to deprive me of the coronership.

'It's been done before,' he said darkly. 'In my grandfather's time.'

'What? A coroner thrown out of office by the Corporation? They don't have the power.'

'We are subject to election every October, are we not?'

'There's never been an election, though! No one has ever wanted this job except me, fool that I am.'

'If the Mayor's court impeaches you, an election will be called next month, and you will be debarred from standing. Your time as Coroner will be over.'

'They would not dare. The Lord Lieutenant will refuse to allow it. Lord Derby has always been my protector.'

'He is a lord, with interests in this town. He will put those interests first, as they all do.'

'You say it has happened before?'

'Aye, there was a coroner in the last century, Wilson by name, that killed a man. Murder was not proven but he was disgraced and left the town for ever, I believe.'

'But this here is a triviality by comparison. Wilson would not have been impeached for doing what I have done, as it was done only to save life – Lady Rickaby's.'

'What was an utter triviality a hundred years ago may be an utter gravity now. The weather changes, Mr Cragg.'

'No, Furzey, it is incredible. Stop fooling. Have you gathered news of our jurors? Shall we be able to resume the inquest tomorrow?'

'There's no chance of that. Half of them are as hoarse as donkeys; they're all mortally afraid. Word has gone around that the fire was set on purpose. After what we all went through they don't want to have owt to do with this inquest.'

I sighed.

'They will have to in time. Oh well, let us wait two days and speak to them again.'

Chapter 12

THAT EVENING I acquainted Elizabeth with the Mayor's accusations and threats. In spite of my earlier jocosity, the suspicion had begun to nibble at me that Furzey was right, and that I really might be ejected from the coronership in this ridiculous way. As for my wife, she took the news indignantly.

'That Lady Rickaby! How she draws attention to herself. It is nothing but pride, and quite unseemly as well as absurd. But you must be careful, my love. The Corporation has little love for you and they will pick up this charge by Lady Rickaby as a stick to beat you with.'

'A very thin and absurd stick. It would not hurt me.'

'Don't be so sure. It might if you charge into the Scroop family accusing them of concealed pregnancy and baby killing.'

Later, I lay uneasily in bed for a long time, turning this way and that, while my wife slept beside me. As Elizabeth had said, the matter was very delicate. Abraham Scroop was a powerful man. Without presentable evidence of the fact, or at least a strong indication, his daughter could hardly be asked the question direct: had she been with child? With that problem still foremost in my mind, I did at last sink into sleep – only to awake an hour later from a fearful dream.

What the devil is the mind doing when it dreams? Lucretius wrote – if I read him right in Book 4 of his poem – that dreams are the worn-out thoughts of the mind, cast off in sleep as snakes shed their skins. I have also heard it said that dreams are the games of a childish brain given licence to caper around all forgetful of decency and decorum. Yet some dreams are more dreadful than we dare to think of waking, and raise terrors that linger long in the memory. They seem charged with meaning and portent, according with our much older belief that gods and spirits talk to us through dreams.

In this dream I was in our vegetable garden out beyond the Friar Gate Bar, and there I found to my great surprise a tan-pit exactly like those I'd seen at the skin-yard. Approaching it I saw the dead newborn baby floating there half submerged, its unformed face and swaddled body lying ghost-like in the tanners' stinking, leather-making soup. I bent and reached down to pull the little victim out, whereupon its eyes flashed open and stared at me with horrid accusation. Then a hand – its own hand it seemed to me – appeared out of the swaddling clothes and seized my thumb and gave a sharp jerk. Pulled off balance by what seemed incommensurate strength, I found myself pitching helplessly forward into the vileness of the pit, when I jumped awake covered in a hot sweat of horror.

I have just offended against the rule that I once read in *The Spectator*, 'Never narrate your dreams. You enjoy telling them, but no one enjoys hearing them'. Very well, but I cannot help it, for the dream did not just frighten me, it convinced that I must proceed with care, or I would end up falling into a trough of shit.

That morning as I dressed I meditated on the problem of Harriet Scroop, and how I could ever find out if she had been pregnant and given secret birth. At breakfast, bringing me the food, Elizabeth bent and scrutinized my face.

'You look tired, my love.'

'I didn't sleep much.'

I was on the point of telling her the dream, but restrained myself, not wanting to look foolish in her eyes.

'It was this very delicate Scroop business. I cannot come out and ask Harriet Scroop if she has been pregnant. We must find it out another way.'

It was then I thought of how Elizabeth might help.

'I wonder if you would by any chance be calling on Mrs Scroop, my dearest?'

I asked this in a sidelong sort of way but, as quick as a pipit, she grasped my intent.

'Titus, are you asking me to spy for you?' Her eyes sparkled with amusement. 'I don't know what the town would say to your using your wife as an agent.'

'I am asking you to try the air of the house, that's all. You have the most sensitive nose that I know. You can smell trouble. I would like to find out how that household *smells*, if you catch my drift.'

'Well, I have the very thing in the cold press to take with me: a restorative milk jelly that Matty made this morning. I will carry it to the Scroops in such a neighbourly way that no one will guess my ulterior motive.'

'A junket! Shall *we* not have any junket, then?'

Elizabeth laughed at my fondness for the dish.

'Matty will make another immediately. It will restore you, too.'

In the evening at supper, as helpings of Matty's second junket lay before us on the table, Elizabeth gave me a full report on her visit.

'Of course I asked first for Mrs Scroop, but she would not or could not see me.'

'She is very reclusive, it seems.'

The milk jelly was cool, but with the musty tang of nutmeg. I enjoyed the slipperiness of it on my still-rough throat as Elizabeth continued.

'So I requested the company of Harriet Scroop instead and she came in to me. So far, so good. Harriet is still only fifteen, but I fancy she has grown up since I saw her last. She is more composed than the stammering girl that she was. And she has not quite lost all that puppy fat. Anyway, I gave her the junket and we exchanged a few polite words. I asked how her mother was and the children, and then her busy father. Of course we did not touch on the nature of his business but I had the impression he is very occupied with it, and a great deal absent from the family. After a little time she asked about myself and then after you, which gave me my opportunity. I described how you were absorbed in the case of the murdered newborn child, and in how to restart the inquest, and that you had even been as far as Wigan making enquiries. I affected to know no details – being just a wife, I made her understand – but I kept an eye on her manner as I raised the matter. There is no doubt, Titus. Her interest in it is keen, very keen. "Was your husband looking for that Kathy Brock, then?" she asked. I pretended not to know, and asked why she thought you might, and she said she knew Kathy was in Wigan, and that the word was she was suspected of murder, and that she, Harriet, wouldn't put it past her, as when she was a servant in the household she had always been saucy and a hussy. "And now she has run away to her uncle in Wigan, hasn't she?" she said. "Does not that prove her guilt? I hope she is brought back and made to confess her guilt."

'Then she became rather quiet for a moment, and it seemed she might have had something to say but found it difficult to put whatever it was into words. Then Dr Harrod came in. You know he is such a friend of the family that he comes and goes almost as he likes in the house. His joining us only increased Miss Scroop's difficulty and she began actually to stammer. "Now, now, my dear," he said. "Don't say your stutter has returned, that I took so many hours to cure you of?" But still she failed to produce words and instead she fled from the room.'

I have given Elizabeth's account shorn of my own interrupting exclamations and superfluous questions, just as Cervantes does in *Don Quixote*. This may not be how people talk in life, but it keeps the matter brief. However, at this point I asked her a question worth recording.

'What did Dr Harrod say about this?'

'Oh, he made light of it, before changing the subject – complimenting me on bringing the junket and telling me what a busy day he was having.'

'He has a wide practice and is much respected, though not by Fidelis, who calls him a medical buffoon with his astrology and old-fashioned nostrums. As for me, I am inclined to think his nostrums have stood the test of time, and his talk of the constellations is only an embroidery to cover the rather less pretty facts of disease.'

'He is very popular with the ladies. He does not discuss their insides with them.'

'Yes, and by God, one of them's . . . How could I have forgotten? A minute before I opened the inquest, Harrod told me he was in a hurry to give his evidence, as he had been called to the bedside of a lady with a very bad bandaged abscess.'

'What is remarkable about that?'

'Because he told me the lady's name. Lady Rickaby.'

'How odd. Lady Rickaby was in the inquest room.'

'Exactly. And, unfortunately for me, I saw her legs. There was not a bandage to be seen. So why tell this lie? Why would she pretend to her doctor she was ill?'

All the threads of this inquiry were getting confused, just as fishermen's lines tangle in the wind. Everywhere was the suspicion of underhand dealing and lies. I did not know why the fire at the Skeleton Inn had been started, and nor could I tell the Mayor's reason for hurrying me to judgement in the matter. As for the lies, what credence could I give Kathy Brock? And why had Lady Rickaby lied about her health?

And all the time that friendless little body lay in the bath house. Still no prayers had been said for it, and no grave dug, and I knew I would feel the tugging of this, even as I went about my mundane legal tasks – for now my story begins a new day, being Wednesday.

The sky this morning was broadly patched with blue between white scuts of cloud, and it was pleasant to walk about town. After breakfast, I stepped out into Cheapside and turned left towards the top of Friar Gate. My job this morning was to go the rounds of our coffee houses in search of an executor who had repeatedly dodged all my attempts to obtain his signature on a letter. However, the elusive fellow I was seeking was not in any of the coffee houses I put my head into, but when I came to the last, the Turk's Head, I saw Luke Fidelis sitting, with a pot of coffee before him, as he studied the *Preston Journal*. The air in the room was spiced with the smell of tobacco and roast coffee beans, and I breathed it with pleasure as I joined him.

Fidelis called for another cup and poured for me.

'It is the coffee our grandfathers used to drink,' he said. 'Plumtree tells me his supply of Jamaican beans has been interrupted by a shipment to Liverpool going down in a hurricane. He's obtained a supply of Arabian beans from somewhere in London. I fancy it will sharpen you up.'

'I require sharpening up,' I said, tasting the brew. It was darker and more bitter than what we were used to. 'I am getting nowhere with the case of the dead baby and now I am accused of assaulting a lady.'

'I have heard. The woman is a fool. You must take no notice, Titus. Have a pinch of snuff with your coffee instead.'

He placed his snuffbox on the table between us. I picked it up and saw that it was of unusual design, being circular and with a motif in a foreign alphabet.

'I haven't see this before. It is handsome.'

'A lady gave it to me,' he said. 'I am fond of it.'

I tried to flip the lid up with my thumb in the usual way, but nothing happened. Fidelis watched me intently, but offered no help until I had revolved the box in my fingers and found I could not nick it open from any point in the circumference.

'How the devil do I open it?'

'Oh, the lid twists,' he said, rising now and heading out by the back door towards the jakes.

I continued to struggle to open the snuffbox. Taking a firm hold of the lid with the fingers of one hand and of the base with those of the other, I twisted. There was a slight movement and then it stuck entirely. I put the box down and waited for Fidelis to return.

'I cannot open it,' I said. 'It is too tight.'

Fidelis took the snuffbox and had it open in seconds.

'You see?' he said. 'It is not too tight, you merely tried to open it in the wrong direction. This is an old Russian box. The thread on the lid is counter and so you must twist it counter.'

I took a pinch of what was evidently good Seville tobacco dust and said, 'I have read that Russians cross themselves by touching the right shoulder before the left. Do they by the same token screw lids in the other direction also?'

As I snuffed, he laughed.

'A delightful idea, but the truth is better. A hundred years ago Tsar Michael forbade all tobacco taking. He specially hated snuff and punished those caught taking it by having their noses cut off.'

'He was a harsh ruler.'

'But a stupid one. The courtiers had their snuffboxes made on this pattern, so that the Tsar would be unable to open them and discover what they contained. Now, you must tell me how you do in proving Kathy Brock's story?'

I sneezed and at once my head seemed clearer, my brain less oppressed.

'Not well. Jack Thwaite has spoken to me. He raised this absurd idea that I attacked the lady, and then said I was negligent in dragging out the skin-yard inquest. He does not like the place and considers all its inhabitants degenerate. Kathy he sees as the only possible culprit in the matter and he wants to hurry the thing along.'

'It is not for him to decide.'

'Well, he is chief magistrate. He can if he wishes take the matter into his own hands even though it would be customary not to do so until he knows the inquest's outcome. But this haste to blame Kathy Brock looks dubious, I think. A matter of policy, not of justice. There is a project to remove the skinners from the skin-yard in order to set up a new tannery or something of the kind, and it will be easier to turn the Brocks and the Kites out of the skin-yard if one of them is tainted as a murderer.'

'Where is Ephraim Grimshaw in this? Let us not forget the Grimshaws are curriers and themselves have an interest in the products of the skin-yard.'

'Yes, they must make powerful allies for Scroop – even without the addition of Lord Grassington's nephew. However, there's a part of me, too, that wants to get this inquest over and done. I wish it had not been thwarted and we had got to a verdict, one way or the other.'

'It would have gone against her, I think. Margery Brock's evidence was damning.'

'Yet it was about another state of affairs, another man and last year. I wish Kathy had had the chance to speak for herself.'

'And that would have helped her, you think?'

His tone told me he thought not.

'You are probably right,' I said with a sigh of regret. 'If she did come back, the gallows or transportation would almost inevitably await her.'

'Then it is up to you to sort the lies from the truth.'

I laughed ruefully.

'Lies! I have already found one out, though I don't know the meaning of it. I haven't told you, have I, what Dr Harrod said to me when we came back from viewing the body? It seems remarkable, but I don't know how. I only last night remembered it.'

'What was it?'

I told him that the doctor had informed me he was hurrying away to a patient whose leg was eaten by an abscess.

'What is remarkable about that?' he said. 'I see one of those every fortnight.'

'I'd wager you can't guess who the lady was.'

'You would be right: I can't.'

'Lady Rickaby.'

Showing no surprise, and little enough interest, Fidelis took another pinch of snuff.

'So I want to know this,' I went on, 'and I hope you will tell me: if the lady had an abscess, I mean a bad case of it, would she have been able to go out and come to the inquest?'

'I doubt it. If it was indeed a bad suppuration, she would have been resting in a curtained room with a poultice on it. She would hardly have been able to attend an event in public without it being lanced. Where is this leading, Titus?'

'To the question why did she call for him to lance it and then miss the appointment? Did she make an unexpected recovery? You know I saw her legs. There was nothing. Was it all pretence?'

Fidelis sighed, impatient at the dragging pace of my thoughts.

'No, Titus. At least, not on her part. She might have pretended to a migraine, perhaps, but would never have made up anything so easily discovered as an imaginary abscess. Ergo, Lady Rickaby did not lie to Dr Harrod. It was Harrod who lied to you.'

'Well, I am at a loss to see why.'

'He did not want to waste time. He wanted to give his evidence early, so he invented the appointment.'

'It probably doesn't signify and was only a whim of his.'

'Perhaps he had some assignation. It is whispered here and there that the good doctor is a man with secrets, by which I suppose they mean he is a lady's man.'

'In which case, that is his business and I revert to the more important question – how to proceed in this matter of the baby's death. I am checked in every direction.'

'You are not, Titus. Let me suggest two ways you may go. Remember the state of the baby's navel cord? It had been tied and cut – it had been dealt with by someone who knew the necessities of childbirth. So here is my first suggestion: find the person who tied that knot. It would be one with some experience of childbirth.'

'A mother? A midwife?'

'Those are two possibilities.'

'And what is your second idea?'

He tapped the snuffbox.

'Do not the French say *cherchez la femme*? I say, turn the question the other way, like the lid of this box. Look for the man in the case. The seducer of Kathy last year may be the same man as the father of the baby we are dealing with this year. If you can find him you may discover the truth.'

Chapter 13

BY MIDDAY I had crossed the river and gone to Penwortham. The morning's bright weather had faded now and the wind had dropped, so that the air felt oppressive. I walked up through the woods to the west of the village, taking what began as a lane, became a ride and finally thinned to a muddy path. The trees were still green, but it was a desiccated, dull, September greenery, which depressed my spirits. After less than a mile the woods came to an end, and now there was a view down across moss and reed beds towards the river. But seeing the pig-iron sky and muddy river in spate did little to relieve me, and I felt more misgivings than ever for my mission. I had to force myself to press on.

I had passed no house, or hovel among the trees, and there continued to be none in sight until I came to a dip in the turning road. Here, at the bottom, and a little apart from the path, stood the tumbledown home of the woman I sought – Crazy Daisy, which was the only name I knew for her.

My visit was a direct consequence of my conversation over snuff and Arabian coffee with Luke Fidelis. Daisy's name had been mentioned as someone that had recently been near the skin-yard. She was a midwife – and she also had a name for her strange dealings. These three facts about Daisy created a strong pull in her direction.

I hammered on the cottage door-post. It was shaky, and decay was creeping into it from the ground upwards. After a while the old woman came out to me – a bent and wizened creature whose age looked anything between fifty and seventy. Only her bright and piercing eyes did not look aged.

'You've come for a potion.'

It was not a question.

'No, I—'

'There's one I've just made up: mace, comfrey, bullrush root, and more. Come in, come in, and see!'

I've been inside hundreds of cottages like Daisy's in the course of my work. Downstairs there was just one room, with earth for its floor. The walls were mud and lath and the only sturdy part was the stone chimney, at the bottom of which a reluctant fire smouldered in the hearth. In a corner a sagging stair led upwards.

She shuffled across to a table on which stood a small boiling cauldron, and a few earthenware bottles.

'You're wanting to cut a stiffer pen, am I right?'

'No, I—'

'There's nowt wrong with a stiffer pen. Every girl wants one as well as men. Don't be blushing over it.'

'I am not blushing, Daisy. And I don't require a stiffer pen.'

'Most of the gents coming here are after a stiffer pen, or else a cure for the gout.'

'It's not that either. I would like you to tell me something.'

'Telling? Oh, time was I could do telling. Don't meddle with it now. Cost me dear did telling.'

'It's to do with your work as a midwife.'

'Midwife now? Yes, I do a little midwifing, if you can call it that. Folk come to me when they're in straits.'

'Well, that's exactly *my* meaning too. People that come to you in trouble, hoping you will help them. Women. Girls.'

She shot me a wary glance.

'What're you asking *me* for? I hope you're not thinking I've done owt that's wrong.'

I took a more masterly tone.

'As I am sure you already know, Daisy, I am the Coroner of Preston. I am making enquiries pertaining to that position.'

My words had the opposite of their intended effect.

'And I am the Queen of Sheba,' she told me. 'I am keeping my mouth shut, also pertaining.'

At that very moment of impasse came the sound of a man's voice approaching the cottage door.

'Mother!'

A moment later he appeared framed in silhouette by the doorway itself.

'Who's this?' he asked.

'Coroner from Preston,' said Daisy, 'with questions that I'm not answering.'

I stood and faced the man, and it was only then that we recognized each other.

'Why, it's Jass Spungeon, isn't it?' I exclaimed.

He darted forward, snatching the hat from his head and extending his hand.

'And you are one of the gentlemen I met near Wigan Lane. The very kind gentlemen. Coroner, are you?'

'I am that. I had no idea you were Daisy's son. How is Henrietta, after her adventures in Wigan? She bears up, I hope.'

We shook hands.

'She's tip-top, Sir. And glad not to be a side of bacon. Is it to do with her that you've come?'

'No,' broke in his mother. 'He's come wanting your old ma to confess to crimes.'

Jass looked uncertain.

'Oh, aye?'

'Not at all,' I said. 'It's true I am looking into the case of a baby that was found dead near the wharf across the river. But I only come to your mother because she has much skill and experience of child-birth and such things. I am wanting her advice, or her suggestion.'

Jass turned to the old woman.

'Then please give it, Ma. This is an honourable gentleman. If he says he's not come to make criminals of us, you can be sure of it.'

'My only hope is to gain a little enlightenment, Daisy,' I added. 'Your son is at liberty to witness our talk, and see fair play.'

She sniffed, by which I understood she had agreed, if only to a qualified extent.

'What do you want to know?'

'A person at the skin-yard mentioned you and—'

'Skin-yard? Don't say she's got another one.'

'Who? You mean Kathy? Kathy Brock.'

'I don't say I mind her name. About a year back this one came to me, a lass towing a lad behind her. Said she lived at skin-yard. Asked me for a potion that would lose her the babby. All the preg-nant ones do, unless they're married and want to know the sex of their child. She wasn't married, but right determined she was to take summat away with her in a bottle.'

'And did you give her something?'

Again that look. Daisy was not as crazy as she appeared to be.

'I gave her a mixture to purge her stomach. Nowt wrong with that.'

'What about the lad that was with her?'

'A ginger-top he was. A lot of airs, he gave himself, but under it all he was fretting. I said to myself, he's a servant in a fine house and she's told him she'll tell all and make him lose his place, unless he pays me for the potion. And that he did, mister. Not enough, but he did pay. No, I didn't know him by name.'

'I must ask this, forgive me. The girl who came to you from the skin-yard, that was last year. Do you know anything about the baby that's just been found? Did any girl come to you wanting to be rid of it? The same girl, perhaps?'

Daisy bunched her lips and shook her head.

'No. There's been no one like that come to me.'

Though I was not sure I could believe her, I sensed that it was her final word and that our interview was over.

After thanking her sincerely, I walked with Jass out as far as the road.

'My mother is right clever with herbs, Sir,' he said. 'So folk do come up here time to time asking for all sorts – charms, mixtures. But she'd not do owt wrong. She'd not kill a babby in the womb.'

'I would not accuse her of any such thing, Jass. The baby was not killed by abortion, so there is no accusation against either of you. But, though you may not see it, your mother has been a great help, and for the time being any road I won't trouble her more.'

I raised my hat and retreated down the path. The sky was still dark and menaced rain, but my mind was much less clouded than it had been coming up.

'When you were visiting the Scroops, did you see the manservant?' I asked Elizabeth on reaching home. 'His name is Jon.'

'Yes, I did. The redhead. It was him that showed me into the parlour. Now drink this.'

She placed a glass of Nantz and hot water in my hands. I had been drenched by a short but violent deluge crossing the river on Battersby's ferry and had been firmly marched to the fireside to dry out.

'What did you make of him?' I said, taking a sip of the brandy.

'He's Irish, about twenty – and thinks he is the cock of the walk, the way he looks at a woman.'

'I didn't see that when I was there.'

'Men don't.'

And, very slightly, she blushed. It was enough for me. By following Fidelis's first suggested course of action, I had unexpectedly achieved the second. *Cherchez l'homme* he had told me, and now what did I have in view? A servant from a fine house, with red hair and an eye for a woman.

On my return to the office, the clock was striking five. I sent Furzey out to fetch the urchin Barty, who often ran messages and errands for us.

'Barty,' I said when he arrived. 'There's a red-headed young man named Jon who works at the Scroops's house on Water Lane. I fancy he also lives in the house, but I want a word with him away from there, do you see?'

'You don't want them Scroops knowing you're talking to him, right Sir?'

He was a boy with a mind sharp as a razor.

'Exactly right. And I am quite sure there must be an alehouse he goes to. I want you to find out which it is and then, if you can bring me intelligence of when I might find him there, you shall have sixpence.'

An hour and a half later Barty returned.

'I found out his whole name's Jon O'Rorke, Mr Cragg. I watched the house and saw him leave. I followed him to the Pride of the Pit, but I never went in.'

'How long ago did he go in?'

'Just a few minutes.'

'Then I had better get over there.'

The Pride of the Pit Inn used to go by another name until the present keeper came in. He had a special interest in cocking, and even gave his yard over to the fancy, allowing those that could not have cock-pens at home to keep their birds there. Inside it was not crowded or loud with talk, so that it took only a moment to be certain that Jon O'Rorke was not there. I cursed inwardly, thinking the fellow must have quit the place while Barty was bringing me news of his whereabouts. I asked the landlord if he knew where O'Rorke had gone.

'He's in the yard, at the coops. He's seeing to his birds.'

'His birds?'

'Of course. He's fighting two in the Michaelmas Main. He's got preparations to make.'

I ventured out of the back door of the inn and into a cobbled yard, which was lined on all sides with narrow coops in four tiers, with a hut in the centre. I recognized the red-headed young man kneeling to bring a bird out from one of the bottom coops and greeted him. Turning his head, he did not look very pleased to see me.

'You are tending your fighting birds, Mr O'Rorke?'

He grunted.

'As you see.'

'And they are due to perform in the Michaelmas Main of Cocks, I believe.'

'They might be.'

He extracted the bird and carried it by the feet, head down, into the hut. The cock, a lean, sleek bird, twisted his head this way and that, the eyes fiercely protesting against the affront to his dignity. O'Rorke placed him on a table and attempted to shut the door on me. As politely as I could I planted my foot in the way.

'And do you have good hopes for their success?'

Still holding the bird down on the table he turned on me with a look of anger.

'That is private information, Mister. If you were a cocking man you would know not to ask. Now, if you don't mind . . .'

There was on the table a pot containing some sort of liquid preparation. O'Rorke picked up a broad painting brush and dipped it, then began painting the cock's feathers. The bird became immediately content, closing his eyes and croodling in appreciation of the attention he was receiving.

'Mr O'Rorke, I have not come here on cock-fighting business, but a legal matter.'

He grunted and carried on working.

'I can see however that the moment is not convenient, as you are preoccupied. Perhaps you would be good enough to call on me at my office in Cheapside as soon as possible. Tomorrow morning, in fact. Your employer will possibly send you to town with some messages, and you can call in then. May I add that I mean in no way to cause you trouble?'

I left him then, passing back through the inn where I stopped and ordered a glass of wine. The landlord, Charles Foster by name, put it down in front of me.

'You have business with that boy?' he asked.

I said that I had, but gave no particulars. Foster laughed as he picked up a cloth and a glass and began polishing it.

'He has two interests, has Jon O'Rorke,' he said. 'His cocks, and his cock, as you might say. You'll be hard put to get him to expand on any other business.'

This sounded promising.

'I take your meaning, Mr Foster. Something of a Lothario, is he?'

Foster favoured me with a sight of his gappy teeth.

'Put it like this: I wouldn't leave a daughter of mine alone with him. But he's a capital trainer of birds, I will say that.'

'I'm sure he'd be interested in money also,' I said, casually. 'If he happened to have some coming to him.'

I drank my wine and wished Foster good day. He had not

answered my suggestion, but I'd seen a flash of curiosity in his face – curiosity enough to make him acquaint Jon O'Rorke of the hint I had dropped. It might just be enough to bring the lad trotting obediently along to Cheapside in the morning.

On Thursday morning I had no sooner sat down behind my desk than Furzey appeared bearing a letter sealed with the imprint of the Corporation. He placed it with a perceptible flourish in front of me.

'This came in last night, Sir. For you.'

He spoke these words in a funereal tone.

I said, 'Do you know what is in it?'

'I do not. But I can guess.'

'And what is your guess, Furzey?'

'Retribution. From Lady Rickaby.'

Waving him from the room with a sigh, I broke the seal and unfolded the paper. It was in the best legal hand of the town clerk.

To Titus Cragg Esq. Coroner. Sir, I beg to inform you that on the order of His Worship the Mayor you are required to attend at the Court Leet next Friday morning the twenty-second instant, there to answer charges of lewdness prejudicial to the good order of the borough and to the honour of the office you hold. Be advised that the case will be heard and judgement is liable to be made notwithstanding your absence.

I groaned. Furzey had been right. But the question now was whether it would be better to try to head off the charge before Friday, or to simply go to court and defend myself. It would be best if the matter could be snuffed out in advance, and never publicly aired, but I had only twenty-four hours before the hearing and could not see much prospect of changing Thwaite's shuttered mind in so short a time.

My thoughts were interrupted by voices in the outer office, and a moment later, to my great satisfaction, Furzey showed Jon

O'Rorke in to me. It was shortly after ten. Warily he accepted my offer of a seat but sat alertly on its edge.

'I was told this is something I may take advantage from.'

'I don't know why you were told that,' I lied. 'I'm afraid you are mistaken. I am looking into the death of a baby – the one they found dead in one of the tan-pits at the skin-yard. You have heard of this?'

More wary than ever, he said that he had.

'How long have you been a servant of the Scroop family?'

'Two years and a bit.'

'And in that time was Kathy Brock also employed in the house?'

'Yes. What's this got to do with me?'

I noticed a note of belligerence edging his tone.

'I think you know. You and Kathy walked out together, isn't that right?'

'I'll not deny it.'

'And do you see Kathy still? Do you still walk out together?'

'I don't know that it's your business, but I'll tell you as there's nothing to hide. Not now, we don't. Not since she left the job.'

'And before that, did you know each other well?'

A slight smile curled across his lips.

'You might say that.'

'Did you have knowledge of her in the, er, biblical sense?'

'You mean did I fuck her?'

'In a word.'

'I'll not say I did, or I didn't.'

'I shall be candid with you, Mr O'Rorke, as so far you have not *quite* been with me. From the very start suspicion in this case fell on Kathy. Her mother has given evidence that the girl had been with child last year. She aborted – naturally or otherwise – long before the baby could live, but in the meantime it appears that Kathy went together with yourself to old Daisy Spungeon to ask for a mixture.'

'It wasn't what you think.'

'Don't be perturbed. I am not concerned in the least with that visit, except that it may point in a certain direction. I am only interested in the child that was found last week, and in the identity of its mother. And its father, of course, who would lead to its mother.'

'Not if she's been with a lot of men, I'd say.'

'Let me be blunt. You say you have not walked out with Kathy since she left the employment of Mr Scroop. Who then are you walking out with? And is that girl the mother of the dead child that was found?'

His eyes would not stay fixed on my face. They darted around the room, at the window, then back to me; at the walls, the door and Furzey, sitting and taking his notes, then back to me. Jon O'Rorke was feeling trapped, but he would not reply. I tried another approach.

'Let me ask you something else. Have you any children of your own?'

'No.'

'Have you ever been present at the birth of a child?'

'No, course not. What do you want to know that for? You're trying to trip me into saying I had something to do with this child.'

He got up, bristling now with righteousness.

'I'll not stay here and be tripped up by you like some ladeen mooching off school. I'm leaving, and I'd be obliged if you would keep your distance in the future, Mr Coroner.'

With that, he was gone.

Chapter 14

∞

THE FIRE HAD occurred just a week ago but, as I approached the Skeleton Inn, I saw that demolition had already begun. Men were crawling ant-like around the ruined structure and every few minutes a shout would ring out and a basket of roof tiles would be swung to the ground, or a blackened beam let fall with a loud bump.

Watching them in concentrated disappointment from the pier was the forlorn figure of Clarkson. He looked what he was: a man who had run out of expectations. I approached and greeted him.

'He's lost no time, has he?' he said, tipping his head towards the demolition work. 'I told you he wouldn't, didn't I, Mr Cragg?'

'Are these Abraham Scroop's workmen, then?'

'Aye. And Lord Grassington's, I'm sure. I've cried about it all over town. I've protested. Nothing would stop it. They could rebuild it as it was and we could have stayed on, but no. They must flatten all – all we worked for. Our home.'

He jerked his head backwards in the direction of the pier, where I saw his entire family, the children huddled around their mother and a heap of baggage, waiting beside a boat at the quayside, the *Maid of Man*. The tide now being at the top, her crew were readying for departure.

'You are leaving Preston?'

'Aye, on the tide. We'll sail far as Liverpool and then we'll see what we'll do.'

'We are met just in time, then. I wanted to speak with you about how the fire started. Are you still convinced it was arson?'

'There is no question. Set on purpose.'

'By whom, then?'

'I collected a few bits of evidence but the Mayor would not listen to me or look at them. But I'll tell you what . . .'

He rummaged in his coat pocket and pulled out a few roughly folded sheets of paper, which he thrust upon me.

'Here. You have them, Mr Cragg. They're no use to me now; I'm done with this town. But you might find the truth in these notes, if you've a mind to do so.'

I glanced at the bundle. The papers were covered in not very elegant writing. I saw various names noted down and a rough drawing. But before I could examine them, there came a shout from the boat. Clarkson looked behind him. A sail was being readied for hoisting and men were in position on the quay to cast off.

'That's our call to go on board, Mr Cragg. I'll be saying good-bye.'

He hurried back to his wife and children and, following him to the bottom of the gangplank, I watched the family file across it. A burly sailor helped Clarkson transfer his belongings and, a few minutes later, the *Maid of Man* was drifting away from the berth, her blocks squeaking as the crew hoisted sail. Silently the family stood in the boat's waist, the children snivelling and their parents grim-faced. I raised my arm and they, dolefully, returned the wave just as the sail above them filled with wind. The craft heeled a fraction and then slowly turned until she was under way. I watched as she grew smaller along the meandering channel that led to the sea.

I sat in the Turk's Head with Clarkson's pieces of paper spread across the table in front of me. There were three. Two contained lists of names, some of them with notes beside them, and the third was a drawing.

I knew already that these papers were to do with Clarkson's search for evidence of arson of the inn. Glancing at one of the papers I found my own name, among many others, and soon realized that this was an attempt to list every person that had attended the inquest in the upstairs room. The other paper, I saw, was also filled with names, many of which I did not recognize. Then there was the drawing. Clarkson was no draughtsman, that was clear, though nothing else was.

The design was a rough rectangle drawn lengthways and divided into three areas – a narrow rectangle at the left which stretched from top to bottom of the diagram and a small one at the right, placed in the centre of the right side. This was striped horizontally and overdrawn with what looked like the outline of a hand. Various names, many only initials, were written in the different boxes, some of which had a line through them.

Reminding myself that the papers represented Clarkson's attempt to work out who might have set the fire, I guessed that the drawing was a plan of the ground floor of the inn, with the individuals present at the time written in, and that the 'hand' was the flames on the stairway. It looked as if Clarkson had come to the same conclusion as Fidelis and I: that the fire had started in the area of the stairs.

He had told me he himself had gone into the pantry at the time the alarm was raised, so it followed that this must have been his recollection of the *status quo* a few moments beforehand.

A shadow fell across the table and I looked up.

'What is this?' said Fidelis, removing his hat and sitting down beside me. 'Papers, lists of names, a diagram! I am intrigued.'

I showed him the papers and told him how I had obtained them.

'Clarkson was trying to create a picture of the ground floor of his inn at the moment when the fire broke out, in particular who was there. He must have believed that one of these names is that of the supposed arsonist.'

Fidelis studied the pages.

'Not necessarily: he might have been identifying witnesses. Some of the names are crossed out. Perhaps they are men Clarkson spoke to. Those uncancelled were yet to be seen.'

'In that case he was being commendably systematic. But surely if anyone in the room had seen a person setting the fire, it is inconceivable that they would not have come forward immediately to tell their tale.'

'Sometimes various witnesses see various things, which mean nothing by themselves. Put them together and they may acquire significance. You know this well, Titus, from your work in the courts.'

'I do. But is there need in this story for an arsonist? Here is how I think the fire started. You remember the day was gloomy and there were candles lit inside. One was placed in a sconce on the wall halfway up the stairs, which were crowded with people both standing there and jostling to come up or go down. Eventually someone knocked the candle out of its sconce and it fell through one of the many holes and gaps in the staircase, and into the panelled cavity beneath. There it continued to burn until, in course of time, it set fire to the wood inside the cavity – the wood from the log store.'

Fidelis was looking intently at the rough plan of the Skeleton Inn's downstairs room.

'You are right to seize on the candle: I myself am sure that it instigated the fire. But it is surely only a distant possibility that this was accidental.'

'I should be obliged if you would tell me why.'

'Because it's much more likely that the candle was dropped into the log store by a human hand. First, if it had happened by accident, the chances are very strong that someone would have noticed. There were many people present.'

'If someone had done it deliberately, that would still have been the case.'

'No, you ignore the difference between accident and agency. The moment of the one is random; that of the other is chosen. Criminals generally choose to act at times when their deeds will not be noticed.'

'Very well. What is your second reason?'

'Simply, how could the candle have got accidentally through the stairs?'

'As I said, the stairs were old and decayed. In some cases the steps and the risers had split and cracked. Several holes had appeared.'

'Yes but those cracks and holes were small, and again, for a lit candle to fall through one and not go out would be an incredible chance, do you not think? On the other hand, what could be easier for someone all unnoticed to kick in one of those risers while standing on the stairs and then, when the chance arose, to pick the candle from the holder and drop it through into the log store below? It would take time before the effect was noticed – a lag sufficient for the fire-starter to make himself scarce.'

I would have preferred not to acknowledge it, but Fidelis might have been right.

'Then why, Luke? Clarkson thinks it was only done to deprive him of the inn.'

'I don't believe *that*. The thing happened in the middle of an inquest. The arsonist must have been trying to halt or delay the proceedings – and, in fact, succeeded.'

'It might have been the skinners, then – one of the Brock family. The evidence against Kathy was beginning to look formidable at the time.'

'Remember that I was close by, Titus. I don't think any of them were on the stairs. They were in the body of the room, listening to the evidence.'

'Who did you see, then?'

'People moving up and down. One or two standing on the stairs waiting to get up into the room. But let's see from the drawing who Clarkson places there. He was recording the names of those he saw there in the moments before the fire was detected.'

The names transcribed exactly as Clarkson had written them were 'Brumshaw D.R.S. Scroop serv? Phillips'.

'Phillips might be the carpenter who lives in Ashton. I have treated his family and we talked together briefly.'

'Brumshaw – that's the baker with his shop on Spaw Brow. Who is D.R.S.?'

'I don't know, but I am more interested in "Scroop serv". It must mean one of the servants in Scroop's house – the sex is not stated. But this might be Jon O'Rorke.'

'He is not the only male servant of Scroop. There are several more outdoors, I am sure. But he may be the only indoors man.'

'The real point is Clarkson did not know who it was. He only recognized the livery – its colour is distinctive enough – but not the face.'

'Did you not see him there yourself?'

'I didn't.' He tapped Clarkson's drawing. 'But this may have been while I was giving evidence. Did you not notice him yourself, at any point?'

'No. From where I sat there was merely a mass of people at the end of the room and around the stair. If only I had seen this paper when O'Rorke was with me this morning, I would have asked him the question direct.'

'He came in answer to your request, then? You have questioned him?'

'Yes, my small subterfuge successfully lured him to the office.'

'And?'

'Questioning him was like trying to open that damned snuffbox of yours, Luke. The harder I tried with him the tighter he became.'

'A pretty conceit. A touch of lubrication will ease the lid off, I think.'

'Lubrication? I suppose you mean of the fermented kind.'

'Yes. The kind that comes in pewter pots. I will do it myself, if you agree. I'll seek him out at the Pride of the Pit Inn and oil him well.'

'I went there myself. I got nothing out of him.'

'But you are a stranger to the place – and a stranger to the fancy. I can do better. I am tolerably well known in cocking circles and there'll be no surprise at my appearance. The place is particularly busy just before a main of cocks, you know, and it is only nine days now until the Michaelmas Main. One goes to the inn to strike wagers and for intelligence of the more likely birds.'

'I don't know how you will ever get O'Rorke to speak more about his adventures in love, though. The man is forewarned now, and on his guard. I wish I had not let him know he is suspected. He will never speak honestly again on the question.'

Fidelis shook his head and smiled in a way he had when knowing better.

'Quite the opposite, Titus. His grievance will by now be fully developed. He will be sore and glad in his drunkenness to find a sympathetic ear. He will soothe himself and at the same time betray himself – if there is anything to betray.'

'Ask him whether he was present at the fire, while you're about it. I would like to establish that.'

'If that was him on the stairs, which seems more and more likely, I fancy we may have our fire-starter – and a direct link to the mother of our dead baby. The coincidence would be too great for it not to be so. The solution to this puzzle is almost in our grasp, Titus.'

I shook my head, gloomily. I felt oppressed by Fidelis's heady optimism.

'If he were both the fire-starter and the baby's father, he is not likely to admit it. It is as a bragging seducer that you will best pursue him, Luke. In that way maybe we shall find whom he seduced and so be led to the girl that gave birth to the baby in the tan-pit. When will you go to the Pride of the Pit, by the way?'

'Tomorrow night is the night when it will be full of cockers. I'll go then.'

Gloom and oppression did not leave me, and even my wife's company at home could not lift them entirely. Of course, the true cause was not my prospects in discovering the truth about the skin-yard body, it was the thought of my impending trial in the morning at Court Leet, about which I now could summon no levity of any kind. Elizabeth and I did not mention it directly, and yet it lay between us with the food on our table, on the fireside rug as we sat together after supper, and in the six inches of feather mattress that separated us in our bed as we lay reading our books before sleep.

I opened Dr Mandevil's book, and in time came to a passage arguing that 'Honour in its figurative sense is a chimera without truth or being, an invention of moralists and politicians. In great families it is like the gout, generally counted hereditary, and all lords' children are born with it.'

In spite of myself I laughed, and read the words aloud to Elizabeth, as I often did in bed when struck by a passage of literature. She, who was reading her *Don Quixote*, gave a distinctly sorrowful sigh.

'Oh dear! Poor Don Quixote is fighting against exactly the

same cynicism, you know. His high notion of honour is mocked on almost every page of the book.'

'Mandevil says here that Quixote was the last upholder of ancient honour on record.'

'What does he mean by ancient honour?'

'In his formula, it meant to be truthful, to rate the public interest over one's own, to do no fraud and to let no affront go unanswered. He says we moderns have discarded all these principles except for the last – which is clearly the case with Lady Rickaby, as we know.'

'Hers is only pretended modern honour, my love. Yours is real and ancient. You must have faith that it will help you to prevail.'

'I cannot understand how she rates my glimpsing her drawers as being of greater significance than my preserving her life. Is it because she married into the nobility, in whom honour is bred like the gout, as Mandevil says?'

Elizabeth gave a scornful laugh.

'Hardly! She is as common as we are – an iron-master's daughter from Derbyshire. Did you know, by the way, that being the widow of Lord Rickaby connects her to Captain Strawboy and so to his uncle Lord Grassington?'

'In what way?'

'She is sister-in-law to Grassington's sister-in-law, who is Strawboy's mother.'

'Say that again, please, more slowly.'

'The sister of Lady Rickaby's late husband, Lord Rickaby, married Lord Grassington's younger brother, who was Captain Strawboy's father.'

I shut my eyes and repeated this mentally.

'So Captain Strawboy is nephew to both Lord Grassington and Lady Rickaby?'

'Yes, on different sides of his family. And furthermore he's been heir to Grassington, and due to inherit his fortune, ever since his lordship's own son died. He was a wastrel, they say, with terrible debts. The Captain seems a better fellow and I hope a more honourable one – in the ancient sense.'

I hoped so too, but was beginning to doubt it. I suspected some underhand dealing in Lady Rickaby's complaint against me, and that the young projector might be playing some part in it.

Chapter 15

'Y ou've done no wrong, Mr Cragg,' whispered the toothless woman who sat beside me on the long bench. Her name was Betty and we were in the passage outside the courtroom, waiting our turns with three or four others. Betty had with her a goat on a string; from time to time, it punctuated the conversation with a rasping bleat. 'You've only saved the rotten woman's life, unless *that's* a wrong, though it may be as her rotten ladyship's not from round here.'

She gave a cackle of laughter. From time to time Court Leet heard complaints involving people, like Lady Rickaby, from out of town, but these were not the court's main business. That was three-fold: to regulate the market, keep the town's bailiffs and searchers up to the mark, and settle arguments between neighbours. The latter was the case with Betty. Her goat had been accused of eating the nuts off a neighbour's walnut tree, and Betty had brought the animal to court, so she told me, to enable Mr Thwaite to see what an honourable and law-abiding goat she was, who would never descend to the theft of a few nuts.

I consider that all goats have a shifty and pragmatic look, but I suppressed the thought and thanked her for her belief in my innocence, adding, 'That fine animal of yours looks remarkably free of guilt itself.'

Heavy footsteps on the flag floor approached and I saw it was Jonathan Kite, his large bulk suddenly making the passage feel narrower. He had come to answer the charge which I had seen made against him by Abraham Scroop during the previous week – that of selling inferior goods, and without a market licence.

'Eh, Mr Cragg, I'm right sorry about this complaint against you,' he said, sitting down on the bench against the opposite wall. Everyone by now, it seemed, knew of my indictment. 'They've only brought it because that woman's a nob, and Burgess Grimshaw's wife's sister.'

'You are very kind, Kite,' I said. 'And I am just as sorry that you have been brought here. The charges are equally unwarranted, I am sure.'

'It is the third time in three months! They do persecute us, which is a fact. And it's because they are set on killing off the skin-yard, which is another fact.'

We three defendants, all equally convinced of our innocence, sat like children awaiting the schoolmaster's pleasure. Betty and her goat were called in first and came out only a few minutes later having been pronounced guilty and ordered to pay a shilling in recompense to the walnut grower. The goat, looking so entirely free of shame, cannot have helped the case for its own defence. I was in the midst of sympathizing with Betty when the old usher, Danks, hobbled into the room and spoke my name. Obediently I followed him to the courtroom.

The room, which was used also for the magistrate's court and the quarter sessions, was panelled in oak and furnished with brass rails, making it far more imposing than the makeshift courtrooms in which I was accustomed to hold my inquests. It was furnished with a high platform for the Mayor's great throne and alongside it other not quite such great chairs for the Recorder, Thwaite's fellow magistrates, and the judges at quarter sessions. Below these in the court's well were the usual clearly defined spaces: jury box, witness box and an assortment of chairs, pews and benches for the use of councillors, clerks and lawyers. At the back of the room was an area best described as a pen for the public. It was a space fenced by barriers and occupied by friends of interested parties and one or two others, such as Miss Colley and Mrs Bryce, who derived amusement *gratis* from attending trials and hearings. I knew also that Elizabeth was there, though I did not look for her. I had tried to dissuade her from it altogether.

'I cannot possibly be absent when my husband is undergoing such a trial,' she had said.

I took my place in the position appointed for those answering complaints against them, a boxed stand that formed the dock when criminals stood trial. There was, of course, no jury present on this occasion, since at Court Leet the Mayor was sole juror and sole judge. He sat, however, with the Recorder Matthew Thorneley and two burgesses, one of whom was the former Mayor William Biggs, a man with no love for me. The other was Abraham Scroop.

Danks asked me to confirm my name and then the town clerk swore me in and read the indictment in his usual wavering, reedy voice.

'. . . that on Thursday last, the fourteenth instant, at the Skeleton Inn, you did lewdly, indecently and concupiscently unclothe Lady Rickaby and exposed her body without her consent, thereby causing her dishonour and distress, harming and depraving the good name of your office of Coroner and giving scandal to this ancient borough of Preston.'

'What do you say to this charge?' barked Thwaite.

'I deny it,' I said. 'It is ridiculous.'

'We shall soon see about that,' said Thwaite. 'Call Lady Rickaby.'

The lady, supported by her sister Mrs Grimshaw, appeared and took her place in the witness box. She looked pale and wary, but resolute.

The story her ladyship told under examination was that of a man – me – using his superior strength to subdue and affront a lady – her. Far from being overcome by smoke, far from being out of her senses, she maintained that, though coughing and in discomfort, she had been moving away from the fire and towards safety at the moment when I seized her and dragged her by main force to the window.

'And what did the Coroner do then?' Thwaite asked.

Her eyes became wide.

'Why, he ripped off my skirts, Sir. He exposed my nether clothing in a most brutal, shameless and violating manner.'

The room was suddenly quiet, intent on hearing the evidence.

'And did he speak?'

'He pushed me half through the window, head first, so that my . . . my other end was towards him, and then he placed both his hands on me, and pushed me to my great shame and distress and with great force out on to the sloping roof, down which I slid and then fell to the ground.'

'Surely you were hurt by such a fall!'

'No, Sir, I landed softly, but with extreme loss of dignity. I was caught in a canvas sheet which, as I learned afterwards, was a sail held out for the purpose by brutish, laughing sailors whose coarse language in reference to myself I could not possibly repeat in this room. It was vile and beastly, Sir. It was demeaning.'

I heard some whispering and a few stifled laughs from the public behind me.

'Thank you, my lady. I shall not distress you more by making you further recall these unfortunate events. I think we have your testimony complete, and you may take a seat. Now, we had better hear from Titus Cragg himself, I suppose, and learn what he has to say.'

It was a strange sensation, submitting to examination in a court of law, as it was I that usually did the examining. Thwaite's voice, more full than ever (it seemed to me) with bluster and self-regard, boomed out his first question.

'Is this true, Cragg? Did you violently tear and remove Lady Rickaby's skirts?'

'Yes, I did. If I had not done so, she—'

'And did you push her in the indecent manner she described through the window.'

'I wouldn't call it indecent but, yes, I did push her through the window.'

'But you do admit that you put your hands to her rump? That you seized and pushed her buttocks? That you—'

Hearing the word 'rump' caused the lady and her sister each to give out a piercing squeal, but 'buttocks' had an even stronger effect. Clapping their hands to their ears, both ladies shut their eyes tightly and jammed their chins into their chests in spasms of embarrassment and shock. Thwaite turned to them.

'I cannot apologize to you, my lady, or to you Mrs Grimshaw, for my choice of language. Here in this court a spade must always be called a spade, you know. You may answer the question, Cragg.'

'Well, it is true that I did that, yes. I was trying to save her life, you see, and I was extremely pressed for time under the circumstances we found ourselves in.'

'So you say, so you say. But it appears you were trying with an unnecessary degree of, to put it in its best possible light, zeal. You gave no thought to the scandal you would cause.'

'No, indeed I did not, because I—'

'Because you thought to gratify a baser instinct with this lady.'

I almost let out a guffaw, but just managed to check myself. Lady Rickaby was ten years my senior, and in terms of physical charms her palmy days were well behind her. I drew a breath.

'I assure you, Mr Thwaite, that my only instinct was to preserve Lady Rickaby's life.'

I gestured towards her with a smile.

'In this, as you see, I happily succeeded.'

Now without warning Thwaite jumped to his feet. He was snorting like a war horse and his eyebrows writhed like a pair of black caterpillars.

'Will you make a joke of this, Titus Cragg?' he thundered, shaking his finger at me. 'Well, let me tell you. Let me tell you how you succeeded. You affronted the lady, and her family. You yourself have admitted in this court to carrying out the actions complained of. By which you have further succeeded in shaming this great town of ours.'

The public were buzzing like a beehive now, as I attempted to continue. I meant to say that both Lady Rickaby and myself could have lost our lives, and that it was imperative to make our exits from the burning room as quickly as possible, in which case considerations of modesty did not apply. But Thwaite, who had still not resumed his seat, shouted me down.

'No! No! No! No! NO! Hold your tongue, Cragg. We have heard sufficient pleas in mitigation and I have made my decision according to the facts. Therefore I shall proceed to judgement.'

He reoccupied his seat and the four men on the dais put their heads together to confer in whispers. It took less than a minute before they parted again and Thwaite composed himself. At last, adopting the gravity of a hanging judge, he intoned,

'Titus Cragg, I find that, by your own admission, you did indeed take advantage of and indecently assault my Lady Rickaby, here present, in the manner and on the day specified in her complaint. Such actions cannot be tolerated in one holding a public office. It is therefore my duty, my very painful duty, to order your immediate retirement from the post of Coroner of Preston, and I order further that you be disbarred from standing in any further election to the said post for a term of five consecutive years. Next case, please.'

I stood there for a few moments in a state of considerable amazement. What had I expected from this absurd process? An admonishment, perhaps. A requirement that I make some form of apology to the lady, at worst. But not this. I had been Coroner of Preston for almost a decade, the direct successor to my late father. Now suddenly I was turned out. It was hard, no, it was impossible to believe.

Elizabeth took my arm as we walked the short distance to Cheapside.

'How will you fight this stupid decision, Titus?'

'With everything I have.'

'Quite right. You are a fine Coroner and devoted to the job. You have been shamefully abused by that woman.'

Just ahead of us as we neared home I saw Furzey going into the office from the street. He had a ledger tucked under his arm.

'I had better go into the office and tell Furzey the news. We will discuss what action to take.'

I let Elizabeth go in by the door of the residence, while I went in by the corresponding office door.

'I have just been at Court Leet, to answer this matter brought by Lady Rickaby,' I said to my clerk. My voice was trembling. 'Thwaite wouldn't listen to me for a moment. The fact that I was saving the woman's wretched life carried no weight at all, with the upshot that I am precipitately expelled from the office of Coroner for moral turpitude, beginning now. I am thrown out like a dirty old shoe, Furzey.'

'Yes,' said Furzey, 'so you are.'

'In addition, I am disbarred for five years from standing for election again. How can they do that? I cannot believe it. Can you? All in the space of ten minutes.'

'Forgive me for reminding you, Sir, but did I not mention it might turn out so?'

When being proved right, as he quite often was, Furzey would usually sound a guardedly triumphal note, but now his voice was funereal. This decision affected him as well as me.

'I can't help the feeling that it is connected with this skin-yard inquest,' I said. 'Thwaite threatened me about it the other day – not in so many words, but he made it clear he was in a great hurry to get Kathy Brock found guilty.'

But Furzey was not convinced by the case.

'There is a better explanation, Sir. If you recall, certain members of the Corporation – certain mayors, in fact – have been plotting to remove you for years. Maybe it's not the present case that precipitates Mr Thwaite's actions, but his old desire to turn you out. In short, I think he has seized on this business with Lady Rickaby expediently because he wants the office for himself.'

'Well he can't have it, can he? It is an elected post.'

'But once upon a time it wasn't elected, Sir, not directly. Before the time of Oliver Cromwell there was never a poll for Coroner in Preston. Instead the Mayor did the job *ex officio*. It was Oliver's parliament that took it off the Mayor and made it elected, and when the King came back no one thought of going back to the old way. Or not until now, is what I'm thinking.'

Sitting at my desk I put my head into my hands and thought about it. But all I could see was Thwaite telling me darkly to get Kathy Brock found guilty of murder. I shook my head as if to dislodge the memory and concentrate on Furzey's proposition.

'Well, it is true they've been gunning for me for years, the Corporation,' I said. 'Perhaps that is it: pure expediency. They've seized this as a chance to bring me down, as you might seize the first ripe plum on the tree. Well, I believe I shall appeal to Lord Derby. As Chancellor of the Duchy he will reverse the decision. He must.'

Furzey looked doubtful.

'I fear his Lordship's powers, though they are considerable, may not extend to reversing a mayoral decision *ex cathedra*, as you might call it, and nor may he wish to.'

'We can only try. I shall need a written record of what was said in the court – that would help. I must make a memorandum of it immediately. His Lordship will be unable to credit what he reads.'

Furzey took a step towards me, opened the ledger and placed it in my hands. I looked at the page, which was covered in his shorthand.

'It is all there verbatim, Sir.'

'You mean . . . Furzey, were you there in court? I never saw you.'

'I was in the public benches. I thought it best to attend and get the proceedings down on paper, foreseeing the possible need of a record afterwards. Like I've told you, I'm doubting an appeal will do much good, but I knew you'd be trying.'

'You knew right – by God you did! Thank you, Furzey.'

I went through to the house for dinner. Elizabeth received me calmly, though not complacently, for her first action was to embrace me and plant a kiss on my lips.

'You will defeat these evil forces against you, my love, I am sure of it.'

'Well, I might begin a case in the Duchy Chancery court, though it would be extremely tedious. I'm not sure the Mayor's behaving constitutionally, but the history of the coronership in Preston is obscure and very shadowy. Furzey believes Thwaite wants the coronership back in the hands of the Mayor, as it used to be before they changed the rules during Cromwell's Commonwealth.'

'Thwaite is voracious for power, my love. But a case in Chancery would be a frightful expense.'

'I know. It would probably ruin us, and fail besides or, if not, run on for years. My first thought is the best one, which is to appeal personally to Lord Derby. Furzey thinks his lordship has no power in the matter, but he is Chancellor of the Duchy after all, and his mediation would be powerful I believe.'

'Then it is lucky he has arrived back at Patten House this very morning. He has returned from Knowsley Hall for tomorrow night's Assembly. Oh! I am sure he will save the day. He has always been kindly disposed to you. You must go there immediately after dinner.'

'What stings me most is the idea that I would have exposed Lady Rickaby's legs, and shoved her by the arse, just for my own pleasure.'

'There are few in town who think you would, Titus. It is all a nervous fiction of Lady Rickaby's, that the Mayor has fashioned into a boot to kick you with.'

'Well,' I said with a rueful laugh, 'the man's a cobbler, when all's said and done.'

'It does me good to hear you laugh, Titus.'

Chapter 16

THE STANLEY FAMILY had over the years found excellent ways of deterring public access to themselves. Patten House, their town mansion, stood in its grandeur a hundred feet back from an entrance on Church Gate, with a high enclosing wall and an imposing gatehouse. It was garrisoned at all hours by a retainer enjoying the absolute power to deny entry to anyone he judged unworthy, or suspicious. If you should happen to get past him, you approached the house by an alley walled in brick on either side. In summer this flagged walk was aromatic of flowers and herbs, but the flanking walls were too high to allow sight of the gardens beyond.

On arrival at the main door you found a short flagged passage with an anteroom on the right and a small writing room opposite. Here presided a second commissary, in this case one of the household clerks, with the duty of being every way as obstructive as the first. So you negotiated once more as he fixed you with a searching look, asking sternly for your explanation, your brief, your letter of introduction. If he, too, was satisfied, you were shown into the anteroom to wait.

I had handed in a carefully worded letter requesting an interview with Lord Derby, and was now sitting in the anteroom with three or four others, all of us hoping for an audience as we listened to the light drumming of rain outside. One young fellow – dark, slim and with eyes so intense that they seemed to burn inwardly – sat beside me glumly eating currants, which he shook out of a pouch that hung from his belt. He'd carried in with him what appeared to be a hatbox. We fell into conversation.

'My name is Joss Kay,' he told me, 'and I am an apomecometrist.'

'You are what?'

'You do not know the word? Not many do. In common terms, I am a surveyor of land and I received an instruction that I was required to conduct some apomecometry – a survey to you – for Lord Derby. I went of course immediately to Knowsley Hall to receive my commission, but after much delay I could not obtain it, as Lord Derby had upped and left to come here. I was forced to follow, all at my own expense.'

'Why not wait at Knowsley at his expense? He would be bound to return.'

'What? Wait idly and indefinitely? No. I find it impossible to be without employment. And besides, you never know with these lords where they'll fetch up next. It's best to keep on their tail. It was the same with the Duke of Portland when I had dealings with him.'

'Surely you don't have to wait on the Earl himself at all. His bailiff at Knowsley must be able to give you the office.'

'Not he. Said he was not empowered. Nor would he tell me what the job is. No more would the steward, or the farm bailiff. For all I know this is all a fool's errand. You are passed from one official to the next, and nobody has the authority to tell you anything. They only say that I must have my commission from Lord Derby in person, or I'll not have it at all.'

'Well, maybe you will not have long to wait now.'

'Maybe!' Kay repeated bitterly. 'That is just my difficulty. Everything is "maybe" and nothing is "will be". I have been here all day. I cannot fritter such time away in waiting. I must know if

I am to be taken on, and as soon as possible, or I shall look for work elsewhere. I am not a petitioner, I am a professional man. Am I to be kept at bay indefinitely? Oh, I am tired of this. And these currants are all that I have eaten since breakfast.'

He put another into his mouth and sighed, and I sighed in sympathy for at that moment I felt as tired of waiting as he, though not as hungry. I had no way of knowing if the note I'd so carefully written and sent up to Lord Derby had been received; or, if received, opened and read. As Kay and I talked, men passed through the room, men of business carrying portfolios and brandishing documents, confident men and each with untrammelled access to the great earl. We eyed them sourly as they came and went.

After a while, I nodded towards the hatbox by his feet.

'What hat have you there?'

He behaved as if I had said something highly peculiar.

'How do you mean, what hat? This contains the tool of my trade. My apomecometer, or theodolite as you would probably call it. It is of my own invention – new and much improved, in every way.'

He opened the box and reverently brought the object out. It looked like some kind of spyglass with brass fittings mounted inside a polished mahogany box. He began earnestly to explain its working. After twenty minutes, with azimuths, altazimuths and alidades spinning around in my barely comprehending head, I looked at my watch and saw I had been waiting almost three hours without satisfaction.

Presently a note came down, addressed to Mr Kay. He put away his instrument and perused it.

'I am being fobbed off, again!' he exclaimed.

'How are you fobbed off?'

'I am referred to another. I must it seems apply not in person to Lord Derby, as I have been told all along, but to this underling.

Oh well! It is only to be expected in dealing with lords. You never know how long they will keep you waiting, or how long it will take them to make up their mind.'

I got to my feet.

'Well, I have no more time for this today myself. I doubt his Lordship will see me so late. Would you therefore do me the honour of taking some refreshment at my house? It is close by, and no man can live by currants alone, you know.'

He said he would and, after I had informed the clerk I would return, we quit the premises.

The clouds had passed and now shafts of sunshine made the puddles gleam under our feet. On reaching the church I saw a small gathering of townspeople around the entrance of Moot Hall. To my surprise they were being addressed by Furzey, and with considerable vehemence. He jabbed the air with his finger and flexed his knees so that he appeared to be bouncing up and down. He did not see me as we joined the back of the group, which at this point numbered no more than a score of people.

That Furzey was addressing a meeting did not altogether surprise me, as he was very earnest in his politics – they were of the Whig persuasion – and he had been known to play the demagogue before. I was, however, taken aback to realize that this time he was talking about me.

'I say it is not just, friends. The Coroner is a man of conscience and probity. He has ever done right by this town, and now he is being done grave wrong by the Mayor and the Corporation.'

One or two in the crowd murmured in a grumbling way, though whether saying yeah or nay I could not tell. Furzey now pulled a paper from his pocket and held it high in the air.

'I have here a petition drawn up by myself. I hope you will sign it, and all men and women of this town that have reason to thank

Mr Titus Cragg and who say no to his being put out of office on this trumpery of a charge. I shall proceed to the reading of it: To His Worship the Mayor, we the undersigned . . .'

He paused to clear his throat, then continued in a ringing voice.

'We, the undersigned, following your worship's finding against Mr Titus Cragg in Court Leet, do demand the rescinding of the dismissal of Mr Cragg from the position of Coroner of this borough of Preston, and his immediate reinstatement. We hold that the said charge against him of molestation was made upon a false, unfounded and vexatious accusation of which he is wholly innocent, free of blame and untainted by guilt, being only at the time carrying out his duty of preserving the life, limb and safety of another.'

He looked up from the paper for signs of support. But the little assembly remained more or less impassive.

'There I have left off, ladies and gentlemen. As Mr Cragg's clerk I am well versed in the ways of the law, and of legal language, and you will appreciate that I could have written more.'

'Aye,' called out one of the audience. 'More rubbish.'

Furzey ignored him.

'But as any lawyer's clerk will tell you, brevity in petitions is a great virtue, for the party petitioned might find the matter tedious or lose the thread of the argument.'

'It's tedious already,' called out the heckler. 'And we've lost it.'

'Hold your tongue!' said a bonneted woman, turning to confront the objector. 'Are you not ashamed?'

I saw that under the bonnet was an indignant Miss Colley. The fellow pointed at Furzey.

'He's only trying to save his own job,' he said. 'And that's all this is.'

'He is not!' she squeaked. 'He's speaking up for dear blameless Mr Cragg who has been foully traduced.'

'And besides,' Furzey now went on, raising his voice further, 'keeping it brief leaves more room on the page for your signatures, does it not?'

'Not mine, any road. Not for you, Robert Furzey, or any black-guard Whig traitor.'

This remark, which came from another quarter, was also contradicted, and soon the meeting – which had noticeably grown in number as it took on the character of public entertainment – was jostling and exchanging choice insults. I made my way to the front and stood beside Furzey.

'What are you doing, man?' I said in his ear. 'Am I to become a political football to be kicked up and down the street?'

Furzey made a show of astonishment at my words.

'I do this to defend your name, Mr Cragg. The Corporation must know the will of the people.'

'That is absurd. We will talk about this later. Enough now!'

I turned to the meeting.

'I thank you all,' I said. 'I am hopeful there will be no need for your signatures. Please be so kind as to disperse.'

They began to do so, still arguing amongst themselves. I looked for Joss Kay and saw that he had wandered a little way down the street to peruse the window of Arthur Holdsworth's print shop. As I strode towards him, Miss Colley caught up with me.

'You can have my poor signature, and gladly, Mr Cragg,' she assured me.

'It would hearten me, Miss Colley. But I shall allow this petition to go no further.'

'Well, I am right sorry for you. It's a disgrace and I am sure no one else could make a better Coroner.'

I bowed, saying I was grateful for her concern and support. I re-joined Kay. The enterprising Holdsworth had set out a show of cock-fighting prints in honour of the coming Michaelmas Main. If he had any interest in what had just occurred in the street Kay gave not the slightest sign of it.

'There is a prime bird indeed,' he said, gesturing at a portrait of Derby's Old Dander, a famous fighter of a past era. 'As fine a specimen as ever you will see.'

I was encouraged that he seemed to be cheering up.

'You take an interest in the fancy?'

'Oh no, I find it barbarous. But even in unworthy pursuits there is always the spirit of improvement – in this case through rational breeding. I take an interest in that.'

Having eaten a plate of potatoes and cold salmon, and taken several glasses of my port wine, Joss Kay shed the last vestiges of the lassitude that had enwrapped him in Lord Derby's ante-room. Indeed, so energetic was his talk that my wife and I had to concentrate our attention with a degree of tenacity to follow him. He discoursed entirely on improvement, in all its forms.

'Improvement is my religion,' he explained. 'I do not say the Bible is untrue; I say it is old. I do not say its counsel is useless; I say it is unimproved, and there is nothing on God's earth that cannot be improved by God-given human ingenuity. You will agree that the way things are done is determined by the way they have always been done. But will you agree that this weight of tradition is a dead weight? Will you agree that the traditional way is a circular way in a dark forest? We must pursue the direct way in order to pass out of the forest of ignorance and into the light of improvement. There are few things in any house that cannot be improved. In yours, for instance—'

'We have an improver at work here in Preston,' I interrupted. I felt I had better put my oar in now, or nod off, as I sometimes do during sermons.

'Lord Derby, I hope,' said he.

'Well, his lordship, too, I suppose, but I mean Captain Strawboy. Do you know him?'

'He is the very man to whom I have been referred. What improvements does he say he is engaged in?'

'Among other things I understand they include re-opening our cold bath as a spa, and reforming the manufacture of leather. He has money put at his disposal by some of our merchants as well as the promise of money from Lord Grassington in return, of course, for a share in the profits.'

'Improved leather-making, is it? I look forward to meeting him. I myself have twice been employed by large tanners.'

'In what capacity?'

'Helping to improve the process. Building new tanneries. Designing tan-pits. The difficult thing is to construct them so that they don't leak, or drain away. The other matter is the smell. The position of the prevailing wind must be seriously considered before establishing a new leather works. But there is also hope of manufacturing less odorously with new methods, and making it faster and more profitable.'

Suppressing a yawn, I furrowed my brow and leaned forward.

'Can you do that with our tannery here in Preston?'

'Oh yes, no doubt of it. Where the right spirit rises, it sweeps obstacles away like cobwebs.'

'How would you do it?' asked Elizabeth.

He gave her a look of surprise.

'By improvement of course. That is what I have been saying, Mrs Cragg. The spirit of improvement. Tannering has always been a long and tedious business – but it is done that way because it always has been done that way. It is circular and does not progress. Thank you Mr Cragg, just another glass would be very agreeable. So we must work to make tannering less tedious and sweeter smelling, which we can only do by understanding it. We know that oak bark and alum salts will preserve skins, but what other barks and other salts will do the job better and more cheaply? What machinery can be made to assist the tanners in their long labours, or to abbreviate those labours? When we answer those questions – as surely we will – the old tanneries will be swept away. Out with the old, and in with improvement, that is the whole burden of my belief. I hold that there is no walk of our life that cannot be made infinitely better by improvement and by sweeping away the old. In this house, for instance.'

And so began a lengthy discourse on better soaps, hotter cooking ovens, brighter candles and many other household items that were in need of improvement. But he rose from his chair at last and patted his belly.

'Well! What a happy evening,' he said. 'I have enjoyed your food and wine and you have enjoyed hearing of the benefits of improvement. Everyone is satisfied. But now I must bid you good-night.'

Later that night Elizabeth sat before the looking glass in our bedroom and I unpinned her hair while telling her of Furzey's unwanted attempt to raise a petition about my case.

'He is a loyal servant,' she said. 'We are all threatened by this.'

'Furzey *is* loyal to me, but he is more loyal to himself.'

'That is natural.'

'Anyway, I am not taking issue with his loyalty. It is his method. He proposes to bring the will of the people to bear and make the Mayor turn his decision around in that way.'

'The general opinion may be to our advantage.'

'Opinion is not the same as will. But anyway what *is* the general opinion on this matter, or any other? I doubt there is such a thing as a general opinion, let alone a general will. Or, if there is, I don't see how it can ever be known. And even if they did know it, the burgesses would not care.'

'That is true. They manage without it and always have.'

'So, Furzey's idea of a petition will only make matters worse. It will harden our enemies against us. I cannot condone it.'

'But what *can* you do? You must do something.'

'A personal petition to Lord Derby – that is what I am intending at the moment. Except that he doesn't give me an interview. There's nothing for it. I'll have to speak with him at the Assembly Rooms tomorrow night.'

She turned in her chair.

'You cannot, my love! It is business, and the Assembly is pleasure. He will take it as an affront.'

'If I choose my moment carefully, I may get a word. Now, I must take Suez out before I sleep.'

It was midnight and most of the town were in their beds as I gave the dog a run around Market Place, as was my habit. Just as we were crossing the entrance to Friar Gate I noticed Luke Fidelis making his way up the otherwise empty street towards me. He was walking with a certain unsteadiness and carrying an enclosed wicker basket. He hailed me.

'Titus! A man on whom one may rely. A man of substance. And my very dear friend. Well met.'

He stood before me swaying slightly, his eyes narrowed as if he were having trouble focusing them. As with many young men without wives, it was not infrequent for Fidelis to became the worse for wine. But tonight he was unusually well cut, his face flushed and his wits disguised.

'Luke, you are drunk.'

'Yes. I will not pretend otherwise. I've spent the whole evening in the company of cock-fighting men. Splendid fellows. Huge capacity for drink.'

'You have spoken with Jonathan O'Rorke, then?'

'O'Rorke? Oh yes, with him and with Lord Strange and

Captain Strawboy, and all of 'em. Highly informative evening. And I've come away somewhat enhanced. I have a proud new property.'

He indicated the basket. Something moved and rustled inside it.

'What sort of property?' I asked.

He tapped the basket with his finger.

'I seem to have won myself a fighting cock.'

Chapter 17

I HAVE NEVER MUCH liked cock fighting. Luke on the other hand is passionate for it.

'Why do you care for the game?' I asked him once.

'Because it is elemental,' he said. 'You cannot bribe a gamecock. All he wants is to fight and have the pit to himself. You can never persuade him to back away: he will fight or he will die. There is nothing more simple and magnificent I think.'

'I would rather play bowls. It is usually less bloody.'

Preston had its own cockpit off Church Gate, not far from Lord Derby's house. There was fighting every month or so, but these were mostly training bouts or matches for betting. The big prizefights – the mains, with silver trophies and awards of money for the winners – were held at Preston just three times a year: at Shrovetide, during the July races and at harvest end, on the twenty-ninth of September, Michaelmas. I have heard it said that in the old days, on farms where the corn had been safely cut, a cock would be imprisoned inside the last stook of corn, which was then set fire to. The ashes of that fire were kept until next season, when it was mixed with the seed corn before planting. This, I suppose, is why cocks are still linked to the Michaelmas season.

Fidelis had gone, as he said he would, to the Pride of the Pit Inn, where he found a rout of customers plunged in noisy conversation about the birds: of the cut of combs and the looseness of wattles, of the protuberance of spurs and the sleekness of sickle feathers. Disputes broke out over diet, grooming and keeping. Coarsely expressed views were aired on how often a bird should be exercised, and how long it should be allowed to roost.

Most of this talk was concerned with particular cocks. There was much exchange of news about wagers struck on the forthcoming contests, and of which birds are the betting favourites, and which the rag-tags. Public favouritism in betting is thought to be the most reliable guide to identifying likely winners. Second only to the gambling is the condition of the cocks themselves. A bird is rarely fancied that does not stand out in his physical appearance, with a clear eye, plump breast and gleaming feathers. Any sign that he begins to moult, or any loss of appetite, will damn him to defeat in the fancy's eyes. My friend took part in these debates as hotly as anyone and at the same time drank deep.

He was standing beside O'Rorke, as they listened as a gamester detailed at exorbitant length the martial qualities of his favourite bird. After a minute of this, Fidelis drew the Irishman a little to one side and gestured towards Captain Strawboy. Sprawled on a wooden settle at the end of the room, with his captain's tunic unbuttoned and a pot of wine in his fist, he was hailing each serving girl as she passed in front of him. Some would stop and banter, and every so often one would put down her jug of punch, or her plateful of pies, and sit for a moment on his knee to be kissed and fondled.

'The Captain is playing Lothario with a will tonight, is he not?' Fidelis observed. 'No maid within reach is safe.'

'That's the Captain for you,' agreed O'Rorke, 'with a jug or two of brandy inside him he's a terror.'

'I'm told you have a way with the ladies yourself.'

O'Rorke was drunk enough by now not to be offended. He took a pull from his tankard.

'I see a lot of girls, yes I do. I plant a few cabbages here and there.'

He laughed at his own heroics. Fidelis prodded him further.

'Kathy Brock, for instance?'

'Oh, Kathy? Do you know her? Well yes, I did niggle a bit with her, as we worked for the same family, and a very saucy piece she was, too. But that was last year. She's taken to prudery since, and won't be enticed no more.'

'What about these other cabbages you've been planting?'

'There's three or four, if you want to know. There's a girl in Ashton who doesn't mind showing her bubbies to a fellow in the haybarn. There's a butcher's daughter I know an' all who'll oblige if you give her enough sweet talk. Some of them do it because they want a man's attention. Others just for the tickle of it. It's all the same to me, as long as I can do it whenever I fancy.'

'What about your master's daughters? I'll warrant you've had a grab at them?'

He dropped his voice.

'You're joking. Too young for me. I did try to kiss Harriet once, after she'd just turned fifteen. She acted very odd. She didn't slap me in the face. She didn't tell me she'd have me dismissed if I forgot my place again. She didn't act the little tartar. She certainly didn't make out that she wanted it, like. She just froze. Rigid in her lips and her body. It's a funny thing though. Most little ladies are glad of a man's interest – a man's, not a boy's – but none of those Scroop lasses are, not in the slightest. They are all mortally afraid of nature, so they are, or that's what I think. A mite different from their mother and father, I will say. *They're* at it like rabbits, seeing as how much they're always breeding. But those girls . . . no. A man knows when one's got interest in it. Those ones'd rather jump off a cliff.'

One of the group shouted to O'Rorke a question about a fighting bantam he'd once put out against a full-size gamecock, and the bantam had won. With relish the whole story was told and Fidelis had no more chance to question him about his amorous life.

The evening continued increasingly boisterous until, towards midnight, Fidelis found himself contesting a drunken game of two-yard Card-in-the-Hat with Mr Fairbrother, a boastful farmer from the Yorkshire up-country at Scrafton. Fairbrother had come a laborious journey to Preston with his prize bird, the Sultan of Scrafton, to take on Lancashire's finest at the Michaelmas Main of Cocks. He was unshakeably confident of victory. He claimed that anyone from, as he called it, Lancastershire would be bested by anyone from Yorkshire without breaking sweat – or wind. And what was true of a cock-fight was even truer of two-yard Card-in-the-Hat.

The rules of two-yard Card-in-the-Hat are the essence of simplicity. An ordinary tri-corn hat is placed on the floor and a circle is drawn around it with chalk on the end of a taut string two yards in length, that detail being what distinguished the game from three-yard Card-in-the-Hat. The players take it in turns to draw a playing card and according to the suit and denomination must challenge their opponent to flip a minimum number of cards from a stance outside the circle and into the hat. He must then match or over match the score his opponent achieved. Fairbrother considered he was an expert and was backing himself against Fidelis with increasing sums of money.

He lost every rubber they played.

'Come on, come on, young man,' he laughed as his ace of spades veered through the air and landed six foot wide of the target. 'Don't you know I'm toying with thee? We'll double up again and I'll take thee this time, no danger. No danger of *that* not happening!'

This time Fairbrother failed to land a single card in the hat. Obliged yet again to open his purse and pay the bet, he found he had insufficient money left. Flicking a glance at the men of

Lancashire that had gathered on all sides to watch the game, he addressed Fidelis, for the first time, with a measure of caution.

'I find I am a little short, young man. You'll take my note, no doubt.'

He glanced around, like a man standing at a fork in the road with no signpost. The onlookers growled. They had grown sick of hearing him sing the praises of Yorkshire, and the excellence of its puddings, cheeses, horseflesh and woollens. Fidelis was no less surfeited with the Yorkshireman's boasting and in drink had himself grown as truculent as any in the room.

'Your poxy note won't serve, Fairbrother,' he said with spirit. 'I'm calling in the bet and I'll be obliged if you'd pay instanter and in specie.'

'Well I've not enough coin with me.'

'Then you must furnish me some thing of equivalent value.'

For the first time Fairbrother's bluster faltered. Through the mists of strong ale he had become dimly aware of where their discussion was leading.

'But my *note* is equivalent, Sir. My note is—'

'He'll not take your note, Mr Fairbrother.'

This was landlord Foster, taking a burly, belligerent stance almost nose to nose with the Yorkshireman. Fairbrother took a step back and lifted his arms away from his sides.

'But I've nothing else just to hand, you see. Nothing of equivalence.'

'I say you do,' replied Foster jerking his thumb towards the inn's rear door. 'It's out in the cockyard, and it's covered in feathers.'

Fairbrother's mouth fell open.

'You don't mean—?'

'Yes I do, and so does the doctor: the Sultan of Scrafton.'

Half an hour later Dr Fidelis stumbled out of the Pride of the Pit Inn carrying a wicker basket, whose occupant squawked and scrabbled, being angry at having been disturbed in his roost. Immediately behind them emerged Captain Strawboy, with one of the barmaids on his arm. They were both flushed with wine and laughter. The captain, in great good humour, hailed Fidelis.

'Doctor! Doctor! Do you realize what a prize you have won here tonight?'

'I do, Captain,' replied Fidelis, rapping on the basket. 'I've won what I have been told *ad nauseam* is a remarkably fine fighting bird, bred from champion stock. The egg that enclosed him as a chick was hard as china, yet he shattered it easily when the time came to make his triumphant entry into the world.'

'You take the word of a Yorkshireman on that?'

Fidelis laughed.

'Well, I'll indulge you on the question of the egg, but I need not take the word of a Yorkshireman that he is a champion. I use my own judgement. This cock looks a good fighter. *How* good must remain to be seen in the pit. But he has fire in his eye, as anyone can see.'

The captain was swaying a little from side to side but his own eyes, far from being dulled by drink, sparkled and his handsome mouth smirked. As a soldier, nothing more invigorated him in drink than a difference of opinion in a sporting matter.

'I fear you must think again, Sir,' he said. 'For I have to tell you that my own bird Dr Faustus has been matched against yours in the Main next Saturday. And Faustus is a champion supreme, is he not my pretty Doll?'

He had turned to the girl, who pouted.

'I don't know owt about that, Captain. But my name is Moll, you know.'

Strawboy patted her bottom fondly.

'So it is, so it is. Now, Doctor, we must have a side-bet. I know as a gentleman you will not be satisfied by merely losing the prize.

You must make it more interesting by losing your own money. Shall you back your Sultan, then, in his hopeless cause against me and Faustus? Shall we say an even five hundred to settle the matter?'

'Five hundred crowns, Captain? I would be honoured.'

Fidelis had not completed his bow of assent when he heard the captain spluttering.

'Crowns, Sir? You are joking. Crowns are for corn millers and oyster farmers. I deal in the gentleman's unit of account. I will bet only in guineas.'

'Very well,' said Fidelis without pause. 'Five hundred guineas it is that my Sultan will win the pit against your Faustus.'

Sober, Fidelis would have been astonished at his own bravado. Instead, astonishment was left to the girl. Her eyes had widened. Five hundred guineas was more money than she was likely to see in her whole life.

She looked from the doctor to the captain, then hooked her arm into the latter's arm.

'Well, Captain Strawboy, what a demon of gambling you are! If I could have just one of those guineas I'd be in clover.'

'Then clover shall cover you as an eiderdown, my pretty Polly, if you will just lead me to your chamber and show me the bed.'

As they set off down Fisher Gate, giggling together like children, her voice was heard telling him,

'Only it's Molly, Captain. My name's Molly.'

Chapter 18

THE SATURDAY OF the Assembly dawned cloudy, but the sky did not lour as oppressively as on the morning before. I do not know if this reflected, or infected, my mood, but feeling some of the previous day's gloom had dispersed I came down to breakfast with a faint spring in my step. Elizabeth had told me the previous evening that she planned to spend the morning with Matty mending and enhancing her best silk dress, which she had not worn since the celebration of the Guild Merchant a year previously. They would be similarly overhauling my own pale blue damask coat, which had not seen the light since I wore it for the present Lord Derby's inauguration as Lord Lieutenant two years earlier. I had wondered if I was not really too old for such fancy cloth. I even questioned, since I stood in such disgrace, if we should go to the Assembly at all this year.

'Don't be daft,' said Elizabeth. 'Of course we must go.'

'But how will you feel if someone chooses to insult me in public – or insult you?'

'Pooh to that!' Elizabeth said. 'We shall shine tomorrow night, my love, and that is why I have the damask coat in hand. This is the moment to show spirit, not skulk at home. These bloodhounds that are trying to run you down will all be there. You must outface them. You must go bravely suited and outface them.'

My wife was right, of course, as I could see clearly in my braver frame of mind this morning. To dodge the Assembly would show weakness at exactly the wrong moment – apart from being a great betrayal of the faith Elizabeth placed in me. And, besides, I needed to speak to Lord Derby.

This morning she had the coat waiting for me, draped over my breakfast chair, and I consented to try it on even before the food was put before me.

'You are fatter than when you last wore it. The arms are all right but we shall have to do some tailoring to let it out. Yes, if we can just let it out down the seam of the back it will do very well.'

She took the coat off me and felt along the seam.

'There's plenty of spare cloth. It will let out an inch, I am sure, which will make the coat much more comfortable, and less liable to split during the dance.'

'You even expect me to dance?'

'Of course I expect you to dance, Titus. And to enjoy yourself thoroughly.'

After breakfast I went through to the office braced for a wasp-ish exchange with Furzey (who was working his Saturday half-day) over his attempt to turn my dismissal into a political debate. But I found him unexpectedly rueful.

'Mr Cragg, I must tender an apology over my action yesterday. I have thought it out and you are right – it was rash and premature to try to stir up public outrage over our dismissal. Not at this stage. We must certainly speak to his Lordship at the first opportunity, and why not just mention the possibility of a petition on our behalf? Public feeling can sometimes strongly sway politicians.'

Furzey used the words 'we' and 'our', just as Elizabeth had last night. Then I had thought his support merely self-interested but now I was unexpectedly moved by this third-person plural. Furzey had held his position as Coroner's clerk since my father's day but, as I fell from grace, so fell he, and if he chose he could have held me responsible and turned dead against me. Yes, he had a stake in me and my standing – so had Elizabeth, yet I did not call her support self-interest, I called it love. What, then, of Furzey? Had I come so far under the cynical influence of the author of *The Fable of the Bees* that I could no longer distinguish self-interest from love?

Feeling privately abashed, I accepted his apology, whereupon he picked up a thick ribbon-tied bundle of documents and let it fall again with a thump.

'Here's all the papers in the baby inquest, Mr Cragg. The Recorder's sent for them. What shall we do: accede or obstruct? We could easily mislay this bundle – d'you follow me? It could have dropped out of a saddlebag, or been mistaken for some other bundle and accidentally sent up to Lancaster Castle. We could elaborate a story.'

The papers included all the statements we had assembled and would be essential for the self-appointed Coroner Thwaite to complete the interrupted inquest quickly. No doubt his legal adviser, the Recorder, had told him that unless he had them he would have to start again from the beginning.

'No, Furzey, we won't obstruct. It would be futile. The Mayor will conduct his inquest one way or another. It will be a travesty, of course, but I don't want to be seen standing in his way. Remember there is a dead child still unburied.'

'I'll send it over, then.'

'No, Furzey. Let me take the papers to the Recorder myself. I should like to have a word with him.'

Matthew Thorneley had held the office of Recorder of Preston continuously for twenty years. The Mayor and bailiffs whom he served took office for just twelve months at a time, before being jostled out by the next man in the queue. The great advantage of the recordership, therefore, was its permanence. Thorneley himself had no principles beyond furthering his own advancement through assiduous service, but he understood the intricacies of the law as a rat knows the hidden cavities of your house.

Calling in at the Recorder's place of business, which stood opposite Moot Hall at the junction of Church Gate and Fisher Gate, I was told he had spent the morning at home. Declining to leave the inquest papers in his clerk's hands, I carried them instead to Thorneley's house, near the gates of Avenham Walk. The Recorder cultivated a dull, homespun image in his dress and demeanour, but the house, which stood surrounded by its own ground, with stables, lawns, a parterre and a walled kitchen garden, was sizeable and luxuriously appointed. The place had belonged to the Langtons, an old and once powerful merchant family who'd invested all they had and more in the South Sea Company two decades before. As the bubble burst they had lost the lot, enabling Thorneley to get the house for a pittance. It had unusual features, including a large double-height entrance hall in the classical style, with wall- and ceiling-paintings commissioned by old Absalom Langton at the height of his prosperity.

Left by the servant alone in this hall to await Thorneley, I placed the inquest papers on a broad table on which also stood the family mailbox. Another bundle of documents, thinner than mine, was already waiting there. It tweaked my interest, as it was labelled 'Private Instructions re: P.M. – Mr Kay', but I did not want to be caught looking more closely, and so glanced up instead at the domed ceiling. It presented the artist's idea of the fall of Phaeton in highly colourful style – the chariot spinning down from the sky, the crazed team of horses and the desperate, overreaching boy hauling ineffectually on the reins. I couldn't help smiling at this image of a son's reckless disobedience. Thorneley's only heir had become notorious for dissipation at Cambridge, and was now confined to a madhouse near Manchester.

Thorneley kept me waiting for a carefully judged interval. When he appeared, I pointed up at the dome.

'Who was the artist?'

'Oh, a fellow called Parmentier. A Frenchman who came over from York in the last days of Queen Anne, I have been told. I don't know what to make of the decorations myself but my wife can explain them all. Now, what can I do for you, Cragg?'

I indicated the bundle on the hall table.

'The papers you wanted in the inquest on the child found dead at the skin-yard. As Coroner it is my only inquiry in progress.'

Thorneley crossed to the table and unlooped the bundle's ribbons.

'And all the witness statements are here, and clerk's notes from the hearing up to the point of being unfortunately interrupted?'

'They are.'

I waited while he leafed through the pages. Thorneley had always seemed to me an ill-dressed toad, who existed cravenly to give the Corporation the sort of legal advice they needed to pursue their own ends. But now, standing in his house for the first time (Elizabeth and I had never been on visiting terms with the Thorneleys), I began to see that this servile, slovenly image was largely a pretence – a cover, perhaps, for the lavish scale on which the Recorder had feathered his own nest. Despite his plain woollen coat and down-at-heel shoes, he had grown much richer than most of the burgesses whose actions and decisions he underwrote with his legal advice.

Putting the bundle down, Thorneley efficiently re-tied it.

'Good. Then I need detain you no longer, Cragg. I am sure you have much re-ordering to do, since yesterday's sudden alteration in your life.'

There had been a certain sneer in his tone, which required a counter-thrust.

'You must see that this whole business of transferring the coronership to the Mayor *ex officio* is nonsense, Thorneley. He is, of course, egged on by Scroop and Grimshaw. They have made him actually believe he should be Coroner by historical right and, since he is vain enough, he does now *want* to be Coroner. But you know, as well as I know, that Thwaite couldn't conduct an inquest any more than he could conduct an orchestra.'

'The Mayor will be advised by me. There will be no difficulty, I assure you.'

'That is my point. You, as legal officer, will be the *de facto* Coroner of this town, Thorneley: do you really want all that extra work? There's little or nothing in it of remuneration.'

Thorneley looked at me for a moment, and I sensed he was tempted to make an admission. Then he hardened again, shaking his finger at me.

'It nevertheless seems *you* want to keep the job, Cragg. Is there not something in it for you?'

'Oh, that is only my pride, Thorneley. Like Mayor Thwaite I enjoy the social standing, you know: the sense of importance. But you cannot benefit from that, as you will be only an elevated sort of clerk, will you not?'

'By heavens, Cragg, I'll have you know I am no clerk!'

'No, that is my point, Thorneley. Can a mere clerk call all of this his own?'

It was mischief, I suppose, that made me indicate the house and all its fine fittings. It was the wrong play, however. The Recorder was furious at my jibe about his being a clerk; nor did he like my implication that he was more interested in his own enrichment than the public good. He now stepped smartly towards the door and grasped the knob to open it for my departure. But I still lingered by the post table.

'By the way,' I continued casually, 'I have met your ingenious Mr

Kay.' I tapped the file of documents labelled *Private Instructions*. 'Important work he's engaged in, I imagine. I have seen his remarkable equipment.'

It had been a shot at random but it hit a sensitive spot. Thorneley left the door and moved straight back to the post-table where he took up the papers and clapped them to his chest. It was as if he were afraid I might seize them and run away.

'I know nothing of the instrument you refer to, Cragg. However, if there be a Mr Kay in this town, and if he do have any work here – which I do not say he has – it is confidential, private. You will be in serious trouble if you reveal anything you may know.'

'Quite so,' I said with a smile. Then I bowed and picked up my hat. 'Good day, Mr Recorder.'

In the hope that Lord Derby might be prepared to see me, I called at Patten House, but was told his Lordship was from home on business. So I returned to the office where Luke Fidelis awaited me.

'The Sultan of Scrafton thrives, I hope,' I said at once.

He shook his head gravely.

'The Sultan has a morose look this morning. His eye is not as beady as it should be and he is proving a choosy eater. I tried him on maize and sunflower seed but he will touch neither of them. I wonder if he is pining for Scrafton. I had better consult my new friend Jon O'Rorke in the matter, or the bird'll never be in a fit state to fight a week today. Now, you will be interested in this.'

He took from his pocket a letter, which he put into my hand.

'It's from Kathy Brock to me.'

'From Kathy? Where does she write from?'

'From Wigan. By all means read it for yourself.'

The letter was short but it was literate enough.

Dear Doctor Fidelis,

I hope you do not mind. I am writing to you because you were kind to me about my bruises on that day we met in the lane. I want your word on a doctor hereabouts in Wigan – or between here and Warrington, where I go sometimes. Do you know one that would be kind as you are and take my side? I would be obliged if you would give me the name of such and write to him yourself about me so he is warned. Please write me care of Didcott's drapery shop.

Your poor friend, Kathy Brock

'Well! I wonder what that's all about.'

'She may have had some more knocks from Pitt, her uncle. Perhaps she has got a lasting injury and he refuses to acknowledge it or allow her to be treated.'

'But why does she say she hopes this doctor will "take my side". Her side in what? Surely not a formal dispute. She can hardly be taking an action for battery against Terence Pitt, for she would not stand a chance of winning. What will you reply?'

'Well, as it happens I know someone – Dr Hume of Warrington. I worked as his apprentice for a year when I was more or less of a stripling. He is utterly honest, to his own detriment, I may say, since most of the other doctors there are no straighter than ours are here. They hate Jack Hume for his refusal to charge their high fees. No more will he play their astrological games, or prate to the patients about wet and dry humours, as they all do.'

'You will recommend him to Kathy, then?'

'I want to help her and that is the best I can do short of going to see her myself.'

'Could you not do that?'

Fidelis shrugged.

'How can I? I am training a gamecock for the biggest fight of his life. Anyway that's not what she has asked me to do. Hume will serve as well as me – better, in fact. He is a remarkable physician.'

'I suggest, when you write to her, you inform her of how matters are in the case of the dead baby – that the Mayor has taken over the inquest, and that I fear this would not bode well for her if she chose to return to Preston.'

'She won't come back unless she feels in greater danger from her uncle than she does from Mayor Thwaite.'

'Both seem equally threatening, in my opinion. The poor girl is between a very sharp rock and the devil of a hard place.'

Our talk drifted to how the resumed inquest under Thwaite might turn out. I described my visit to Thorneley's to deliver the papers in the case. I also mentioned my curiosity at seeing the 'Private Instructions re: P.M. – Mr Kay'.

'I have had Mr Kay to dinner,' I said, 'having met him when we were both applying unsuccessfully for an audience with Lord Derby. He is a land surveyor summoned by his Lordship, for some reason that Kay had not yet been told. It is to do with Captain Strawboy, I do know that. Kay has been told to apply for his instructions to Captain Strawboy "re P.M.". What is that?'

'Strawboy represents Lord Grassington, not Derby, does he not?'

'It seems Lord Derby has a stake in this "P.M." thing also. But what is "P.M."?'

'Project Something, I guess. They are projectors, after all.'

'And why are surveying instructions passing through the hands of the Corporation's legal officer? And what is the reason for secrecy?'

'I am interested in this fellow Kay. What is he like?'

'A devoted apostle of improvement in all its forms. He talks of nothing else – and I do mean nothing. His conversation was so stultifying that Elizabeth and I could scarcely keep awake. I expect you would like him.'

Chapter 19

THE CITY OF York already had a splendid Assembly Room with no fewer than forty-two Palladian columns, while Bath also had magnificent rooms dedicated to assembly and polite concourse. I have lived long enough to see Preston build its own Assembly Room at last but, until it came, large gatherings with presentations and dancing were always held in the great first-floor dining room at the White Bull Inn, with its long refectory tables removed for the purpose. Refreshments were served in the downstairs coffee rooms.

The conduct of the Assembly revolved around the presiding family, which was naturally that of the Earl of Derby. The opening ceremonies were ones of arrival and announcement. The Derbys took their places in chairs arranged on a raised dais at the end of the hall, and there held court while music played and Billy Wilkinson the town crier, having scrutinized tickets at the door, bellowed out the names written on them. Each ticket holder then entered the hall, walked the length of it to the dais – under the close scrutiny of those who'd preceded them – before bowing or curtseying to the Earl and Countess.

It took some time to get everybody in, and those waiting to make an entrance formed a queue which, at its longest, stretched down the stairs, out of the door and into Market Place. I noticed, as Elizabeth and I took our place in line, that women whispered behind their fans and several people avoided greeting us, though they stared, then looked away at the instant we looked back. Possibly they disapproved that we had shown our faces, or were just surprised. Ahead of us waited James Starkey and his wife. I tapped him on the shoulder.

'Hello Starkey. I'm ready for that game of bowls,' I said.

Starkey kept his back turned, pretending not to have noticed. I looked at Elizabeth and loved her for the way she wrinkled her nose fiercely at his back. It is a curious feeling to suffer ostracism, even to that petty extent, but easier to bear when you have such a wife as mine.

We ascended the stair and with each step the orchestra was more clearly heard, and the accompanying buzz of chatter. We reached the top of the stair and gave our card to Billy. He hesitated and looked at us as if uncertain what to do.

'Come on, Billy,' I said. 'Announce us.'

He cleared his throat and turned to the room.

'Mr and Mrs Titus Cragg!' he roared.

There was a noticeable drop in the level of conversation as we walked arm in arm up the centre of the room, flanked on both sides by Assembly-goers watching our every step. I tried not to think about what they were whispering, but kept my eye on Lord Derby, looking for a friendly sign, or some indication of what he might be thinking. He glanced at us as we advanced towards him, then turned aside to the Countess and said something behind his hand. She tightened her mouth and his eyes betrayed a moment of laughter, though when he removed the hand his mouth showed no sign of it.

'What was so funny?' I murmured after we had made our obeisance and moved to the side.

'Who can tell what amuses a Lord?' she said. 'But I still think he is on your side, Titus.'

'I wish I could be sure of that.'

We were now watching the Grimshaws progressing up the room, the former mayor pouting his chest and looking self-importantly around while his wife kept her eyes on the Derbys. She was looking in particular, I thought, at the women's dresses. It was a byword of Elizabeth's that studying what the Stanley ladies wore on special occasions was the most direct way of finding out the London fashion.

The Grimshaws were followed by a succession of burgesses, with their wives bedizened by pearl and precious stones. Eventually my nemesis appeared, surprisingly escorted.

'My Lady Rickaby and the honourable Captain Strawboy,'

She looked straight ahead while the Captain smiled and nodded to one or two acquaintances.

'Why is she with Strawboy?'

'Because they are related, remember? Old Sir Grimes Rickaby was Strawboy's mother's brother. So they are aunt and nephew.'

Not far behind these two came the Scroop family, or half of it. Scroop himself fat and prosperous; his wife, who had not been seen since her confinement, looking exhausted, hardly doing justice to her expensive silks. Trailing behind their parents came the misses Scroop – an anxious-looking Harriet and her two equally nervous nearest sisters who, with rounded shoulders and blushing cheeks, kept their eyes on the floor as they came forward under the collective scrutiny.

Lord Derby was about to call an end to this first phase of the proceedings when one last arrival was heralded by the stentorian voice of Billy Wilkinson.

'His lordship, thee – Viscount Grassington!'

I was very curious to see this peer, who had never before been in Preston (to my knowledge) but who was now taking such an interest in improving our town. He was a tall, spare-looking man in his fifties, with prominent cheekbones, a nose that I would call sub-aquiline and a thin mouth. He came into the room unaccompanied, stalked the length of it and gave the dais a perfunctory bow. Then he held out his hand to be shaken by Derby, who was already out of his chair and descending from the dais. The two lords went off talking closely, with their heads together, no doubt to get a glass of wine or punch in the room below.

'They seem to be friendly enough,' I said. 'Is there no Lady Grassington?'

'He's widowed,' said Elizabeth.

We were now joined by Luke Fidelis, who admired Elizabeth's Wigan coal necklace and asked if she would keep a dance for him. Fidelis was a much more skilful dancer than myself and she agreed, but insisted I must go out on the floor with her first, as a show of unity to the world. Then Elizabeth's cousins Mary-Ann and Grace, with the latter's new husband, sought us out, and they too admired the necklace. Grace and Arthur Arkwright had been married only six months, and were still in the first flush of love, that is, taking every opportunity to touch hands and exchange burning looks. After hearing the history of the necklace, Grace expressed the wish to have one of her own. But Mary-Ann, forthright as ever, changed the subject. She had angry words to say about the Court Leet's decision to depose me.

'It is a crying shame, Cousin Titus. You must be reinstated as soon as possible. We shall not rest until you are.'

'I fear there's not much you can do, my dear, though it is most kind of you.'

'I can speak out and I have done so. I've heard remarks being made about your presence at the Assembly and I've given those people a piece of my mind, I do assure you.'

'Please don't get into a quarrel on my account.'

'Quarrel? I'll not quarrel with them. I'll tell them.'

A quadrille was called and this suited me well, as I did not want to take part in a set with many couples and run the risk of an insult during the dance. The Arkwrights agreed to make up the four and we spent ten minutes walking up, and walking back; skipping this way and skipping that; turning and being turned. I watched the faces of Grace and Arthur and remembered with pleasure the freedom and silly bliss of first love. When the band sawed their final chord we were a little out of breath and pleased at having got through the dance with all its complications and not tangled feet or tripped over.

A visit to the refreshments was proposed and we went downstairs. While young Arkwright set about finding jellies for the ladies, and punch for us all, I looked around the room for Lord Derby, wondering how to get some time alone with him.

I need not have worried. I had only half finished my glass of punch when I heard a voice beside me speaking my name: it was the Earl himself.

'I have read your note, Cragg,' he said. 'Very sorry I couldn't see you yesterday, but I had much business and not a moment to spare. However, I think we might have a small word now, if it does not disturb your enjoyment.'

We walked apart from the others into a corner of the room. Derby was very friendly. He was in general not the warmest human being you might meet, but he knew how to speak amicably with people in all walks of life, and this he did with me. The act seemed a calculated challenge to the town's tittle-tattle: no one could hear what we were saying, but everyone could see that we conversed seriously and in friendship. For a peer of the realm to talk so with a commoner on a social occasion could only be seen as a mark of favour.

'I start by saying I do not approve the action of Mayor Thwaite in removing you from the coronership,' the Earl told me.

'I am deeply grateful, my Lord. Can you make him reverse it?'

'Ah! That's another thing. My position is delicate, especially at the moment.'

'If you were to read the record of my hearing at Court Leet, I think you would agree it is an arbitrary judgement.'

'I am sure, I am sure. But to speak candidly, I need to be friends with the Corporation just at the moment.'

'Of course, I do understand that, but—'

'I must not give them any cause to oppose me, you see, as I have plans which . . . well, never mind the details, but I may very well need their support, and soon. I don't think the law would smoothly support me in overruling a decision by the Mayor, so it would have to be a dirty fight and, value you though I do, Cragg, I cannot afford such a fight now. So you will have to bear your misfortune, I fear. But I do deplore all this whispering against you personally. Lady Rickaby is a ninny and very silly, and I hope by my speaking here to you openly, and in front of all these people, that the obnoxious woman's credit will be dinted a little.'

'I am grateful, my Lord.'

He patted me on the arm and smiled.

'It's nothing. Perhaps you would like to come and shoot with us next month. The pheasants will soon be fat and ready. I'll ask my secretary to suggest some dates.'

He left me with a final encouraging smile. I was not sure what to make of this. On the one hand he had told me he would not help me. On the other he had gone out of his way to show his support for me in public, and asked me to shoot. As a mark of favour, that outweighed the enmity of the Mayor by some margin.

Our party – now swelled by the addition of Nick Oldswick the watchmaker, another old friend who had not deserted me – decided to return up the stairs to the dancing room. Just as we entered, an angry female shout rang out above the general noise. Beside the door as we came in we found an argument had broken out between Abraham Scroop and his eldest daughter. Such things are not unusual at balls and assemblies, of course. Fathers see their little girls flirting with unsuitable men; daughters flash with anger when they are told off, and there is much hectoring and flouncing. But this was different. Harriet did not strike me as a defiant sort of girl: more the opposite. Yet she and her father were standing with Dr Harrod, who stood blinking and glancing back and forth between father and daughter, in what looked like benign bafflement.

'I *shan't* dance with him!'

'You shall!'

'No, I shan't because I won't! I refuse!'

Harrod made pacifying gestures with his hands.

'Let's not get too upset about this, Abe,' he said. 'And dear Harriet. Would one dance for your father's sake be so terrible?'

She sniffed and shook her head. Scroop was growing red in the face as another wave of anger rose up in him.

'If I say you shall dance with my friend, then you shall, my girl.'

'I won't! I won't dance at all, ever. I don't like dancing and I don't like—'

Scroop grabbed his daughter by the wrists and pulled her round to face him.

'Listen to me, Harriet Scroop. I shall not let you add insult to your refusal. You will dance!'

Harriet was trembling now and crying, as her mother came hurrying up to make peace. She asked her daughter a question, inaudible from where I stood. Harriet closed her eyes tight, as if in pain, then leaned towards her mother's ear and spoke for about twenty seconds with passionate urgency. Mrs Scroop took a moment to take in what had been said, glanced at her husband, then at Harrod, Harriet and finally at Scroop again.

'We are leaving, Abraham,' she said firmly, when she had recovered herself, and loudly enough to be heard by those of us standing nearby. 'This is no place for us tonight. We must all go home at once. At once!'

So, amidst a storm of gossip, and despite anything Scroop himself had to say about staying on and not causing scandal, his wife bundled him and their daughters out of the White Bull an hour and a half before Lord Derby would be expected to call time on the Assembly.

'Who's she refusing to dance with? Did you hear?'

'No, but it must be the Captain. It's him she's being pushed towards – and she doesn't much like it.'

I thought of Jon O'Rorke's assessment of Harriet Scroop: 'afraid of nature'. This was evidence of something of the sort, but it did not accord with what I had seen at Water Lane, the encounter between Strawboy and Harriet in the morning room. She had blushed then and become a little breathless in the Captain's presence. As far as I remembered, it was he that had been cool. So what had she said to her mother that forced their so sudden departure?

Several people were asking Dr Harrod what was the matter, and why the Scroops had left, but he merely smiled and said he was sure it was nothing – nothing but a young girl feeling overwrought and a mother understandably concerned for her daughter's delicate health. Then, despite this show of complacency, he hurried out after them.

In the next half hour Fidelis danced with my wife, and then partnered Mary-Ann, while Elizabeth took a turn with Nick Oldswick. I myself moved around the room. The public show of support from Lord Derby had already had its effect. People who'd previously turned their backs now miraculously acknowledged me and even asked after my health. I didn't tell them that I was restless and felt hot. Lord Derby's kindness had had its strict limits: if he had wanted me back as Coroner he could have made it happen. There were other desiderata, over which my own fate could claim no priority. I was conscious of a rising headache and a sense of oppression.

After a while I found myself near Lord Grassington, who was standing beside his nephew. They studied to give the appearance of two men watching the dancing while, in reality, discussing something quite different. Manoeuvring myself so that I stood a little in front of them, and myself pretending to watch the dancers, I was able to pick out a few of their words. The topic seemed to be the skin-yard, as I heard reference to Scroop 'not growing too suspicious' and this was in relation to the Marsh. There was mention of Lord Derby, the skinners, and then 'that surveyor fellow'. Finally I caught the words 'difficulties in that direction' and a reference to a sum of some thousands of pounds – I could not hear the exact figure. But the upshot (I decided) was that they were discussing finance for the clearance of the skin-yard, while considering the possible obstacles still standing in its way. There were also some words which might have been expressing the hope that Scroop would 'hold steady'.

'Cragg!'

I was clapped on the shoulder by someone approaching from behind. I turned to see with surprise it was James Starkey, my opponent at bowls and he who had earlier snubbed me.

'Terrible unfortunate business this matter of Lady Rickaby and her accusation,' he said as if nothing had happened on the stair on our way in. 'Nobody takes it very seriously – well, Thwaite has done, and maybe Grimshaw and Scroop and a few others. But no one else. We don't ostracize you or hold you guilty in any way, Cragg.'

'Thank you. You would support my reinstatement, then?'

'Ah! Not sure I would go so far as that. Strictly speaking of course an offence was committed. Still, no hard feelings, I hope, and all is friends and jollity again – eh?'

Starkey did not fool me. He was not a bad man, but merely one that always grazed with the herd. Having turned his back on me at the start, but then witnessed my friendly chat with Lord Derby, he'd now reckoned it was safe to resume relations himself.

I said, 'We will have to see about our . . . our game of bowls, then, shall we not? Ah! The dance is finished. I must re-join my wife.'

Elizabeth was flushed and looking young and so pretty that as I joined her my heart turned over. Then I felt a similar sensation, but a more threatening one: a thump of the heart, a flush of heat in my neck and a small pulse of pain in my head. The atmosphere in the room was warm and humid with the smell of bodies and the stickiness of air breathed many times over. I pulled a handkerchief from my pocket and tried to mop my brow but fumbled it and dropped the handkerchief. The pain in my head was growing and a dizziness was overcoming me.

'I think I need to sit,' I said, but before I could do so I was aware that my knees were giving way and then I was unaware of anything. Only later was I told that the seam of my fine coat split all the way down the back as I hit the ground.

Chapter 20

I KNOW NOTHING ABOUT the next thirty-six hours, excepting what others have told me. I was carried across Market Place and home on a litter and lay in bed largely insensible of the activity around me. Luke Fidelis superintended my medical care, calling at the house repeatedly; Matty made me hot drinks under his direction; and Elizabeth sat beside me almost continually, determined to be at her post when my fever broke.

Fidelis told my wife I was suffering from an acute ague brought on by late events undermining my constitution. The outcome of such a fever was very uncertain, he said, but for the time being the best care was to keep me calm, cool my brow and give me plenty of beef tea to drink. There was no single drug to cure me, but a camomile and tansy root infusion and a little fermented elder juice might do some good.

The fever raged throughout Sunday and at certain moments Elizabeth even feared for my life. Much of the time I was in a febrile dream. She said I muttered about death and seemed to be holding dream inquests, but whether about old cases or imagined future ones she could not tell.

But on Monday I rallied. The fever abated and for several hours I slept deeply. As I lay unconscious, the real inquest, that had been taken from me by the Mayor's Court Leet decision, was reopened under Thwaite's newly fledged coronership. As he had done at my own 'trial' at Court Leet, Furzey attended with his pen and ink-horn and brought a transcript of what had been said to Cheapside where, by eight o'clock the next morning, I was well enough to sit up in bed and demand to see it.

Only two witnesses had been heard by the reconvened inquest, the first of whom was Kathy Brock's mother Margery, resuming the testimony that had been interrupted at the Skeleton Inn. Thwaite's questioning of her was a little more direct than mine.

'You have already – have you not? – testified that this daughter of yours is little better than a whore.'

'No, that's not true! She's just—'

'That she was with child last year, unmarried, and would never say who the father was?'

'Well, yes, but—'

'And you have no idea who this man was – none at all?'

'No, Sir.'

'Even though you have testified . . .'

Thwaite cleared his throat and picked a paper from the bundle in front of him.

'You testified "We were that close, since her father left us." Your own words. You were "that close" – and yet you didn't know which young buck she'd been rutting with?'

'No, Sir, I—'

'Not even a suspicion?'

'No, none.'

'Well, it is a likely story! A likely story! So is this behaviour of your daughter typical of the skinners generally, this loose morality? Are you all at it?'

'At what, Sir?'

'This shocking ungodly lasciviousness. You yourself, for instance? How many bastards have you had?'

'Me, Sir? None!'

Thwaite selected another document from the pile.

'This is a transcript of the register of St John's church. It gives your daughter Kathy's birth date as the sixth of June 1726 – is that right?'

'Yes, that's right.'

'And a page later on the fifteenth July it is written: "Married John Brock, tanner, and Margery Turner, spinster." Is that you?'

'Yes.'

'So when you conceived and gave birth you were still a spinster.'

'Well, John was away. He—'

'Yes or no – did you conceive a bastard?'

'Yes, in that way she was, but—'

'No "buts" – you are admitting it. Earlier you denied the same thing, under oath. That is perjury. You may expect to hear more of that, Margery Brock, as the law punishes perjurers with great severity. You may get down.'

Having thus terrified Margery Brock, and proved to his satisfaction the whole turpitude not just of the Brock family but of the skin-yard in general, the Mayor now put Jon O'Rorke in the witness chair.

O'Rorke gave resentful testimony. It seemed that he blamed Kathy Brock for putting him and his habits of life under public scrutiny and, though he passionately denied fathering the child that was dead, his answer to Thwaite's questions about Kathy's morals went further than what he had told Luke at the Pride of the Pitt tavern.

'So you did know Kathy Brock well?' was the question.

'Yes,' was the answer.

'Did you have intimate relations together?'

I imagine O'Rorke smirked.

'What do you think we did – make daisy chains?'

'I am not here to think, O'Rorke. Did you father a child on her?'

'I don't know.'

'You knew she was with child, did you not?'

'Yes, but that girl went with a lot of lads. She was like that – she enjoyed it, you know? Sporting with a lad was what she liked to do best.'

'Was she not afraid of conceiving a child when she did this . . . sporting?'

'No, she told me she knew what to do then.'

'You mean murdering the child, of course. So! What wickedness in this town of ours! What monstrous perversion of religion! You may get down.'

Thwaite turned to the jury and told them that Kathy could not herself be questioned, as she had absconded (which weighed very heavily against her) and he therefore proposed to proceed straight to a verdict. They were left in little doubt as to their duty and so, dutifully and within a few minutes, they returned their decision: 'murder by Kathy Brock'.

Thwaite heard the verdict with a look, so I was told, of pure satisfaction. He felt he had managed the case with supreme finesse and in less than an hour. He did not mind if he congratulated himself.

'I will say in conclusion only two things,' he told the court before dismissing it. 'First that I am pleased to have finished this matter with the kind of dispatch rarely seen under the previous Coroner; and second that I have uncovered a serpent in this town and it lives in the tannery. This progenitor of evil shall poison our society for, as the scripture puts it, "he that cleaveth to harlots will become impudent". And in case you doubt that, remember the disrespectful bearing of the witness O'Rorke, and the shameless perjury of the witness Margery Brock. The serpent must therefore be dug out, I say, and its breeding-ground laid waste. As Mayor I shall now make that my business.'

These concluding words were a dire enough threat against the skinners, but the verdict alone might spell death to Kathy if she ever came back to Preston. I wondered how long it would take Constable Mallender, having made his way to Wigan with a warrant for her arrest, to prise the girl from the determined grasp of her uncle and to bring her back for trial. The confrontation between the two men – town constables of similar obduracy but unalike in almost every other way – would have been a sight to see, though I was not very happy at the prospect of Kathy being hauled back from Wigan to face the Preston grand jury, and be committed by them for the assizes.

But news runs faster than nature, as they say. Kathy heard of the verdict naming her long before Oswald Mallender had even got his palfrey saddled, and immediately took the action that she may have planned from the start. We learned about this on Wednesday afternoon, by which time I was well enough to leave my bed and sit for an hour or two by the parlour fire. I was thus installed, wrapped in a woollen rug, when Fidelis arrived. He was carrying a letter from his friend Dr Hume of Warrington, which had just been put into his hands. I have this letter in front of me now.

Dear Fidelis,

I have the honour of writing to you with regard to Miss Kathy Brock, the skinner's daughter whom you have referred to me. She appeared today without warning at my rooms and I found her an unexpectedly intelligent and well-presented young woman. She came straight to the point and asked me to examine her. I enquired what complaint she had and she said none and merely wished to submit to an examination and that a memorandum be then made of the result. I followed her wishes. I found several contusions and bruises about her person and a loose tooth – all the result she told me of the disciplinary methods of her uncle in Wigan with whom she had been living – but there were no broken bones or no other sign of malady arising. Questioned about any abiding symptoms she suffered, Kathy told me she felt sore from these deplorable beatings but had no internal pains and no other unusual physical effects. She then, to my great surprise, pointed out that I had not made a vaginal examination (though not in exactly those words!) and asked me to do so. After I had complied, and told her that I could find no disease, she said to me,

'That is not what I want to know, Doctor.'

'What, then?' I asked.

'Tell me, have I given birth in the last three weeks?'

'Good heavens!' I laughed. 'This is something you must know yourself.'

'I do know. But it is no laughing matter. I am accused in Preston of having had a bastard baby and killed it, just two weeks ago. From what you have found, could I have had that child?'

'No. There is no evidence whatever of a recent parturition.'

'Will you put that down in writing, that I may bring it out on my defence if I need to?'

I gladly provided her with the paper, which she folded and put away in her pocket, asking that I also communicate the result of our consultation directly to you in Preston – a duty which I hereby discharge. We then spoke about what she might do next. She would not risk a return to her parents, but nor would she stay under the roof of her uncle, whom she calls base and a brute. So she intends leaving the County Palatine altogether and going far away – though whether to London, or America, or some other place I could not prevail on her to tell me. She tried to press a few coins on me by way of a fee, which I refused to accept. I then had my house-keeper give her some food in the kitchen and so at last she went on her way.

I hope you will be able to put this information to good use in Preston, by clearing the name of this personable and unfortunate young woman.

Your servant,

John Hume M.D.

Postscriptum. Please send me your latest observations on the use of the turpentine clyster in cases of urinary obstruction. In return I will let you have some of my own results in opening the cephalic vein to relieve the megrim.

On Thursday morning, after another better night, I re-entered the office for the first time since my illness. Furzey handed me a list of cases we had in hand.

'While you've been lying on your back, the work's been building like hair on a barber's floor. There's Mr Fleming's will that's in draft and needs finalising, Miss Colley's latest codicil to put into legal language and the signature for notarizing on the deed

you drew up for Mr Caddick. I also have two bills we are protesting, and you need to see Mr Oldswick. He was here yesterday,
enquiring after your health and also wanting advice about a case
he's bringing against Simon Parbold at Court Leet for selling him
rotten fish.'

I sighed.

'I suppose I should be happy that I still have a legal practice.
First I'll go and see Mr Oldswick at his shop. I haven't been out of
the house since Saturday and will enjoy the fresh air.'

I was fond of Oldswick, the watchmaker of Friar Gate whose
passion was going to law. He once sued a dancer for stepping on
his foot, and another time next door's dog – by way of its owner –
for not barking in the night at a thief that was robbing Oldswick's
house.

Oldswick was one of the twenty-four burgesses of Preston, but
his own trade was modest compared with those like Scroop who
saw no horizon to their ambitions. He was thus without personal
power in the town but was nevertheless one of a strong and vocal
Tory-minded party in the Corporation, which opposed the Mayor
and his Whiggish friends who constituted the other powerful group.
A third part of our ruling body was not committed to either side,
but floated between them from issue to issue. One of the issues that
always raised hackles was change – almost any kind of alteration
to the way in which things were done – whether it be the conduct
of the market, the enclosure of common land, making toll-roads,
or strengthening the Game Laws. The Whigs were all for these
projects and reforms, but Oldswick and his associates invariably
opposed them, finding they offended against their traditional free-
born rights.

After asking how I did in health, and deploring what he
called the despicable act of Thwaite in 'pitching you out of the
coronership like an old straw mattress', Oldswick consented to

discuss the business of the bad fish. We dealt with it quickly. It appeared the questionable items, two grayling, had been bought on Parbold's stall the previous Saturday. However, since neither Oldswick nor his old servant Parsonage had become ill in the eating of them, I had to tell him his case was weak, and getting weaker with the lapse of time and the continuing absence of illness.

'But it tasted foul.'

'Tastes differ. They cannot be enshrined in law.'

'We might get sick yet.'

'After four days? Perhaps it would be best to let this drop, after all.'

'I want everyone to know that Parbold is a lazy lying cheat. His father was a hard worker who caught the fish himself. Young Parbold never casts a net or a line. He buys his fish from poachers and God knows who, and never asks a question before he sells them on.'

'Write a satire against him in rhyming couplets. Report him to the market viewer of fish. But don't sue him for damages – you'll lose.'

I was surprised at Oldswick's response. Instead of sulking and threatening to take the business to the none-too-scrupulous firm of Rudgwick and Tench, as he often did, the watchmaker tamely agreed to suspend any action unless and until some sickness ensued in either himself or Parsonage.

This business being dealt with, our talk turned to the week's main topic in Preston, the naming by Thwaite's court of Kathy Brock as a murderess.

'What will happen to her?' Oldswick asked. 'Won't she be brought back for trial?'

'I believe she has got away free.'

'Yes, but she'll be a fugitive. A warrant for her arrest has been signed, I hear. She could be tried and hung, which some people are thinking would not be good justice.'

'I know it would not be justice, but I think she will be safe all the same, Nick. As long as Kathy is not foolish enough to return to this part of the world, no one will take the trouble to pursue her. The only real victim in this crime – which I am sure she did not commit by the way – was the baby. It is dead. Who is there who'll seek true justice for its murder? The Mayor only pretends to love justice.'

'Aye, there's a politician for you. He has no method except shouting the loudest.'

'I don't believe he'd waste money chasing a skinner's daughter around the country.'

'No, you're right. He loves money as he loves himself. That is why he is for Scroop's and Grassington's projects. It is a vicious marriage of vanity and avarice. He can feather his nest as an investor in the bath, the racecourse, the skin-yard, or whatever it is, and have his term as mayor fondly remembered for them into the bargain.'

'That could be a point in their favour, though. These improvements may turn out useful for Preston. I've been reading a book that argues private vices have a way of turning into public goods.'

'That sounds an ungodly sort of book, Titus. Vice is vice, after all. And I don't like to see Thwaite, Grimshaw, Thorneley and Scroop treated like public benefactors when they've acted only in their own interests. And then, what if it all goes wrong, which it probably will? What if Thwaite and company have killed off our tried and tested way of doing things, only to find that their wonderful new projects don't work? The skin-yard for instance. It's been there for centuries and these men will sweep it away without even telling us where our leather will come from after.'

He snorted dismissively.

'Cobbler Thwaite, Rag-and-Bones Scroop, Trimmer Thorneley and Grubber Grimshaw: the Cabal of Improvement. God help Preston, that's what I say.'

Chapter 21

∞

THREE HOURS LATER, after a refreshing nap and dinner with Elizabeth, I was ready to go out once more. I had to collect Dr Hume's letter from Fidelis, for I meant to take it to Kathy's mother and let her see that her daughter was exonerated by it.

I found my friend, not in his rooms, but by the chicken coops in the yard at the back of the Lorrises' house. He was not in a position to pay me much attention as he had the Sultan of Scrafton in his arms and was much too agitated to listen to a tale of conspiracies and a Cabal.

'Two days to go before the Main and look! The Sultan is still off his feed. The case is desperate. He will be in no shape to fight if he doesn't eat. I attribute it to him being lodged near to Lorris's chickens.'

'Is he love-sick?'

'It's lust, my friend, not love. He thinks he's acquired a harem. But I'm going to disappoint him. I'm moving him further down the yard to the rabbit run where he'll not be distracted by lascivious thoughts.'

I followed Fidelis as he carried the cock to the rabbit-run, remembering how he had once used it as the location for an inspired experiment with a rat. Now the enclosure was to be the gamecock's training paddock. Tenderly he placed the cock inside the gate, shut him in and stood back to watch what he did about the bowl of feedstuff that lay waiting for him. He stalked around for a while, making his small woodwind clucks, the aquamarine feathers of his neck and crop gleaming in the watery sunshine.

'What are you feeding him?' I asked. 'Maybe he doesn't like it.'

'If only I knew what he liked! Every cockman has his favourite feed. Some say sunflower seeds, others swear by hemp or flax. I've heard of men putting garlic juice in the feed, and others that use dried ground beef. I've been unable to compare the merits of all these diets in the short time I've owned him, so I've decided to combine them.'

He pointed at the Sultan's feed bowl.

'And there you have the result. Apart from the dried beef, which I think is against nature, there is everything in that bowl that I have ever heard was good for a gamecock. It was the only logical way – a grand composition.'

Having paced the enclosure from end to end, the Sultan was now approaching the feed bowl. He inspected it, turning his head this way so he could use one eye, and then that way to bring the other eye to bear. Finally he seemed to make up his mind and picked out a speculative seed.

'Good! Very good!' whispered Fidelis, pulling me a few steps further back.

The Sultan raised his imperious head, looked around, then lowered it to peck again a little less tentatively.

'Not until he takes a third peck will I feel vindicated.'

But now the Sultan went for another walk. Stepping with the exaggerated care peculiar to many birds, and jerking his head to left and right, he made another complete circuit of the pen. We waited.

'Infuriating bird,' hissed Fidelis. 'Why doesn't he make up his mind? Ah! That's better, look.'

The Sultan was back beside the feed bowl, where he began pecking, selectively no doubt, since he had so much choice from Fidelis's mixture, but now with more will. Husks and unwanted elements of the recipe flew this way and that as he began at last to help himself with appetite.

'Come away,' said Fidelis. 'We must let him enjoy his dinner in peace. Later I will be able to check which ingredients he has rejected.'

We walked back towards the house where Fidelis, coming some way back to himself, asked about my health.

'I feel much better, but I would be glad to sit down for a moment.'

We went up to his room, which was untidy as usual with a litter of glass retorts, vials of differently coloured liquids and papers dark with dense figures and calculations. The fire was lit and I sat down at the hearthside to enjoy its warmth, but Fidelis still could not relax either his body or his mind. So he fidgeted about the room, lifting a paper here, a book or a bottle of something there, while I gave an account of my conversation with Nick Oldswick.

'He used the word Cabal,' I said. 'Thwaite, Scroop, Thorneley and Grimshaw making secret decisions that will greatly affect Preston, but entirely for their own profit.'

'Profit from what?'

'The skin-yard, certainly, and perhaps the Marsh.'

'A few pits making cheap quality leather. A riverside bog. I don't see big profits there.'

'Well, the other burgesses are feeling left out, even before they know what they're being left out of. They see the nobility joining in – Grassington, Strawboy and even Lord Derby, in his usual cautious way – and they suspect underhand dealing.'

'I will agree there has been some of that.'

'Not least in the treatment of Kathy Brock. She stands

condemned by Thwaite, who was determined to do it, and yet we know she's innocent. My conscience isn't easy about her, or about the murdered baby, who deserves justice.'

'You are no longer concerned in this now, Titus. What can you do?'

'The least I can do is show Kathy's mother the letter from your friend in Warrington. The poor woman must be miserable after being so vilely abused by Thwaite, and hearing her daughter branded a murderer.'

A few minutes later, and carrying Hume's letter, I left Fidelis's rooms and set off for the skin-yard and Margery Brock.

The laborious production of leather went on at the skin-yard just as before. I found Margery on the job that was usually done by her daughter – giving the tan-pits their daily agitation by the procedure of 'handling' with a long-handled paddle. She continued this work impassively as I read out the Warrington's doctor's account of his meeting with Kathy. When I finished the message her face still showed no expression until, suddenly, she frowned.

'She would not tell the doctor where she was going?'

'No, just where she wasn't going – neither back to Wigan nor back here.'

'But this doctor – Hume, did you call him? – he's proved she did not give birth. So why can't she come home? I know what my brother can be like: we wouldn't have let her go there except it looked so bad for her in this town that it seemed the lesser evil. But that's all changed now. She should be safe in Preston now that she can prove her innocence.'

Very gently, I said, 'Not necessarily, Margery. The Mayor is powerful. If he really wants her to be guilty, he can make it so. Your daughter is a clever girl and she knows this.'

'But you know the truth! You can tell them.'

'I have been turned out of the Coroner's job now. I have no influence. I am just a citizen, like you.'

When I left Margery I walked along the lane towards the wharf, where the remains of the inn had now been completely removed. I saw nothing but flattened brick-dusty earth, bordered and divided by pegs and string to denote the footprints of what looked like more than one new building coming in the old inn's place.

The vessel *Maid of Man*, that had taken Clarkson and his family away, was tied up once more, leaning at a drunken angle as it rested on the low-tide mud against the side of the jetty. Large bales were being unloaded on to the wharf. I asked the Captain what news of the former innkeeper and his family.

'They went ashore in Liverpool, which is where we turn around. That were the last I saw of 'em. He were a good innkeeper – said fool things sometimes, but honest.'

'Do you merely shuttle between here and Liverpool?'

'This is an Isle of Man boat. We do a three-way trip. We bring all sorts of goods from Liverpool to Douglas, which we exchange mostly – this time of year, after harvest – for this raw flax here for the linen manufacture, which we ship here to Preston. From Preston, it's mainly passengers like Clarkson and family, which we unload at Liverpool dock and so do it all again.'

He sighed, as if disappointed with his lot.

'It is a repetitive life,' I said. 'You would like more adventure in it, no doubt, being a seaman.'

He looked at me doubtfully.

'You've never been to sea, if you say that. The elements give us all the adventure we require. No, I'd only like to turn around faster at this port here. I am always standing off the mouth of the estuary waiting for the tide, or I'm waiting for a berth here at the Wharf. More room for more ships, that's what they need. We'd land a deal of Isle of Man flax here if they had more berth-room. We won't be able to leave here now until Sunday.'

I took my leave and wandered back along the lane. Looking to my right across the Marsh, I noticed a slight figure at the far edge of it, close to the largest of the Marsh's ponds, known as Colt Hole. He was looking through some sort of sighting device mounted on a tripod. I immediately turned on to the Marsh, following a raised path that snaked around the clumps of tree and reed and the claggy holes containing a mixture of fresh and salt water. Here and there cattle and sheep grazed. A curlew cried and a small flock of shell-duck got up and flew away.

I reached him in little more than five minutes.

'How do you do, Mr Kay?' I said shaking hands. 'I looked for you at the Assembly on Saturday but did not see you.'

'I do not attend assemblies,' he said. His response to me was a little cold.

'Oh! You should. You cannot work all the time.'

'I have much to do – sightings to take, and measurements. The figures are many, making the work extremely mathematical.'

'But what are you doing out here on the Marsh? I did not think your business was here.'

He looked warily at me.

'I am doing exercises. I am testing my apomecometer.'

'You are not surveying any part of the Marsh, then?'

'We have been working at the site of the Skeleton Inn: they need new buildings after the fire – another inn, harbourmaster's office, customs house and so on.'

'Not the skin-yard? You talked about your interest in tanneries when you supped with us.'

'Did I? No, I have not just been asked to survey the skin-yard.'

'"Not just" you say – then part of a larger survey, is it?'

Kay did not answer but asked me instead, and a little huffily, to kindly leave him, if I pleased, to his work. Nonplussed by the man's lack of friendliness, I left him to it and returned by way of the meandering footpath towards the road.

You will remember that there are two ways from the top of Watery Lane to Preston, and that the broader and easier of these is Water Lane, the address of the neighbours Burgess Abraham Scroop and Doctor Basilius Harrod. It was the way that, on this occasion, I took in making my way home.

I was striding along when I came to the Scroop house. A small crowd had gathered around the gate that opened into the short drive, at the end of which, in front of the house, I saw a small funeral carriage. This was drawn by a single plumed black pony and stood ready to receive the coffin, for the bringing out of which the house's front door stood open. But who I wondered was dead?

I approached the group of watchers.

'What has happened here?'

The nearest of the spectators, a toothless woman called Jean Garnish, shushed me and clattered my elbow with hers.

'Look, Mr Cragg,' she said, pointing.

The coffin was now coming through the front door carried fore and aft by two undertaker's men. As they turned to slide it on to the carriage, we could see the coffin broadside. It was barely two feet long.

'One of the children,' said Jean, crossing herself. 'And the babby, by the size of that box.'

Following the coffin out of the house were the Scroop family, the adults looking sombre, the children in tears. Bringing up the rear was Dr Harrod. They walked in this order behind the carriage as it circled around and headed towards us at the gate.

'*Requiescat*! Rest in peace!' called out some as the cortege passed into the road, and several crossed themselves. But the mourners paid no attention, looking neither to right nor left.

'Where are they going?'

Instead of turning in the direction of Preston and of one of our two churches, St John's or St George's, the little funeral procession turned down Water Lane and towards the junction with the road that led westward along the shore of the estuary. Some of the group around the gate began to straggle after them. Jean Garnish, who did not follow their example, banged me with her elbow once more.

'Likely they're burying it at Kirkham church. It's a bonny grave-yard they've got there, and more than one Scroop grave's in it already.'

'Aye,' said the woman standing on her other flank. 'It's a bonnier spot than St George's, is Kirkham. And quieter.'

'That's right,' said Jean, looking after the funeral carriage. 'You don't want a big to-do when a babby dies. You want to let it go quietly. I did with three of ours. Quietly and quickly, that's all that me and Charlie wanted. A few prayers, word of the Book, nod of the head, and into the ground sharp.'

She sniffed. I took a sideways look but she showed no emotion.

'The Scroop's baby son has died.'

I found Elizabeth at home counting washing and making entries in her washing-book.

'I know,' she said. 'It had been sickly in the afternoon, I've heard, and then in the evening it had a fit and seconds later was dead. Very sudden.'

'Strange, how all their sons die, while their daughters thrive. Scroop will be sorry. I wonder if this new Coroner of ours will be holding an inquest.'

'There's no call for that. Doctor Harrod was in the house at the time. He pronounced it dead of natural causes and made a certificate. Oh dear! I'll be patching this sheet soon. See?'

She held the sheet up to the light to show where it was worn.

'Ah yes,' I said, looking. 'A bit threadbare. If it was me, I would have Luke examine it first.'

'Why would Luke examine this sheet?'

'Don't be daft. I mean the body. What's niggling me is the way that, the whole time I was investigating the tan-pit case, the Scroop family kept getting in the way.'

Elizabeth looked at me in kindly exasperation.

'Titus! Let it go! You're not Coroner now. Whatever goes on in that house is no longer your business.'

'I expect you are right.'

I went to bed early, immediately after supper. 'Let it go', Elizabeth had said. Yet I couldn't. My habits of thought remained those of a coroner. I had trained myself for years, as assiduously as Fidelis was training his Sultan, to apply myself to death, the reasons for it and the consequences of it. So this dead baby girl – found in a tan-pit, denied the chance to grow up, and now buried in the unmarked grave of a pauper – would not relax the grip of her tiny fingers on me. I lay in the dark, thinking the whole case through, from the very beginning when sensible Ellen Kite had found the body while 'handling' the tan-pits, to the end when Thwaite took over my duties and so mishandled the inquest and wilfully – I couldn't help this, I really did think it was wilful – pointed his finger at a purely innocent girl.

No, it would not let me go, and nor could I let it go.

Chapter 22

THE NEWS OF the arrest of Jon O'Rorke, and his incarceration at the House of Correction, came early in the morning. The Mayor had decided to question the servant after Oswald Mallender's return from Wigan, where he'd gone with his constables the Parkin boys in an attempt to pick up Kathy Brock. Returning without her, Mallender had not had much to say publicly about his reception at the irascible Terence Pitt's house. The plausible speculation was that the two rival headboroughs had locked horns, and that Mallender had a few points broken off his antlers. It is also said that Pitt had told Mallender that, if he was looking for a murderer, he should forget about Kathy, wayward though she be, and look no further than the servants' hall at the house of Abraham Scroop.

There was a set of cramped and stygian prisoner cells beneath Moot Hall, where men were kept under suspicion awaiting either the magistrate's questioning or the grand jury's decision whether to commit them for trial. O'Rorke could therefore not normally have expected to be held in the relative comfort of the house of correction, but on this occasion the lock-ups at Moot Hall were even less habitable than usual, being flooded by the building's water tank leaking directly into them.

I was on friendly terms with the keeper of the House of

Correction, Arnold Limb, who had frequently helped me by look-ing after bodies awaiting inquest. This time, however, he was a little less sure than usual that he wanted to help, and needed persuasion.

'If it should come to the attention of the Mayor that I let you in to see the prisoner I may be censured.'

'He won't know if we don't tell anyone. Look, Arnold, this is the case that Thwaite's used to discredit me and destroy my coronership. I know he has got it terribly wrong. Help me to find out what really happened.'

'Is O'Rorke innocent? Do you think so?'

'I am certain of it. But he might go to the gallows yet, if Thwaite has his way.'

'Very well, Cragg. You can have twenty minutes with him, and no more. And if anyone asks how you spoke to him, it was through the barred window of his cell, and entirely without my knowledge.'

I had to work hard also to bring O'Rorke around, as he was in a foul humour – pacing his cell, wringing his hands and cursing.

'I have two birds going to the pit tomorrow,' he railed. 'After months of preparation, they're primed and ready to fight for their lives. But they're out there and I'm in here and I'm buggered if I can do anything about it. And on top of that I'm out on my ear from the Scroops'. See?'

He waved a paper at me which I took and read:

To Jon O'Rorke,

With this letter you are to consider yourself summarily dismissed from my employment, and must remove your belongings from my house immediately. If you do not, they will be thrown or given away.

Abraham Scroop.

I handed the letter back to him.

'I imagine you are not surprised.'

'Nothing surprises me with the English. This is all a plot to keep me out of the Main of Cocks, of that I am sure. They are afraid they cannot beat my birds in a fair fight, so they put me in prison. I have large bets with Lord Strange, Mr Shuttleworth and other gentlemen. If I don't turn up with my birds, there will be no contest, and they will be mightily frustrated.'

'How do you, a servant, have the means to strike large bets with such rich men?'

'Borrowing, Mr Cragg. I will not say who from, but I have had support.'

'Then cannot this backer or backers help you get out of here?'

'On the mortgage system, may it be damned, I cannot rely on them.'

'Your birds are mortgaged?'

'Yes. So, if I don't pay up, they take the birds. The men I've mortgaged with may prefer that outcome.'

So it was not until I showed him Dr Hume of Warrington's letter that he began to be pliable. He proved to my surprise to be perfectly literate and read it through in disbelief. Then he read it again and realized it was no prank, and no illusion, but his manumission, his ticket of leave.

'This proves that Kathy was not this dead baby's mam!'

'Yes. She cannot have been.'

'So there's nothing to connect me to the tan-pit baby.'

'Precisely. It exonerates you, O'Rorke, as well as her.'

'Then for God's sake make it public. Go out and exonerate me, as you put it.'

I was not ready to let him off as lightly as that.

'All in good time. First—'

'I don't *have* time – the Main is tomorrow.'

'But first, my own time with you is even shorter, and I would like you to tell me about the Scroop family, if you please.'

He gave me a cunning look.

'But you're not Coroner now.'

'Let's say I have unfinished business.'

'Very well, I'll answer your questions if you promise to take that letter to Mr Thwaite immediately you leave here. Immediately.'

'I promise.'

'What do you want to know?'

I asked him first how the Scroops were with each other: what was their give-and-take as a family. O'Rorke, a natural talker, soon settled into the narrative mode.

'They're not a happy lot, Sir. All that money, the big modern house – you'd think they'd be content. I came up out of the bog, where every day I'd the same food, and with nothing in my head but whatever the hedge school had to teach, but I'm happier than what they are. They bicker all the time, and never laugh. Old Scroop hates the house. He's almost never there, but always at work, or somewhere else – with his fancy woman, if you can believe the gossip in the kitchen. Mrs Scroop doesn't care. I think she hates Scroop. The way she is kept all the time expecting another little Scroop, only because he wants a son to inherit his money. She's got him a few, but none of them's thrived – this one that's just died is only the latest in the line.'

'What about the daughters – how are they?'

'They've one thing in common. They never do rough and tumble, fun and games, not even the youngsters. And they certainly don't go in for loving fun – you know? – kisses, tickles, cuddles. Those girls're not natural that way. I'd rather be kissing a carriage wheel than Harriet or Amelia Scroop, the oldest two of 'em.'

'Why did the family come home early from the Assembly last Saturday?'

'Oh, yes! There was a row in the carriage coming home, and it was even angrier than usual, I can tell you. It was about something Harriet said to her mother, and old Scroop wanted to know what it was.'

'I saw it!' I exclaimed. 'Just before they left the Assembly, they were arguing and I saw Harriet whispering in her mother's ear, and I saw Mrs Scroop's reaction. It was she who insisted that they all go immediately home.'

'Harriet wouldn't repeat it to her father, anyway, and nor would her ma. Got himself into a right passion about it, Scroop did, first of all talking about a dance Harriet was supposed to have with someone—'

'Do none of the other servants know what this was all about? Mrs Scroop's own maid perhaps?'

'No one knew anything for sure. That woman doesn't confide in her maid – or in anyone at all. Self-contained, she is. In the carriage Scroop was shouting that he had a right to know why they'd left the Assembly before the Derbys left, that it was humiliating and they must tell him. But neither of them would say one word. Doc Harrod had ridden with us into town for the Assembly but, when he came out along with them, Mrs S told him sharply he had to make his own way home. Cook – who's been in the family longest of all – when I told her about this, said the truth's yet to come out from that direction.'

'Can you tell what she meant?'

'I'll tell you something, and it's interesting. Scroop and Harrod have known each other for years, but Scroop doesn't go into Harrod's house – not ever. Harrod, now, can't keep away from the Scroops. He's always in there, playing cards and games with the girls, reading to Mrs Scroop, running errands, doing any little thing he can – nothing is too much trouble for Dr Harrod in that house. He's there more often than the master himself and I do not exaggerate.'

'So what does the cook mean?'

O'Rorke tapped the side of his nose confidentially.

'Harriet's growing up at last, and seeing the kind of thing kids can't ordinarily see, Cook says. So now, after all these years, the girl's added up two and two – the first two being her mother, and the other two being Harrod. Understand me?'

He showed the two first fingers of each hand and clasped them together.

'Two plus two, yes?'

'Ah! I see.'

It would not be the first time, I thought, that a man had found himself in love with his best friend's wife – or that a wife had fallen for the family doctor, come to that. Anyway this was only hearsay of hearsay – it was all in the mind of the cook, apparently, and I had no time to pursue it now. My twenty minutes had nearly expired.

'But all this recent fretting and arguing in the family,' I continued, 'couldn't it be from the strain of having the new baby, the son? Everyone would surely have been anxious about its health and survival. They'd lost so many already, after all, and they have indeed now lost this one. Had he been sickly from the start? How did he look to you?'

'I never saw him.'

'What about the other servants?'

'None of us saw the baby. The mother kept him close to her, fed him from her own breast, apparently, stayed with him all the time. No one else except the doctor had seen him yet. His report was just that the baby was very small and sickly.'

'So they *were* anxious about him.'

O'Rorke shrugged.

'If they were, they didn't say so.'

A knock came at the door and there was Limb telling me I'd

outstayed my time and please would I leave? Before I did, the Irishman reminded me of my promise.

'Very well, Mr O'Rorke, I am on my way to Moot Hall directly.'

'There's one more thing, Mr Cragg, before you go. You no longer think that I might have set fire to your inquest, I hope.'

I had forgotten that I had ever harboured such a suspicion. Now I was able quite truthfully to reassure him.

'No, no. I don't. Not any more.'

'That's something I would also appreciate being known around town, if you can arrange it.'

I decided that I would fulfil my promise to O'Rorke by submitting the document in evidence at the Recorder's office, rather than at Moot Hall, where it might go astray in the chaos of Mayor Thwaite's office. But I was not going to be fool enough to part with the original. Instead I would get Furzey to write it out, and then find a couple of witnesses to attest Furzey's version as a true copy of the original. This copy could then be furnished to the Recorder along with a note from me explaining how it came into existence and asking that it be taken in evidence in any hearing or trial of Jon O'Rorke in the matter of the tan-pit baby.

All this done, I found Thorneley at his place of business.

'You will have to stop pursuing Kathy Brock and let O'Rorke go when you read this,' I told him as I handed him the copy of the letter.

He quickly did so, pursing his lips in what I hoped was disappointment.

'Hmm. As you say, it does tend to justify the Brock girl, though whether it gets O'Rorke out of hot water we shall have to see.'

'O'Rorke's only come into the story as Kathy Brock's old beau. If she is no longer suspected, he cannot be.'

'As I say, we shall have to see.'

'You must let him go today. Tomorrow his gamecocks are fighting in the Michaelmas Main.'

Thorneley's head rocked back, his face crumpling in a comic show of disbelief.

'Of all the— You are not serious, Cragg. We must let him go because of a cock-fight? Are you out of your mind?'

'You may be, if you keep the man locked up. Mr Richard Shuttleworth has an interest in this cock-fight – a large pecuniary interest, I am told. So has Lord Strange. Neither of them, I fancy, will thank you very kindly if Mr Jon O'Rorke cannot bring his birds to the pit tomorrow.'

My mention of these two members of Parliament, one of them none other than the heir of Lord Derby, was decisive. Thorneley could ill-afford to stand in the way of his betters' betting, which could be on such a scale as to bring water to your eyes. He dropped Kathy's letter down on to his desk, then ushered me out of the door. As I left, I heard him shouting for his clerk and, looking back, saw the writer slide on to his desk-stool and pick up his pen. The Recorder was about to draft something, and I was confident it was a warrant for the release of O'Rorke. This he would then take across to Moot Hall for Thwaite's signature. So the Irishman would be free to fight his birds at the Michaelmas Main and the Mayor would have to start all over again in his search for someone to prosecute.

Fidelis, looking pale, harassed and very agitated, was making his way up Fisher Gate. He ran across to me.

'You look as if someone's been shooting dried peas at your bedroom windows all night,' I observed.

'It's true, I got no sleep. I only hope the Sultan did. He gave a mighty crow this morning at dawn, I do know that. Just one more dawn and then this will be over, one way or the other. Then I can breathe freely again.'

'How far are you committed? Will you lose much if the Sultan loses his bout?'

'The Sultan losing is unthinkable, Cragg. Inconceivable. Unconscionable.'

'I see. So you are very much hoping for his success.'

'I will be ruined if he loses. I have struck such bets as you would not believe. I am heading for arrest and a spell in the compter, Titus, if the Sultan doesn't come through.'

'Anything I can do, Luke, short of actually attending the contest, which I wouldn't like at all, you know.'

'Well, that's the very thing I was going to ask you, Titus. I have to have a second.'

'A second? As in a duel?'

'No, no, not as in a duel, as in a cock-fight. It is the rules of the Main. Every cocker with a bird in the pit must have a second man behind him to hold his coat, or the said cock shall be disqualified and the victory awarded to its opponent.'

I laughed.

'You are quoting? That sounds like rules all right – pompous and pointless, very often. You should read the rules of bowls.'

'You will do it?'

'I am hardly the right man, Luke. I have just once been to the cockpit, I admit a long time ago, but I hated every moment of it. I see no reason why I should like it any better now.'

'You were just a stripling then. Now you are a man and less sensitive. And besides the game has changed. It is more civilized and less savage. Please. Be my second.'

When I told Elizabeth that I was to be Fidelis's second at the cockpit tomorrow she seized me by the collar of my coat.

'You have *not* been gambling, Titus! I should be very much distressed if I knew that you had, or intended to, risk our money.'

'I have my faults and vices, my love, as you know better than anyone. But I have never engaged in gambling.'

'That's not true. I have seen you buy tickets for the horses at the August races.'

'Oh well! That signifies nothing. Everyone in Preston does it, even the vicar.'

'And we play piquet for money.'

'For pennies, Elizabeth. These people go in for stakes that are on rather a different scale – hundreds of pounds at a time.'

'Titus!' said Elizabeth, tugging for emphasis on the flaps of my collar. 'That is what I am afraid of. You may go there with the best of intentions, that you will not lay a bet, or take a bet, or however you say it – that you will not put our money at risk. But then after a few glasses of wine, who knows? I shall not be there to restrain you. You may throw caution away.'

'I shall not need you. I am there on official duty as Fidelis's second, as he must have one or his bird will be voided from its fight and he will lose his own bets.'

'He has gambled?'

'I fear so. And without me he will surely lose, or so he says. Out of friendship I must go in to support him.'

She softened and kissed me.

'Of course you must, my Titus, or what is friendship for?'

Chapter 23

WHENEVER A MAIN of Cocks is held at Preston, the streets around the cockpit attract a throng of idlers and gawpers jostling to watch for the gamesters arriving with their birds, exchanging late intelligence on the fights and then, from reports relayed through the open windows, trying to form a picture of the action inside. There is also the usual contingent of jugglers and fiddlers, trinket hawkers and piemen, storytellers, ballad mongers, orange sellers and ribbon peddlers, and always one or two religious fanatics preaching hell-fire and damnation to anyone who bought such tawdry.

Pushing our way through and into the building, we ticket holders found a six-foot circle contained within a parapet that reached no higher than a man's chest. This was surrounded by a space for standing room and then by seven circular rows of spectators' benches rising and receding like a small Colosseum. Behind the top row of seats was a landing where men could take relief from the action, strike bets and obtain wine and food at several times the market rate. In the wall were the windows through which commentary and results were conveyed to the outside world.

It was only when Fidelis and I got in there, and the fighting began, that I began to suspect I had been tricked. When I'd earlier

asked him about the duties of a gamester's second, Fidelis had been
vague and assured me I would pick it up as we went along. So,
during the first bout, and again during the second, I looked down
from the high surrounding benches to see what these other gamesters' seconds were doing, that I might copy them and creditably
carry out my role, whatever it may be. But I could not even see one.
Most of the gamesters had a few fellows in attendance, but none
of these performed any useful service, only shouted and guffawed
from time to time, and passed around bottles.

'What exactly am I to do, as your second?' I asked.

'Oh, you know, hold the towel, mop my brow when things get
hot, that kind of thing.'

'The towel? Just show me anyone holding a towel around this
arena.'

'Well, I—'

'Luke, there are no seconds, are there? There is no earthly reason to have them. It was all just a ruse.'

He nodded his head contritely, then gave me his most mischievous smile.

'I'm sorry, Titus. I just couldn't think of another way of getting
you in here. If you were not here I should lack your steadying hand,
you know, at my moment of triumph – or catastrophe, whichever
it's to be. The Sultan and I need you, d'you see?'

He clapped me on the shoulder.

'And we're right glad you've not let us down.'

Those two initial bouts showed me that the order of cock-fighting had not changed much since I'd seen it as a young man during
my time studying at the Inns of Court. The first contestant is called
and loosed in the ring to strut around and be assessed by the
crowd on points of beauty, strength and haughtiness. He is then
picked out so that his opponent may similarly show off his best
points. The birds are then simultaneously lifted into the ring on

opposite sides and held or bated by their owners for one timed minute, out of reach but in full sight of each other. This bating 'sets' them, in the jargon, that is, it gets their hackles up so that, by the time the timekeeper's bell sounds and they're released, the fighters are ready to go at it with all the murderous hostility at their command.

Not all cock-fights unfold in the same way, which, as the fancy will tell you, is what makes the game into a sport. Often there is an initial phase of wary circling in which the birds try a few tentative attacks. But this is not invariable. Some birds launch into the fight with everything they've got from the moment their feet land in the straw, their flightless wings cocked, their spurs and beaks slashing as feathers fly up and float in the air between the gouts of flying blood. The initial attacker is not always the winner, however. Staying power, gameness or stomach are thought by many to count for more than early aggressiveness, which is even reckoned a fault by some, a sign of juvenile inexperience. Wily old birds of the ring are practised at defence and happy to wait for the first storm of attack to blow itself out before moving in themselves to strike the killer blow. One way or another, the contest is decided when a bird goes down and is no longer able to fight back. Often he is dead, or beyond help, though defeated birds may be nursed back by their owners to fight another day. In many cases these survivors, if they profited from the first experience, can go on to win the next time.

The Sultan of Scrafton's all-important contest was listed towards the end of the programme, so for much of the time Fidelis and I were spectators. Once the sequence of fights was under way, I felt disinclined to watch each one as it came along, but observed instead the extraordinary passion of the crowd. This was quite beyond anything one sees in elections, mad-houses or even the racecourse. I am persuaded that the volume of hoarse, hellish noise, the flying spittle, the obscene curses and imprecations, the tears and the abandon are all multiplied by their confinement to the cockpit's small and circular space.

I felt Fidelis's elbow nudging me and saw that Captain Strawboy had arrived, accompanying Lord Strange and two or three other young men, all of them drunk. No sooner had they settled into their places than Strawboy spotted us and made his way over.

'Dr Faustus is most pleased with himself this morning,' he said. 'He is crowing with delight to be taking on a rival doctor.'

He laughed, then added laconically.

'And one that will inevitably lose the prize, and also our wager, I am afraid. I suppose you'll be good for the money, Fidelis.'

My friend was incensed. He jumped to his feet and stood nose to nose with Strawboy, his fists tight.

'Only a scoundrel would ask a gentleman such a question.'

'Oh let us not fight, you and I,' said Strawboy, negligently. 'We have our gamecocks to do it for us, after all.'

He spun round and returned to his companions, who were now cheering Lord Strange as he carried his gamecock Hector Hardrada to the side of the pit.

'Are you by any chance good for the money, Luke?' I asked.

He turned to me, still furious.

'He was taunting me – goading me. Oh, it is very unwise of him. He does not know which bird will prevail, he cannot, and if it is mine I will make him choke on those words yet.'

'But are you good for the money?'

Fidelis's expression softened.

'It is five hundred pounds, Titus. I can manage that but there are another five hundred or so in side-bets. Let us say I shall be a very penurious doctor indeed if the Sultan does not do me proud.'

The master of ceremonies now called the next bout, between Lord Strange's Hector Hardrada and the first of Jon O'Rorke's fighters, a bird called Sir Lancelot. The latter's owner, freed since yesterday from the House of Correction, was a striking sight at the ringside, holding his bird in the bating position for the prescribed sixty seconds, his face a mask of intense concentration. Sir Lancelot was a tawny fowl, with deep red comb and wattles to outmatch his master's own bright ginger hair, and he was straining with some spirit to get at the opposite fowl, as if O'Rorke's own fierce will to overcome was being transmitted into the bird through his finger-ends.

Moments later O'Rorke and Strange heard the bell and released their birds. There was no preliminary sparring but an immediate clash so ferociously equal – with first one and then the other gaining the advantage – that even after a full minute of tangled and bloody conflict no one could have predicted the outcome.

I looked at O'Rorke at the side of the ring. He was jiggling uncontrollably up and down, his features distorted, his cheeks red with arousal, his fists pounding the rim of the parapet, and his mouth open howling from uninhibited blood-lust. These transports did not last long, however, for now Strange's bird gave up the fight as abruptly as he had hurled himself into it, flopping down into a submissive posture, wings outspread on the straw, and no longer attempted to reply to the assaults of the beak and spurs of the other. Half the house gave a collective groan while the other half roared with delight. Within a few more seconds the contest was done and O'Rorke's bird was crowing his supremacy.

That the dismissed servant O'Rorke could bring a bird of his own to the pit and defeat Lord Derby's heir shows the levelling nature of the pit-side. Indeed one may speculate that it's for this reason and not the savage blood-letting that so many call for cock-fighting to be suppressed. The surrounding gallery behind the top row of seating is no less easy-going in matters of class, wealth and education. Here men of all stripes meet and argue, wager and drink together, and in doing so quite forget, for a while at least, the distinctions that normally divide them. Who is to say this is a bad thing? Not me.

I was walking around this gallery five minutes later on my way from the jakes, seeing several that I knew including the captain of the *Maid of Man* and Dr Harrod, accompanied by a sallow youth – his son Abel. Then I came face to face with the surveyor Joss Kay.

'You said you were not a follower of the sport,' I said.

He pulled a sour face.

'No. I do not like it very much, as it has little of improvement in it.'

'Do you not approve after all of how the birds improve by careful breeding?'

'I may have said they do, but for what? The bird is a fighting engine, good for nothing except quarrelling and killing or being killed. And when it is killed the flesh is bitter and stringy to eat.'

'So why are you here?'

'Let's say I am diverted by the sight of so many men in tears. Are you fighting a bird yourself?'

'No, I am second to Dr Fidelis. You've finished surveying the Marsh, then?'

'The Marsh? Who told you that?'

'I saw you at it, did I not?'

'But I told you at the time, I was merely practising. I was setting up my apomecometer.'

'Whereas I know that you were taking real measurements and I strongly suspect those measurements covered the whole of the Marsh.'

The heat of the cock-fighting had perhaps made me speak with less reserve than I might usually.

'Why would I do that?' he challenged.

'I don't know – perhaps you don't yourself.'

He came closer to me and spoke into my ear.

'I have been sworn to secrecy. What I know and what I do not know is also a secret.'

He was speaking most decisively. I patted his back in a companionable way.

'As long as we agree you have apomecometrised the Marsh for reasons still to be determined, I will make an end to it for now. But it bears on a case I was engaged in, Kay, and in a way I still am.'

I went back to my seat and found Fidelis missing. I glanced at the programme and realized that he must have gone down to the bird room to collect his contestant. The Sultan of Scrafton was on his way to the pit for the next fight.

'Gentle-men,' shouted the master of ceremonies two minutes later, in his laborious and oddly emphasized manner, 'we announce the tenth bout of the morning, which is for a challenge cup of gilded silver to the value of ten guineas, and to contend for it will you please welcome the first contestant, FROM the cockyard of Dr Luke Fidelis, and weighing in at one pound and fourteen ounces, I give you: thee Sulta-an of SCRAFTON.'

The Sultan was undoubtedly an impressive bird. First of all he was visibly proud in the extreme. Second, he appeared bursting to fight as he took his measured steps around the ring, evidently appreciating the wild cheers and plaudits of the crowd. Thirdly, he looked fit – light on his feet and alert, his eye most fiery and his comb exuberant.

No contest is won on splendour alone. It was not until Fidelis reached out and gathered the Sultan back into his arms that his opponent's name rang from the mouth of the master of ceremonies to remind us he must prove himself in action.

'Gentlemen, once again will you now welcome his opponent, FROM the cockyard of Captain James Strawboy, and weighing in at two pounds and two ounces I give you: Doctooooor FAUSTUS.'

More cheers, more waving of hats and programmes, accompanied Strawboy's champion as he stalked to and fro in the straw, flicking his head this way and that as if to say any challenge, any test, and he was equal to it. Faustus was not as beautiful as the Sultan; not as bursting with aristocratic *hauteur;* and certainly not as colourful, being largely white. On the other hand he had one big thing in his favour: he was two inches taller and, on the scales, four ounces heavier.

I was, without realizing it, sitting on the utter edge of my seat and straining upwards to see everything that could be seen.

The two cocks were now presented in the bating position, to get them properly set. The timekeeper held up his watch with one hand while the other hovered over his handbell. Fidelis's face was uniformly taut, white and strained, but exactly as the bell rang and he released his bird, he puffed out his cheeks and two bright spots of red came on to them. The die was cast – but which way would it roll?

The Sultan and Faustus took a cautious approach from the start. They were behaving as if they felt they were well matched, despite Faustus's advantage in size. This way and that they went for twenty seconds, then thirty. Soon they must engage. Cocks that do not start to fight within sixty seconds are both scratched and the contest called null.

That humiliation was avoided a few seconds later when the Sultan made a furious attack. He raised both wings and went in talons first, trying to slash with the metal spurs on his heels that augmented the somewhat smaller ones that nature provided him with. Faustus dodged with his own wings upwards and turned the Sultan around.

For a moment a flush of excitement passed through my own

body. My throat was dried and constricted, my heart worked harder and I heard a yell – my own – burst suddenly out. The Sultan had got a beak-hold on Faustus's wattle, who in turn was trying to peck out the Sultan's eye. Twisting this way and that, striving to get the other bird off its feet, they both lost their footing and came down together to a great shout from the crowd.

What emerged from that storm of beating wings and slashing spurs was that the Sultan somehow achieved supremacy. He seemed to screw around in an instant, levered himself upright, and was now standing on top of the other bird's body, stabbing down on to it with murderous slashes of its beak and claws. At that moment (though I did not realize it until later) I understood what previously I had found incomprehensible – the ecstasy of the crowds in Rome's Colosseum, their frenzied joy in the gory defeat of lions, the dismembering of Christians and the evisceration of gladiators. Blood was being spilt and I was excited, heady, charged up with what I can only call demonic joy. I cannot explain it, as I am a peace-loving man in most respects. It is simply the fact.

It was over and the Sultan of Scrafton had won his ten guinea prize and a hundred times more in bets for his owner. I said to him, as we jostled our way out of the cockpit at the end of the programme, 'That was extraordinary, Luke.'

'You have become a convert to the game?'

'No, but I'm sorry to say that I did enjoy it. I trust I satisfactorily carried out my duties as your Second.'

'That was your only duty – to enjoy it.'

'I hope the Sultan's eye is not badly hurt. It was one of his handsomest features.'

'It may be entirely saved. I am hoping it appears worse than it is.'

'And what will you do with all that cash?'

'I believe I shall buy myself a home, Titus, and become a devoted householder. It is a prime example of your Dr Mandevil's philosophy: vice leading directly to virtue.'

Chapter 24

THAT NIGHT WE ate our Michaelmas Eve dinner of roasted goose, after which we sang songs until midnight and the next day lay late in bed, getting up only when it was time to go to church.

'Oh, take me for a walk,' said Elizabeth, after the service. 'It is such a fine day and there is an hour or more before dinner. Let's go and see how work is progressing on rebuilding the Inn at the wharf.'

So we made our way in the direction that had become so familiar to me in the last two weeks. At the wharf we found the old inn was being replaced by rising wooden spars and connecting struts that would be the framework of the new building.

'The skeleton of the Skeleton Inn,' said Elizabeth. 'I hope they will not change the name.'

A figure came into sight from Watery Lane, and headed straight on to the wharf itself. He wore a cap, a great coat and carried two wicker baskets. It was Jon O'Rorke.

I called to him. The dismissed servant strolled over to us with something of a swagger and we exchanged greetings. I introduced Elizabeth.

'Your lady wife, is it?' he said, looking her up and down. 'And very nice, too.'

'What brings you down here?' I asked.

'I'm bringing the last of my things to the boat – my fighting cocks,' he said. 'I have everything else on board.'

'Are you leaving?'

'Yes, I'm off, never to return. I sail by the *Maid of Man*. There's nothing for me here and I go back home with a few guineas in my pocket, which is satisfactory.'

'I'm sorry you have been dismissed.'

'I am not. I have been a good enough servant, but I have higher aspirations.'

There was a shout from the quayside.

'I must be away,' said O'Rorke. 'The tide's turned and they're sailing.'

Again he nodded his head towards Elizabeth, this time a little more deliberately, and said in a slow, savouring way, 'Madam, there is in your eye something that promises a man great pleasure. I congratulate you – and you sir. Good-bye and good luck.'

We saw him on board and then watched as the crew went through the routine of casting off, hoisting canvas and bearing away on the turning tide. The water was just past its fullest; the river was swollen and the mud banks and shoals well covered as far as the eye could see. We waved and the figure standing in the waist of the ship raised his rustic cap in farewell.

Over the next night September gave way to October, with the new month breaking dry and breezy, though with the ever-present promise of showers. Indeed, by dinner time, rain had fallen with sudden, brief ferocity, after which the extraordinary news began to spread around town that Abraham Scroop was missing. It seems he had ridden to Kirkham in the early morning to speak to the mason about his infant son's gravestone. Three hours later his riderless horse came cantering back through Ashton and into the end of Water Lane.

The first presumption was that Scroop had been thrown when his horse spooked at an unexpected noise, or reared when a dog snapped at its pastern. Kirkham is some seven miles distant and it was thought that surely, given time, the rider himself would turn up alive, albeit bruised, footsore and ill-tempered. After another couple of hours and with still no sign of him the alarm was raised, which shortly reached the centre of town. Thereupon a mounted party assembled in the Market Place with the object of going along the Kirkham road to search for him. The party, made up of fewer than a dozen riders, had been raised by Dr Harrod, who had heard of the emergency on his return from a round of country calls. I decided to join the searchers myself and, a few moments after I had done so, Fidelis too rode up with the same intention. Blowing a short brass horn, Harrod called us into a ring around him.

'We shall ride directly to Kirkham and, if we do not find him along the way, we shall scatter with each man returning by a different route so that one of us must find him. Everyone should have a hunting horn to assist communication.'

The still country air felt cleansed, for, after a gusty start to the day, there had been an hour of rain around midday and now, in stiller air, sunlight picked out beads of water hanging in the hedgerows. From time to time a game bird got up out of the hedge and rattled away into the distance, squawking and scattering the water drops behind it.

'Perhaps that was the cause of the accident,' observed Fidelis. 'His horse startled.'

'He may have been taken into some wayside cottage and is being tended as we speak with vinegar and brown paper,' I said.

There were a few such dwellings along the road and we enquired at each of them but no one had seen Scroop, either horsed or on foot. Nor did we meet him on the road, or find him lying in the verge.

So we arrived at St Michael's churchyard in Kirkham, where we dismounted beside a fresh and unidentified heap of earth – the Scroop infant's resting place. Harrod had sent a man galloping ahead with orders to fetch the stonecutter with whom Scroop had had his appointment, and now we all gathered around to hear the man, a wiry fellow with a blind eye and a crooked back.

'Oh ay, Mr Scroop were here,' he said. He gestured in an actorly way at the bare mound of earth, much moistened by the recent rain.

'He fetch me here to this spot and told me the words to be carved on his little laddie's stone. Then we talked about what kind of lettering I had to cut, and how to set the stone.'

He dug in the pocket of his leather apron and produced a paper covered with writing.

'See here, he've writ it all down, which I needed him to, so odd it was, the inscription he wanted.'

He held up the paper and waved it in the air. I just caught sight of the baby's designated name – 'Loammi Scroop' – before he had folded it and slipped it back into his pocket. I hadn't seen the inscription but it certainly seemed an unusual name.

But Harrod was not concerned with the wording of the gravestone.

'What time did Mr Scroop set off again for Preston?' he asked.

The mason shrugged.

'It was just after a quarter before eight when I left him. I noticed because the church clock struck and he'd got out his watch to set the time and then wind it. I never saw him ride away as I went back to my yard.'

He looked around at the encircling Preston men, his good eye rolling around and looking particularly bright beside its cloudy and sightless counterpart.

'So what is your purpose here, gents? Is it a hue and cry? Have you come to arrest him and take him to the gaol? What's he done wrong?'

Harrod clicked his tongue irritably. His customary geniality had deserted him.

'Are you trying to be funny, man? Of course not. His horse merely returned without him and we are concerned for his safety. Mr Scroop is a prominent citizen of Preston, as you well know. You may as well leave us if you cannot be of more help.'

Now that the mason had been dismissed, Harrod gave us his orders.

'You are to search in pairs, each along one of the different ways he might have ridden. He that finds Mr Scroop is to give rapid toots on his horn – and to keep tooting, mind, until I join him.'

We spent a few minutes discussing the different routes available and agreed a different one for each couple of searchers. Fidelis and I, having ensured we were paired together, were to ride a route that would take us through the hamlet of Treales to the north of the road we had taken getting here.

We reached Treales, a scattering of mean homes centred on a tumbledown alehouse, and asked if anyone had seen Scroop riding through. None had, so we continued along the lane towards an even meaner settlement known as Treales Cottages, where our enquiries had no better result. For the next two miles there were no dwellings of any kind, and no sign of Scroop, either on foot or lying in or near the road.

'Did you note the name given to the dead child?' I asked as we entered on a bridle path bisecting a field of stubble.

'Yes. Loammi. Very peculiar. Biblical, do you think?'

'Undoubtedly, yet very strange. I don't know which book it's from, and I have never heard of the name being used for a christening.'

'Nor I.'

We talked for a while about names and their significance, which we agreed express parents' aspirations for their child.

'So what was your parents' hope in naming you, Titus?'

'They wanted me to make good connections in my life, I suppose. They were thinking more of Titus, the friend of the Apostle Paul, than of the traitor Oates. And you? Were you named Luke because the evangelist was a physician?'

'My father was an apothecary. He desired I would climb one or two rungs higher than him in the ladder of medicine.'

Our idle talk was interrupted by the sound of tooting coming from the south across the great stubble field that we were crossing.

'There it is. Scroop is found, I guess. Let's hurry.'

We turned off the bridleway and spurred our horses into a canter across the field, in the direction of the sounding horn. After half a mile we broke through a hedge and into a rutted track. Looking along it we saw, a little further on and beside a small wood, or copse, saddle horses and dismounted men standing in a small knot at the wayside. When we came up and ourselves dismounted I realized they were gathered around the form of a man lying in the verge of long grass that separated the road from the trees.

I straight away recognized him as Abraham Scroop, in riding clothes and lying on his front, with his arms spread, legs crooked and head twisted at an extreme angle, with the right cheek and nose resting on the earth. The uppermost eye was wide open, as if surprised, but there was not a spark of life in it.

As we joined the group, Dr Harrod was crouching beside the body and I saw him turning the head and attempting to close the eyes: they merely flipped back open again.

'His head's crushed,' Harrod said in a doleful voice. 'My dear friend and neighbour.'

One of the others held up a pocket watch, the glass smashed.

'Mr Scroop's. Broke it in the fall.'

'What time does it say?' put in Luke.

'It stopped at ten thirty-four.'

'There's nothing to be done for him,' said Harrod. 'He fell off his horse, I suppose – no, it's more likely he was knocked out of the saddle by that low branch there, and broke his skull when striking the ground.'

Harrod pointed back along the road to the branch of an oak that hung half across it. This was at such a height, more or less, that it would have to be avoided, or ducked, by any passing horseman.

'He was distracted, it must be,' Harrod continued, in a subdued voice. 'He didn't see the danger as he rode towards it. A terrible mishap which happened a little after half past ten this morning – as the broken watch confirms – while poor Abraham was riding back from Kirkham.'

The gleam of a tear appeared in his eye.

'At half past ten I was at the bedside of another dead man, Peter Chimpton over at Cottam. Well, he wasn't dead yet, but barely alive and he will certainly have gone by now. The stars were terribly against him. As a doctor I cared for him, of course, but I have seen so many patients dead. When a true friend dies, and in this senseless way, it is different. One feels the tragedy of it more.'

'The mason left him before eight,' said one of the others. 'What was Mr Scroop doing in the meantime?'

'Who knows?' said Harrod. 'Praying for his son. Riding about without any particular aim. Grief makes us do unaccountable things, does it not? In any case, we can say for a certainty that the horse came home just before eleven, well lathered. He was caught at the edge of Preston and taken to his stable at Water Lane without delay. Even at the trot – even if it found some juicy grass to eat along the way – he couldn't have taken more than half an hour to get there. So he must have parted company with Mr Scroop about half past ten.'

'It might have been a footpad that knocked him from his horse,' said another of the party.

'On this little road? It's not very likely, is it? But let's turn the poor fellow over. We may see if he's been robbed.'

It was quickly done, and Harrod ascertained that Scroop's purse contained coins. A silver snuffbox lay in his waistcoat pocket.

'That settles it,' he said. 'This was not a robbery, but a very unfortunate mishap.'

'And yet the Coroner must be called, Sir,' I put in. 'No one has witnessed this accident. In the absence of witnesses there will have to be an inquest.'

Harrod stood and turned to me.

'Had this happened a few weeks ago it would have been unnecessary to *call* the Coroner, as you, Cragg, are here already. But now you are no longer in office, I suppose we shall have to send for the Mayor, yes?'

'I'm afraid not, Sir,' I said. 'Remember where we are. This is five miles from Preston and outside my old jurisdiction. It is therefore also outside Mr Thwaite's. We must call one of the County Coroners.'

'Who's that?'

'The nearest County Coroner lives not far away fortunately: Mr Thomas Matthews of Poulton-le-Fylde.'

Harrod smiled and patted me on the shoulder.

'We are lucky to have you here to guide us, Cragg, with your special knowledge of these matters.'

'And in the meantime,' I added, pointing down at the corpse, 'Mr Scroop should lie exactly where he was found.'

Harrod looked around at the circle of men.

'So who will ride post-haste to Poulton? Dr Fidelis, I believe you have the fastest horse.'

Fidelis was kneeling beside the corpse, not in prayer but in order it seems to inspect it more closely. Rising immediately and without looking in the least put out, he said,

'I'll bring him as quick as I can.'

'Good, good! Meanwhile we'll find a cottager willing to mind the body. I am sure we all have business and cannot loiter here for the rest of the day. I certainly cannot.'

'I am at leisure this afternoon,' I said. 'I'll watch over the body until Mr Matthews comes.'

Harrod fixed me with a quick yet deliberative stare. I wondered if, for a moment, he had doubts about leaving me to guard his friend's corpse. However, he only said, 'That's right neighbourly of you, Cragg.'

By this time I was legging Fidelis up the flank of his horse. Once seated, and as the other men were laying a horse-blanket over the corpse, my friend leaned down to my ear.

'You will have a good look around?' he murmured. 'It will be almost dark by the time I get back.'

'Of course,' I replied equally quietly. 'What am I looking for?'

'First his hat. And then anything material to the fact that Scroop was murdered.'

'*Murdered*?'

'Of course. Did you not see that for yourself?'

With no further explanation he kicked his horse and clattered off back in the direction of Kirkham and beyond that the road to Poulton.

Some of the search party lingered for a while, but within half an hour they had all cut off back to Preston and I was left alone.

Two hours later, still waiting for Fidelis to return with Matthews, and now in the dusk, I had made a thorough examination of the place. I did not find the hat. Nor was there anything to substantiate Fidelis's idea that Scroop had been murdered. On the other hand, nor was there any sign of the accident having happened at the spot as Harrod believed. The overhanging branch showed no marks of collision, and the ground below was not dented to suggest a heavy fall.

Finally Fidelis returned in company with Tom Matthews. The County Coroner did not look well. I had been slightly acquainted with him over the years, and he'd always appeared a hearty fellow that lived for outdoor pursuits – shooting, angling and fox hunting. On this day, having formerly been plump and ruddy, he was lean-faced and pale; his old trumpet-voice sounded more like a scrannel pipe.

'I have a slight ague,' he said when I enquired after his health. 'Nothing serious, you know. Dr Fidelis told me his opinion of the case as we rode along. You are experienced in these things, Cragg. What is your view? Has this man been murdered, as Fidelis believes?'

'I can see no indication at all of how Mr Scroop met his death, Sir. Why do you suspect foul play, Luke?'

'It's perfectly simple. Scroop died some time in the early morning – between eight and nine. And he—'

'One moment,' I interrupted. 'How can you be so precise? Dr Harrod reasoned that he died about ten thirty, which was also when the man's watch was broken.'

'There are certain things that cannot be altered, and others that can. I deal in things that cannot. For instance, the first thing I noticed was that the dead man's eyelids would not stay down when Harrod tried to close them. The time then was a little after half past two. Now, eyelids are among the first parts of the body to be affected by *rigor mortis,* but *rigor* doesn't commence less than five hours after death. On that reckoning alone, Scroop cannot have died as late as ten thirty.'

'But the watch?'

'Unlike *rigor mortis* a watch can be set at will. And so can the position of a body.'

'What do you mean by that?'

'The second thing I noticed as well as his hat being missing was that the ground under the body was soaked with rain.'

'God's hooks, Luke, that's interesting!'

I lifted the blanket and felt the front of the dead man's waistcoat. He had been lying on his front, and it was soaked through.

'It didn't rain until after eleven. He must have been put down here at some time after that. The ground was bone dry before.'

Matthews, who had been listening attentively to all this, now put in,

'Might there not have been dew in the grass?'

'It was a windy morning, Sir. By eight o'clock any dew would have evaporated, and we know Scroop was then still alive, and in Kirkham. No. On the mason's evidence he died after eight, and on the evidence of the *rigor*, he died before half past nine.'

'And on the evidence of his wet clothes, he was moved here about three hours after he was dead and without his hat.'

'Precisely,' said Fidelis with satisfaction. 'The question is, why?'

Chapter 25

THE QUESTION OF why Scroop was murdered occupied Fidelis and me for much of our ride to Preston. On the way from Poulton Tom Matthews had ordered a cart to come up behind him for the corpse, since it had to be brought back into Kirkham, where the County Coroner's inquest would be held. We had helped load it and then, as twilight gave way to darkness, said good-bye to Matthews, both of us promising any help that we could give to his inquiry, including inquest testimony if necessary. When I shook hands with Matthews, the lamplight gleamed in his pinkly tinged, rheumy eyes and I could see that his face was lightly sheened with sweat. As he rode off alongside the squeaking wheel of the cart, I heard a hollow, wheezy cough tearing the breath from him.

'It is certain this is not the work of a footpad – are we agreed on that?' Fidelis was saying as we rode off in the opposite direction, towards the scattered cottages of Ashton.

'A footpad would have made himself scarce very quickly. He certainly would not have stayed for hours and then moved the corpse.'

'And besides all that, no money was taken. No, the one who killed Abraham Scroop did so out of malice.'

'It may have been simply a quarrel that ended in blows, one of them fatal. It may not have been planned by the killer, whoever it was. But naturally, he still wanted to conceal his crime, and that must have meant making us believe that Scroop died in the late morning, when in fact the deed must have been done earlier, and quite likely in a different place. Why?'

'There is no mystery about the placement of the body, Titus. He wanted to make it look like an accident and to do that he needed to leave it near that overhanging branch. The contrived timing was another matter. I am guessing that he did it to ensure his safety – to be able to plead an alibi should he happen to be questioned.'

We reached the crossroads on the edge of Preston where the skin-yard stood. Its great gates were closed as usual, but now the porter-door was also shut tight. Yet we clearly heard sounds of laughter and singing from within, and someone playing wildly on the fiddle. There were also flames visible, leaping high enough in the air to be seen over the top of the surrounding wall. A large bonfire had been lit.

'They have something to celebrate, it seems,' Fidelis remarked in a tone of dark innuendo.

'I know what you're thinking, Luke,' I said. 'But I also know those people, and I don't think they would resort to murder.'

'You can't deny they had a motive, though. They'd heard Abraham Scroop threatening to destroy them and their livelihood. They can only have hated him for that.'

I didn't deny it. The skinners certainly hated Scroop, as I had heard with my own ears. But I remained reluctant to call them killers. Sometimes I think of how fortunate animals are. They never impute evil motives – or any motives at all – to other creatures. This imagining of others' thoughts is something to which we humans alone are condemned, and which frequently and fatally divides us. It is particularly so when we imagine what is not true, as we do so often, not just from being mistaken, but because we are not impartial when we look around us. I am too partial to find malice or fault in one that I love – in Elizabeth, for example – but I am quick to see it in someone I detest, even though my detestation might originally have been stirred by nothing more menacing than the shape of a nose, or a grating voice.

The truth was that I liked the skinners. I liked their spirit and the way they conducted their affairs according to their own lights, without bowing to any man outside their own circle. They had a certain fibre to them, a steadfastness, and I could not see them doing evil.

'I agree they hated Scroop,' I said. 'But anyone can resort to violence, and not only from hatred, but also from fear. And the skinners were surely not the only ones to hate or fear Scroop. He was a powerful man.'

'Well, one thing is sure,' said Fidelis, 'all Preston will be agog at his death. And something tells me that, as soon as they know this was an assassination, most will point their fingers at the skin-yard.'

'Then I suggest you and I say nothing about murder, Luke. Let them believe it was an accident for the time being. It is for Matthews, and not us, to make the case for murder, and he must see for himself in which direction the fingers are pointing.'

'How do you think Matthews will do in this?'

'Matthews has long experience and is no fool. He will do very well.'

As expected, the death was being discussed that night and all the next day, in all the taverns, shops and coffee shops, and at every street corner and market stall. The first intelligence had come from Harrod, and the others that had ridden back with him, so the story being told everywhere was that Scroop had killed himself by the mischance of being struck from his horse by the oak branch as he attempted to ride beneath it.

Besides providing something to gossip about, Scroop's untimely end was being taken as a matter of serious consequence in some quarters of the town. I heard this myself on entering Gilliflower's barber shop on Wednesday morning, where I found Recorder Thorneley in the chair ahead of me.

There was no man in Preston more discreet, and none with more temptations to be indiscreet, than old John Gilliflower. In all his years of dewhiskering and hair cutting he had been privy to every kind of secret. He never solicited them – indeed Gilliflower never initiated a conversation at all, but merely carried on cutting, trimming and shaving, apparently regardless as his customers rattled on about their woes and opinions. All he did was interject an occasional soothing 'Sooks!', or an 'Is-that-so?', to punctuate the monologue.

A man cannot talk whilst being shaved but, as the barber wiped the razor and picked up his scissors, so Thorneley picked up the thread of the one-sided conversation. He was oblivious that I was now sitting in one of the waiting chairs not three yards away. I nevertheless opened a book that I carried in my pocket and pretended to read.

'It's damnable, Gilly,' Thorneley was saying, 'damnable and damaging of that fool to get himself killed – and by a tree, of all the contemptible things! Rode smack into it – a horizontal tree branch, nothing more deadly than that, and broke his skull in the fall. And we need him, by Heaven we do. We need his money to be more exact. The whole of our scheme by his carelessness is now in danger of collapse – complete collapse! It is designed for the greatest possible benefit and future prosperity of this town, and he was the greatest investor. I suppose you want to know what it is, the scheme?'

Gilliflower made no indication of either wanting to know, or of not wanting to. He continued cutting and shaping the hair without any comment whatsoever.

'Well, Gilly, you will certainly be astounded by the size of it when you *do* hear – but that can't be yet and it won't be from my lips. They are sealed. If any details should become known there are certain people . . . well, I may say no more at all. No more at all.'

Thorneley sat on, fuming and apparently wishing he could unburden himself to Gilliflower, but I guessed he was after all conscious of the presence of another in the shop – even if he didn't know who it was – and was guarding his tongue. When he got up to have his coat brushed down he did not show surprise at the sight of me, though he glowered and gave a small snort before snatching up his wig from the head-shaped barber's block that stood on a stand beside the chair.

'Scroop had as much sense as this block,' he muttered, 'getting himself killed in that untowardly way.'

It was almost noon, with my chin smooth and my hair pomaded, when I returned to the office and found Furzey at his desk. He had not shown his face all morning, but now was sitting with his head propped by his hand and a cup of ginger infusion steaming in front of him that he had got from Matty in the kitchen. He told me he was feeling a little 'hippish' as he had spent the previous evening as a guest at the table of Abraham Simcox the town clerk, who was a cousin of his.

'He entertained you well?'

'Too well. My writing will have a shake in it today.'

'What news did he have from the Town Hall?'

'They talk of nothing there, he says, but the fatal accident of Abraham Scroop. Some are seeing it as God's wrath; that Scroop over-reached himself and was struck down for it. It is the nemesis of a rag-and-bone man that over-reached.'

I brought to mind the knowledge I had, unknown to anyone

else, of the manner of Scroop's death. The wrath I thought was that of his murderer, not of God.

'His nemesis, Furzey?' I said. 'You grow Classical in your reference. I know that Scroop was ambitious, but how did he attract the wrath of Zeus? How did he deserve the fate of Prometheus?'

'He seemed to talk as if the gods themselves were his investors in those improvement projects of his. That was overweening, as some see it.'

'Do they? He kept his plans so very dark I'm not even sure what these projects were – not in detail. Something to do with the skin-yard, I believe. I suppose Simcox must know.'

Abraham Simcox was the perfect type of a town clerk. He knew the resting places of all the burgesses' secrets – petty and great.

Furzey said, 'Abe has not survived in his job for more than ten years by running off at the mouth. He certainly knows about Scroop's projects but will not divulge any details, neither for pie nor pence. He told me one thing touching you, though. I asked him particularly about the coronership of Preston, seeing that you are pining to be re-appointed.'

'Am I pining?'

'Oh yes. You're like a dog looking for its own nose.'

'Don't tell me you don't miss the work as much as I do, Robert Furzey. So what did Simcox say? Might we be reappointed when all this nonsense is over and my lady Rickaby's taken herself off to pastures new?'

Furzey gravely shook his head.

'No. I'll bet on a sparrow swimming the river first, and a trout flying over it. Those are Abe's own words by the way. No, Thwaite's enjoying himself too much. He's grown as fond of dead bodies as he is of pudding.'

'Thwaite's term of office is expiring. He won't be in the job a month from now. His successor may be less enamoured of corpses.'

'That isn't the point. Their chief delight in the matter is that you are ousted. The Mayor will hang on to coronership just to keep you out. They are cock-a-hoop on it.'

The bell at the door jangled as a boy came in, panting and bearing a letter for me sealed with the Derby crest. It was from his lordship inviting me to wait on him at Patten House at my earliest convenience. I reached immediately for my hat.

'So! Mr Cragg! We find ourselves thrown together once again, awaiting the pleasure of his lordship.'

The speaker expressed a sigh. It was Joss Kay. I had found him seated once again in the ante-room inside the front door of Patten House, just as he had been when I'd first met him. He spoke congenially and seemed to have entirely forgotten our abrupt encounters on the Marsh and at the cockpit, so I pretended to forget them, too. I explained that this time I was here because Lord Derby had sent for me in person.

'Which makes me believe that he will see me, though what it is about I am at a loss to say. But, Joss, tell me why you're in attendance here again.'

Kay gave another sigh.

'Because my governor, the one that had agreed to pay the fee for my work, well, he's kicked the bucket.'

'You don't mean the late Mr Abraham Scroop?'

'I mean no other. I am sure he was everywhere regarded as kindness and virtue itself, but to me he has played the scoundrel by being dead before a penny of money's been paid me for my apomecometry. Who will it come from if not from him? Grassington's left town. Captain Strawboy hasn't a piece of tin to his name, never mind gold, and I've been warned against even approaching the Corporation for money. So it must be from Lord Derby, or if not, I don't know how I will get it.'

'The fee you hope to get – what survey work is it for?'

'Confidential work, as I have mentioned to you before. Highly confidential and not to be spoken of in public. Those were the terms of my employment, Mr Cragg, and I must abide by them, else I risk never being paid at all.'

I could not pursue the matter further for now a servant came in and called me up to the presence of his master.

Edward Stanley, 11th Earl of Derby, was sitting in his business room in a gilt chair beside a gilt desk, at which his secretary sat poised to write. On the wall behind him was his lordship's portrait by his personal artist Hamlet Winstanley, which I had seen once before when it had then been on the artist's easel and still in progress – but that is another story. A sheaf of papers rested between the peer's knee and his left hand while, with his right, he held a single sheet up to the light to peruse it.

'Ah, Cragg!' he exclaimed as I came in. He tucked the paper he was reading in with the others. 'Good of you to come express. I fear I have received a sad piece of intelligence this morning. It concerns Mr Matthews of Poulton.'

'The County Coroner?' I said.

'Yes. He is dead.'

'Dead? No, Sir! I was with him only on Monday.'

'Well dead he is. Perhaps he was already ill when you saw him?'

'Now you mention it, he was, my Lord. He complained of an ague, but said it was nothing serious.'

'Yet it was a fatal ague, I'm sorry to say. I have received notice this morning. He expired yesterday having arrived home the previous night after a long ride, whereupon he was overtaken by a fiery fever and a painful shortness of breath.'

'Lord! That is sudden news, and very sad indeed. He had been much exerting himself in the case of the late Mr Scroop that was found dead near Kirkham, which perhaps he should not have done, being unwell. He was a good man.'

'I won't disagree but, what's more to the point, how am I to shift to find me a new County Coroner? I am very anxious to have the inquest into Mr Scroop properly conducted.'

Fool that I was, I did not immediately catch his drift, or see why this concerned me.

'Well, I may be able to give you the names of one or two suitable gentlemen, my Lord. There is Mr Perry of Garstang, who I believe is of sound judgement.'

'Confound Mr Perry of Garstang, Cragg. I look to you. You'll have to take the job.'

'Me, my Lord?'

'Who else, man? You're vastly experienced in the work and, at the moment, without employment in it. Some of the burgesses of Preston won't be pleased, of course. But it's no concern of theirs and they couldn't stop your appointment even if it were. The responsibility's mine as Lord Lieutenant of the county and I'll be damned if I won't have my old friend Titus in the job.'

I hesitated. It is a ticklish matter to question the decisions of a peer.

'If I may remind your Lordship, the County Coroner is an elected official.'

Derby clicked his tongue impatiently.

'Yes, yes, I am aware of that. But to arrange an election is not the work of a moment. I am proposing to install you *ad interim* pending an election – in which you shall not only stand but, if I have anything to do with the matter, win.'

'You are most kind, my Lord.'

'Not a bit of it. Always thought highly of you and I know you won't let me down.'

I sensed my face flushing with emotion as I realized what a sudden change of fortunes this was. I performed a little bow.

'I will try to be worthy of your trust, my Lord,' I said, almost stammering.

'That's settled, then. We'll draw up your commission right away and you can come in and be sworn tomorrow morning. Would that suit? And then you can get along with the inquest into the late Mr Scroop.'

I am not in general possessed by affection for the nobility. They exist, after all, in a different sphere, condescending to the rest of the world only from time to time and when the fancy takes them – or more particularly when it is in their interest. But Stanley, for all his occasional hauteur, had a practical and sensible way about him and he had more than once lent me his direct support against Burgess Grimshaw, and my other enemies in the Corporation. So I had always had a certain regard for the man; now I felt ready to kiss his feet.

Having stammered my thanks as best I could, I left the noble presence in a state of high elation, even of triumph. I was Coroner again. In the cock-fight of life I had trodden my enemies down. How I could crow now! And how crestfallen they would be!

Full of the news, I went straight home and told Elizabeth what had happened. She let out a scream, hurled herself at me and kissed me fully on the mouth, all in front of Matty, which I doubt she had ever done before.

'I really should not rejoice, my love, because a man had to die to bring this about. But I cannot help it. It is so wonderful for you. Oh! I could dance.'

'It's good to see those beautiful eyes shining,' I said, kissing her forehead. 'Now I must go and tell Furzey, and then Fidelis shall know.'

I went through to the office where Furzey was bent over his writing. He showed no emotion at my news – I mean not through his face. But he laid down his pen and scrubbed his hands vigorously against each other for a moment. Whatever mustiness of the head remained from his dinner with Simcox, it had been instantly swept away.

'We'll be taking on the Scroop inquest, then?'

'Yes, Furzey, without delay. On Friday I think.'

'It's an interesting one, is that.'

'So it is. It is not quite what it seems.'

And then, suddenly, my clerk favoured me with his particular notion of a smile – he tilted back his head and shut his eyes while his mouth formed a leering, twisted grimace, almost as if he were in pain.

'That's always the beauty of it, Sir,' he said, opening his eyes again. 'When death comes by surprise it is very likely not what Simple Simon thinks. It is very likely many spits deeper.'

'And we shall dig, Furzey, be assured of that. In the meantime, go to Kirkham and find us some jurors.'

I went out through the street door and made my way to Fidelis's lodging, where Mrs Lorris told me her lodger was out.

'Looking at a house, he is,' she said. 'He's given us his notice and is intending to buy, so he says. We'll be right sorry to lose the doctor, Mr Cragg, though, as I told Mr Lorris, we won't miss the smells, with him making up his chemicals at all hours of the night. And we won't be sorry to lose that rooster of his, crowing in the garden at the crack of every dawn.'

'I do commiserate, Mrs L.,' I said. 'Dr Fidelis's habits can be vexingly irregular at times. Would you mention when he comes in that I have news to tell him and hope to see him at the Turk's Head as soon as he returns?'

Chapter 26

WHENEVER SOMETHING FORTUNATE happens to me, I like to celebrate by giving myself a new book. So, reckoning I had a good half hour before Fidelis could possibly appear, I returned to my favourite shop, Sweeting's. Sitting in the bookseller's place behind the counter I found a youth of perhaps seventeen, deeply absorbed in reading.

'Is Mr Sweeting here?' I asked.

He glanced up from the page and mumbled something from which I heard only the word 'out'. The youth seemed familiar but for a moment I couldn't place him.

'You are minding the shop, then?'

He mumbled again.

'Speak up, young man. I can't hear you.'

This time the mumble was a fraction louder and just comprehensible.

'Yes. I'm 'prentice.'

'Is that so? You must have signed recently, then.'

He made a blushing bob of the head. I looked at him more closely.

'Wait a moment, I know you. You're Abel, Dr Harrod's boy. I saw you with your father at the cock-fighting, did I not?'

He nodded again.

'So you've decided to take to the bookselling trade. A very good choice, if you are at all bookish. You will learn much from Sweeting. He is extraordinarily learned in literature. What's that you're reading?'

He picked up the book and showed me the spine of the book. It was *Robinson Crusoe.*

'Ah, what a book! You like it?'

Abel Harrod brightened.

'Oh yes, Sir, I do. I can't give over reading it.'

I took the book from him and turned to the title page.

'This must be a new edition. I have it in the original printing, which I've read more than once. But I envy you the pleasure of coming to it for the first time. It is a marvel of a book.'

We were interrupted by Sweeting, who came in dragging behind him two bulging rough-cloth sacks. These he dumped on the floor.

'I've been to the widow Scroop's house,' he announced. 'She sent for me expressly.'

He paused. Sweeting, who was usually so composed, was breathing with a pronounced wheeze

'It's a most extraordinary thing,' he said at last. 'The husband's only two days dead and she's gone through the house and packed up his things, all of them. She means to get rid of everything of Scroop's as quick as can be. I saw bags of his clothes and shoes lying all in a heap, and she expected me to buy and take away all his books.'

I nodded at the sacks.

'Which you did?'

'Only some of them. He wasn't much of a reader. She's burning the rest of them, with his papers.'

'Oh dear!'

I shudder when I hear of the burning of books.

'Most of them were worth little. There were three copies of

The Pilgrim's Progress, but only one of them worth the taking. I did bring away a few plays and Bishop Andrewes's sermons, which might be saleable. Best of all, I've got the *Cyclopaedia* complete, which there is always demand for. Abel, give me a hand here.'

Master and apprentice began to take the books out of the sacks and to pile them on a sideboard. I picked up one of the pair of fat volumes of Chambers's dictionary – or *Cyclopaedia* as the author called it – and marvelled at the breadth of learning that it paraded, in alphabetical order from Abacus to Zythum. I noticed that some-one – Scroop, I guessed – had inserted paper slips to mark certain articles of interest to himself and, out of curiosity, I looked through them. On each marked page a head-word had been underlined with pen and ink: clay, manure, marl, peat, soil. The paper of these slips was clean and recent: evidently Scroop had lately been taking a particular interest in agriculture.

No sooner did I have this thought than another thought stung me.

'My God!'

I closed the book with a snap.

'Did you say she was burning Scroop's books *and papers*?'

'So it seemed.'

'Then she must be stopped, immediately! Excuse me, Sweeting, I shall return. Please will you examine all the books and keep any stray papers you may find inside them?'

I left the shop. First I went back to the Turk's Head to see if Fidelis had come in: he had not. I scribbled a note for him saying I would return at five o'clock and then hurried off to Water Lane, which was a walk of about twenty minutes.

I have observed that widowhood takes women in different ways. Many like to preserve everything of the deceased as if it were in sugar, under the pretence that their spouse had never gone at all. The suits of clothes remain in the press, the buckle shoes are kept brightly polished, the last worn wig sits forever on its stand. Others, by contrast, act as if they never want to be reminded of their loss. They quickly dispose of everything reminiscent of their loved one, as if afraid of putrefaction. The latter seemed to be the case with Mrs Scroop, and in extreme form, but I should stop it if I could. A dead man's papers give paramount evidence of his life and, when the death itself is doubtful, the Coroner must carefully examine and take them into account.

I was out of breath when I arrived at the door. Pausing for a moment to regain composure, I could hear voices calling inside, with hurrying footsteps and the banging of doors. Then, in almost instantaneous answer to my pull on the bell, the door was snatched open and I confronted a woman in a servant's apron and cap. But she was no servant; she was Mrs Scroop herself. Her hair was disordered and her face red, as if she had been exerting herself.

'Mr Cragg,' she said.

In her disdainful mouth my name sounded vile – as if it were another way of saying excrement. Nevertheless I removed my hat and bowed.

'Madam, I have the honour to have been appointed in Mr Matthews's place who, I must inform you, has yesterday passed away.'

'Matthews? Matthews? I don't know the man. What is this to me?'

Helena Scroop had always been a forthright body.

'He was County Coroner, and had lately begun enquiries towards an inquest into the regretted, er, passing of Mr Scroop. But Mr Matthews being himself now unexpectedly deceased it has become my duty to take up those enquiries and to hold the inquest into your husband according to law.'

'I thought you were turned out in disgrace,' she said with something like a sneer. Her tone still discomforted me.

'I was formerly but Coroner of the town,' I said. 'Now Lord Derby has seen fit to appoint me as temporary Coroner for the county in Mr Matthews's place. Later there will be an election for the post.'

'I repeat, Sir, what is this to me?'

'It is in connection with the inquest into Mr Scroop. I must to ask you if there were any circumstances I should know about. And I would like to look at his recent correspondence.'

'I have nothing to say to you about circumstances. Nothing whatever. As to the late Mr Scroop's letters, we are destroying them.'

I held up my hand in a staying gesture.

'Madam, you must not! They may contain important evidence.'

She hesitated for a moment, then her face suddenly softened a little.

'We cannot help it! We find it unbearable to keep anything relating to the late Mr Scroop. We do not wish to be reminded.'

'That is understandable, Madam, after such a sudden loss. But surely you will not destroy everything. You must at least spare his Will and his legal papers.'

'If you are interested in all that, I refer you to Messrs Rudgwick and Tench, his attorney. I am concerned with what he kept in this house.'

'Madam I really must insist that you allow me to look at that first.'

'Very well, I will allow you to look. Come in.'

Mrs Scroop led me through the house, whose interior was in a state of some disorder. Furniture had been pulled away from the walls, while drawers and cupboards stood open, and unhung pictures leaned against the wainscot. In all this disorder servants and the Scroop daughters scurried around with bundles in their arms. Passing the open door of what, I could see, had been Abraham Scroop's study, I saw that his bookshelves were bare, and his desk drawers had been pulled open and emptied. Seeing me pause to look, the widow plucked my arm.

'No, not there. Follow me and you shall see.'

We passed right through the house and outside again by the yard door. I immediately smelled smoke.

'There,' said Mrs Scroop, gesturing towards the yard's end. 'His papers. But you haven't very long to look over them.'

A bonfire was blazing with fierce hunger. It was being fed by two of the Scroop daughters who, standing at a respectful distance, were casting into it the last few armfuls of letters and ledgers, papers and prints. As these were committed to the fire, the flames leapt blue, orange and red, and an impenetrable plume of the thick grey smoke rose above them into the sky.

I found Luke Fidelis at the Turk's Head on my return to Fisher Gate, where he was eating a late dinner of roasted fowl. He had looked for me at Cheapside and had already heard of my appointment from Furzey. Now, on seeing my approach, he found it impossible to contain his glee. He leapt up and punched me hard on the shoulder.

'This is the finest news I've heard this year,' he said. 'And that, I may say, includes our valiant King's humiliation of the French at Dettingen.'

'Yes, it is very good to be in business again, and with a wider scope of responsibility,' I agreed.

'The wider the better,' said Fidelis, as we settled at our table. 'You have the whole county under your eyes, and you can work without the interference of Grimshaw and the rest of them.'

'I am not so sure we can count on that in the first matter I have in hand: Lord Derby seems particularly concerned that I pick up the traces of Scroop's inquest at Kirkham. It has grown exceedingly complicated.'

I then told him of my visit to Water Lane in connection with Scroop's death, and of Mrs Scroop's bonfire. I also mentioned Elizabeth's feeling that Scroop's behaviour had been that of a guilty man. Fidelis, a slow eater, examined a cube of meat on his fork before easing it cautiously into his mouth. He chewed reflectively and swallowed.

'So, why has the widow disposed of all her husband's belongings so quickly after his death? What is she wanting to hide?'

'It may be no more than what she told me: an expression of her extreme grief. She wishes to expunge her husband entirely in order not to be daily reminded of her loss and that of her children.'

'That might account for her actions in the normal way, I agree,' said Fidelis. 'But in the light of her husband's murder, it may carry a different significance, may it not?'

'But if she had a guilty reason, something to hide as you say, she would still only be doing this if she knew there were suspicions about his death. But there are none, or not publicly. And even if Helena Scroop were attempting to destroy evidence, she would surely confine herself to the destruction of incriminating documents, whatever they might be. She surely would not burn everything.'

Fidelis began to saw through another chunk of chicken flesh.

'Unless she does not know for certain what is incriminating.'

At this moment a shadow fell across our table and we looked up to see Captain Strawboy.

'Fidelis,' he said. 'How is your Sultan? I doubt he is yet recovered from the mighty contest.'

The Captain was a little the worse for wine. His stock in Preston had gone down since the surprising death of Abraham Scroop, his partner in business. Those that had previously sat and feasted with Strawboy, and toasted the captain's name under Scroop's presidency, now avoided him. Being the heir of Lord Grassington, which had once lent him glamour, now seemed to isolate him, since his

Lordship himself had left the town. Meanwhile Strawboy's friendship with Lord Strange seemed to have cooled and his aunt, Lady
Rickaby, had also gone away. She had mounted a private coach
loaded with luggage and driven back in pomp to Derbyshire. With
the noble widow gone, even her brother-in-law Grimshaw now
avoided the captain.

So Strawboy was reduced to the company of cockpit men
and tavern gamblers with whom he passed the time in wine and
bawdry. Now he was swaying gently and his face wore a light
sheen of sweat.

'The Sultan is still weak in body, and his eye is not yet healed,'
said Fidelis. 'He is strong in spirit, however.'

'He is certainly spirited, we've seen that. So, Doctor, what d'you
say to another bout? I have just acquired a new bird even gamer
than the last, that I'm sure will give me the prize this time.'

'We must see, Captain. I fear I cannot commit the Sultan to
another bout until he has made a full recovery.'

Strawboy gave a drooping bow and was about to withdraw.

'Captain Strawboy,' I said. 'I hope the shocking death of Mr
Scroop does not affect your joint projects for Preston. Do you and
Lord Grassington intend to proceed with them?'

Strawboy adopted a puzzled expression, as if I had spoken to
him in a foreign language.

'I don't construe your meaning, Sir.'

'In the first place, I refer to the improvement of the skin-yard,
which you suggested to me was necessary when we met at Scroop's
house. But are there not other projects under your eye – the bath
house, the racecourse, the Marsh?'

No longer able to pretend he could not follow me, Strawboy
was flustered.

'The Marsh? That is not— I mean to say, I cannot say anything
about the Marsh.'

I pressed on.

'Mr Scroop's investment was to be a considerable one, or so I hear. D'you suppose that money will now be withdrawn?'

Strawboy's eyes narrowed. His thoughts arranged themselves a little more geometrically.

'I don't know how you obtained this intelligence, Cragg, but let me tell you, it's —'

'And if Scroop's backing is withdrawn, will those projects collapse?'

Strawboy straightened his back, as if remembering his military rank.

'I came to speak to the doctor on a sporting matter, Sir, and not to you on business. I therefore wish you good evening.'

When he had gone, Fidelis said,

'What was all *that* about?'

So I told him about my visit to Thorneley's house, and the plans I had seen signed by the surveyor Joss Kay, and how I had later met Kay on the Marsh.

'He was working with instruments, though he denied he was carrying out a survey of the entire Marsh. He maintained he was only calibrating his gear before using it at the skin-yard. Captain Strawboy had already told me that he and Scroop were concerned with the tanning business, and I know for a fact that Kay is here working for Strawboy and Scroop, though it seems Lord Derby and Lord Grassington are also concerned in the matter.'

'I can't see what business any of those gentlemen would have with the Marsh.'

'All I know as a certainty is that the brief I saw on Recorder Thorneley's hall table was expressly marked "Private Instructions re: P.M.". Now, having seen him at work there, it seems a good guess that this refers to Preston Marsh.'

'No doubt they plan to do some work on the Marsh – drain it or improve it in some way.'

'Improve it! Not an easy task. An Act of Parliament would be required. The Marsh is common land. It has many ancient rights and easements attached to it, going back God knows how long.'

'But improvement is improvement, is it not? What's in this to be so secretive about?'

'If you even think about interfering with the Marsh you will raise anger. Haven't you noticed the way in which improvement always seems to require enclosure? A decision is made by a few placemen in London and, handy-dandy, that's more of our stock of common land disappeared into private hands for ever. That's the reason for the secrecy. If these projectors want to improve some part of the Marsh, to drain it, for example, the last thing they want is a public discussion. What they require instead is a *fait accompli*.'

Fidelis had been leaning forward, listening intently. Now he sat up straight and a beatific smile lit his face.

'How very clever of you, Titus. I believe you may have accidentally uncovered the reason for Mr Abraham Scroop's untimely death.'

At nine the next morning I was again at Sweeting's shop. The books taken from Scroop's library still lay stacked on a sideboard. I asked if any stray papers had been found in any of the volumes. 'Only this,' said the bookseller, handing me a single printed sheet. 'It's a page from *The Gentleman's Magazine*.'

I took it and looked over the item. One paragraph in particular had been underlined, which read as follows.

> May I advert your readers to a curiosity I have noted in Sheffield amongst the cutlers? The handles of their excellent table-knives being fashioned for the most part from

cattle bone this is shaped by being turned on a lathe. Beneath this piece of machinery the bone dust falls into a tray which is emptied from time to time into a particular area of the yard, and this has extraordinary results, viz. that the herbiage growing where the bone-dust has been deposited does so with twice the vigour and to twice the size as that in any other part of the yard. Can it be that this same bone-dust has powers of fertilization previously unknown to agriculture? It cannot be beyond the wit of our Royal Society to conduct experiments that would confirm such a startling and useful discovery! I am, etc.

Scroop's interest in this article was no surprise, when I thought about it. Was he not among other things a dealer in bones? And was he not also a man full of energy and zeal for improvement?

Chapter 27

∽

A<small>T TEN</small> I <small>ATTENDED</small> Lord Derby once again. This time I was not shown into the downstairs ante-room but directed straight up to the peer's business room. The ante-room door, as I passed, lay ajar and I was afforded a glimpse of the leather case, like a hatbox, that contained Mr Kay's measuring instrument. The land surveyor evidently was still waiting for his interview with his Lordship.

I had a further reminder of Mr Kay no more than three minutes later. The business room was empty as I was shown in and told that if I would indulge him for five minutes or so Lord Derby would join me to conclude the business at hand. I took a seat in front of the desk and settled down to wait – as one always waits on peers of the realm.

On the desk in front of me were several bundles of papers, tied with ribbons, being mostly parliamentary business or matters related to the county. The one nearest to me, however, was different. It was concerned with Preston, and I recognized it: it was the file I had last seen in Mr Matthew Thorneley's hallway. I knew as soon as I saw it that I would not restrain myself. Listening hard for any approaching footsteps, I rose and turned over the top page, which was blank save for the identification 'Private Instructions re: P.M. – Mr Kay'. The document immediately below this was a letter, which I rapidly read through.

I later obtained a copy of this letter as being of evidential interest. It read as follows:

To the Earl of Derby at Knowsley Hall, Lancashire.

My Lord: I am in receipt of your letter regarding the works at Preston proposed by Mr Scroop and others, and am sincerely flattered at the regard you express for myself and for my previous improvement projects, and gratified by your request that I participate in Mr Scroop's scheme. However, I am presently engaged at Newry in Ireland in a most difficult engineering project which absorbs all of my energies at present. I can do no better therefore than to recommend to you a young man who has been in my employ. I refer to Mr Joseph Kay, who is a skilled surveyor and zealous believer in improvement. If you will send me your assent I shall direct him to wait on you at Knowsley.

I am your most obliged servant, Thomas Steers.

I had no time to look further into the file of documents, for now two sets of steps approached the door, and I hastily replaced the file's title page and stepped back as Lord Derby and his legal secretary for the affairs of the county of Lancaster swept into the room. The business was summarily executed. I was handed a card with the words of a loyal oath, which I read with my hand on a Bible. His Lordship then pronounced me duly invested as a temporary incumbent, and presented me with my commission, a document furnished with elaborate decorative lettering, pendant seals, and the signature of Derby under the designation Lord Lieutenant.

When all was done, we shook hands and I left Patten House in a position which only three days earlier I had not the slightest inkling of: Coroner of the Duchy and County Palatine of Lancaster.

Scroop's body was being kept under the care of the churchwarden at Kirkham and, as it is not in my nature to procrastinate, I had sent word even before Lord Derby had sworn me in that I would be inspecting the body during the second part of Thursday morning. Luke had agreed to come with me and to give his own opinion.

However, I had some other business in mind first.

'Before we look at Scroop's body we'll be passing the mason's yard,' I told Fidelis as we rode into Kirkham. 'I want to call there and talk to him, as he will have to give his testimony at the inquest.'

The stonemason's name was Joseph Twiss and we found him kneeling in his yard chiselling letters into a smooth slab of granite. Skinny in body, he possessed a large head which, when he stood up, he canted forward as if to counter-balance the humped right shoulder. His body was all out of kilter, but the look in his good eye was lively and intelligent.

'What can I do for you, gents?' he asked.

'A little information, if you please, Mr Twiss,' I said. 'Perhaps you remember that I was with the group of men from Preston who came out here the other day looking for Mr Abraham Scroop.'

'Oh, yes, I do,' said Twiss. 'And you found him, too, knocked off his horse by a tree, I've heard.'

'Just so. It is the kind of death where there must be an inquest to determine what happened, and I am holding it, you see. You must have been one of the last to speak to Mr Scroop.'

'Happen I was,' said Twiss.

'Can you tell me the reason for your appointment with him that morning?'

'He'd sent word to meet at the graveside of his baby. He wanted to give me a paper that he'd prepared with the words for its headstone.'

'Can you show me the paper?'

'I can do better,' he said. 'Come along.'

He put down his mallet and chisel and led us to the end of the yard where his store of flagstones lay in orderly stacks according to their size, with a number of rougher boulders interspersed. There was also a row of finished carvings – urns and garlanded tablets, and a remarkable angel with furled wings who rested on one knee. I stopped to admire the angel.

'This is a fine piece of work,' I said.

The statue had the preternaturally beautiful face and elegant neck of a young man in a Greek or Roman bust. The hands, however, though resting on the pommel of an unsheathed broadsword, were more like those of a girl. I touched one of them, to feel the almost silken texture of the stone.

'The hands are my wife's,' said Twiss. 'She had the fingers of an angel. Not ugly like mine.'

With a gappy grin he held up both hands. The fingers were large, knotted and much calloused.

'Nevertheless, yours are the hands of an artist, Mr Twiss.'

'I thank you sir. I like to think so. Now, this headstone. It's over here.'

The stone that he showed us lay propped on a wooden pallet. It was no more than a foot and a half high, by a foot wide, and was etched with elegant flowing letters. The largest of these spelled out the name 'LOAMMI SCROOP' under which in smaller script 'Born and died 1743'.

'You completed the work?'

'I did it the same day, before I knew Mr Scroop was dead. I'd have waited else.'

'So this is the inscription he asked you to put.'

I lowered myself to the posture of Twiss's angel and read the words aloud.

'"*Plead with your mother, plead.*"'

A strange injunction. Luke, do you recognize these words?'

'No, I cannot place them.'

'Mr Twiss, did Mr Scroop tell you what they mean or why he wanted them on his son's tombstone?'

'He didn't.'

I let my forefinger trace the curl and sweep of the lettering and found that the stone gave the same illusion as the angel's hands, of being soft instead of hard.

'First this peculiar name for the infant – Loammi – which we think biblical, and then the obscure inscription. Might it be from scripture also?'

'You are asking the wrong person,' said Fidelis. 'My knowledge of holy writ is selective at best.'

'But it is such a very bald injunction – "plead, plead". Was Scroop in his right mind?'

'Oh yes,' said Luke. 'I fancy the man was sending a message. It would certainly be useful to find out who it was for, and what the message means.'

Scroop's body lay on a table in a damp, stone-walled room at the base of the church tower. Bell ropes mutely surrounded him, hanging down through slots in the vaulted ceiling. While Fidelis opened his medical case, took out a small candle and lit it, I cast my eye over the corpse. It was a study in the diminishment of mortality, for death had entirely undone the substance of the man. His confident living face had crumpled and his body seemed too shrunken, now, for the riding clothes he had died in.

The first thing we did was strip these accoutrements off him.

As I went rapidly through his pockets – finding nothing of note – Fidelis used a measuring rule to take the dimensions of the livid head wound just above Scroop's right eye. The dent in the forehead bone was two and three-quarters inches long, half an inch wide and a quarter of an inch deep.

'The wound looks quite deadly,' I said. 'But is it actually serious enough to kill him?'

'It might not be. The effect of a wound in the head is always variable. However, in this case, I would doubt it did for him instantaneously, as Harrod believed. On the other hand it would certainly have knocked him unconscious.'

He lowered his head and using the light of the candle examined in minute detail the wound, and then the rest of his head, with particular attention to the dead man's mouth, nose and ears; but it was only on the left ear that he lingered.

'Well, well!' he said. 'I wonder what's here.'

He selected a pair of narrow tweezers from his bag and, inserting them into the ear, withdrew a plug made from a small piece of white cloth wrapped in a ball. He held the tweezers to the light and we saw that the cloth was darkly stained on one side.

'That would be blood,' said Fidelis. 'And therefore I think we have found the true cause of death.'

As he often did, Fidelis was running strides ahead of me.

'And that is?'

'If I open the skull, I would expect to find that the brain has been pierced through this left ear by a long, thin, spike-like instrument, and fatally wounded.'

I formed the scene in my mind.

'So at a place other than the spot where Scroop was found his attacker smashed in his head with some object, or knocked him down in such a way as to smash his head, then carefully killed him while he lay unconscious.'

'And the manner of his execution?'

Only then did I grasp the import of this.

'He died in exactly the same manner as the baby in the tan-pit!'

'Exactly the same: through the ear with a long needle or spike.'

It took a few more moments before my astonishment cleared, and I saw the implication.

'My God, Luke! I've never seen such a type of attack before, and now we have two. The deaths must be linked.'

'I'll go further, Titus. I'll stake the life of the Sultan of Scrafton, and all the money he won for me, that they were done by exactly the same murderer. Now, if you will allow me, I shall open him up.'

I did not stay. Post-mortem dissections are hard on the layman's stomach, so I took the opportunity to go to the largest inn in the town, where I engaged its biggest room for the inquest, and then sought out the constable whose job it would be to distribute jury-summonses. By the time I had re-joined Fidelis, I was glad to find him sewing the corpse back together.

'It is just as I thought,' he said, with much satisfaction. 'A thin spike into the brain via the ear. The brain bled profusely inside the skull, which is generally fatal. He would have died very soon after.'

My first thought on reaching home in mid-afternoon was to tell Elizabeth about the infant Loammi Scroop's strange tombstone inscription.

'Tell me what you think,' I said to Elizabeth. 'I have seen the writing Abraham Scroop ordered for his child's gravestone just before he was killed. "Plead with your mother, plead." What can that mean? Plead for what?'

Elizabeth repeated the words softly to herself, and added,

'Plead for her forgiveness is likely, I would say.'

'For what offence, though?'

'For some wrongdoing by Scroop himself. He's asking the

innocent child in heaven to intercede on behalf of his sinful father still on earth.'

'Intercession is a papist notion, Lizzie. The Scroops were very much of the Protestant faith, you know.'

'It is not very Protestant for the wife, as soon as her husband is dead, to destroy or dispose of all his possessions. It looks like vengeance, Titus, and "vengeance is mine, sayeth the Lord".'

'Why would she seek vengeance?'

'Suppose that he broke his marriage vows.'

'Abraham Scroop? He gave his wife a string of children. You really think he was unfaithful as well?'

Elizabeth laughed.

'Titus, my love, he would not be the first man to do both.'

Even when she is laughing at me, I love to hear it. I put my finger against her lips.

'Are you mocking me, wife? In my eyes Scroop was a righteous man. We may not entirely approve his ruthless way of conducting business, but I am much deceived if he was an adulterer.'

'Faithless men make deception their business.'

'Maybe the point is not whether Scroop was deceiving her, but that Mrs Scroop might, rightly or wrongly, have thought he was. She may have overheard her servants gossiping. O'Rorke told me there was talk amongst the Scroops' servants that he had a fancy woman.'

'That decides the case. Servants always know what's what.'

'Well these servants seem more than a little fanciful. O'Rorke went so far as to suggest something untoward in the conduct of Dr Harrod and Mrs Scroop.'

'Titus, this is not to the point. Whatever her own conduct, and whatever she believed about her husband's, I do not think Mrs Scroop murdered her husband on the road out of Kirkham.'

'Harrod might have. But he was on his rounds seeing patients.

Let me tell you what else I have found out today, with Fidelis's help.'

I told her of the spike-in-ear method by which Scroop had been killed, just like the tan-pit baby.

'Fidelis considers with much reason that the two murders were necessarily done by the same hand. He believes it is something to do with the improvement of Preston Marsh, and not just the tannery.'

'I can have no opinion on that, Titus my love. But it seems to me that if what Fidelis says is true you only have to catch Mr Scroop's killer and you'll have the one that killed the newborn in the tan-pit. That will be an excellent thing, after all the trouble the case caused you.'

'Even if it turns out to be one of the tanners? I am very sorry to feel I may have been wrong about them. Not only was the little child found in their yard, but it is known the tanners hated the sight of Abraham Scroop. What's more, they're leather workers as well as tanners; they have strong needles and spikes in their gear as a matter of course. I have seen them in use.'

'It would be a strange thing for Scroop, if he were wicked in that way, to be punished instead for doing something perfectly legal, such as improving the skin-yard.'

'But, if you are right about him, fortune is evidently better advised than us. It runs its course and gets its way.'

I went into the office to confer with Furzey, and see what names he had for Saturday's jury. Within half an hour we had made out the summonses and engaged a messenger to take them to the constable of Kirkham for distribution. I also made out witness summonses for Captain Strawboy, Dr Harrod, Mrs Scroop and Bartholomew Lock, Scroop's foreman.

'You won't have heard the rumours, then,' said Furzey, when we had finished.

'About what?'

'About Mr Scroop being attacked deliberately, and not killed by riding into a low branch.'

'Who's saying this?'

'Everybody. It's all over town.'

My first thought was that, despite our agreement not to speak of it, Fidelis had been expanding on his murder theory in some tavern. I had doubted my friend unfairly, as soon became evident, because the talk had in fact reached us from Kirkham. The late Mr Matthews's gardener had brought some produce to market there, and reported that it was common talk in the Matthews house that the late coroner had believed Abraham Scroop was the victim of an assassin. It did not come out that the idea had come from his speaking with Luke Fidelis.

By evening the murmur of murder grew to something more like a roar, and my hopes of keeping it under seal until the inquest had vanished like smoke. Now all the talk in Preston's taverns and coffee houses was of mortal force and malice aforethought, and there was much ado over it, too, at Moot Hall. The burgesses may often have had their differences and their cliques, but collectively they were a club, and they considered any act against one of their members to be an assault upon the whole. So it was announced they would sit in session the next morning to debate the emergency and, that evening, the Mayor sent for the town sergeant, Oswald Mallender, to demand that immediate action be taken to limit the danger of this terrible act. A simpering Mallender asked just what could he do? Thwaite (as Furzey was later told by his cousin Simcox) barked at him, with spittle flying, that he must take measures immediately, measures to satisfy the burgesses when they convened, and nothing short of someone in custody would do the job. In short, he must make an arrest.

In all the public discussions about who the felon might be, one name predominated. Had not the Irishman O'Rorke just been dismissed from Scroop's service? Had he not made himself scarce and furthermore did he not have red hair, the sure sign of violent dispositions? Some of those in cock-fighting circles had grown fond of O'Rorke and did their best to speak up for him, but their voices could not outweigh the majority opinion – that Jon O'Rorke must have been the killer.

Mallender entirely shut his ears to this talk. It was in part because, absurdly, he considered himself independent of mind; but also because the theory that O'Rorke was the felon was no use to him now, since the Irishman had sailed away from Preston. Mindful of the Mayor's express instruction to find the culprit, Mallender therefore fixed his mind upon another doubtful foreign character on whom he actually could lay a hand: Joss Kay. The land surveyor had been going around loudly complaining that Scroop died owing him money. Mallender had interpreted this to mean Scroop died precisely *because* he owed Kay money – from which a short step led him to form the idea that only Kay himself could have done the murder. When the sergeant heard report later in the evening that the young man had been seen near the bottom of Water Lane at midday on Monday, at the same time as Scroop's riderless horse had appeared from the direction of Kirkham, and further that one witness actually saw Kay catch the reins of the horse, Mallender's suspicion solidified into certainty.

In logic it made no sense, but logic is not the driver of gossip, or of prejudice, or even of political expediency. Joss Kay was a stranger, and strangers are always the first to be accused when accusation is called for.

Chapter 28

'SOMEONE MUST HAVE been telling lies about me, Mr Cragg,' called out Joss Kay. 'They came for me before I had even had my breakfast.'

It was true: at daybreak on Friday Kay had been made a prisoner and it was now ten in the morning. He was being marched by the Parkin brothers to Moot Hall, to appear before the magistrates' bench. I was coming out of my house just as the small group passed on its way along Cheapside, whereupon Kay caught sight of me. His wrists were shackled and his aggrieved voice quavered.

'Keep your head above water, Joss, and all will be well,' I called back.

He was hurried onward by his captors and, feeling sorry for him, I followed. If I could snatch a few words more with him before the hearing I might be able to help him. I could suggest some lines of argument for his defence, but I would also have the chance to discover whether he should give testimony at the next day's inquest.

The magistrates' courtroom was closed, however. The Mayor, and all the bench, were in council with the rest of the burgesses, so the hearing of Kay's case was delayed and the prisoner was thrown into one of the half-flooded cells to wait his turn. A couple of shillings in the palm of Tarlton the turnkey bought me half an hour's conference with the prisoner in his damp and dripping cell.

'I hope I am right in supposing you're innocent,' I said.

'Of course I am. And I am keeping my head above water.'

We both looked down at the two inches of water in which we were standing.

'Were you at or anywhere near Kirkham last Monday morning?'

'No. I was working on the Marsh – taking my readings.'

'Did you catch hold of the loose horse?'

'Yes.'

'How did it happen?'

'I was going back to my lodgings for dinner. I reached the junction where the bottom of Water Lane meets the way to Ashton, just by the skin-yard. There was a commotion. They were trying to catch a horse that was running around riderless. He was spooked and nervous. I lent a hand, that's all I did. I had grabbed hold of the reins for a moment, before someone took them off me. It was just a moment. It doesn't make me a criminal.'

There was a catch in his voice.

'You are right, it doesn't. What did you do then?'

'I went on my way.'

'Good. So, if they bring it up, that's all you need to say on the subject. But how will you reply when they charge you with holding a grudge against Scroop because he did not pay you what you say he owed you?'

'He *did* owe me. Don't you believe me?'

'I am speaking as the court will speak in accusing you.'

'I see. Very well. Yes, I was angry with Scroop. He owed me a great sum of money – well, it was a great sum to me, though not I suppose to him. Anyway, I still expected him to pay me in the end. Why would I kill a man from whom I hoped to receive a sum of money? No one would do that.'

'That is an excellent reply. You were engaged for this work on the recommendation of Thomas Steers, I believe.'

Kay was startled.

'How did you know that?'

'I heard it somewhere. Who is Mr Steers?'

'He is a prominent citizen of Liverpool and a skilled engineer. He is extremely distinguished.'

'And will you tell me, please, exactly what work you were engaged to do on Mr Steers's recognizance?'

'I am sworn to secrecy about that.'

'You will swear in front of the bench to tell the truth. How will you reply when they ask the same question?'

'They won't.'

'Why not?'

'Because they already know the answer.'

'Is it for the improvement of the Marsh, Joss?'

He flared with sudden anger, and raised his hands, jingling the chain that bound them.

'I must warn you not to press me too far on the Marsh, Cragg! But yes. Why else would I come to this backward town, but to improve it?'

'What sort of improvement, though? Agricultural? I understand Mr Scroop was becoming interested in fertilizers and suchlike.'

Kay let out a laugh that echoed around the damp cell.

'No, no, no! This is a much grander thing than mere fertility. It is what we apomecometrists would call a "topographical hyster-on-proteron". That is all I can possibly say to you on the matter.'

Joss Kay was certainly clever, though the oddest combination of self-confidence and self-pity that I had ever met with. Even though I was not sure he properly understood the force that weighed against all strangers in Preston, I apprehended that he did not want to be schooled by me in defending himself. I went to the door and hammered on it for Tarlton to let me out, then reached into my pocket.

'I'll leave you, then, with my best wishes for your early release. Meanwhile, here is a paper for you.'

'What is it?'

'What we lawyers would call a summons. It requires your appearance at Kirkham as a witness at tomorrow's inquest into the death of Abraham Scroop. I shall want you in the morning. If you are still in custody the Sergeant will be instructed to produce you. Until then, I wish you well.'

As I walked up the mossy stone stairs towards the daylight, my shoes squishing wetly, I could hear the voices of the burgesses in council. It sounded like a lively discussion. I wondered what on earth a topographical hysteron-proteron might be.

I had no sooner reached the open air than I heard my name called from across the street. It was Luke Fidelis dressed for riding and on his way to the livery yard.

'I'm off to Cottam to see a patient,' he told me. 'It's one that you might find interesting. Why not ride with me?'

On the eve of an inquest, with everything ready and nothing more to do, I am often restless and in need of distraction. Fidelis's invitation would meet the need so I agreed and went with him to the horse-yard.

'I hear Mallender's made yet another injudicious arrest,' Fidelis told me once we were mounted and on our way.

'Yes. I've just been to see Mr Kay. There isn't any evidence against him though Mallender's got a face like the King of the Cats since he made the arrest. But tell me about this patient we are going to see.'

'It is Peter Chimpton at Cottam.'

'Chimpton? But surely he is dead! We both heard Dr Harrod say so.'

Fidelis laughed.

'For a dead man, he played pretty well on the harpsichord when I saw him on Wednesday. The corpse was in good voice, too.'

'You mean he was not poorly at all?'

'Oh yes, he is poorly. He suffers in his liver and his heart is not strong. But so far he remains alive. Dr Harrod's prognoses will always be doubtful as long as he relies on astrology to tell him when a death is due.'

Peter Chimpton's house was charming but very old. The original builders had made it of stone, and roofed it with slates, which was fortunate as these materials kept wind and rain out of the dwelling. Inside, though the house was more or less dry, it had been allowed to fall into ruin.

Chimpton had once been prosperous, with many acres of fertile land for crops and grazing. But thirty years ago disease had swept through his herds and, at the same time, his crops were entirely blighted. People believed it was God's judgement on him for taking the Pretender's side in the '15 rebellion, and whether true or not (I keep an open mind about such things), nothing about his farm had thrived since. In the first years following the disaster, Chimpton worked like Hercules to replace the beasts and replant the fields, but every season came the same failures: misshapen calves, still-born lambs, blackened potatoes. Finally, having exhausted all his reserves of money and will, Chimpton yielded to his fate. He let his fields run to tares and bramble. His sheepfolds were empty; he abandoned his pig pens and milking barns. Now he lived on with only a couple of milk-cows, a senile manservant and a harpsichord for company.

We could hear him playing even as we dismounted in the yard, a river of notes running on and on in a spate of quick rills and plunging chords. Fidelis hammered on the door and, though the music never stopped, we heard a voice from the inside telling us to wait on. Finally a spindly, wisp-haired ancient heaved the door open. It was the servant, Cargill.

Without a word spoken we were led into a gloomy stone-flagged parlour, where Chimpton sat playing. He looked up and, recognizing Fidelis, immediately raised his hands from the keyboard.

'Most men of my age can't do that,' he declared. 'I still have capacity in my fingers, Doctor, if nowhere else in my body.'

'You play excellently, Mr Chimpton,' said Fidelis, who was no mean musician himself. 'What was that you were performing?'

'Something from Dr Byrd. His music's a hundred and fifty years old now, but nothing has ever surpassed it.'

'I'll wager there are few farmers in Lancashire who can surpass your playing.'

'Former farmer, Doctor, that's how I describe myself. And one that should be dead and buried, if Dr Harrod's to be believed. Who is this with you? Forgive me, Sir, my eyesight is not what it was.'

'I am Titus Cragg, Mr Chimpton.'

'Welcome, Mr Cragg. I regret we have nothing to offer you, unless there's a glass of Cargill's fermented apple juice. Cargill!'

Before the servant could reappear, we hastened to decline the offer of the home-brew and Fidelis reverted to his role as doctor. He asked how the patient was (middling), took his pulse (a trifle rapid), listened to the beat of his heart through an ear trumpet (a touch watery) and sniffed the water in his chamber pot (a definite tang of yeast).

'I would recommend that you eat more red meat,' he said at last.

Chimpton shrugged. 'Alas! I cannot afford to. Cargill gives me a hot pot from time to time, but money's short. I can say this, and I'm proud of it: I owe nothing. But I *have* nothing neither, so I scrape by, and that is all. Most of my valuables have already been sold so there's not much to look forward to from that quarter.'

'Your harpsichord is a fine instrument,' I said.

'If by that you mean I should sell it, no Sir. I will starve before I do. Music gives life, did you know that, Doctor?'

Fidelis smiled.

'I have heard it said, and would not deny it. But you mentioned that Dr Harrod told you that you would die. When was this?'

'Oh, it was on Monday. I had felt dizzy and fallen over, so I sent for him. He told me when he came that he had prepared his calculations and it was in the stars that I would die – indeed that I should already be dead – and so I must prepare myself.'

He shrugged again.

'Well, so I did. I sent for the priest. I said the prayers he told me to say. But look at me: still here and still playing William Byrd's music.'

His eyes had the slightest sparks of laughter in them.

'When precisely was Dr Harrod here?'

'Nine o'clock on Monday he was here, or just after, by that clock there.'

He nodded towards a tall and solemn long-case clock that stood against the opposite wall. Surreptitiously I checked it against my watch: it told the right time.

'And did he stay long?'

'No, the man seemed in a hurry, which I thought a trifle bad-mannered in him, as he'd just told me of my death. He was here, oh, fifteen or twenty minutes, no more.'

'And he has not been back.'

'No, he said I would unhappily not see him again. Ha! I have been thinking of surprising him with a letter to tell him his horoscope was all cock-eyed and he should cast it again. And, mind you, to give me some medicine while he's about it. But I don't need to, now that you have adopted my case and told me there's a teaspoonful of life in me yet.'

Fidelis took a small bottle from his case.

'Indeed you don't, Sir. And speaking of teaspoonfuls, see here, I have made up a draught for you to take. Just give yourself a spoonful in the morning and evening.'

'It is surprising that Chimpton is still alive,' Fidelis told me as we rode away ten minutes later.

'Harrod was not wrong, then?'

'Not in principle. The patient is seriously ill. But I believe that accidentally Harrod did him a favour by informing him he should already be dead.'

'It seems an unfeeling thing to do.'

'It is certainly a chancy one. Tell a man that he is shortly going to die, and there can be one of two contrary outcomes. Either he despairs and the thread of life thins and thins until it breaks. Or he says "Be damned! I'll not die!" Then, somehow, the vital spirits rise up against the death sentence; they flow back again, and he survives. It was the case with Mr Chimpton, I am sure of it.'

'Will the effect last?'

'No, he will meet his maker quite soon, I fear. But he's lived long enough to give some excellent information about the doctor and the death of Scroop, and that's a good thing, don't you agree?'

'I might if I knew what you were talking about.'

'The timing, Titus. What Chimpton just told us exposes Basilius Harrod to a serious accusation.'

'Which is?'

'That he killed his friend Abraham Scroop.'

I laughed.

'You think Harrod's the killer now? He is such a mild-mannered fellow. It hardly looks likely.'

'We have heard tales of how he is enmeshed in the Scroop family, have we not?'

'Tales! There may be nothing in them beyond a mild infatuation. It does not tell us why.'

'You always want to know why, Titus! Think instead about the fact. Harrod lied about what he was doing at the time Scroop was killed. He said he was with Chimpton at ten-thirty when in reality he left at a quarter past nine. He would not do this unless he wanted to conceal his presence at the scene of the murder. From there it is not a long step to believing that he himself delivered the fatal thrust of the needle into the ear. Does it not strike you as the kind of murder a medical man might commit, and hope to get away with?'

'For Heaven's sake, Luke, if this is true, then by our own surmises he must have killed the skin-yard baby, too, and I cannot think why on earth he would do that murder. And how does it sort with your suspicion of the skinners when they celebrated Scroop's death?'

'It may have been just that – the celebration of a welcome deliverance. The finger now pointing to Harrod is much more firmly directed.'

'I wish your finger would point me in the direction of what improvements of the Marsh were being discussed. It would help if only I knew who Thomas Steers was.'

'Thomas Steers? How is he involved in this?'

I told him of the letter from Steers in answer to one from Scroop, in which he declined the offer of employment and recommended Joss Kay instead.

'But Kay won't tell me about Steers, or anything about the project he was hired for. He makes a great mystery of the thing.'

'There is no need to be mystified, Titus. You should have asked me. Steers is very well known in Liverpool and is a titan of achievement there. Though he is not a native he is one of the town's favourite sons.'

'What sort of achievement, Luke?'

And so he told me – and suddenly the reason for the secrecy

that had obscured all Scroop's dealings with Lord Grassington, Captain Strawboy, and even with Lord Derby, became clear.

'I'm going to bring all this out at the inquest,' I said grimly. 'I'll be damned if I don't.'

Chapter 29

EVEN AT PRESTON, home to much and various legal activity, the public treated an inquest as a form of entertainment. In a small market town like Kirkham, it sucked people in like a raree-show. The upper room of the inn at Kirkham was therefore packed even more solidly than my last inquest at the Skeleton Inn, with arrivals from Preston competing with local people for room on the public benches.

'Let us begin by hearing from the first finder, Dr Basilius Harrod. Please come up to the chair, Dr Harrod.'

We had already sworn the jury and viewed the body, and now the interesting part of the inquest began. Harrod was all smiles and ease as he made his way to the front of the packed room. The audience looked around to follow his progress and he greeted one or two friends amongst them with a wave of the hand, or a small bow for the ladies.

Once he was sworn in, I asked him to take me through the events leading up to his finding the body of Scroop.

'I had been seeing a patient at Cottam. I returned to Preston to hear that my friend Scroop's horse had come back riderless. I learned that he had gone out to Kirkham on some business relating to the headstone of his poor dead child. After another two hours he did not appear, so it was decided to form a party to look for him.'

'What time did you set off?'

'At half past two, or thereabouts, as you very well know, Cragg. You were of the party.'

'Yes, Doctor, I do know. I merely ask for the record. What happened when you reached Kirkham?'

'I had sent ahead for the attendance by the infant's graveside of the mason that Scroop, as we had been told, had seen first thing in the morning. This man confirmed that he had a conversation with Mr Scroop about the wording on the headstone before eight o'clock, and that they had parted shortly afterwards.'

'What did you do then?'

'We divided up into pairs, each undertaking to search along a different path towards Preston. As it happened I was the one to find the body lying on the wayside. He had obviously been knocked from his horse and died from the fall where he lay.'

'Which road was this on?'

'It was not quite a road – a track or ride just north of Newton Mill, at a point where it passed through a small wood known, I believe, as Carter's Copse.'

'And how did the body lie?'

'On its front, until we turned it over to see whether poor Scroop had been robbed. We searched his pockets.'

'Did he still have his valuables?'

'His watch, chain, pocket book and snuffbox were all there. We concluded he had not been robbed.'

'Was his death caused in your opinion by the injury to his head?'

'Yes. It had broken his skull.'

'Would that have killed him, necessarily?'

'No, not necessarily. Someone hurt like that might lie for a time unconscious but alive. However, in his case, I suggest that the injury resulted in bleeding in the brain and that this would have led to his death very soon after he hit the ground.'

'Did you see anything that might have caused him to be thrown from the horse?'

'There was an oak tree branch a few yards back. It overhung the track at about the height of a rider's head. I believe that Mr Scroop was not paying due attention as he rode, and was struck from the saddle after his head had violently collided with the branch. He may have been trotting fast, going at a canter or even a gallop at the time.'

'But a man who strikes something with his head whilst riding is generally hurled back over the rump of the horse, is he not? He then lands, I would have thought, in the road rather than on the verge.'

'I see what you mean. In this case I think he must have some-how retained his seat in the saddle for a pace or two more, until unconsciousness overtook him, whereupon he fell to the ground.'

'Very well. There is a gap in time of more than two and a half hours – isn't there? – between his last being seen by the stonemason and the arrival of the horse back in Preston. Could Mr Scroop have lain there dead or dying on the ground for as long as that?'

'I don't think he did. Consider the horse. It would surely have made its way directly home once the rider was out of the saddle. We all know that horses do not dawdle on their way homewards. They want their oats.'

Some slight laughter over this commonplace rippled through the room.

'So if what you say is right, and we allow for a half-hour jour-ney by the horse, from the place where the body was found to the point at which it was recaptured, the horse and rider would have parted company at about ten-thirty.'

'That is my belief. And furthermore it was at that time that his watch was broken by his fall.'

I looked to my right and left. The jury were listening intently and one or two of them were nodding their heads sagely, to show they understood the significance of this.

'So what was Mr Scroop doing in the meantime?' I asked. 'You knew him well. Can you enlighten us?'

'No, as I have said I was neither with him nor privy to his plans. But Abraham Scroop was a man with many business concerns in many different places, which much occupied his mind. Nor was he one to waste his time. I would guess he had further business out that way and that this detained him in the area until ten-thirty.'

'Thank you Dr Harrod. May I ask you to stay with us in case the inquest has any further need of your medical knowledge?'

Next I called Joseph Twiss to the chair. He confirmed the time at which he had seen Scroop, before eight o'clock.

'Did he say where he was going after your meeting?'

'He did not.'

'What frame of mind was he in?

'A very sober one – as you would think he would be when talking about the burial place of his baby son.'

'Will you tell the court what words Mr Scroop had asked you to carve on the child's headstone?'

'"Loammi Scroop, born and died 1743. Plead with your mother, plead."'

There were whispers in the audience.

'Did he tell you anything about that inscription?'

'No. I told him I'd not seen those words written down before. He ignored me.'

'And the unusual given name, Loammi? Did he mention it at all?'

'He didn't. We just talked about the kind of lettering and the layout on the stone and that was it. We shook hands and I went back to my work.'

I excused him, and called Bartholomew Lock, who had been

Scroop's right hand at business, and whom I had last seen as a juror in the case of the skin-yard baby. I asked Lock if he was aware of any other business apart from the headstone that might have occupied Scroop in the Kirkham area. He knew of nothing.

'Mr Scroop were very busy with the plans he had for various improvements. It were likely summat to do with those that kept him over there.'

The answer naturally led me to call my next witness, who I hoped would tell us more of those very improvements – James Strawboy. The Captain spoke out in a loud, straining voice, as if the duty of giving his evidence was something unnatural to him. Equally unnaturally he seemed intent on keeping his eyes fixed on mine throughout my examination.

'You were a business associate of Mr Scroop, I believe.'

'I was.'

His eyes bored into mine.

'In what business precisely?'

'In one or two projects around Preston. Improvements.'

'What were you planning to improve?'

'It is no secret that Mr Scroop wished to clean up the tanning yard. The idea was to move it from its present site, and there run it himself in a more salubrious way.'

'But Mr Scroop was not a tanner. How would he know how to do this?'

Still that intense look – was it attention or fear in his eyes?

'He would take advice, naturally.'

'Would he need the advice of Mr Thomas Steers of Liverpool, for instance?'

At the mention of Steers Strawboy turned pale then looked down for the first time. The pitch of his voice was lower and quieter.

'I, er, don't know who you mean.'

'Mr Steers is a distinguished engineer established in Liverpool.'

'Is he?'

'Captain Strawboy, I think you know he is. I shall put it to you straight. Is it true that you and Mr Scroop, with some funding from others such as your uncle Lord Grassington, were planning a huge project for Preston Marsh, a plan that would entirely alter the character of that very useful and much appreciated stretch of wet land beside the river bank?'

Strawboy's face had begun to redden now.

'I regret I am not at liberty to say more on this subject.'

'You won't be at liberty at all, Captain, if I decide to press you on this.'

'But it is quite irrelevant to the present inquiry.'

'That is for me to decide, Sir. But – ah! – I see one has arrived who might relieve you of the duty of helping us.'

I meant Joss Kay who, flanked by the Parkin brothers, had just been led into the room. We had heard that Kay had been ordered back to prison by the bench, pending his appearance before the grand jury. Asking Strawboy not to leave the court, I let him down and called Kay in his place.

'Mr Kay, the court has heard Captain Strawboy's words, viz. that "it is no secret that Mr Scroop planned to improve the skin-yard". However, there was more to this scheme than just the tannery, was there not?'

Kay, already facing legal troubles of his own, looked trapped and miserable as he tried to weigh the perils of perjury against the secrecy of men who might yet help him out of facing a murder charge. Finally he must have decided it was too great a risk to lie. He nodded his head.

'Clerk,' I said to Furzey, who was writing furiously, 'please note that the witness assents. Tell us more if you please, Mr Kay. This was indeed being kept secret, I think.'

Kay cleared his throat.

'It was thought best not to speak of the project until the moment was right. It was thought there would be unrest. Protests. Not even the majority of the Corporation knew about it.'

'Who did know? Had you been told the full extent of the project?'

'Not I. Mr Scroop, he was the prime mover. The Earl of Derby. Captain Strawboy. And the Captain's uncle Lord Grassington also, I believe, though I don't know the nobleman. There was also a group of men among your Preston burgesses who were interested in investing.'

'But surely you yourself became privy to this secret also?'

'Some of it. I was asked to make a survey, wasn't I?'

'Yes, and on the recommendation of Mr Thomas Steers of Liverpool, I believe.'

'Er, that is so.'

'Who is at present employed in Ireland – making a canal I believe – but who became known in Liverpool for something else. What was that?'

Kay's answer was in two words that came out in a hoarse low whisper.

'Speak up, Mr Kay. You must make up your mind to tell the court in plain words.'

The witness straightened his back. He had decided, it seemed, which side of the scales weighed heavier.

'It was the dock,' he said, quite clearly now. 'Mr Steers designed and built Liverpool's enclosed dock on top of the Pool.'

'Ah! Did he indeed? And the work you came here for – tell us about that.'

'It was to do a complete survey of the Marsh.'

'With a view to?'

'Doing the same for Preston's Marsh as Mr Steers did for Liverpool's Pool. To turn the whole place into a dock.'

'Go on. Tell us why he wanted to do that.'

'Anyone can see that the present wharf at Preston is not adequate. Our project is to replace it with an enclosed dock so great it would be one of the wonders of England, and far larger than Mr Steers's first dock.'

'And would it really consume all of the Marsh?'

'Easily. It is a huge enterprise requiring much toil in excavation, drainage and embankments.'

At this point one of the jury interrupted. He did not know what was meant by an 'enclosed dock'. I turned back to Kay.

'For the benefit of us inlanders, would you explain the construction and purpose of an enclosed dock?'

'It is a man-made basin surrounded by quays and dug out of the river bank or, in this case, out of the Marsh. It allows shipping to come into it at high tide through sea gates. These close behind it, keeping the water level up even when the tide outside is low.'

'So the ships inside float rather than, as now, sitting high, dry and a-tilt on the mud?'

'Exactly.'

'But why do this in Preston, Mr Kay?'

'To bring more sea trade. Loading and unloading will be easier, but more important are the many extra berths that will be provided, as well as warehouses and the like. Capacity at the moment is woefully low – four or five ships at a time, at the most. Such a dock would take ten times as many. And of course the profits arising will especially benefit the town's life and manufacturing. Preston would be a great port and a happier town because of it.'

'You are very confident there, Mr Kay.'

'I am. I have based my whole life on the belief in improvement of all kinds.'

'But not everyone would agree with this improvement. There are those who uphold the traditional employment of land – in this case of the Marsh in grazing and other uses. They would say your scheme rates private profit ahead of ancient public rights. So, from your own observation of him, was Abraham Scroop afraid that his plans would meet with this kind of opposition?'

'He knew they would. He said there might be violence.'

'Violence! That's interesting.'

'Unrest happens in many other places where improvement is pushed through by energetic men against the dead hand of ignorance. Unfortunately windows get broken and life is endangered. That's why it was thought best to complete the calculations and working plans for the dock, and if possible get the Act of Parliament passed, before—'

I interrupted.

'A parliamentary Act is required, is it?'

'Yes, or the work would not be legal.'

'And the idea was to pass this Act before the people of Preston woke up to what rights they were losing?'

'That is so, more or less.'

The whispering in the room had become a buzz, a murmur of debate and a flurry of under-the-breath comment.

'You have described Mr Scroop as the prime mover in the enterprise. Do you know if he feared violence against himself, if this news became public?'

'I don't know. He may have. You must ask someone closer to him.'

'I intend to. But it has not escaped my attention that you have been questioned by the magistrates in Preston. They think you are concerned in the death of Mr Scroop. What do you say to that?'

'No. I am quite innocent. I had done work for Mr Scroop and he owed me money. I was waiting to be paid, that is all.'

'Thank you, Mr Kay, your testimony has been enlightening.'

He left the chair and I now called Mrs Scroop. She had been

present from the beginning in her widow's weeds, alongside her three equally black-clad eldest daughters. One of these, Harriet, helped her mother to the chair, then returned to her seat. I addressed the new witness.

'Tell us what you know about your husband's plans for the day on last Monday morning.'

'I know nothing. My husband did not confide his plans to me, not ever.'

'What about his personal safety? Did he say anything to you on this subject? For instance, in relation to this scheme for a dock we have been hearing of?'

'No.'

'Very well, Mrs Scroop, here is another matter. Why have you given away or burned all your husband's clothes, books, papers and personal things since he died?'

'Because I do not like to be reminded of him. It is painful.'

'I fear it will be painful also for you to answer my next question but I must ask. Did you choose the name Loammi for your baby son?'

'No. My husband did.'

'Do you know why he chose this curious name?'

'No. But I imagine one cannot be barred from having what name he prefers.'

'What about the inscription Mr Scroop asked to be carved on the headstone? Did he not consult you about that? It refers to yourself, after all.'

'I know nothing of it.'

'It seems to address the dead child. "Plead with your mother, plead", it says. Plead to you for what, Mrs Scroop?'

'I don't know. It was all his idea, from beginning to end.'

'You cannot tell us what it might mean?'

'No.'

The audience conversation now rose towards a hubbub. I had asked a string of questions and Mrs Scroop had remained as closed to me and as icily calm as ever. On my side, I was no nearer to knowing the truth, but my questions had been so many crumbs thrown into a fishpond and the carp were beginning to boil in the water around them.

I quietened the crowd and, dismissing Mrs Scroop for the time being, called Dr Fidelis up to replace her.

While he was making his way forward I said, 'May I appeal to all of you present: if anyone can shed any light on the words Mr Scroop had chosen to inscribe on his son's headstone, I urge you please to come forward. Ah, Dr Fidelis! Will you take the book in your right hand please?'

Once he was sworn in, I asked for his opinion of Scroop's death.

'It was murder,' he said. 'He was killed with malice aforethought.'

The room of course had been expecting this. They buzzed about it like bees, but did not roar in complete surprise, as I have once or twice heard in court.

'You are very definite, Doctor.'

'When I first saw the body I noticed that the eyelids would not close, while the extended limbs – the fingers for instance – were still loose. The stiffening of the eyelid is the first sign of the general stiffening of the muscles that begins to creep over a body five or six hours after death. Since I was examining the body at about two thirty in the afternoon I concluded that Mr Scroop had died between eight and nine in the morning.'

'That contradicts the suggestion that Mr Scroop was knocked from his horse at ten thirty, dying shortly afterwards.'

'It does. At the finding place, I looked for his hat and could not see it. Indeed it was not found, I believe. So I was not surprised when I noticed that the clothing on Scroop's front – and he was found lying on his front – was wet, while that on his back was dry.'

'What conclusion did you draw from that?'

'That he did not die in the position in which he was found. I believe that he was moved to the spot, and this cannot have happened until after it rained at about ten thirty that morning.'

The jury had continued to listen intently but this flummoxed them. Their agitated hand signals told me they needed help in understanding what had just been said.

'The body was lying on its front,' I explained. 'The front of the clothing was wet, meaning the body must have come down on wet ground – that is, after it had been raining. But the only rain that morning was a heavy shower which began at ten thirty. Therefore Dr Fidelis draws the conclusion that the body – which was already dead for the reason previously given – had been deposited at that spot by another person after the shower had come and gone. Note – the *back* of the body was dry. Have I caught your meaning, Doctor?'

'Yes. That is what I observed when I first saw the body.'

'And did you have the opportunity to examine it more closely later?'

'I did on the next day, at your request.'

'What did you find?'

'I noticed blood in the ear and from it removed a plug of material thickly soaked in dried blood. I then opened the skull and found that the brain had been assaulted via the ear canal by some thin instrument such as a spike or needle and severe bleeding had been caused, which would have brought about death in a few minutes.'

'Could this injury have been self-inflicted?'

'No man or woman could do that to themselves.'

'Have you ever seen such an injury before?'

'Only once, and that was recently. It was a death you held an inquest over at Preston – the baby found in the skin-yard.'

'So you are telling this court that that baby and Mr Scroop died in the same way?'

'Exactly the same.'

'Thank you, Dr Fidelis.'

The room had been taut with concentration. Now, as Fidelis walked back to his seat in the audience they released a collective out-breath and began to speak amongst themselves again.

I let the chatter continue while I meditated my next step. We had heard all the evidence about the circumstances of Scroop's death and were no nearer identifying his murderer. Did that matter? Strictly speaking the duty of the inquest ends when it has determined a cause of death, and I felt confident Fidelis's evidence would have convinced the jury to find murder. There were still some details I would like to give them such as the meaning of the words on Loammi Scroop's headstone. Perhaps someone would come forward with an explanation if we had an adjournment. I was about to ring my bell and call this when a folded paper was placed on the table in front of me, with my name on it.

And behold the people knew not, as of old they had known, the word of the Lord. And the Lord therefore hid his face from the people covering them with ignorance, yea, as he has covered the very frogs and toads and creeping things of the Earth.

Chapter 30

THE NOTE WAS unsigned. I read it through three times, and came out from behind my table in order to speak quietly to the front row of the audience. The woman that had handed me the letter said it had been passed up from behind her. I enquired behind, and identified some of those that had handed the letter forward from the rear of the room. None, however, could say who had written it.

I called for order and immediately adjourned the inquest. I sent the jury to the room in which their dinner awaited, telling them they could discuss the case – how could I have stopped them? – but must make no attempt to reach a verdict until after they had heard my summary which would be delivered after we had all eaten. Then I took the Bible that we used for swearing in, and shut myself in the small adjoining parlour where my own meal was laid out.

I did not touch the food at first, but stood at the window and looked out across the busy Saturday market place. Sellers shouted their wares. Customers came and went between the stalls, stopping to feel a piece of worsted or test the ripeness of a plum. Draught animals stood with infinite patience between the shafts, twitching their ears at the flies. A puppy lay asleep in a patch of sunlight.

Under the market cross at the centre of my view a fellow was climbing with some difficulty on to a mounting block. He was dressed in black and held in his hand the same book as I had in mine. Having perched himself on thin legs above the heads of the passers-by, he got ready to preach, holding up his Bible just (I couldn't resist the thought) as I have seen hucksters and quack doctors hold up their bottles of patent medicine.

On a sudden impulse I went out, down the stairs and into the open air. What had that note tried to tell me? The one question not answered during the morning's proceedings had been the meaning of the words Scroop had carefully chosen for his son's tomb. Was this person – I supposed he or she was too shy to speak openly – pointing to their source in the Bible and saying the reason no one had identified them was because of widespread ignorance of the scriptures?

This marketplace preacher would know his Bible, however. The book was his touchstone, and the source of his power. He had no need for ordination, or a tap on the shoulder from a bishop's crozier. So long as he could come up with a biblical quotation to fit every human situation, so long as he could show that he knew the word of God as intimately as he knew his own mother's face, he would never lack legitimacy, whether in a meeting house or in the open air.

I stood in a small group watching the man's Adam's apple jerking up and down as he denounced the ways of the world, in a voice surprisingly rich in one so skinny. After ten minutes he stopped to wipe his perspiring brow and take a swig of cold tea from a bottle in his pocket. I took this opportunity to step forward.

'I wonder, Sir, if you can identify a quotation from Scripture for me?' I asked.

He looked down at me warily.

'I do not perform tricks of memory, Sir. I am not a fairground attraction.'

'It is nothing like that. I am the County Coroner, and I am

enquiring into some words that may originate in the Bible.' I nodded towards the black volume in his hand. 'I hope you can tell me exactly where they occur.'

The preacher now stepped down from his perch and took my arm, drawing me a little apart from his other hearers.

'I will help you if I can, Sir, but not in public. Of course it does me credit with these people if I succeed in placing the words. However, by the same token, I cannot afford to fail, which I might do. The Bible is a very long book. What is it you are looking for?'

I showed him the anonymous note, which he studied, frowning and with his lips pushed out, before handing it back to me.

'No. These words seem biblical, but I regret I can't place them. I would like to, as they are extremely apposite to most Christians in the world. I will search for them.'

'Then what of the words "Plead with your mother, plead." Can you place those?'

He immediately looked happier.

'Oh yes! Yes, indeed, I know those. The Book of Hosea. The most difficult of all the prophetic books. The edicts of the Almighty it gives are puzzling to say the least. "Plead with your mother, plead". Yes. I think you'll find the words near the beginning of the book. I'll leave you to construe them as you will, however. I must get on, if you'll excuse me.'

Back at the inn's parlour, while eating the excellent mutton pie provided for me, I turned the pages of the Bible as far as Hosea. I had not read more than a few lines when I knew I would have to recall Mrs Scroop immediately to the chair.

The crowd may have been disappointed to discover they were not going to have an early verdict, but they were compensated by the chance of hearing more from Helena Scroop. They were all agog.

'You have heard Dr Fidelis's evidence that your husband – in his opinion – was murdered somewhere in this locality, and later moved to the place where he was found. You will understand that in cases where murder is suspected a coroner must ask hard questions and bring to light unpleasant matters.'

She looked at me with unmixed hostility, but said nothing.

'It is my duty therefore to tell you I now know the source of the words your husband chose to put on your late child's tomb, and I know why he chose to call him posthumously by the singular name Loammi. The import of these words and this name are also very clear to me, but may be very shocking to you and to many of those here present. I therefore ask you to prepare yourself.'

There was no talking in the room as I opened the Bible. Every rustle of the pages I turned could be heard.

'I now read from the Book of Hosea, Chapter 1. "And the Lord said unto Hosea, Go, take unto thee a wife of whoredom and children of whoredoms: for the land hath committed great whoredom, departing from the Lord."'

I looked up to see if these words had any effect on the witness. She merely looked stonily ahead. I went on.

'"So he went and took Gomer, the daughter of Diblain."'

I looked up from the book again.

'I omit a passage in which his wife gives birth to a son, a daughter and finally another son. About this last child the text continues. "Then said God, call his name Loammi for ye are not my people and I will not be your God. Plead with your mother, plead: for she is not my wife, neither am I her husband, let her therefore put away her whoredoms out of her sight and her adulteries from between her breasts."'

The room had gone so quiet you might have heard a leaf hit the ground.

'Mrs Scroop, we know of your husband's murder. We have also

been told that his secret improvement project for Preston might have attracted the enmity of some in the town. But now we find that the words on your son's memorial had nothing to do with his business. Instead they had to do with you.'

'Not with me!'

'But it is in plain view. With these words your husband is accusing you of misconduct. He says to you "put away your whoredoms and your adulteries". He even seems to say that you are not his wife, and that you and your children are not God's people. Can you give this inquest any explanation for these accusations?'

She sat with her left hand clamped tightly around her right wrist, as if to restrain it.

'My husband and I were lawfully married, Sir.'

'But it is common speech that an adulterous spouse is not a true spouse, is it not?'

The witness merely tightened her lips and said nothing. I persisted.

'Mrs Scroop, the court must hear from you on this matter, however painful and awkward the truth may be. I put it to you that you had formed an attachment with another man, that you conceived a child and that Mr Scroop discovered he was not or may not have been the father of that child— Good God! The child! I hadn't thought of it until now. It must be examined!'

I had spoken these words out loud, just as they had come to me, in a confusion of mental associations. I asked the court for a moment's grace, and had an urgent whispered conference with Furzey.

'There may have been a third murder!' I said. 'Draw up an exhumation order – now! The name is Loammi Scroop and the burial place is St Michael's churchyard. Dr Fidelis *must* examine the child, and do it today!'

I then turned back to the witness and cautioned her to remain in or near the courtroom for further questioning if necessary. Then to the astonishment of all I adjourned the hearing for two hours.

An exhumation is a serious matter and cannot be obtained without the Coroner's signature being endorsed by a member of the bench. Fortunately I was able to enlist to the cause a gentleman of the town, Mr Marmaduke Flitcroft, and so within half an hour I was standing by the little grave of Loammi Scroop, together with Magistrate Flitcroft, the vicar the Reverend Phillips in surplice and stole, the parish sexton with spade, Luke Fidelis holding his medical bag and most of the audience from the inquest.

While Mr Phillips read aloud from the Psalms, the sexton forced his heart-shaped blade into the loose soil that covered the grave, laying each spadeful carefully aside before driving it powerfully in again. Every eye that could get a view was fixed on that spade. Some were perched precariously on nearby headstones. Others had climbed to the top of the church tower so that they could see it all from above.

In only a few minutes the spade struck wood with a hollow thump. Sixty seconds later the child-sized coffin was in sight. Excavating around the edge, the sexton loosened it, and breathing in grunts eased it out of the slot where it had nestled. Straightening his back, he looked between Phillips and myself for his instructions. The vicar moistened his dry lips with his tongue.

'Shall we take it into the church – for privacy, you know – the vestry, perhaps?'

I looked around at all the people expecting to view the result of the exhumation and made up my mind not to disappoint them.

'No, let everyone see. Bring the box over to that tomb there.'

I pointed to a nearby grave, which was covered by a wide stone slab. The sexton placed his burden there and then produced a short crowbar.

'All right, Sir?'

I nodded and he slipped the sharpened end of the tool under the lid. The strained nails creaked, creaked more loudly, and then popped. The lid came loose, but instead of lifting it the sexton swept the loose earth from it and stepped away. I came forward.

'Is everyone ready?'

Everyone was. I grasped the lid, raised it and peered underneath. The first thing I noticed is that there was no smell.

The elongated shape wrapped in some rough dowlas or cheese-cloth was easily lifted out. It had the shape and firmness of a short bolster, and was roughly stitched at each end. I picked a hole in the cloth, which I enlarged by driving a finger into it. When I took my finger out a dribble of wet sand dropped from the hole.

I looked up. Phillips, who usually looked ashen-faced, had turned even paler upon realising that he had lately read the funeral rites of a sandbag.

I stormed back to the inquest room and rang my bell furiously. The empty coffin had charged me full of rage and demonic determination to reach the truth. But I was looking at rows of empty benches.

'This inquest is in session again,' I shouted. 'Where's the jury? Furzey! Find that Foreman and tell him to herd the men back in here.'

When at last the bewildered jurymen had returned to their places, and the audience settled itself, I was able to continue my examination of the widow. I prefer my manner towards witnesses to be one of courteous, infinitely patient enquiry; but now I could not prevent acidity from creeping across my tongue.

'Mrs Scroop, you have deceived us. You have deceived the vicar of this parish. You have deceived the world. Now you must tell us the meaning of this outrage. Where is the body that all supposed had been buried in that grave? Where is your son, Mrs Scroop?'

Helena Scroop held herself rigid and unyieldingly composed. She looked straight ahead of her – or rather she did not look at all but affected oblivion to the room, and to me. She was physically present yet she had withdrawn her attention from the proceedings. I repeated the question in a thunderous voice, but with the same result.

'Oh! If she won't tell, then I will!'

It was a high-pitched voice from the middle of the room, and it belonged to Harriet Scroop. Dressed as neatly and sombrely as her mother, but with her face betraying considerably more emotion, she came out of the crowd and approached my table, where she immediately snatched up the Bible.

'I swear by Almighty God to tell the truth, the whole truth and nothing but the truth. There, I have sworn, Mr Coroner. Ask me your questions.'

The procedure was not quite orthodox, but I agreed with a tilt of my head towards the witness chair.

'Very well, Miss Scroop, will you take your place in the chair?'

The chair, however, was still occupied by her stony-faced mother, who showed no sign of moving.

'No,' said Harriet. 'I will stand.'

'If you prefer. Now, please will *you* tell us about your baby brother. What happened to him? Where is he?'

Harriet did not hesitate. To general astonishment, she plunged into one of the strangest family stories I have ever uncovered.

'There is no baby brother,' she declared. 'There never has been.'

At this point her mother leapt from the chair.

'No! Harriet, no! You will bring ruin down on yourself!'

'I am ruined already, mother. There's no escaping it.'

Helena Scroop started to cry. She pressed a handkerchief to her mouth and nose, but kept her eyes fixed on the empty air in front of her. Some kind soul from the audience came forward and led her away.

I said, 'Please go on, Miss Scroop. You said there never was a baby brother.'

Harriet now sat down in the vacated chair. She seemed as composed as ever.

'My mother was not expecting a child, you see, she merely made a pretence of it.'

'Why would she do that?'

'To protect me. It was me that was with child, Sir.'

I quelled the burst of surprised cries from the audience and, gently now, asked Harriet to say more.

'We managed to keep it secret, though I came to think my maid Kathy Brock suspected it. Once she left our house it was easier. I did not go out except to church, where I wore a wide cloak, and so my condition was not revealed even towards the end. Meanwhile, my mother let it be known she herself was expecting another child. Our intention was that when I eventually gave birth she would tell the world the baby was hers.'

'Did something go wrong, then?'

'Yes. My mother was away visiting her brother in Hull when my baby started to come. It was born two weeks early.'

'But what happened to it, Harriet?'

'It died.'

'And then?'

'I don't know. It was . . . disposed of.'

'In the tan-pit at the skin-yard, not far from your home?'

'I . . . I don't know. It wasn't me that did it.'

'Who was it, then? Who, Harriet?'

She did not reply, but stood blinking away the tears in her eyes. I tried another approach.

'Was it the father of your child who took this action? Tell us his name. Who seduced you?'

'It was . . . oh, well, what does it matter? It was the

footman who worked for us. O'Rorke. It was him that was responsible.'

I was astounded. She had spoken quite clearly yet I wanted her to repeat herself.

'Jon O'Rorke? Is that who you mean?'

'Yes.'

'I see. And did O'Rorke take the baby away from you when it was born?'

'Yes. I never saw it again.'

'And what happened to O'Rorke? '

'My father dismissed him. I had told him nothing of O'Rorke's part in the matter, but he suspected him and that was enough.'

'Were *you* fond of O'Rorke?'

'No, I was not.'

'So why – forgive me – did you yield to his persuasions?'

'I don't know. But I did.'

'Did your father know about your transgression?'

'He realized in the end that I had been dishonoured. But only because of your enquiries at the time, Mr Cragg. From those he worked the truth out for himself.'

'My enquiries were interrupted by a serious fire. Do you know anything about that?'

'No, Sir. I was not present.'

'Could your father have had a hand in it?'

'I don't know.'

'So, meanwhile, your mother had come back from Hull still masquerading as pregnant.'

'Yes. When she returned she had to go through the motions of birth. We pretended that the child was a boy, and very feeble, to explain why no one heard him cry. Then after a few days we said that he had died.'

'Was your father party to this deception?'

'No he knew nothing about it. He only thought about business and hardly cared about babies.'

'Did he not ask to see the baby in death?'

'He did not.'

'So whose idea was it to make the parcel of sand to lie in the coffin and simulate the body?'

'That was me. I made it.'

'And it fooled your father.'

'It fooled everybody.'

'Did it fool your family doctor, who is also your good friend? Did it fool Dr Harrod?'

Harriet seemed to flinch at the mention of the doctor's name.

'Dr Harrod? No. He knew nothing about any of this.'

'But he once told me that he had himself delivered this fictional child. Why would he do that?'

'I don't know. I cannot say.'

'Very well. May I turn to the headstone inscription your father chose for young Loammi? How do you interpret it?'

'I think it means he was even more angry with me than I knew.'

'But there is something I don't understand. His anger led him to choose the Bible quotation "Plead with your mother, plead". I have read the relevant passage out, and its import is not only to accuse you. It accuses your mother also, doesn't it?'

'I can only think that is because of her deception – of *our* deception. He held us both equally responsible for it – for the whole thing, really.'

'Harriet, one more question. Do you know who killed your father?'

'No, Sir, I don't. I only know that I myself had nothing to do with it.'

I looked into the room, searching for Dr Harrod. He appeared to have lied – but he might have been mistaken – about the time he'd been with Chimpton, and on this supposed lie rested Fidelis's theory – his latest theory, mind you, contradicting his earlier theories – that Harrod was in fact the killer of both the tan-pit baby and Abraham Scroop. Harrod had certainly lied to me about delivering the non-existent Scroop son, and that was before its supposed death. I realized I ought not to give my summary of evidence before I had him back in the witness chair to answer for himself.

'Would Dr Harrod please come back to the chair?' I asked.

But Harrod was no longer in the hall. When I repeated my request someone stated that he had been urgently called away to a patient in Clitheroe, which was a day's ride away. I realized I would have to make the best I could of it without him.

Chapter 31

MY INQUEST MAY have uncovered a number of dark facts about Abraham Scroop, his family and his business, but the name of his killer had not emerged. In my summary, therefore, I set the scene and gave a careful account of the testimony, with strong emphasis on Fidelis's view that Scroop had been fatally attacked through his ear, possibly while he lay incapacitated on the ground. After that – and here I considered was the point of difficulty – I attempted to divert the jury away from any rash accusatory verdict, such as 'murder by Jon O'Rorke' or 'by Joss Kay'.

I pointed out that O'Rorke had left Preston by boat on Sunday and that evidence against Joss Kay was lacking. The fact that Mr Kay had been taken into custody must not mislead us.

'You have to weigh the evidence,' I said, 'just as you would expect the tobacconist to weigh your snuff when you buy it. Remember that you may always include the word "murder" in your return without naming any individual murderer. That would then leave matter to be dealt with by the magistrates.'

It was an untidy conclusion and I didn't very much like it. I knew how perverse the magistrates could be. They might yet pursue O'Rorke, or even the hapless Kay, though they would not go after one of their own – Harrod, for example, in spite of his lies and evasions.

The old doctor had escaped scrutiny at the inquest and it was my own fault. I'd had a liking for the man or I might have taxed him when I'd had the chance about his movements on the morning Scroop died. Admittedly I had no real grounds to do so, merely Fidelis's surmises about the visit to Chimpton, and some unreliable gossip about Harrod and Mrs Scroop. It is true that an inquest is in essence a forum for guessing and gossip, yet one of the Coroner's most important jobs is to keep this from straying into tittle-tattle. I could well see how Harrod might be guilty; but based on what the inquest had heard in evidence I could not safely venture his name as a possible culprit.

After the first twenty minutes of their deliberation, the jury foreman came to see me.

'Just a small matter, Sir. We don't like this doctor, see? Very suspicious of him, we are. We wonder what you think of him yourself.'

'Well he is a close friend of the Scroop family, you know. He must know more than he is saying, but perhaps he does not say it to protect Mrs Scroop and the girls as much as he can. I must say I would like very much to have questioned him further before we finished. I couldn't, of course, as he had left the court.'

'Left the court? No he hadn't. He was there at the end, I saw him.'

'You saw Dr Harrod? But didn't you hear me call for him? He'd gone.'

'No, no! Not Dr Harrod, Sir. He's a very pleasant gentleman. It's that other doctor, the know-it-all who thinks Mr Scroop was murdered through his ear, or something like that: he's the one we don't trust.'

'Dr Fidelis? I assure you he is the soul of trust and unparalleled in the examination of a body *post mortem*.'

'Not for us he's not. He cuts bodies up and takes bits out of 'em and suchlike. Made a terrible mess of Mr Scroop's head, he did.

Well, I'll go back to the lads. We'll have a decision for you shortly and then all you Preston folk can bugger off home.'

When the verdict came back it was not what I wanted to hear: 'death by manner and means unknown'. As a matter of form I thanked the jurors before discharging them, but it galled me. They had utterly failed in their duty, of course, but I blamed myself. I'd concentrated on the witnesses and quite neglected the jury. Formerly as Coroner in Preston I had known most jurors in person and they knew me; here, as County Coroner, I was a stranger, an object of suspicion come in from the big, bad neighbouring town. This prejudice, I told myself, was the entire reason why Fidelis's findings and my own summary had not made its mark with them; indeed, many had wanted to depart even further and designate the overhanging oak tree as Scroop's killer.

'You can take comfort from having escaped that humiliation at least,' as Elizabeth pointed out to me in bed that night.

'But why is no one questioning Harrod's conduct?' I asked. 'He seems untouched by all this. Goes around saying Fidelis and I tried to lead the inquest up the garden path.'

'Ha! But in fact you led them up the churchyard path, and did you not find a fraudulent burial and an empty grave? You also uncovered Harriet Scroop's pregnancy, and the truth about the baby in the tan-pit.'

'But I can't see the whole picture. Harrod's not just a liar, but a murderer, I'm sure of it now. I just don't know why.'

So matters stood until a fortnight later, when I learned the answer to this question in dramatic fashion.

For Preston's leaders, if not for me, the Scroop inquest had ended quickly and satisfactorily. Now life in the Corporation could resume, though not exactly as before. Open debate of the future of the Marsh, and the need for a dock, had previously been prevented as a matter of policy. Now – as a matter of policy – its discussion was being vocally promoted by the politicians as a healthy thing, a necessary airing of views which would assist the town's esteemed leaders in making the right decision. Such sudden reversals of direction are commonplace in politics but, in fact, the bruised knuckles and bleeding noses that were then suffered in the course of these free discussions were all in vain. The future of the dock project had, in truth, already been determined.

Lord Derby was so pleased with the Kirkham inquest that he wrote me this letter.

Dear Cragg, I congratulate you on your conduct of the inquest into Scroop, your first as County Coroner. A pity you could not quite reach the verdict of accidental death, but by unknown causes is almost its equal. My main wish now is to see an end to all the scurrilous talk in Preston of murder etc., but I expect this to die away naturally as the weeks and months go by. I take this opportunity to renew my invitation to you, which I mentioned at the Michaelmas Ball in Preston, for a day's shooting. Come out to Lathom next Sunday with your gun. You will be expected at eight a.m.

Derby.

Riding south in the early morning towards Lathom with Suez bowling along the road beside me, I had mixed expectations. It was regarded as an honour and privilege to be invited to shoot on the Earl's private land – and one that no man would dare to refuse. But who would I be shooting with? A day out and a friend for company is a delightful activity; alone it would be less so, though with Suez at my heel I would still enjoy it; but with Lord Derby walking stiffly at my side, and on his own estate, it would surely turn into a torture in which, at any moment, I might do or say the wrong thing.

I quickly learned, however, that Lord Derby was not to be my shooting companion, as the peer had gone off to London on the previous day for the sitting of Parliament. Nor was it any friend of mine, such as Luke Fidelis or Nick Oldswick – nor even my bowls rival, stationer Starkey. Instead I found that my chosen shooting companion would be Dr Basilius Harrod.

When I arrived, Harrod was chatting amiably with the gamekeeper in the stable yard at Lathom. He had a game bag and a flintlock rifle, as I did. He turned to greet me.

'Ah, Cragg! Excellent! Mr Clarke here recommends we begin with an assault on his lordship's woods which, if we walk all the way through them, will lead to the lake and some fine duck-shooting at dusk.'

I greeted Clarke, who said we had the freedom of the western woods and that there would be no one but ourselves legitimately there.

'If you see anyone else,' he said, 'it'll be poachers. You have my blessing and his Lordship's to shoot them.'

For half an hour as we moved deeper and deeper amongst the trees, taking pot-shots at wood pigeons and rabbits here and there as we went, I could find little to say. Harrod, on his part, was just as he had always been with me – good-humoured, free, easy. It was as if there had never been an inquest into his friend Scroop's death, no decision by Mrs Scroop to leave Preston with her family (as they had already done), and no suspicion in my own heart that he was a killer. Was it possible he didn't somehow know that I suspected him of two murders? I studied the man several times when he was loading his piece, or stalking ahead of me towards a bird. I only saw the same easy-natured man I had known since childhood and, again, I found myself doubting Luke Fidelis's thesis. How could this kindly, twinkle-eyed doctor have done those terrible things – and more importantly why? In company with him like this it did not seem credible.

We reached a place where stone had once been quarried, a flat grassy space from which rose a sheer cliff fifty or sixty feet high, the rock face being lumpy and heavily mossed.

'Time for refreshment,' said Harrod, taking from his satchel bread, cheese and a bottle containing ale. Elizabeth had provided me with much the same provisions and so we both sat down on cushions of moss to refresh ourselves. I tossed Suez the bone that had been provided for him.

I was just taking a swig of beer and, with my head tilted well back, never noticed Harrod raise his gun. The unexpected noise of its discharge made my chin jerk downwards. The sticky liquid fizzed painfully back through my nostrils and on to my chest. Suez looked up from his bone and barked.

'Got it!' shouted the doctor in triumph, pointing to the quarry face. 'It was right up there on that ledge! A sparrowhawk, I think.'

Mopping myself I looked around the quarry floor.

'Where did it fall?'

'It didn't. It's still up there, lying on the ledge. Be a good friend, Cragg. Climb up and get it, will you? I suffer from vertigo or I would go myself, of course.'

I have no notion of how I allowed myself to be talked into it. Some people have such powers of persuasion that it is practically impossible to say no to them. Harrod told me that he badly wanted that bird. He knew he couldn't eat it, but he desired to have it stuffed. It would look so amusing displayed in his dining room in a bell-jar. He really must have it. It would be perfectly safe for me to climb up. It's the sort of thing an adventurous young fellow like myself rather enjoys doing. The boy Titus, that he used to know and remembered so well, would certainly do it. I would be up there and down again in less than a few minutes. It was perfectly safe.

A few minutes later I was thirty-five feet up, working my way along the ledge. Spying the place from the ground I had not realized how narrow it was: three hand's-breadths at most. I was inching along it, urged by Harrod's pointing finger.

'It's just there, don't you see it? No, a little further along. Keep going. Keep going.'

I couldn't make out the bird. My back was pressed to the cliff face, my hands too. It would be practically impossible to pick this sparrowhawk up from the level of my feet without losing my balance, even if there were a sparrowhawk. I now had begun to doubt this as it occurred to me – how could I have been so stupid? – that perhaps a game was being played with me. If there really were no bird of prey up here, was I in fact the prey?

'Be damned to this Harrod. It's not safe. I'm coming down.'

I began to move by slow degrees in the reverse direction, the one from which I had come. My mouth was dry and I tried to control my shaking limbs. I felt the lurch of a fall in my stomach and my head, and imagined the jagged wounds I would get when I hit the rocks below. I would die, that was fairly certain. Looking down, I expected that Harrod would be following my movements with his eyes, exactly as Suez was doing. But the doctor was not watching me. He was re-loading his gun.

I had just turned, to test the next place on which to put my weight, when there came a booming report. It started down where Harrod was standing, continued a fraction of a second later with a splitting crack near my feet, and dissipated in an echo that ran round the quarry. A piece of rock the size of my head fell away almost immediately below where I was standing and split into shards on impact below. I don't know how I kept my balance.

Harrod was still holding his gun in the firing position, the barrel smoking and pointing at a target immediately below my feet.

'Don't imagine that I missed you, Cragg,' he called up. 'I am an excellent shot.'

I took another small sideways step towards the place where I had begun my journey along the ledge. It was still at least twenty-five feet away.

'Whatever you're doing, it's a mistake, Harrod.'

He was busy again with the gun, finding a ball, ramming it, pouring powder into the pan, cocking the hammer.

'The mistake is yours, Cragg, and such a simple one. But you know I always thought you a rather simple boy, though for a while a pretty one, I'll admit – if my taste had run in that direction. But it didn't, you see. It's the young female that's my passion.'

He took aim and his gun roared a second time, taking another chunk off the cliff face below where I was standing. The ledge still held.

'Female children, Harrod?'

'No, not children. I am not quite so perverted. Young flesh is what I crave, just at the age when the bud is opening, if you get my meaning. Being a doctor is extremely helpful in satisfying that craving.'

'Being the friend and doctor to a family with six little girls – and all in the house next door – that must have encouraged you particularly.'

'Oh, I arranged all that myself. Mrs Scroop was an easy mark. Her husband was so distracted that he became complaisant, and it was quite a simple matter to inveigle myself into her bed.'

He laughed.

'The act itself was somewhat difficult for me but I stuck to it manfully, if only for the benefits it won me with her daughters.'

His laughter was vile. It was the same laugh he used all the time, and which everyone praised for being such a pleasant laugh. Now it made my gorge rise.

'Yet it went badly wrong,' I called down. 'Harriet conceived.'

'Yes, silly girl. I shouldn't have kept on with her but, even at fifteen, she hadn't completely lost that look of the waif she'd had at thirteen. I simply couldn't stop myself.'

'Did she not resist?'

'She didn't dare.'

He raised the gun and fired again. The rock held firm still, losing only a chip where the ball struck. I took another little sideways step on the absurd plan that he might not notice the movement.

'Don't think I can't see you creeping along, Cragg. You won't get there you know. In a few moments that ledge you are standing on will give way and you will fall. Then I am going to walk away and – not too urgently – seek for help. By the time I return with some good samaritans you will be dead as a result of what all will accept as a foolish climb and a foolish fall.'

It seemed best to keep our conversation going. I said,

'Why did you not stop the pregnancy? You must know how to do it.'

'I am no Crazy Daisy, Sir! I am no abortionist. Besides I learned of it too late. So I devised a better and cleverer plan. At the end of it no one would have been hurt. If only the baby hadn't come early, with its supposed mother far away in Yorkshire, all would have been well.'

'But instead, when it was born, you killed it.'

'Yes, and I had to see to it immediately – which is why I had recourse to the long bodkin, whose use your friend was lucky enough to stumble on. One scream from that baby and the whole house would have known, while its supposed mother was sixty or seventy miles away. Harriet, the little temptress, she understood it was for the best. And I had thought of the perfect place to put the bundle, or so I thought.'

His gun being loaded again, he raised it and fired upwards a fourth time. The bullet buried itself harmlessly in the trunk of a young tree growing below me out of the face of the cliff and I continued to shuffle along my ledge by minute degrees.

'Here's a question I would like to know the answer to. Did you set fire to the Skeleton Inn?'

'That was no doing of mine. My guess is that it was arranged by Scroop, who was the inn's owner. He told me months ago that he wanted to get that ridiculous man Clarkson out and regain possession. He wanted to build on the site – and now we know why. He was planning this dock.'

'You also had reason to do it, though. You were afraid of what would emerge from the inquest into the child you killed.'

'Afraid?' he scoffed. 'I was not. I'd nothing to fear from the inquest, since there was every reason to think Kathy Brock was the guilty one – which if you recall is what was concluded by Mayor Thwaite.'

'It was a convenient verdict for you, though.'

'Oh, it wasn't reached for my convenience but for Scroop's. He was the one with money and power and he wanted to hound the skinners off the Marsh.'

'But you were friends, and you killed him.'

'We were not friends. I hated him. When I got the opportunity to end his life, I was gratified. I loathed his plans – all this "improvement" that he loved so much. Nothing *ever* improves, Cragg, believe me. But I didn't kill him for that. I did it because he had begun to suspect Harriet.'

'He suspected that you . . . ?'

'Fucked his daughter? Ha-ha! No. As long as the girl said nothing I was above suspicion. Even Scroop who suspected everyone didn't suspect me. He distrusted his wife, and his daughters; he distrusted Captain Strawboy and in the end – on my advice, as it happens – turned him out of his house; finally he distrusted the manservant, O'Rorke, and eventually dismissed him, too. But by this time the older girls had been fretting. There had been a scene at the Michaelmas Ball – remember? He had begun to form these ideas about sexual misconduct in the house, and we were afraid he would next discover his eldest daughter had become pregnant. Your damned friend Fidelis was right about the rest of it. I couldn't allow that inscription to be used so I waylaid and killed Scroop after he'd seen the stonemason. I hid the horse and body in a disused barn until I was ready to set the scene of his supposed riding accident. Speaking of which, it is now time for your own terrible accident, I think.'

It happened suddenly. A fifth bullet was ready for firing. Harrod raised the gun, there was a crack and a puff of smoke. The ball hit immediately beneath me and all at once the ledge crumbled away like a pastry crust under my feet. For a brief moment I had the sensation of standing on air, and then I plunged downwards.

The outgrowing tree caught me. I was in it just long enough to get a firm grasp of a green branch and keep hold so that my fall was slowed. When therefore I came to ground – though one of my feet twisted as it glanced off a boulder – I had an otherwise soft landing. I rolled over and saw Harrod fiddling another ball into his gun. I got up and ran towards him, barging him with all my strength. The gun went one way, he went another. I heard the crack of a bone and his yell of pain.

We found later he had sustained multiple fractures of the arm. Now he lay on the grass whimpering pathetically while Suez stood over him with ears pricked and tail wagging and I carefully reloaded my own weapon.

Chapter 32

'I'M LEAVING. I'M taking ship for America.'

Fidelis and I were drinking together with Joss Kay at the Turk's Head. It was two or three weeks later. Kay had stayed on in Preston at Lord Derby's request – and expense – to continue his work at the Marsh, so the announcement that he was leaving took Fidelis and me by surprise.

'What about the dock we have been promised?' I asked, pouring him a glass of Noah Plumtree's punch.

'Well, my survey is finished – as far as it can be.'

'That doesn't sound finished at all,' remarked Fidelis.

'It's not. Or not in the way we all expected, though I have come to a conclusion.'

'Which is?'

'That a dock can never be built in the Marsh. I have tried everything Mr Steers taught me. I've looked at every angle. I've calculated the whole watershed, and the length and capacity of the pipeage required to drain it. I've taken into account the tidal variations. I've calculated the manpower for digging it out, and how much material in tons would be needed for the dock's construction. But it won't do. There are too many imponderables and not enough money.'

'So we won't have a dock at all?' put in Fidelis.

Kay shook his head decisively.

'No. It will cost far more than Preston can afford. Even with Scroop's investment it would have been out of reach.'

'What about Lord Grassington?' I asked.

'I believe he's left Preston entirely.'

'He has, and vows never to return,' said Fidelis. 'I believe Captain Strawboy's behaviour had much to do with the matter. He'd lately fallen out with Lord Strange over a girl and his gambling debts have reached a dangerous height. The Sultan shan't have his bout against the Second Hercules now, I fear.'

'What does the Mayor say about your damning verdict on the proposed dock?' I asked Kay.

'I gave my report to him and Mr Thorneley yesterday. They met Lord Derby after, to ask him if he could find some more money. But no. Lord Derby's money'll cover only my work so far. So that's the end of it – the Corporation have cancelled the whole thing.'

Most people in Preston would feel greatly relieved, I thought, as they had little desire to see the Marsh disappear. Any profits accruing from such a dock would not be seen for decades of years, and besides it would be bound to go into the pockets of the burgesses not the people. For myself I was only sorry that we would be losing Joss Kay. His love of improvement made for exhausting conversation, but once he was teased away from the subject he became a delightful companion.

'Can you not find some other work that might keep you amongst us, Joss?'

'The Mayor says that, instead of the dock, they're considering a bridge across the river from the wharf to Penwortham. He's asked me to work on that, but I'll not do it. I've got my full fee at last for the dock report and I've set my heart on America now. That's where the best opportunities for improvement lie.'

The very next day he was gone.

* * *

From time to time I saw Ellen Kite and her brother at the Wednesday market, selling their cheap leather goods. I always made a point of buying some trifle or other – a packet of buttons, a dog collar for Suez, or a braided bracelet for Matty.

'Do you have word of Kathy Brock?' I asked one day.

'Oh, she's in London, Sir. Margery's had some letters from her, and she's working in a place called Covent Garden. Do you know it?'

'Yes, I know it.'

'And is it the sort of place a girl can do well for herself?'

I chose my words carefully.

'It might be, Ellen. One meets many fine gentlemen in Covent Garden, and several ways of earning a living.'

I remembered how Kathy had spoken so sensibly of her great plans and ambitions, and hoped she had not simply settled for the life of a Covent Garden whore. But if she had, there was no purpose in alarming her fiends and family, so I changed the subject.

'Now that the position of Searcher and Looker of Leather is for the time being vacant, Ellen, I hope the persecution of this stall has ceased.'

'Oh, yes sir. No one bothers us now, not even Mr Mallender.'

'That's good. A dark cloud was hanging over the skin-yard, but it would seem it has entirely blown away and is unlikely to return soon. The dock project is killed off entirely. Captain Strawboy's surveyor, Mr Kay, has gone away and the captain himself is back in the army fighting the French, so I hear.'

This was true, and the other forces that had combined to try to build the dock and thereby destroy the skin-yard were also much diminished. Strawboy's uncle Grassington stayed clear of Preston, while, with the death of their leader, Scroop's cabal of would-be projectors and improvers among the burgesses had been completely silenced by Joss Kay's negative report. Even Grimshaw seemed a deflated figure, though I expected him to puff up again when a new opportunity to get rich came along.

Scroop's rag-and-bone yard was now in the hands of his old foreman, Bartholomew Lock. He appeared in my office one morning that autumn to consult me about some legal questions pertaining to the continued administration of Scroop's business affairs.

'And do you inherit the late Scroop's ambitions, Mr Lock?' I asked, when we had cleared up the matter. 'They were considerable, I think, even without Preston getting an enclosed dock.'

'Aye, he had some fancy ideas, did Mr Scroop. He thought we should buy raw flax direct from Ireland for paper milling, instead of just selling our rags to the paper makers. And he got a mad idea of getting the farmers to spread bone dust over their fields to get better yields. He thought this would make him even richer than he already was, but I reckon it's nowt but rubbish.'

Occasional word reached us of Basilius Harrod in his cell at Lancaster Castle. He was awaiting the next arrival of the assize judges, who would try him and decide his fate, and it was said he spent each day casting horoscopes to see how the planets and stars would align at the time of the trial. His former lover, the widow Helena Scroop, having consigned her husband's business to the care of Lock, was last heard of living with her daughters in London. Harrod's son Abel stayed on in the Water Lane house and I often saw him, as blank of expression and as slow of tongue as ever, sitting around reading in Sweeting's bookshop. For an apprentice he rarely seemed to do anything that resembled work. Sweeting said that Abel appeared to be content, but it must be hard to know that he faced ruin by Crown appropriation if, as seemed inevitable, his father should be convicted of murder.

As for me, I soon became used to, and to much enjoy, my new responsibilities as County Coroner. More time was spent away from home as I travelled here and there to look at corpses, collect statements and recruit juries in the villages and small towns that were dotted around the Duchy. But my attorney's practice in Preston still continued, so now I had a foot in both worlds – the town and the country.

Elizabeth said it suited me.

'You are slimmer now, and you smile more, Titus.'

'I am riding more. I like going about.'

'It gives you even greater resemblance to Don Quixote than ever, my dearest. You and your Rosinante trotting up and down the world, righting wrongs and doing good.'

'With Furzey as my Sancho!'

We laughed. It was late and we were setting the parlour tidy before we retired. I picked up Cervantes's book from the sideboard – the second volume it was – and put it into her hands. Her eyes, beautiful and glowing, were a little tearful, which I took to be because of her laughter.

'You are nearing the end of the book, then?'

'I am at the end.'

'So you know what happens?'

'Yes, and I will tell you. It is time I told you.'

'What do you mean by that?'

'I mean that in the end Don Quixote discovers his Dulcinea at last, and they live together in his house happily, blissfully happily.'

'What d'you mean, Eliza? No they don't, I'm sure the Don—'

Elizabeth gently put a finger to my lips.

'Shh! Don't spoil it. Where was I? Oh yes, blissfully happily.'

She turned the pages of the book and seemed to be reading from it.

'So they lived their days together in bliss, and slept together too at night with the greatest pleasure. But there was still one thing, one desire among all desires in the world, that remained unsatisfied between the Don and his lady. Until, that is, one evening, when Dulcinea was with him in their parlour, and they were preparing for bed. And I don't know exactly why but that was the moment she chose to tell him that now at last their one remaining desire was to be satisfied.'

'Go on,' I said cautiously. 'What actually did she tell him?'

Elizabeth was no longer pretending to read from the book. She put it down, took my hand and pressed it against her stomach.

'She told him this: "Don Quixote rejoice, because soon, against all the expectations of the world, there will be a baby Quixote, or if not then a baby Dulcinea." And just what do you think Don Quixote said when he heard that?'

I suppose my mouth fell open in surprise and then a kind of euphoria washed over me, a wave of joy indescribably remote from daily life. I saw that Elizabeth's eyes had finally overflowed, and mine too were threatening to flood. I wrapped my arms around her tightly and whispered in her ear.

'Don Quixote said that he was speechless and then proved himself wrong by telling her that he loved his Dulcinea more even than he loved his own life.'

Elizabeth's tears instantly became laughter.

'And, to that, Dulcinea quoted Sancho,' she cried, wrapping her arms around my neck. 'She told Don Quixote that she loved him too, even more than she loved her own eyelids.'

And so we kissed, but it was not exactly a good-night kiss.